SOUTH

# SOUTH

MARIO FORTUNATO

*Translated from the Italian by Julia MacGibbon*

OTHER PRESS

*New York*

Originally published in Italian as *Sud* in 2020 by Bompiani, Firenze-Milano



Production editor: Yvonne E. Cárdenas
Text designer: Patrice Sheridan
This book was set in Bembo
by Alpha Design & Composition of Pittsfield, NH

10 9 8 7 6 5 4 3 2 1



Library of Congress Cataloging-in-Publication Data
Names: Fortunato, Mario, author. | MacGibbon, Julia, translator.
Title: South / Mario Fortunato ; translated from the Italian by Julia MacGibbon.
Other titles: Sud. English
Description: New York : Other Press, [2023] | Originally published in Italian as Sud in 2020 by Bompiani, Firenze-Milano.
Identifiers: LCCN 2022042597 (print) | LCCN 2022042598 (ebook) | ISBN 9781635422047 (paperback) | ISBN 9781635422054 (ebook)
Subjects: LCGFT: Novels.
Classification: LCC PQ4866.O74 S8313 2023 (print) | LCC PQ4866.O74 (ebook) | DDC 853/.914—dc23/eng/20220906
LC record available at https://lccn.loc.gov/2022042597
LC ebook record available at https://lccn.loc.gov/2022042598

FOR RITA AND CARMEN

# THE NOTARY'S FAMILY

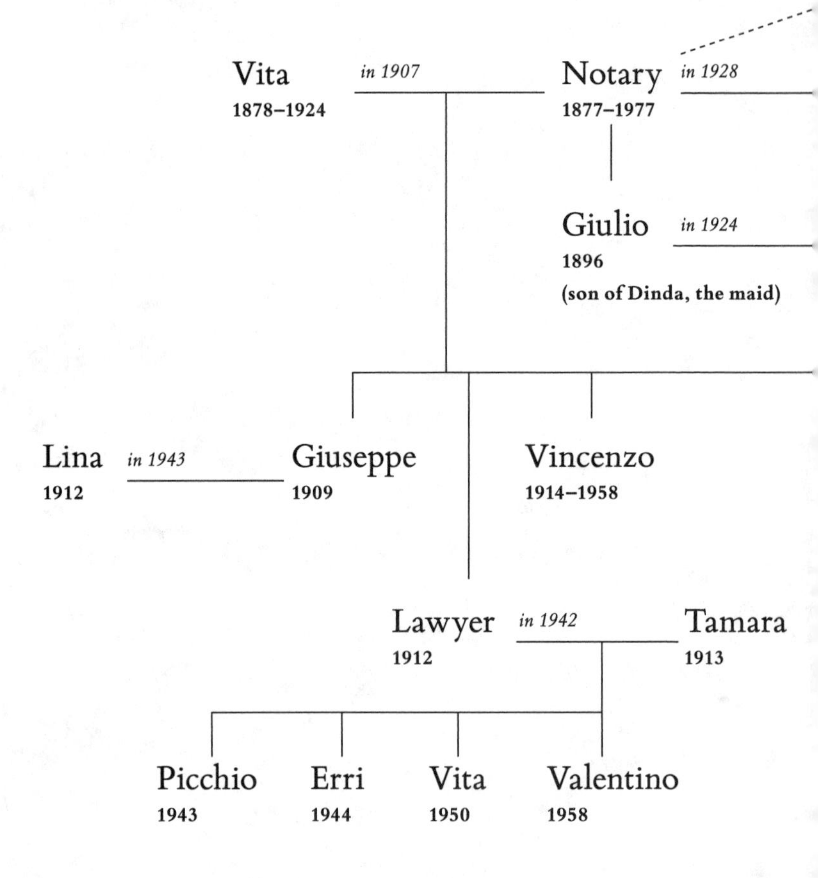

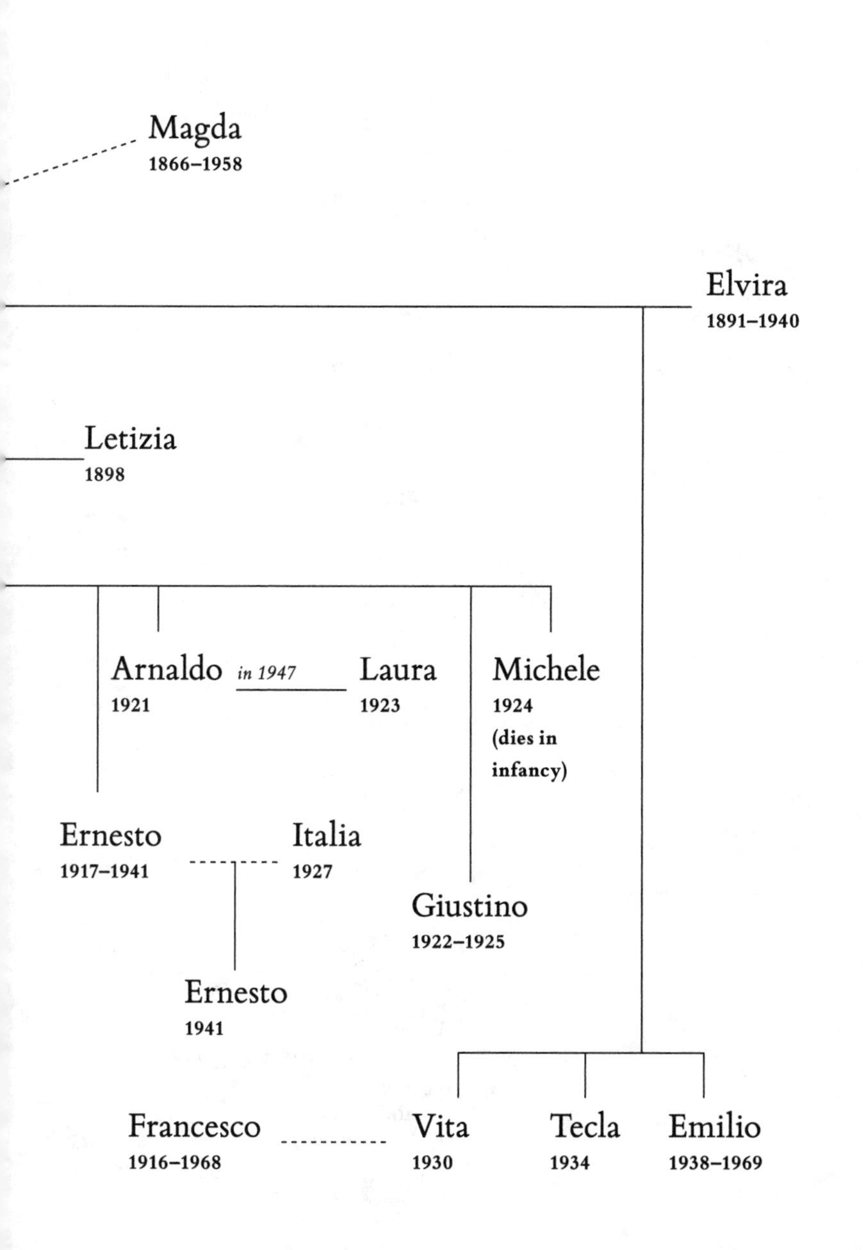

Magda
1866–1958
Elvira
1891–1940
Letizia
1898
Arnaldo
1921
in 1947
Laura
1923
Michele
1924
(dies in
infancy)
Ernesto
1917–1941
Italia
1927
Giustino
1922–1925
Ernesto
1941
Francesco
1916–1968
Vita
1930
Tecla
1934
Emilio
1938–1969

# STAFF

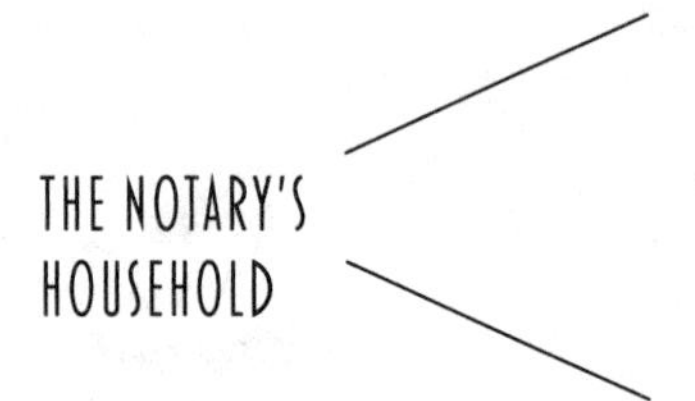


**Cicia**
**1908**
**(married, Emilio's nursemaid)**

**Rosa**
**1924**
**(married, housemaid)**

THE LAWYER'S HOUSEHOLD

**Maria-la-pioggia** *in 1942*
**1917**
**(maid and cook)**

**Ciccio Bombarda** *in 1947*
**1921**
**(chauffeur)**

**Luigi**
known as **Sciammerga** *in 1931*
**1909**
**(domestic servant and general factotum)**

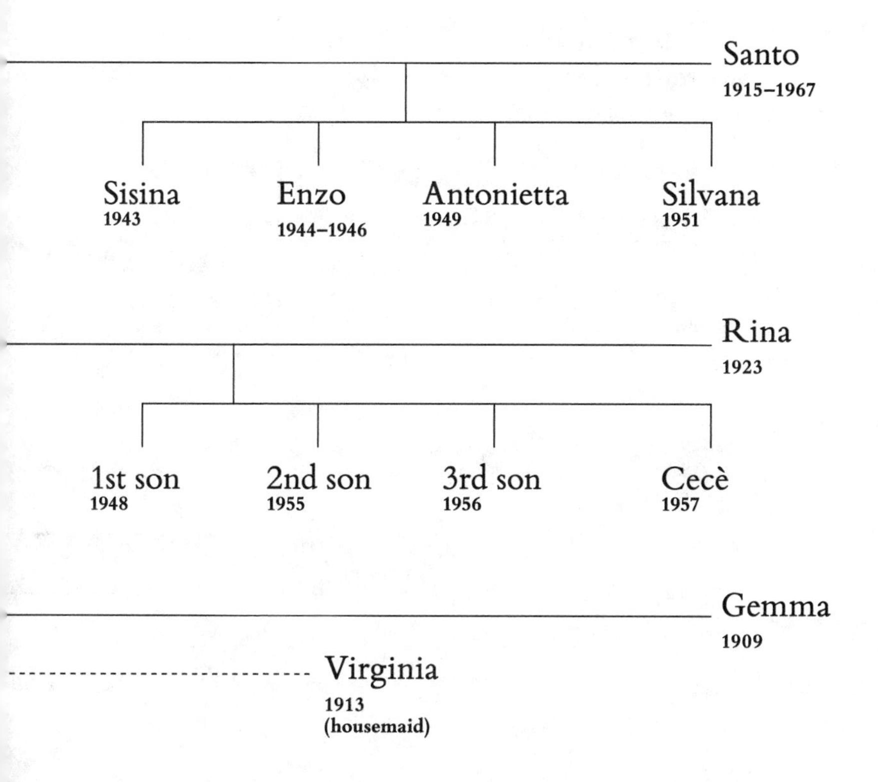
Santo
1915–1967
Sisina
1943
Enzo
1944–1946
Antonietta
1949
Silvana
1951
Rina
1923
1st son
1948
2nd son
1955
3rd son
1956
Cecè
1957
Gemma
1909
Virginia
1913
(housemaid)

# THE PHARMACIST'S FAMILY

Pharmacist *in 1908*
**1879–1964**

boy
**(name unknown)**
**1912–1921**

Uncle Giorgio Attali
**1863–1939**
**(younger brother of the Pharmacist's father)**

Levino *in 1930* Margherita
**1908** **1910**
**(known as "cousins," they are former employees of Uncle Giorgio)**

Maria *in 1939*
**1911**

Lea
**1940**

Pepe
**1941**

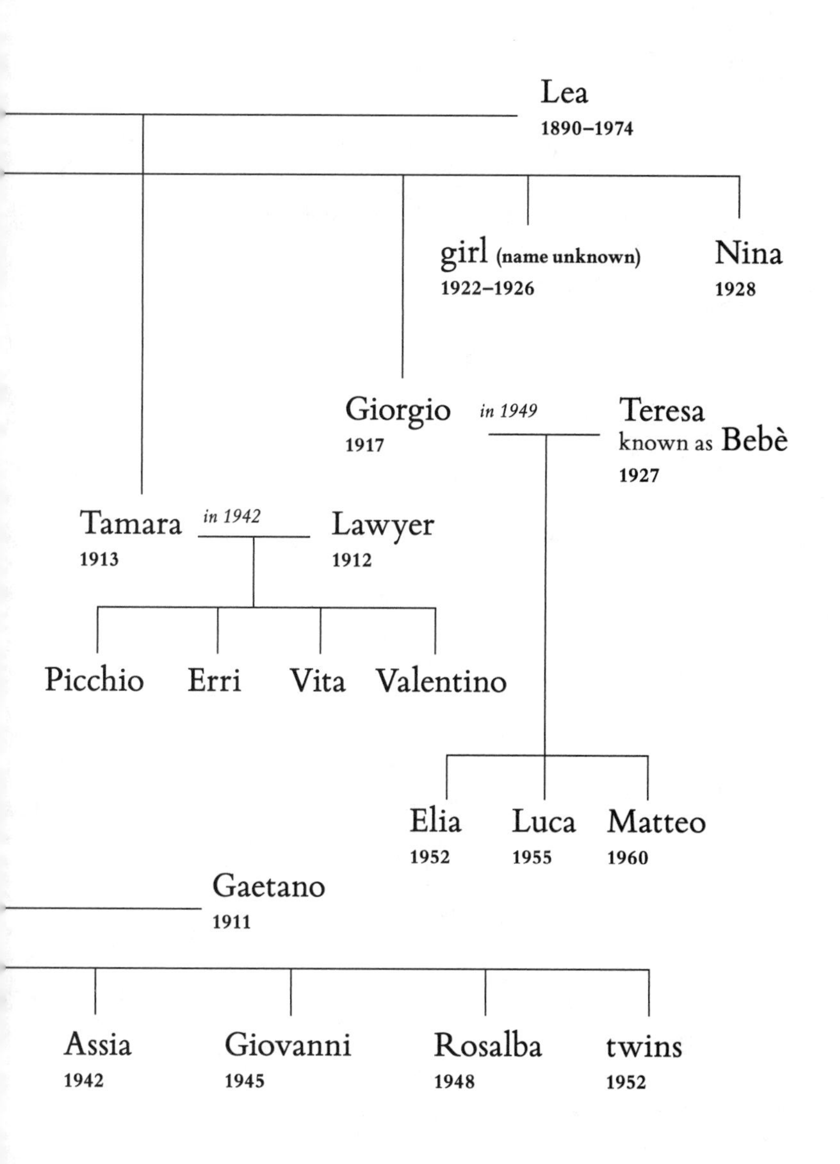
Lea
1890–1974
girl (name unknown)
1922–1926
Nina
1928
Giorgio
1917
in 1949
Teresa
known as Bebè
1927
Tamara
1913
in 1942
Lawyer
1912
Picchio
Erri
Vita
Valentino
Elia
1952
Luca
1955
Matteo
1960
Gaetano
1911
Assia
1942
Giovanni
1945
Rosalba
1948
twins
1952

# STAFF

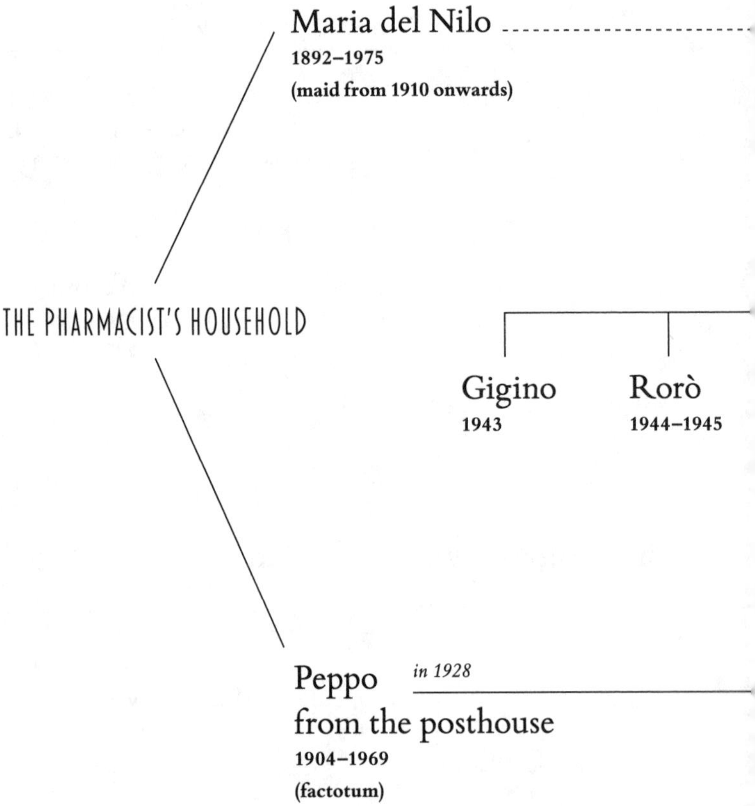

THE PHARMACIST'S HOUSEHOLD

Maria del Nilo
**1892–1975**
**(maid from 1910 onwards)**

Gigino
**1943**

Rorò
**1944–1945**

Peppo from the posthouse
*in 1928*
**1904–1969**
**(factotum)**

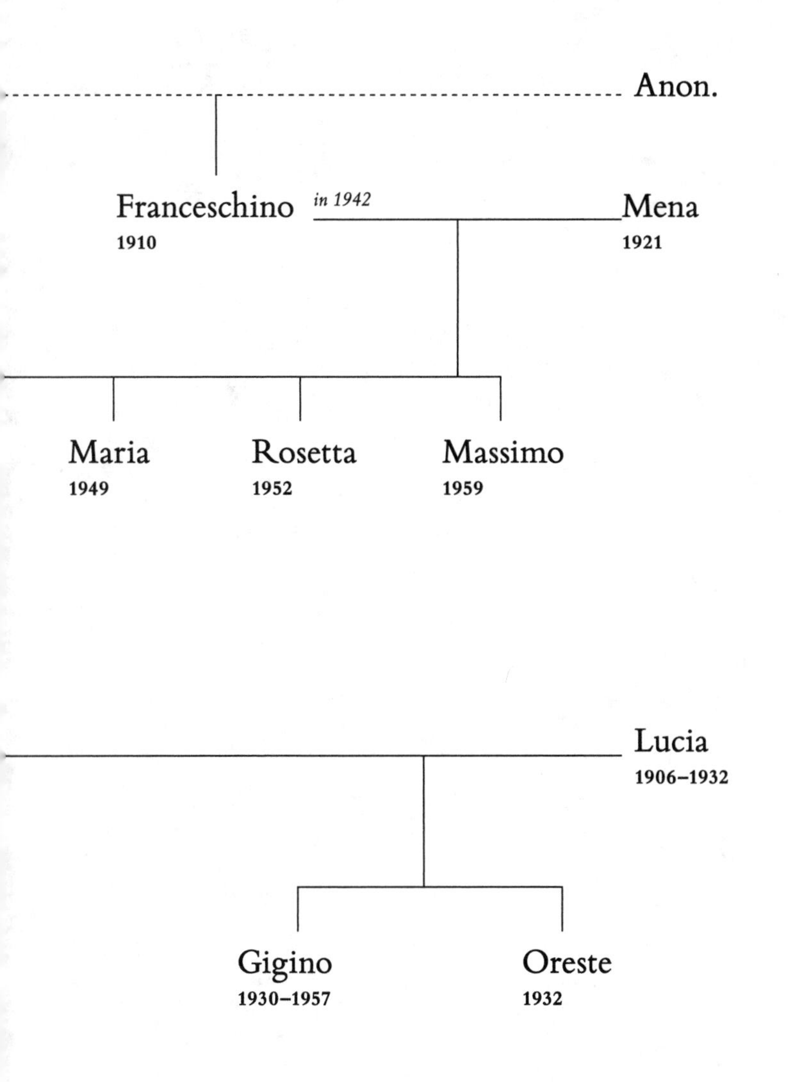
Anon.
Franceschino
1910
in 1942
Mena
1921
Maria
1949
Rosetta
1952
Massimo
1959
Lucia
1906–1932
Gigino
1930–1957
Oreste
1932

# CONTENTS

## CHAPTER THREE



## CHAPTER FOUR



## CHAPTER FIVE

## CHAPTER EIGHT



## CHAPTER NINE

# PROLOGUE

Where are they all? Tamara, whom only her husband called Mara, the Lawyer, with his sidekicks Rosa and Cicia, Maria-la-pioggia ("Maria-the-rain," heaven knows why) and Maria del Nilo (heaven knows why)? Where are the old Notary, with his accidental offspring, and the old Pharmacist, who kept a violin hidden in his wardrobe? And their wives, who were so very different—one shy and gloomy, the other brusque and decisive—and yet both as tiny as children. Where are they? And Peppo from the posthouse, and Nina, who loved ghosts, Emilio, who didn't start talking until he was twenty, Ciccio Bombarda, the chauffeur without a driving license, and Luigi, known as "Sciammerga," with Gemma his wife, Virginia his lover, and the others who never had names. Where are those who belonged to the past historic—up in the hills, cool breezy summers, paths lined with hawthorn, like a page out of

Proust but without any aristocrats—just farmers, the huddled masses, and a scattering of bourgeoisie? And those who inhabited tenses less remote—on the coast, by the sea, all of it humid and smelling of fish: a noisier penury that in the space of a few years would transform itself into *'ndrangheta*?

Where are they all? They once populated the recesses of his dreams. By night he had seen them file by like paper figurines: he had watched them mutate from shadows into bodies and from bodies into statues, and every statue was a story. By day, though, they disappeared into that patchy, inconclusive fog of which memory is made—faces crumbled, words stole away—and he didn't try to stop them or batten them down.

Valentino left at the end of the seventh decade of the twentieth century. He was a boy, and like all boys, he made sure not to look over his shoulder. The world was such an inviting place to dive into. Added to which, Tamara, in other words Mara, in other words his mother, had told him and had repeated until she was blue in the face that he must not stay there, with them, in the south, because it was a land of barbarians and he had better escape to some distant place of safety, as far away as possible. Thus—except in the recesses of his dreams—he slowly forgot them all, discovering that—contrary to popular belief—oblivion is delightful. And for almost forty years he experienced the joy of never quite being himself.

He sped through his youth and then the years of his manhood with the efficient strides of those who carry only hand luggage. The windblown hair of those who are free to live anywhere and reside nowhere in particular. Rome, New York, Rome again, London, Milan, Rome again, Berlin, and, between one waypoint and the next, journeys far and wide, down into Africa, or into Asia, racking up miles and joie de vivre. Meanwhile, little by little, in the oblique and furtive style so typical of death, both the past historic and the past simple began to retreat from his vocabulary. As the picture grew more complex, language grew simpler.

When he lived in England, the thought of Tamara and the Lawyer had once rapped unexpectedly at the wall of his memory, igniting a lonely but nonetheless vehement flare of remorse; but then, as it always does, physiology prevailed. In some ways he had almost not noticed them slipping away—to say nothing of all the others, who had vanished long before leaving this world. He hadn't noticed it for the simple reason that something already erased cannot vanish, in the same way that one cannot lose what one doesn't possess. Time and tenses were an eternal present, busy with pleasant human intercourse, the scenery continually changing—as good a way as any to drag things out. Because with every new backdrop the civilities began afresh, and death seemed to retreat somewhere behind him, into a pleasingly hypothetical location.

The glory of days devoid of memory, the delight of not being oneself, a perpetual childhood for the mind. Voyaging into oneself, as though into a landscape being created with every exploratory stride. And loving those new places, that virginal land inhabited not by ghosts but by people of flesh and blood who possess the immense virtue of being deliberately, carefully, chosen on a daily basis, and not on the grounds of hazy bonds of kinship.

Until one day Tecla, too, disappeared. In other words, the very last panel of the never-completed tapestry of his origins; in other words, his identity. Apart from her name—so orotund and so lovely—he almost didn't know who she was. Tecla. Yet, the instant he learned that that name no longer existed, the entire past historic and all of the past simple came to an end, irrevocably: they were part of a contracting universe, of which he was the final piece. He alone.

So for a fraction of a second, in a final flicker, as a glint in his eye, they returned: Tamara, whom only her husband called Mara, and the Lawyer, with his sidekicks Rosa and Cicia, Maria-la-pioggia and Maria del Nilo (in both cases: heaven knows why), and then the old Notary, with his accidental offspring, and the old Pharmacist, with the violin hidden in his wardrobe, and the wives of each, different but identical, and that strange, largely unexplored, vast, and barbaric world that—being directly descended from one of history's most advanced civilizations, Magna Graecia—lived suspended between hills devoted to Bacchus (the name reserved for Dionysus when in his trance) and that sea called Ionian (after Ionius, great-grandson of Poseidon, accidentally killed by Heracles). Which was how Valentino came to discover something he would have preferred not to know.

# CHAPTER ONE

## 1. ON THE PATERNAL SIDE

The Notary was an only child. Perhaps it was that which drove him to sire a dozen heirs, or thereabouts: it began with a housemaid, Dinda, when he was just eighteen years old, it continued with his first wife and then his second, but it is not entirely clear with whom it ended, because, from time to time and in various locations, other descendants materialized. All three women passed away long before he did, as did many of his children, whom he had once, in one of his frequent fits of ire, defined as "the inadvertent result of a poke or two." In any event, he died a centenarian in 1977, and one can easily imagine that, with a century of life behind one, cynicism becomes rather tempting.

The Notary was a tall man, thin and stern. His sternness was reserved primarily for others; as far as he himself was concerned, he tended toward a certain indulgence. Although cultured, brilliant, and almost obsessively correct, he can't have been a pleasant man, if nothing else but for the fact that he was convinced he was one of the few intelligent people in circulation—a sign that he wasn't, or that he wasn't to a degree sufficient to ensure he nurtured any doubts in that regard. At any rate, he was certainly an uncommon man.

When, in his parents' household, it came to be understood that it was he who had impregnated Dinda, their housemaid, he was packed straight off to Naples, where he enrolled at the university. Jurisprudence, like his father. A student of the legal philosopher Giovanni Bovio, whose republican ideals he shared, he was still an undergraduate when he was invited, first as a trainee and then as an associate, to join a renowned Neapolitan legal firm. And given that, back then, reaching the town of his birth involved catching the boat to Pizzo Calabro—and, from there, advancing along impervious roads infested with brigands before finally arriving at one's destination—he vanished from his father's house for a considerable number of years.

In Naples the young Notary who was not yet a notary applied himself to his own care with the same gusto that other men devote to drugs, and therefore to their own undoing. He read a great deal (a habit he would never abandon), developing a passion for the positivist and Lombrosian theories of his era; he dressed with a maniac's care for detail, investing in expensive suits provided by the very best tailors in Naples and the monthly allowance that arrived from his father; he skipped from one cosmopolitan event to the next, and from one bed to the next, without making subtle distinctions among well-bred young ladies, working-class girls, married women, and prostitutes. The city's cafés teemed with young men who, as he did, cultivated the pleasures of the flesh and socialist ideals. They smoked, they debated, they copulated—in that order of interest. Some of them also imbibed conspicuous quantities of alcohol, but not he: he was almost teetotal.

Having graduated, he began work at the renowned and aforementioned legal firm. He patronized, with equal assiduousness, the halls of justice and those drawing rooms that over a century later would be labeled "radical chic." For roughly a year he frequented a Polish countess, Magda, who had abandoned her husband and children in Kraków to dedicate herself to the cause of socialism and her country's independence from Russia: the woman lived in a vast but gelid flat up on the Vomero hill, gradually selling off the enormous number of jewels she had brought with her when she left her homeland. It was in that apartment, full of drafts and spies, that the young Notary who was not yet a notary went to live, just weeks after having first made the acquaintance of the mature but alluring and feisty countess.

These were the early years of the twentieth century, and the spies who frequented Magda's home fell into the two time-honored classes standard in the sector: the political-ideological category typical of twentieth-century Europe, and the purely mercenary one, present in every era and every clime. Ascribable to the former were those individuals who, feigning friendship with the noblewoman, who notoriously sided with the philo-Bolshevik socialists in her native land, passed information about her and her Italian contacts to the enemy faction, headed up by Jósef Piłsudki, Poland's future head of state. The second category featured the young Notary's fellow Calabrians, who, with the excuse of bringing him letters, parcels, and news from his parents, in reality kept an eye on his private life and—handsomely compensated for their efforts—reported back to the relevant parties. It goes without saying that the mercenaries were in this case (but it is probably a general rule) a great deal more efficient and incisive than their politically and ideologically motivated colleagues. Proof of which is offered by the fact that, while Magda continued for many years to pursue her conspiratorial activities in Naples (she would reenter a liberated Poland at the end of the Second World War, only to flee almost immediately, decrepit and penniless, to Paris), the young Notary was very soon forced to leave the city.

Once informed of the scandalous relationship his son was having with the adulterous and antediluvian Polish noblewoman (thirty-six years to his twenty-five), the young Notary's father wrote him a heartfelt letter in which he pleaded with him to return immediately home: his wife was gravely ill, and from her deathbed, she begged to see their only offspring one last time, after his long—terribly long—absence. Assailed by feelings of guilt—a sentiment he would subsequently erase from his vocabulary—the young Notary hurriedly left Naples, convinced that he would be away for a couple of months at most. In reality many years would pass before he again set foot there—the only true regret in a life otherwise immune to remorse—and he would not see

Magda again until 1948, by which time, the difference in their ages long since nullified, both had grown old.

The Notary's mother did not die before her son arrived, or in the weeks that followed: she suffered quite genuinely from a nasty gastric ulcer, but the condition worsened and took her to her grave three and a half years later. Meanwhile, the Notary resigned himself with surprising rapidity to remaining in the town, thus satisfying paternal hopes, and within a matter of weeks he married. Dinda (the housemaid who had already born him a child) having left the scene, he reencountered (but not by coincidence—their respective families had engineered the event) a girl he had known in the past: a petite girl with a childlike and secretive air to her. Her name was Vita, she rarely opened her mouth, and she bore the Notary, one after another, seven sons, the last of whom died almost as soon as he was born.

They would have named him Michele, but there wasn't time. Fifteen days after the birth, Vita left the house to attend a neighbor's funeral. It was mid-January, and a despotic north wind blew down from the mountains. The woman returned home chilled, with the symptoms of flu. That night her fever rose. It was pneumonia—in those days (we are in 1924) an illness that claimed abundant victims. Vita was no exception. As soon as she died, so did the baby who would have been christened Michele.

Still in his forties, the Notary found himself widowed and with six very young children to care for. The eldest was fifteen years old and named after his grandfather, Giuseppe; the second had just turned twelve, and one day they would all—including his wife Tamara—call him "the Lawyer." Then came Vincenzo, Ernesto and Arnaldo, who were ten, seven, and three years old; the youngest was only two and bore the name of an illustrious great-uncle, but he, too, passed swiftly away, shortly after his mother, and none of them recollected ever having called him Giustino.

## 2. *DU CÔTÉ DE CHEZ* TAMARA

Tamara's parents had distant roots in Haute-Savoie and, even further back, in northern Morocco. In other words, they were Sephardic Jews. In Italy, before settling in the town where Tamara and her siblings would eventually be born, they had lived in Vasto, on the Adriatic coast. From there, still young, they had moved south for work. Nonetheless, even when, in the mid-1930s, some of their relatives joined them, in the hope of being overlooked by a regime that would shortly pass laws promoting racial purity, the townsfolk still considered them foreigners and, not coincidentally, would always call them "the English family."

When Tamara was born, in 1913, the couple already had a two-year-old daughter, Maria, and a comfortable financial situation as a result of the opening of the town's first pharmacy. It was he who was the Pharmacist, but right from the start it was clear to everyone that it was his wife Lea who laid down the rules at work and wore the trousers at home. Lea was diminutive in stature and fair, with eyes of a blue so limpid that they seemed to be made of water.

Like Vita, the Notary's first wife, she resembled a child, but unlike Vita, who was timid and silent, Lea was afraid of no one and could be as cutting and cruel as only certain children know how. By nature she was hard-nosed, tireless, and thrifty, while her husband was the exact opposite: tall and burly, dark-eyed, alert, and ever-worried, the Pharmacist did not enjoy work but earnestly desired a life of comfort. He had a passion for opera, he enjoyed his food ("A good spread doesn't age you," he would chuckle, to which Lea would sardonically reply, "No, it kills you") and, at least up until the early years of the Second World War, he happily played the violin that he kept hidden in a wardrobe—probably for fear his wife would get rid of it. Lea criticized her husband for being lazy, for being an overindulgent father and for not concerning himself with the family finances, but in her eyes it was the violin that summed up and symbolized every one of the man's weaknesses. At the end of the war, however, the Pharmacist stopped playing the violin for good, digging it out of the wardrobe only occasionally to tune and polish it. Because, after what he had learned of the Holocaust, the Pharmacist never again felt like playing, and thus—without being directly aware of it—came to embody Theodor Adorno's theory that, after Auschwitz, it was no longer possible to write poetry. And so none of the grandchildren born after the war ever had the privilege of seeing that big, burly man transformed into the delicate, volatile creature that he became the very instant he settled his cheek on the chin rest.

Prior to the Pharmacist and his wife Lea, there seemed to have been no one. They appeared to have been sired by no one. Their lives sprang from some far-off place, but as far as their respective families were concerned, the couple never proffered any significant information: Lea and the Pharmacist let it be known that they were of merchant stock; they occasionally furnished vague details, but nothing worth remembering. They kept up this reserve at home just as much as they did in the outside world. And even upon the arrival in the town of old Uncle Giorgio—who had no children but did, it was said, possess two suitcases filled with gold and precious stones—and of the cousins, Levino and Margherita, the silence surrounding their family origins remained unbroken. The new arrivals respected the rule and, like the Pharmacist and his wife, declared themselves to be Catholics, despite all evidence to the contrary.

Tamara, like her siblings, was baptized and received an education in every respect identical to that of all the other children in the town. The Pharmacist's girls studied with the nuns, and the boys attended the local school. They, too, suffered premature losses: a girl of not quite five and a nine-year-old boy, both of whom died of pneumonia and whose names—perhaps because they were used for such a short length of time—have been forgotten. (Although the death of the boy provoked the first symptoms of the Pharmacist's depression.) There remained Maria, Tamara, Giorgio, and—a great deal younger—Nina. It was Giorgio who would act as a bridge between the Pharmacist's family and that of the Notary.

### 3. DESTINIES

From the second or third week of school onward, Giorgio and Ernesto, one of the Notary's sons, had been inseparable companions. The former was studious and reserved, while the latter possessed a natural exuberance that encouraged him to scorn his schoolbooks. And so Giorgio did prep for both of them and Ernesto invented games for both of them. They felt united by the fact that both were blond, with pale eyes, which in Giorgio's family was nothing exceptional, but in Ernesto's was so much so that it had led some to suspect that the boy was yet another of the Notary's illegitimate children, and not Vita's son. But that wasn't the case: unlike his siblings, who seemed to be slightly pallid copies of their father, Ernesto conspicuously resembled his maternal grandmother, who, in her youth, had been very blonde.

The friendship, or better, the sense of brotherhood uniting Giorgio and Ernesto, strengthened notably following the death of Vita. Ernesto was seven years old and inevitably in search of attention. His father was absent, as always. His elder siblings did what they could to survive, and he and Arnaldo, who was even younger, found themselves left to the care of the housemaid. Who, furthermore, concerned herself only with Arnaldo, on the grounds that he was the youngest. Inevitably, Ernesto began to spend an increasing amount of his time at his friend's house. Besides, Lea was certainly an austere and rather tightfisted woman, but she felt sincere compassion for this companion of Giorgio's, who was so vivacious and so unlucky, and who, what's more, seemed to fill the void left by the son who had died of pneumonia when he was only nine years old. In short, the Pharmacist and his wife took Ernesto in.

This situation continued even after the Notary married for a second time. In 1928, four years after he had been left a widower, the man married the eldest daughter of a colleague from Gioiosa. Elvira was fourteen years younger than him, and brought with her a substantial dowry and considerable practical gifts. The Notary's two eldest sons, Giuseppe and the future Lawyer, were both away from home: the former had found refuge in the navy, the latter in a boarding school. So there were three left: Vincenzo, Ernesto, and Arnaldo. Vincenzo was a very precocious fourteen-year-old: he disappeared for days at a time and was part of a squad of young men from mixed social backgrounds who were united by a passion for card games and exuberant practical jokes, and also for what northern-European travelers fleeing Protestant prudery thought of as the very last vestige of ancient Greek culture. Elvira was therefore quite happy to concern herself only with Arnaldo, leaving Ernesto to be brought up in the home of a family that was well known to them and well respected, albeit outsiders. Besides, Elvira was herself an outsider.

The boys continued their education at the boarding school in Catanzaro, where the game plan, in a manner of speaking, remained the same: Giorgio studied for both of them, while Ernesto, with the excuse that he was always the life and soul of the party, shielded his friend from the traditional violence of boarding-school life. They left school, where they had studied classics, with different exam grades, but both passed, and they returned to the town wearing jackets and ties, like two little gentlemen. A wonderful summer awaited them, packed with parties, trips to the sea, and stolen kisses. And at the end of that season, which both of them visualized being free, first and foremost, of rules and responsibilities—after so many years in which every minute of the day had been measured out in rules and responsibilities—there glittered the prospect of university, in Naples, no less. In other words, in the metropolis. And in yet other words, in that legendary city where the Notary had lived his own legendary youth.

One of Ernesto's brothers was also in Naples, reading jurisprudence. The Lawyer. And it was, in fact, he who, over the course of that endless and memorable summer, realized that his stomach knotted and his tongue became paralyzed every time he encountered Tamara. Mara. Giorgio's sister.

## 4. THE SUMMER OF '34

Many things happened over the course of the summer of '34. In Germany the Night of the Long Knives took place, a monumental settling of scores at Hitler's orders that targeted his opponents within and beyond the party and the army. In Austria, the chancellor, Dollfuss, was assassinated, although the Nazis who took him out did not succeed in commandeering his country (but would do so in '38, with Italy's blessing). In Poland, in Neudeck, which at the time was Prussian, the German president, von Hindenburg, passed away, allowing the führer to take on every one of the Reich's great offices of state. In the town the Lawyer fell hopelessly in love with Tamara (in his head he already called her Mara) without Tamara in any way noticing; Giorgio and Ernesto realized that their friendship would sooner or later mutate into a bond that it would be more complicated to define, as they had in fact fantasized right from the start; a second child was born to the Notary and Elvira: he had thought of calling her Magda, but then, fearing that his young wife might resent it, had imposed the name Tecla, without explaining that this was in any case a homage to his long-lost lover (Tekla Bądarzewska-Baranowska was a Polish composer whom Madga admired); and finally, after an exhausting journey down from Turin, Uncle Giorgio arrived in the town, along with his suitcases full of treasure, and the cousins Levino and Margherita.

Here it should be explained that Levino and Margherita were not the old man's children, but employees of his who, quite by chance, shared his surname. In short, they were only pretend cousins. No blood ties of any kind linked them to the family of the Pharmacist and his wife. Nevertheless, for the rest of their lives they would always be labeled "the cousins." The pair had followed their aging employer because, having nothing better to do once he had closed down the firm, they had decided to leave Turin, enticed by the sizable gift the old man had promised in return for their help in reaching his family. Uncle Giorgio had built up a small fortune by trading in and selling fabrics, but having no wife or children, he had, at seventy, divested himself of the business, with the intention of spending his retirement close to the Pharmacist and Lea, who, having named a son after him, had offered him an heir and, after a fashion, a future.

Having arrived in the town at the height of a very hot summer, Uncle Giorgio went to stay in his nephew's house: they gave him a reasonably private room, well apart from the other two bedrooms into which the rest of the family piled—with the exception of Giorgio and Ernesto, who were confined to the sweltering attic. What began as a temporary arrangement nonetheless lasted five years, until the old man's death. The room he occupied had the virtue of opening onto the terrace, a feature of no small importance to the uncle. At night he could stroll undisturbed between the pots of basil and the bougainvillea, huffing and puffing to himself about the heat. The cousins Levino and Margherita instead took rooms nearby, in a dilapidated, crumbling building where, crammed into meager lodgings on the second floor, there lived the family of Maria del Nilo, who had kept house for the Pharmacist's family ever since he and his wife had first appeared in the town.

Levino almost immediately opened a little emporium on the main street, where he sold mostly grain and cheap cloth. To do so, he had invested the money that Uncle Giorgio had given the cousins as severance payment for over a decade's work at his firm and as a gesture of thanks for having accompanied him all the way from Turin, down to that godforsaken corner of the south. The couple had no children and had by then come to terms with the idea. With their respective families, who were scattered here and there across Europe, they maintained little contact, and the decision to leave Turin had also been dictated by the atmosphere that had begun to prevail in Italy's cities—an atmosphere which would soon bear the name "racial laws." In the provinces, however, and above all in the south—or so thought Levino and Margherita—anti-Semitism was surely still an unknown commodity.

Their reasoning was to prove correct and farsighted. For the entire length of the war, right up until the fall of Fascism, the two of them would live unmolested, as would the Pharmacist and his wife. Even when, at the beginning of '38, at which point the racial laws had yet to be enacted, an anonymous complaint forced Levino to defend himself against the accusation of having—because he was a Jew—profaned the Italian flag, it would be enough for the Notary, acting in his defense, to make the imaginative suggestion that the man's name was not in fact Jewish, but an Italianized form of the Roman "Lavinius" and evident proof that the accused descended from the purest of Italic stock, to guarantee his salvation. Levino was acquitted and would live out his days in peace.

### 5. MARIA DEL NILO

There were at least two theories as to why Maria del Nilo—who kept house for the Pharmacist and Lea—was named as she was. The first was the most self-explanatory and the least believable: the woman had family roots in Egypt, or at any rate with links to the Nile. Not far from the town, in fact, a rather dilapidated but gloriously positioned archaeological site—on the crest of a ridge overlooking the vivid azure of the Ionian Sea at the point where the coast forms a near right angle—marked the presence of an ancient Saracen settlement. Or an Arab one. Islamic, in any case. It was, in reality, an eighteenth-century structure that had been used as a marketplace, next to which there stood a square tower, built approximately three hundred years further back in the wake of the first Saracen invasions. But although the word "Saracen," which derives from the Greek, is somewhat generic and can also refer to the people of Egypt—which as is well known is watered by the Nile—the truth of the matter is that the invasions to which the inhabitants of the northern Ionian coast were subjected up until the early 1800s originated exclusively in Turkey, which has nothing to do with the Nile.

The second hypothesis—more realistic but equally unfounded—was that the woman was the daughter of, or descended from, a man called Nilo, a name not unusual in the area. After all, in the early years of the twentieth century, women in the south of Italy were often regarded as a man's property, belonging to their father or husband. However, this particular woman's father was called Franceschino, and husbands there had been none. Her only son, who was named after his grandfather, had been given the surname "di Maria," and no one knew for sure who his father was. There was a tenuous possibility that one of her great-great-grandfathers might have answered to the name Nilo, but it seemed highly unlikely, given that the woman's own family had no memory of this being the case.

The truth is that for this sobriquet, "Maria del Nilo" (which had become so routine that, instead of calling them by their official surname, everyone now gave the same name to her son and grandchildren), there remained no reasonable explanation, and at a certain point they all stopped asking themselves what it meant or where it had come from.

Besides which, Maria del Nilo seemed to have been born to pass through the world unnoticed: she was not small of build, but she dressed only in black and seemed as detached and irrelevant as a shadow. She was, furthermore, far from talkative, aloof (maintaining a reserve that bordered on misanthropy even with her son and grandchildren), and, at a certain age, had gone deaf, almost as if to underline, or perhaps to render plausible, her recondite desire for solitude. With the Pharmacist and Lea she had found herself at her ease right from the start, because they left her to her work and barely exchanged a word. Yet, and above all with Lea, the relationship was very successful: when Maria del Nilo went deaf and her voice grew loud because she herself was unable to hear it, Lea was the only person who still occasionally managed to exchange a little gossip with her.

Not unsurprisingly, as the years went by, her grandchildren now adults, the woman increasingly preferred to pass her nights at the Pharmacist's house—in one corner of the large kitchen, next to the fire. For at least two generations—in other words, for the children and grandchildren of the

Pharmacist and Lea—Maria del Nilo served as a sort of unfathomable domestic idol—and like all idols seemed to possess none of the attributes normal in common mortals. First and foremost, mutability. Like the concept of Being in Parmenides, she seemed to have no past and no future. Her face—a perfect lattice of wrinkles—remained unaltered from the age of forty until her death, four decades later. Maria del Nilo inhabited an eternal present, unceasing and indivisible. She never fell ill; despite a lifetime's hard toil, she never seemed tired; she asked for nothing and she always ate alone, hastily and never at the table, but with a plate balanced on her knee.

And yet she would play an important, if not vital, part in the betrothal of the Lawyer and Tamara. She, Maria del Nilo, who could of course neither read nor write, became the paper and the pen the couple used in order to communicate at a distance without the risk of leaving a trace.

### 6. "GIVE ME YOUR KISSES, I'LL GIVE YOU MY LIFE."

The song was called "Primo Amore"—First Love—and the man who warbled it was called Giacomo Rondinella. The Lawyer had no ear for music, but ever since he'd begun hearing that languid refrain in the cafés of Naples his thoughts had unavoidably turned to Tamara, his Mara, and he had developed a sudden and unavoidable devotion to Euterpe, the muse who presides over octaves and opera.

He had never spoken to Tamara. His Mara. She was one of Giorgio's elder sisters. She was tall and willowy. And so elegant. Blonde hair, blue eyes. God, she was beautiful. "*Give me your kisses, I'll give you my life / Together we'll sing / No one ever forgets their first love.*" He had never been brave enough to talk to her, though—with the exception of vague greetings exchanged in the street when he met her out walking or on the terrace of the Pharmacist's house during the parties Giorgio and Ernesto threw after graduating from high school.

She had always been unwaveringly cool and haughty: just as much so during the parties as out in the street. The Lawyer had subjected his brother to full-blown interrogations on the subject of Tamara, his Mara. What did she do? What did she think? What did she like? Whom did she see? He wanted to know everything about her. Ernesto must know her well—he lived more at the Pharmacist's house than with their own family now. But Ernesto's replies were monosyllabic, evasive, imprecise. The Lawyer began to loathe him. He informed Ernesto that, as soon as he, too, arrived in Naples, in a few months' time, he, the Lawyer, would have his revenge and would offer no assistance with any of the practical difficulties Ernesto was inevitably going to confront, from finding lodgings to all the rest of it. But his brother was immovable and indeed continued to grumble and change the subject every time the Lawyer brought it up. Ernesto was so cagey, so vague when he talked about Tamara that the Lawyer began to fear his brother was trying to hide something: perhaps she secretly loved someone else, or Ernesto himself was in love with her, or maybe Tamara, his Mara, dreamed of becoming a nun... Oh god, being in love was such agony. In the blink of an eye the world had become a forest of doubts, and every question foresaw at least a dozen answers. What torture! What an uninterrupted succession of pangs! The Lawyer found it impossible to stay calm enough to study (the summer of '34 flew by in a flash). He tried tagging along with Vincenzo, the brother who played cards for days at a time, or he went hunting, or lounged around with his debonair friends. But the Lawyer was a duffer at cards, and may have appreciated elegance, but hadn't the faintest idea how it was done. As for the art of the chase: on the two or three occasions when he had attempted to practice it, he had gotten as far as jumping out of bed in the morning and arraying himself in his hunter's finery only to discover that it was already noon and that Vincenzo had left the house at dawn wearing his usual charitable grin, and that it was now too late to change into something more suitable before—to the great amusement of all present—sitting down to Sunday lunch.

The Lawyer did love sleeping—a passion that would never abandon him, even into old age. Just as he would never lose his passion for Tamara, his Mara, to whom he dedicated saccharine verses that, as luck would have it, he never dared let her read. Because, had he done so, she—who was exacting by nature and possessed of a notable sense of humor—would never have deigned even to bother refusing him. So, that doggerel, which was intended to have something of the flavor of Giacomo Rondinella's songs, remained a jealously guarded secret, and after a goodly number of years of varyingly clumsy courting Tamara was able to return her verdict and agree to marry him. And, despite all that pungent irony of hers, there would not be a single day in her long life when she ever regretted it.

## 7. A STEP BACK

In the September of 1920 the Notary had been elected mayor, representing a coalition made up of socialists and First World War veterans' associations. His father had held the position before him, and the same thing would one day happen to his son, the Lawyer. When the town council assembled, the Notary could count on a majority of twelve out of the twenty councilors, but was nonetheless elected unanimously. The climate of ecumenism did not last long. First and foremost because the council he led almost immediately increased the local taxes paid by the propertied classes, set up scholarship funds for boys from poorer families, and announced they would be repossessing various plots of public land (and they were extraordinarily numerous) which had been commandeered by the major local landowners, and redistributing them in quotas to the peasants. Added to which there was the question of his character: intransigent, draconian, insufferable. The honeymoon between majority and opposition ended in high drama. Eight councilors resigned in protest. There were physical scuffles. Some accused the mayor of fomenting class hatred, and as a consequence social disorder. In February 1922 the district prefect disbanded the council. At that point things degenerated, and the fresh elections, which were held on 30 July that year, took place in an atmosphere redolent of civil war.

The existing coalition of leftist candidates led by the Notary lost spectacularly, taking only four of the available seats. A conservative mayor was elected, representing the interests of the area's grander landowning families. A few weeks later, Mussolini's March on Rome neatly encapsulated what was happening right across Italy, from the heart of the nation to its outer fringes.

One evening that fall—a fall which would weigh heavily on the entire peninsula for twenty years to come—the Notary was making his way home when he realized he was being followed by three or possibly four individuals. He couldn't see them particularly well, because it was dark—to say nothing of his nearsightedness. Feigning indifference, he kept walking. His legs felt slightly unsteady. The men behind him sniggered, muttering all manner of insults, but softly, so that only he could hear them. Then, when they were just a few steps away from the Notary's house, at a point where the road narrowed to form an alley onto which no windows looked out, the little group pounced and set about bludgeoning him. The Notary had no time to think: he pulled out the little pistol he'd been carrying with him for months now, and started firing wildly. One of his assailants fell to the ground. The others vanished into the night.

Before the night was out, the Notary went into hiding. He escaped into the region's interior, up into the mountains. A supportive network of peasant farmers and militant socialists kept him hidden and safe for several weeks. That was the time it took to find out that the individual he had shot was not dead, but as luck would have it just wounded in one leg, and that no one had reported the incident to the police, and that the situation back in town seemed to have calmed down. And so the Notary headed home. Over the course of those days spent with no fixed abode, some of them spent in the mountains of the Grande Sila and others in the mountains of the Piccola Sila, while deprived of starched collars and impeccable shirts, the Notary had felt briefly emancipated, liberated from a self-image that had confined him to the role of a tweed-suited, gold-rimmed-spectacle-wearing intellectual who condescendingly devoted himself to defending the cause of the lowliest of the lowly. Over the course of those weeks, the Notary had slept in haylofts, had eaten bread and cheese, had washed infrequently and always in icy water—despite it being mid-November and the weather far from mild— and had had to contend with bedbugs and fleas. Nevertheless, at the end of all this he was left with the impression that the words of Marx, or even those of Proudhon—so attentively read while draped across the leather sofa in his office—not only tallied with all the abstract theories he had previously found seductive for almost exclusively aesthetic reasons, but might indeed prove to be sturdy tools for understanding reality. And, above all, for changing it.

During those days on the run, an enduring friendship was also established: his friendship with Pasquale, a very youthful medic from a very poor family, who would one day become one of the founders of the Communist Party in the region and would take a seat in Italy's first postwar parliament.

### 8. A LITTLE HISTORY

For over fifteen years, from 1922 to 1938, the Notary succeeded in practicing his profession almost unproblematically. He certainly wasn't held in high esteem by the local powers that be—they considered him a hothead and a dangerous opponent of Fascism—but even so, he was able to continue working and to continue reading his favorite writers (particularly Benedetto Croce, now that he had written his "Manifesto of the Anti-Fascist Intellectuals").

The man who had been wounded during that ambush back in 1922 happened to live not far from the Notary's house. Although the man had never reported the incident, he was in any event forced to reckon, each and every day, with the consequences of that late-fall evening: he hadn't lost his life, but his right leg had been left maimed. Motive enough that, politics aside, the feelings he nursed toward the Notary were far from warm. His longing for revenge would, however, have to wait a long time before being satisfied. For years and years, every time he encountered the Notary in the alleyways near their respective homes, the man would be forced to repress an urge to pull out the knife he kept in his pocket and to thrust it into the guts of that arrogant, unpunished socialist. Until 28 August 1938, when revenge was finally served as is most fitting. Very cold.

Over the years, a vertical split had formed within the Fascist Party in the town, dividing an elitist wing associated with the grand landowning families and another composed of the so-called social Right. The two leanings took turns at holding power, both of them having to contend with a deep-rooted hostility on the part of the peasantry and the town's laboring class. Toward the end of 1933 and at the beginning of 1934, a series of sizable protests by the unemployed swept from power the podestà, who was linked to the landowning elite; some time later, another protest, which on the afternoon of 28 August 1938 gave rise to violent clashes in the streets, put the opposing faction's podestà under considerable pressure. That podestà, however, saved his job by immediately and violently clamping down on those who had gone out into the streets to protest: dozens of people were arrested, beaten up, and held in prison for months. The podestà was also quick to come to an agreement with the moderate wing of the party, and in so doing, ensured he would remain in the job for a few more years, until the war broke out.

The close entourage of the podestà who survived the brouhaha of 28 August unscathed included the man wounded in the course of the famous ambush of '22. It was he who was entrusted with organizing and directing the roundup that followed the protest march and the violent scuffles with the forces of law and order. And naturally it was he who placed the Notary's name at the very top of the list of the troublemakers who while marching had shouted, "Down with the podestà," and had responded with a hail of stones to the baton charge launched by the Carabinieri. And so the Notary once again had to escape into the mountains of the Sila, this time round remaining on the run for five years, until the Allied forces landed in September 1943.

### 9. LEA'S POINT OF VIEW

Lea, Tamara's mother, had nothing against the Lawyer. He was a serious young man. He had a university degree and a promising professional career ahead of him. Lea had known his mother Vita, who had died long ago, when he was just twelve years old. Despite having lost his mother so young, he had turned out well—that much was in no doubt. No one would ever have described him as dazzlingly handsome, but everyone spoke of him with respect and affection. He didn't make mischief like his brother Ernesto, whom Lea, while adoring him, could not avoid scolding because he studied too little and flirted with all the girls. Yes, Ernesto was delightful, Lea told herself, but he would make a terrible husband.

The Lawyer was right for Tamara, because she too was serious and reserved, for all that sharp tongue of hers. He was just one year older than she, and that was appropriate too. Tamara was perhaps a little too tall for the young man—all the more reason for wearing the low-heeled shoes that were, in any case, quite the thing in the thirties. He was dark as an olive; she had pale eyes and fair hair. An interesting couple, thought Lea: Tamara's slightly pallid beauty sprouted wings with him by her side.

In Lea's eyes the Lawyer had only one flaw, and that was his father. Who in addition to being a subversive was also irresponsible, because from the summer of '38 onward he had been on the run—was not, therefore, working—and his wife and children (with his second wife he had now had three) were practically starving. And that was not a figure of speech. The word in town was that the youngest of the little ones, who had been born at a point when the Notary had already made himself scarce, risked dying of malnutrition.

When he came back from Naples, Ernesto continued to sleep at Lea and the Pharmacist's house, where he still shared the attic bedroom with Giorgio. However, the young man did pay frequent visits to his stepmother and siblings, and each time he went, Lea handed him a little butter, some fresh milk, perhaps a few slices of meat or even a chicken. Elvira made no effort to hide how grateful she was: on the contrary, she wrote Lea brief letters of thanks in which all her anxiety made itself apparent. The small fortune she had brought with her as a dowry had been invested, by her husband, in property that, in his absence, brought in no income. Their not-enormous savings (the couple had lived very comfortably, without penny-pinching) were running out. Poor Elvira had surreptitiously begun selling off bits and pieces of jewelry and smaller items from their vast hoard of family silver. As though that weren't enough to cope with, her husband's flight had been followed first by the death of her father-in-law (who despite his great age had administered the portfolio of properties) and then by Italy joining the war on 10 June 1940. The only person offering her any help—apart from Lea—was the Lawyer, who had reopened his father's office and had begun to make a name for himself as someone a great deal calmer and more prudent than his father.

Lea appreciated the fact that her future son-in-law also took care of his stepmother and younger siblings. It was further proof of the Lawyer's sense of duty and awareness of the value of money. But all the same, with that father of his . . .

### 10. WHAT THE PHARMACIST KNEW

First and foremost, the Pharmacist had a blind faith in his wife's judgment. Lea was not the type to dish out compliments lightly—indeed, she did not, as a rule, dish anything out lightly. What is more, and unlike many women, she didn't place undue value on sentiment. Had Tamara fallen in love with a good-for-nothing, Lea would have done everything in her power to change the girl's mind, one way or another, by fair means or foul: of that he was convinced. Because Lea was not like him. The Pharmacist pictured himself as no more and no less than what his wife had always told him he was, to wit: a man with his head in the clouds. In short: pleasant but weak. Too weak, perhaps. And it cannot be excluded that it was perhaps his weakness that encouraged him to think the world of the Lawyer, almost by default. Nonetheless, he, too, worried that, what with that father . . .

And yet he did like the Notary. For starters, the Notary had taken up the defense of their cousins Levino and Margherita when someone anonymous (the swine!) had accused the pair of disrespecting the flag. The Notary had been the only lawyer in the entire district prepared to take on the job. True, the man was a socialist, so it was only to be expected. In any case, he had shown considerable grit. Besides, the fact that the Notary was courageous had been demonstrated on the night when he had been ambushed and had not run off but had instead pulled out his revolver and fired. It takes courage to shoot at a human being. Although perhaps, in addition to courage, it also takes a certain dose of recklessness; because the Notary had been firing the gun to defend himself from an assault, but could have killed one of those delinquents, and homicide is never forgivable, not even if the law allows for it, thought the Pharmacist. With which he ended up agreeing with his wife on all fronts: the Lawyer was a serious and dependable young man; he would make a good husband for Tamara. But of course, with that father of his . . .

Maybe it was better not to dwell on that. All told, Tamara seemed mature enough and seemed to have her head firmly enough screwed on to be capable of making her own decisions. As far as suitors were concerned, she had already had a few and had not thrown herself into the arms of the first who'd come courting. From what her father could see, the girl didn't seem to be particularly smitten. The young man was probably more in love with her than she with him, but this, in the Pharmacist's eyes, was a boon: it meant that the Lawyer's desire for Tamara would last all the longer, because one doesn't easily stop wanting things hard-won. Although maybe yes, one does stop wanting them all the quicker: because we tire of always yearning for the same old thing.

All these thoughts made a knot of themselves in his head. Anything that concerned his children made a knot of itself in his head. Because his children filled him with immense joy but also with a dreadful anxiety: from this point of view he was undeniably different from Lea, who always seemed so sure of herself. In any case, he would, he decided, ask Uncle Giorgio: What did Uncle Giorgio think of Tamara's suitor? What did he think of the young lawyer?

## 11. UNCLE GIORGIO'S ONION

As, little by little, he made his way into his own sunset—and at this point his eightieth year of life was already a surprising and distant memory, held sadly aloft like a flag at half-mast—Uncle Giorgio sensed that, with each passing day, his life was divesting itself of a pointless patina of ambiguities, conventions, and frills. It was freeing itself and at the very same time diminishing itself, almost as though the time accreting on his body paralleled a fundamental and ultimately regenerative denuding.

Back in the days when he hadn't yet been capable of fully understanding its cruel beauty, in *Peer Gynt*—a play by one of his favorite authors, Henrik Ibsen—he had come across the idea that life is like an onion and that, looking back over it, one cannot help shedding tears. It was an image both simple and artful—he understood it now. And yet it was not the unavoidable tears that struck him most, nor the fact that the onion Ibsen described lacked any true center, so much as the fact (the playwright didn't say as much, but Uncle Giorgio could work it out for himself) that the onion, just like our lives, in reality enclosed a central core of emptiness—the remnant of something lost.

In a sense, ever since he had first set foot in the town, Uncle Giorgio had felt he was getting closer to that core: minute by minute, layers of skin were falling unconcernedly away from him; thoughts he had had were vanishing at a heroic pace; he was shedding weight and becoming a man of no substance. And, in his own way, happy.

For many years he had found it impossible to separate himself from his own past—the childhood holidays at the house in Tangiers, his precocious love of painting, the revelation of Paris—but now he was on the brink of understanding something that all little children know very well, namely that the world is pure surface, and that history is at best a subgenre of fantasy. On the eve of his final journey—in other words, the eve of what, not to put too fine a point on it, people used to call death—old Uncle Giorgio was, in short, becoming the one thing he never had been: an artist. Or, to put it another way, an individual at the mercy of an onion.

He knew no one in town, apart from his nieces and nephews, and so, from the moment he arrived there accompanied by Levino and Margherita, he had felt newly emancipated, just as he had in the period when, as a young man, he had lived in Paris and discovered the city's demimonde. Back then, his parents had divided their time between Tangiers and Lyon; they paid him a discreet monthly allowance and he could therefore permit himself the luxury of imagining a future featuring grand exhibitions, artistic successes, and accolades, even if, for the time being, he wasn't doing much more than staying out late, drinking a great deal, and smoking an even greater deal. When, years later, given that his career as a painter had still not begun, he had had to bow to a paternal diktat that wanted him employed in the family's textile business, and he was therefore packed off to Turin to open a store selling fabric wholesale, Uncle Giorgio had had the distinct sensation that he had left behind in the Ville Lumière the most noteworthy part of himself, the famous core of the onion. He was, however, mistaken; if for no other reason than because, from Paris, he had brought with him—as though it were a means of keeping alive the little flame of that significant, albeit now-inaccessible self—two paintings on canvas acquired for not much more than a bottle of wine and signed by his friend Paul Gauguin.

The paintings hung on the wall at the foot of the bed in the room he had in his nephew's house, while on his bedside table he kept a finely chased silver candlestick that had once belonged to Madame du Barry. Into that high-ceilinged but not especially spacious bedroom, he had crammed the most precious of the treasures accumulated over the course of the decades lived in Turin—alongside the candlestick, a discreet collection of enameled snuff boxes concealing surprisingly erotic figurines, his mother's gold jewelry, four Savonnerie rugs in various sizes, a twenty-four-piece canteen of English-style silver cutlery, a little Flemish-school oil painting of the deposition from the cross, a very small but precious collection of Chinese lacquerwork, a bulging photograph album. Into that circumscribed space he had brought his own world, and there, from the summer of '34 to the fall of '38, he rediscovered the freedom and brio of his youth.

Then all of this came to an end. It happened suddenly, in the space of a few minutes: Uncle Giorgio entered the heart of the onion. Or, to put it another way, he lost himself.

On the morning of 11 November 1938, he read the headline on the front page of *Corriere della Sera* and instantly understood that he was going to die. The racial laws announced in the newspaper banned Italian Jews from doing just about anything. So, the nation that had taken his heart away from him in exchange for a trade was now taking that away too. And little did it matter that the trade was one he hadn't plied for quite a while, nor did it matter that he had long ago converted to Catholicism: those laws took a swipe at, or more precisely obliterated, his past. Which at the end of the day was the greater part of him. His own personal onion. In that past, he had come into this world a Jew, born of Jewish parents, and had constructed, day by day, layer by layer, applying himself to it diligently and stubbornly, his own identity. Now all of this was being taken away from him by law. Now nothing, apart from the empty core of the onion, was left. And so Uncle Giorgio started dying on 11 November 1938 and finished on 24 August the following year. Over the course of the winter he suffered from numerous ailments; he often remained in his room and not infrequently refused to eat. Lea tried to tempt him with the odd treat or two, but Uncle Giorgio appeared to have lost all interests and preferences, which seemed startling to say the least, given that his entire life had been lived under the banner of his relish for delicacies of every kind. All desire and predilections spent, all amusement and entertainments forgotten, at the beginning of the summer—his final summer—one last little flame of vitality lit up in him.

In Turin he had put into storage a large quantity of furniture and other objects difficult to transport, or not especially valuable: the last bits and pieces of what had once been his inheritance. The rest he had already sold (part of the proceeds, in cash, was shut away in one of the two suitcases, which legend had it were full of gold and gemstones). He entrusted the job—of traveling up to Piedmont and selling those last remaining chattels—not to his nephew but, out of prudence, to Ernesto, who in exchange would be allowed to keep 20 percent of the proceeds.

Ernesto completed the mission in little more than two weeks, managing also to sell off the warehouse in which the goods had been stored. From the final sum he detracted the cost of his board and lodging in Turin, in addition to the cut that was due to him, and handed over what was left to its rightful owner. He did, however, ask Uncle Giorgio for permission to keep for himself a seven-inch-wide eighteenth-century reproduction of the *Sleeping Hermaphrodite* from the Louvre, a request which was satisfied and which secretly delighted the old man because his heart always—even in those ultimate days of indifference—thrilled when he recognized in his fellow man the taste for beauty and the pleasure in possessing that had motivated and ennobled his own existence.

It was late June. Uncle Giorgio appeared to be in better form. He began leaving his room quite frequently, and on two occasions even went to the bank, where he had his own deposit accounts jointly assigned to the nephew with whom he shared a name and surname: Giorgio Attali. Then, from mid-July onward, he started to feel restless: he had the impression that his thoughts wouldn't linger for even a second on anything at all. Nothing calmed them. Not the contemplation of the two Gauguins hanging in his bedroom (in the past they had been phenomenal sedatives, and it was no accident that he had—in Paris, and now here in the town—kept them in the room he slept in), and not the silver candleholder that had once belonged to Madame du Barry, the polishing of which represented both ritual and sedative. At night he didn't sleep a wink: he spent the hours walking frantically up and down the terrace, without, however, managing to enjoy the cool air, like a caged animal incapable of sensing anything except the smell of his own fear.

In addition to this disquiet, which during the hours of daylight he did everything he could to mask, Uncle Giorgio was afflicted by another problem: he found himself moved by the silliest of things. On the day when his nephew, the Pharmacist, had asked him what he thought of Tamara's beau, the old man had suddenly begun weeping uncontrollably at the mere thought of that burgeoning love. So intense were his sobs that the Pharmacist, worrying that he had unwittingly reawakened who knows what long-dormant sorrow, had found a way of bringing the conversation to a close, steering it round to talk of the exquisite workmanship of some of the snuffboxes in his uncle's collection. Lea, conversely, seemed impermeable to the old man's emotions, and lately had actually begun treating him rather roughly and brusquely, as though there was something she had to make him pay for.

Round about the middle of August, however, even the weeping came to a halt. Of the ancient onion which had been the life of Giorgio Attali, little now remained. He lost weight. He seemed to shrink from one day to the next. By way of contrast, his hands, and only his hands, appeared to be getting bigger. Taking it in turns, not one but three physicians busied themselves around him, although not at his bedside, because Uncle Giorgio rose early every morning, washed, got carefully dressed, and then, instead of devoting himself to his usual activities, slumped into an armchair he had in his bedroom, next to one of the two French doors that opened onto the terrace. Circling around that armchair, the physicians pronounced their diagnosis: old Uncle Giorgio was suffering from nothing in particular. He was just old.

Early on the morning of 24 August 1939, the two little Gauguins on the wall at the foot of his bed seemed to be astronomically remote. However tightly he narrowed his eyes, Uncle Giorgio could barely make them out. He got out of bed. The summer was still searingly hot. He found time to rejoice in the fresh water found in his basin and flicked it slowly into his face. But then even the sight of himself in the mirror began to disturb him: the features wouldn't come into focus.

Very slowly, with great economy of movement, he put on a pair of light-colored linen pants, a white short-sleeved shirt, a blue jacket with no lining—also in linen. At his throat, the ubiquitous polka-dot cravat; on his feet, rope-soled shoes with laces he didn't seem to be able to tie. He had the impression it had taken him a century to complete this simple series of tasks. It occurred to him that he should slip on the ring inherited from his mother that he always wore on his little finger, but he thought it must be on the bedside table where he usually put it before going to bed, and now that bedside table was so far away that it had faded into nothingness.

Sitting in his armchair, the sunlight still loitering on the far side of the terrace, he heard the voices of the waking household. He thought he could also hear those of his parents, who, he remembered, had talked to one another in Hebrew, a language he himself did not speak. He recognized it, that language full of low guttural sounds that had inhabited only the adults' rooms in the house in Tangiers. It was so ancient, so familiar; it was older than time. Listening to it carefully, with happy astonishment old Uncle Giorgio did recognize it, but did not notice that in the meantime he had died.

## 12. ADIEU

Uncle Giorgio had a Catholic funeral at which very few people were present. Apart from the family, including Ernesto,

Levino and Margherita, there were Maria del Nilo, accompanied by her son and relatives; the Lawyer, with his brother Vincenzo—very elegantly kitted out in jodhpurs—and their stepmother Elvira; Peppo from the posthouse, a young man of around thirty-five who, in recent years, when Uncle Giorgio had still been well enough, had acted as secretary and factotum for the old man, earning a position of trust which he would subsequently be accorded by the Pharmacist as well; a couple of elderly members of the private club the dead man had belonged to; and three professional mourners, in hope of a tip. It was a short ceremony void of elegance. The opposite of what the deceased would have wanted.

By half past six on the evening of Friday, 25 August, it was all over. Back home, the Pharmacist pulled his violin out of the wardrobe and started playing—with rather too many duff notes—some of his favorite pieces (Édouard Lalo's *Symphonie espagnole*, a little Mendelssohn, the usual Paganini). Tamara, meanwhile, let herself into Uncle Giorgio's bedroom and sat down in the armchair next to the French doors, where he had drawn his last breath. For a minute, she thought back over the afternoon just ended.

Unlike her mother and sister, who for the funeral had, in obeisance to local custom, been dressed in black from head to toe, Tamara had wanted at all costs to wear a beautiful dark-green dress with geometrical patterns on it, a dress that reached to midcalf and that clung to and exalted her willowy silhouette (a detail which had very nearly taken the Lawyer's breath away). It had been a gift from her uncle, and for that reason she had chosen to wear it today: it felt like a tribute of a sort to the memory of the most refined man she had ever known.

The two of them had never been particularly close, and Tamara now regretted it. Although he had been kind and pleasant, a man whose courtesy extended to the smallest of details, her uncle had always intimidated her. She didn't know quite why. Perhaps it was precisely that slightly mannered politeness of his, or maybe it was because she didn't feel quite good enough for that elderly gentleman, who had even lived in Paris. Her mother couldn't have cared less, and Maria was blithely unaware of it, but she, Tamara, had spotted the way in which her uncle glanced bewilderedly around him when the table wasn't properly laid, or when the women of the household spoke rather too loudly, or again, when the dresses they wore were dowdy. And then, she had always been struck by the difference between the old man's room and the rest of the house: in that bedroom one breathed a completely different air—it was like stumbling into another world, one crammed with tapestries, precious rugs, and fine objects. Everything seemed wrapped in cotton wool in that world. Even the smell that hovered there was special—a blend of wood and pepper, the aroma of a guarded virility.

Not long after arriving in the town, in the summer of '34, their uncle had given Maria a magnificent diamond broach and had given Tamara a ring with an emerald so big it had shocked her. She hadn't known emeralds could be that size. Their uncle had explained that these were jewels inherited from his mother: after his death he would be leaving them to Lea, and therefore, in a sense, to the two girls and to their younger sister Nina, who at the time was just six years old. He instructed the girls to look after them carefully, just as he had, remembering that they had belonged to a woman of extraordinary elegance—the only woman, he said, whom he had ever truly loved.

Now Tamara thought back to that episode, and in particular to the words their uncle had dedicated to his mother. With the passing of the years, she understood them better, she felt.

After that brief conversation Tamara had asked the Pharmacist to tell her something more of the elderly gentleman whom he, too, called uncle. And so the young woman discovered that in her case the man referred to was a *great*-uncle, in other words her father's father's brother—a much younger brother, with an age gap similar to the one between herself and Nina. Their uncle, she also learned, had been brought up almost as though he were an only child, and had been very pampered. As a young man he hadn't wanted to have anything to do with the family business. He had studied art history in Paris with the intention of becoming a painter and had lived what had in all probability been a rather dissolute few years. But then, lacking cash or any genuine vocation, he had answered the call of family duty, and since he got on well with neither his elder brother nor his father, had settled down in Turin to run an important branch of the business. When first his father and then his brother died, Uncle Giorgio had made the business an entirely Italian affair, had brought his now-ancient mother to Turin, and had handed his pharmacist nephew—who was only sixteen years younger than he—an enormous sum of money, thus buying out the part of the business the nephew was due to inherit. After all, his nephew had no intention of working in the fabric trade: he was studying chemistry, he was already engaged to Lea, and the two of them were planning to live in the south, where he had obtained a permit from the prefecture authorizing him to open one of southern Italy's very first modern pharmacies.

Tamara wondered earnestly whether or not Uncle Giorgio had been happy in their home. Especially toward the end, she had noticed a new tension mounting all of a sudden between him and her mother, something unspoken that seemed to be hurting both parties. There had been times when she had heard Uncle Giorgio muttering to himself in French, and she had imagined that perhaps he was resorting to that language, which no one else in the family knew well, to express freely his disappointment at living out the last years of his life in an atmosphere so different from the one—full of refinement and good taste—he was used to. She would have liked, from time to time, to have conversed with him in French, but had never dared suggest it, and now it was too late.

As she was lifting herself out of the armchair next to the French doors, her brother and Ernesto walked in. She had never before noticed how strongly Giorgio resembled their uncle: the same slightly aloof and elusive look in their eyes; the same way of walking, leaning forward, as though meeting you halfway and simultaneously readying themselves to flee at the first opportunity; the same sartorial vanity, not quite masked by a lick of modesty. Not for nothing, Tamara suddenly realized, was Giorgio the heir-elect. It wasn't just their uncle's name he shared.

The three young people exchanged quick, fond hugs. Making his way toward the bedside table, Giorgio said, "Come into the other room, we'll have a glass of wine in his honor." Ernesto feigned a cheeriness and ease he wasn't feeling. Tamara's eyes raked the room, lingering lovingly on the paintings, the ornaments, the furniture: she could feel her uncle's living presence, almost as though he were hovering there for a moment longer, before disappearing, his hands and his gaze clasping for one last time all the beauty that had been his. As if addressing the old man himself, Tamara murmured, "Adieu."

She noticed that her brother was wearing the old man's ring on his little finger. It looked like it had been there forever.

## 13. INHERITANCE

Ernesto was decidedly behind in his studies. He had already changed his degree twice, squandering almost two years: from medicine, in which he had enrolled solely because that was what Giorgio had chosen, he had moved on to jurisprudence, thinking he might as well toe the line taken first by his father and then by his brother, the Lawyer. In reality neither one quite suited him. Because, as far as Ernesto was concerned, it was university that didn't quite suit him. Ernesto loved the open air, entertainment, and above all female company (but here it should be pointed out that the first two of these could easily be sidelined, if Giorgio's presence was not in the cards). For a brief period Ernesto had also loved sports, but the very idea of discipline was alien to him. And in effect, the open air, entertainment, and girls (not to mention Giorgio) imposed no rules, but on the contrary encouraged the bending of them.

In Naples, Ernesto lived in the same lodgings as Giorgio—an apartment, at the far end of the Rettifilo, where two other young men also had rooms. The house belonged to a lady of an age kinder not to specify, a widow not ugly but with all the elegance of a rotten tooth, and with a daughter by the name of Italia who was pushing thirty (her mother, meanwhile, was known to all as "la Signora," the lady of the house, although there was, if we are to be honest, nothing very ladylike about her).

Following Uncle Giorgio's death, and despite having inherited all his worldly goods, Giorgio's lifestyle had not changed. He continued to dress with care, and as he always had, loved art, opera, and literature, as well as studying medicine: his habits were the same as ever. He now allowed himself occasional extravagances, but they were small things, such as paying for two tickets up in "the gods" at the San Carlo opera house, instead of one, for the pleasure of being able to drag Ernesto or another friend along; or going to the barber more frequently; or perhaps even buying books as gifts and not just for himself. Little things that nonetheless gave Giorgio great pleasure. He had entrusted his mother with the responsibility of administering his wealth until he finished his studies. For the time being, Lea was authorized to withdraw a small monthly sum, which she wired to her son to cover his personal expenses.

By way of contrast, ever since making a very small amount of money in the form of his percentage of the proceeds of the sale of Uncle Giorgio's property in Turin, Ernesto had led the life of Riley. And being—unlike the Notary—generous not only with himself but above all with others, in next to no time found himself penniless (although here we should add that his father, among other reasons because he was on the run, supplied not a cent).

Most of Ernesto's funds had been poured into the city's bordellos. Across Naples, from Via Chiaia to the Spanish Quarter, there were many where the young man was a regular guest. Two very young prostitutes—Spanish Mimì and Dorina-from-Sorrento—considered themselves as good as engaged to him, each unbeknownst to the other. Ernesto was not especially handsome, nor especially elegant (or munificent), yet he enjoyed considerable success not only with experts in that sector but also with the nonprofessionals. Giorgio maintained that the secret—a secret so secret as to be a mystery even to its sole and legitimate custodian—lay in the air of dissolute but, beneath it all, needy youthfulness that Ernesto exhibited—in a manner as unstudied as it was shameless. Perhaps because he genuinely *was* one, the role of the tearaway but sweet-natured half orphan fitted him triumphantly well—financial consequences included.

Italia had a soft spot for him too. Which Giorgio had realized some time back, while Ernesto pretended not to notice. But the signs were very clear. Ernesto was the only roomer to get breakfast in bed on Sunday mornings, and for that matter he found he was given the best slice of whatever was being served when they sat down to lunch at the oval table in the dining room. An evening meal was not covered by the monthly rent, but the young man always managed to cadge a hard-boiled egg off la Signora's daughter, a glass of milk and some cookies, or perhaps even an omelet with the remains of their lunchtime spaghetti stirred into it. The little privileges he enjoyed were countless, which was why, not Giorgio—who could forgive him anything—but the other two young boarders had begun to find him insufferable, and considered him a wily profiteer.

In reality, Ernesto was in no way wily, nor was he a profiteer: he simply belonged to that class of men, somewhat numerous in Italy's south, who cannot help pleasing women. Young or old, pulchritudinous or unlovely, it matters not a jot, since in all circumstances, women—who are not individuals so much as functions-embodied—to wit, mothers, wives, fiancées, or sisters—are to be lied to, always and regardless. As a matter of principle. And so, even if there were mornings when the lady of the house materialized in the kitchen or in the apartment's long central corridor looking every bit as dreadful as an avenging angel from the Book of Revelations, Ernesto never failed to pronounce a breezy "Good morning," followed by the words "bella Signora." To say nothing of the solicitudes he was capable of lavishing on Italia: solicitudes she interpreted as equally lavish declarations of intent, while for him it was simply small talk.

Giorgio warned his friend not once but a thousand times, "You do know Italia intends to marry you and bear you an heir?" Ernesto didn't take the slightest bit of notice. He rolled his eyes and changed the subject. Or even laughed, seeing as she was so much older: she was at least thirty, she had surely given up on the idea of ever getting married. Let alone having a child.

### 14. A WEDDING FAST APPROACHING (BUT NOT BEFORE ANOTHER BEND IN THE ROAD)

The Notary had now been a fugitive for a good year and a half, and there was a whiff of war in the air, but the Lawyer's thoughts were mainly of Tamara, his Mara. How long would they have to continue what was effectively a secret liaison, united by dint of messages surreptitiously exchanged thanks to the good offices of Maria del Nilo? How long would it take to transform that strange routine into an official engagement and then, finally, into a marriage? Of course, the situation was what it was: his father was a fugitive, his brother Vincenzo wasn't achieving anything apart from going hunting and dressing like a dandy, Ernesto and Arnaldo were still busy with their studies (Ernesto had also run the risk of being called up as a soldier for the invasion of Albania in the spring of that year), not to forget his half siblings, the Notary and Elvira's youngest three children, who were so little (nine, five, and one year old) that he felt crushed by the weight of a responsibility as big as it was rightfully somebody else's.

And in addition to that situation, there was the increasing likelihood of war. In April there had been that (fairly catastrophic) dress rehearsal in the form of the invasion of Albania. The Lawyer was not—for now, at least—at risk of being called up, thanks to his advanced age—a full twenty-seven years. But if things got worse? What if, after Albania, Fascism were to launch into a game of catch-up, scurrying eagerly along behind the Germans? If hostilities expanded, there was no guarantee he wouldn't be forced to enlist. Vincenzo and Ernesto would unquestionably end up as cannon fodder. As would Giuseppe, the brother who was almost three years older than he: although he at least was a professional serviceman.

But why, then, was Tamara, his Mara, still apparently hesitant? By now it was clear to everyone, including her parents, that he was smitten. In fact, the Pharmacist and his wife were probably waiting for the proposal to be made and wondering why it was taking so long. So why was she insisting they wait a little longer? At twenty-six, Tamara, his Mara, had reached marriageable age some time back.

Maybe he should throw caution to the wind. Maybe he should just take it upon himself and ask to speak to the Pharmacist and his wife, making his intentions toward Tamara public and official. But how would she react? She, his Mara, didn't have the easiest of characters. Actually, to tell the whole truth, she was imperious and fond of her own opinions to the point of pigheadedness. But he was the man here, and it was up to him to decide.

The Lawyer resolved to write her what would be the umpteenth letter, which he would entrust to Maria del Nilo. He would defend his idea of finally making a move and speaking to Lea and the Pharmacist and perhaps even setting a date for the wedding. The world risked getting into a war that might last who knows how long, and both of them were of an age that made postponements inadvisable. As a coda to his firm but loving peroration, he would attach a few verses written in her honor. He was sure she would find them gratifying. The verses in question were a handful of syrupy rhymes comparing Tamara's blue eyes to a pair of diamonds in the night: those two diamonds lit up the road that led to marriage. Those words, he realized, couldn't have been more mawkish had he tried. All the same, he hoped they might make a breach in the young woman's adamantine position on the matter. He had forgotten, had the Lawyer, or perhaps he couldn't see it, that there was an ironic and mildly sadistic side to his Mara. Who replied to the long, soppy missive with the brief and rather caustic words "The road you refer to has many bends in it."

### 15. PEPPO FROM THE POSTHOUSE

At the age of thirty-five, Peppo from the posthouse was precociously nearing the summit of immutability that Maria del Nilo had already scaled some time back. In other words, he too was well on his way to becoming eternal. His face revealed what could have been any one of a selection of ages ranging from thirty to sixty. It was a face expressing both vigor and ponderation, artfully combined with a dash of inscrutability. Sitting there silently, waiting for the Pharmacist to finish preparing the decoctions and tinctures requested by his clientele, before resuming a conversation the two of them had been having for nigh on two decades, he looked like an enormous heraldic cat sejant, squatting on the back of time. Winter and summer alike, he wore a flat, gray cap that framed and emphasized the feline features of his face. Only once had he ever been seen outside the house without this millinery uniform, at which point word had gotten out that he was bald. The rest of his getup remained an enigma even to the Pharmacist—who saw Peppo from the posthouse every day, having inherited him from Uncle Giorgio as secretary and factotum. Year round, the man forever wore the very same suit, a suit that was slightly threadbare but dignified and, above all, miraculously clean. Given which, it seemed evident either that the suits were at least two in number and perfectly identical, or that this was always the same suit, washed and ironed overnight to be ready to be donned in the morning.

The only element of Peppo from the posthouse's wardrobe that varied with the seasons was his cloak—black, in thick worsted, with two buttons at the neck. If the man was wearing it, one could safely affirm that the year had reached a point somewhere between mid-November and late February.

Peppo from the posthouse had, when very young, married a girl by the name of Lucia, and had, when still very young, been left a widower. Two sons, cared for by their maternal grandparents. For a while, Peppo had played with the idea of remarrying and had therefore, as the phrase goes, cast an eye around—not just in the town but throughout the province. But then he had been overcome by a hopeless melancholy: every time he met a suitable candidate for a trip to the altar, his thoughts turned to Lucia and the early days of their marriage. Peppo from the posthouse remembered those nights when their bodies had rolled endlessly together under the covers, those afternoons when he had found an excuse to break off work and had run home to wrap Lucia in his arms, or even those mornings when he couldn't bear to unglue himself from her. They had made love so often and so imaginatively that he had the impression he'd used up all his reserves, and so, whenever he looked at a woman, thinking he might sleep with her, it occurred to him that it would end up being a bland imitation of things past. The truth of the matter was, no one could ever replace Lucia. And as a result, he never replaced her.

It may well have been that terrible sorrow experienced prematurely that triggered his propensity for infinitude. But whatever the whys and wherefores, at thirty-five years of age Peppo from the posthouse had achieved the status of a person devoid of desires. And therefore of sentiments. And therefore—presumably—of a common or garden ego. Proof of which was in some small way offered by his very name. The posthouse referred to was not the realm of letters and parcels, but an inn (a posting inn) where, as a child, he had worked with his father. In other words, ever since he was tiny Peppo had been associated more with a place and a function than with a family (and thus with sentiments). And ulterior proof was offered by the fact that by the time he reached his dotage, he would no longer (or hardly ever) be referred to as Peppo from the posthouse by anyone in the town, but became Peppo from the pharmacy: almost as if to confirm that his was an impersonal, self-denying nature, definable only by virtue of his place of work.

For all that, the man would represent the sole motive for which, after the war, when the horror of the Holocaust had emerged in all its full detail, the Pharmacist refrained from smashing into smithereens the violin he kept shut in the wardrobe. In short, Peppo from the posthouse would be the reason the Pharmacist didn't kill himself.

## 16. UP IN THE SILA MOUNTAINS

After two years on the run, the Notary had forgotten almost every aspect of his life beforehand. He had forgotten about his profession and his day-to-day routines, he had forgotten his family and what it meant to have ties to that complex system of notions and misconceptions that we all call reality. Like an effect uncoupled from its cause, he was sampling a paradoxical sort of independence: while beforehand personal circumstances had forced him to forswear the wider world in favor of a life in the small town of his birth, now a public (political) motive had obliged him to flee the hole where his roots lay.

He had spent almost eleven months up in the Sila. He had learned to milk cows and lead them to pasture; he had mastered the art of transforming milk into curds and curds into cheese; he had acquired and honed a knowledge of and an ability to read the sky and the winds, and had absorbed the secrets of weather lore, probed with the help of no instruments beyond his own five senses. His friendship with Pasquale (the young communist doctor he had gotten to know a few years beforehand, during his earlier, short-lived time on the run) gave rise to an exchange of ideas and a maturing that, for the rest of their lives, both would look back on as indispensable. While remaining faithful to their respective parties, over those months both Pasquale and the Notary came to see that the doctrinaire inflexibility of the one and the generic humanitarianism of the other were guaranteed to flounder in the fight against fascism, as long as they remained incapable of dialogue. Essentially, they came to understand that, at bottom, competition and clashes of opinion are not synonymous with conflict, and that what results should never be an overpowering: two simple and ultimately commonsensical truths to which, sadly, their respective parties, the Communists and the Socialists, would, in the decades to follow, hardly ever bend the knee, thus condemning themselves in the first place to irrelevance and then to oblivion.

The Notary had begun to love the Sila mountains in summer—on account of the fresh, soft air—as much as in winter, because the snows gave him a new energy that left him feeling endlessly alert. Nonetheless, he ended up forced to leave those mountains, with their forests as thick as those of Denmark and their vistas that, on certain very clear days, like something painted by Morandi, swept from north to south, from the mountains of the Pollino in the north to the Aspromonte massif in the south, while east and west offered glimpses of the Ionian Sea and the Tyrrhenian. After almost a year of perpetual roaming, it was Pasquale who suggested that the Notary leave the area for a while, because in due course even the best-kept secrets risk getting out.

In July 1939, counting on the help of his old Neapolitan friends, the Notary returned, at long last, to the city of his youth. His son Ernesto was studying there, while Magda had very recently vacated the draft- and spy-filled apartment up on the Vomero hill, and was now in Paris, where, for the time being, the Daladier government had guaranteed her protection (she would return to the foot of Vesuvius at the end of that summer, by which time the Notary had already set sail for Nice).

Ernesto managed to meet with his father only once, at the National Library of Neapolitan History, which, back then, stood in Piazza Dante and where Alfredo Parente arranged meetings for many of the city's antifascists. The young man was rather excited to be seeing the Notary again: he had avoided taking part in the invasion of Albania only because his father had intervened; his father happened to be an old friend of the medical officer who had examined Ernesto, thus ensuring he was diagnosed with an acute inflammation of the appendix, warranting a three-week stay in the hospital. Proof that the Notary, despite all the hardships of life on the run, was—thanks to his extensive network of social contacts—still capable of invading his children's lives and changing them. In reality, Ernesto overestimated his father, whom he knew far from well. He was, for example, unaware of the man's almost total lack of sentimentality, against which his elder brothers, Giuseppe and the Lawyer, had long ago learned to build up defenses.

The Notary conceded his son just half an hour of his time. He asked how the boy's studies were going and, without bothering to mince his words, told him he should be worried about an imminent call to arms: following the so-called Pact of Steel, drawn up between Italy and Germany that May, it was plain to see that grounds for conflict in Europe would not be lacking. He, the Notary, would not be able to help Ernesto. The chance to avoid conscription in the case of Albania had been just that—pure chance. From here on in, Ernesto would have only his own resources to count on. As it happened, the same would be true for Vincenzo, who was just three years older than Ernesto. They were, both of them, going to have to cope on their own. At the very most they could ask Giuseppe, the oldest of the siblings, to give them a hand.

Ernesto had just enough time to say "Yes, sir, and thank you, sir," before his father took his leave and rushed off to an urgent meeting. The Notary had not even asked him to send greetings to Elvira, his wife, and the three little ones,

Ernesto's half siblings. The youngest of them, Emilio, had been born mere days after the Notary's flight into the Sila. His father had never yet laid eyes on him.

## 17. POOR ELVIRA

Elvira's first symptoms emerged not long after Emilio's birth, in October 1938. She had a strange fever that came and went—never high, but persistent. The baby was handed over to be breastfed by Cicia, a thirty-year-old woman who lived in the same neighborhood. She was married, was already the mother of several children, and had possibly, at some point in the past, had a brief affair with the Notary, to whom she remained so devoted that she had become one of the region's first female socialist militants. Cicia was small and round, like a chickpea. Which was how she acquired her nickname (Cicia, in the local dialect, means chickpea). She was, moreover, every bit as firm and compact as a chickpea, and like all legumes, could be rather hard to digest when that long tongue of hers got to work.

Elvira had entrusted her with the baby, certain that the woman would make an ideal wet nurse. In her eyes Cicia was a model mother: with what little money her husband managed to bring home as an agricultural laborer, she ensured, at the cost of extraordinary sacrifices, that her children lacked nothing, and the eldest of them all went to school, because all children—said she—are equal in the eyes of God and in the eyes of Filippo Turati, the founder of the Italian Socialist Party. Naturally, Elvira made discreet arrangements to lend a hand financially, ensuring that Cicia was rewarded for her help.

The town's doctor, Italo Gigli, could not work out what was causing the light fever that had now been dogging Elvira for months. After the Christmas holidays—during which she had forced herself to organize luncheons and dinners as though the Notary were at home with them—Elvira asked the Lawyer to make an appointment for her with a doctor in a nearby town who was reputed to be an excellent gynecologist. The gynecologist sent her on to a lung specialist, and the lung specialist sent her on to a colleague of his who was an expert in pleurisy. Thus the months went by and her condition worsened, but she never said a thing to the Notary—with whom she communicated via a pair of shadowy couriers—about her ill health.

At the beginning of the summer of '39, she had herself photographed holding Emilio, and sent the picture to her husband, confident that finally seeing what his son looked like would give him great pleasure. For the occasion, Elvira made herself pretty, and before making her way to the photographer's studio where the sitting had been arranged, tried on several outfits: she didn't want the Notary to notice how wan she looked, so it was important to find a dress that brightened her face and perhaps even lent her an air of gaiety. As for little Emilio: he was so bonny and rosy that he looked like an apple—there were times when, looking at him, Elvira was tempted to nibble at those firm little cheeks. In his case, she had no need to worry about the photograph turning out well.

The picture reached its intended recipient after many peregrinations: one of the two couriers had left it inside a prayer book she used as a hiding place for written dispatches, and forgot all about it for several months. By the time the Notary received it, it was as crumpled and faded as his memories of family life. Straining to make out the baby's face, the man didn't really pay much notice to the image of his wife: he wanted to see whether or not Emilio's features resembled his own. The rest of it didn't matter.

In the meantime, while the Notary, setting off for Nice, was taking his leave of Naples, Elvira arrived there—with the help, once again, of her stepson, the Lawyer. Toward the end of the summer the woman's health had suddenly deteriorated, and it became clear that the treatments she had been undergoing for the putative pleurisy were doing no good. In the hospital where Giorgio was serving his internship on the surgery ward, Elvira underwent an operation on both breasts. Unhappily, the double mastectomy wasn't enough to halt the disease: the cancer had already spread to her lymph nodes. And, from there, to her lungs. Her decline was extraordinarily rapid, almost as if a correct diagnosis had accelerated the growth of the tumors—at that point free, having been recognized and named, to march triumphantly forward and overwhelm the poor woman's body.

She died on 7 January 1940. The funeral took place approximately four weeks later—the time it took for the corpse to arrive home from Naples. And most of the town took part. The fact that she left three young children (Vita, who was almost ten; Tecla, who was six; and Emilio, who was not even two), in addition to her relative youth (she had been born in 1891) and her husband's flight, had tugged at the heartstrings of almost all of them, including the Notary's enemies. Of the Notary himself, meanwhile, there had been no further news.

Via the usual channels, the Lawyer sent a message to his father, informing him of Elvira's demise, but it provoked no response. They would later learn that the message had taken a very long time to arrive, because in France the Daladier government had fallen and numerous socialist exiles—including the Notary, who was in Nice at the time—had left the country, attempting to cross the border into Switzerland. And so the message shuttled uselessly backward and forward across Europe, and when it finally reached its intended recipient, in June that year, the Notary had only just gotten back to Naples. Meanwhile, Italy had joined the war, and little Emilio had stubbornly failed to start talking. The war would last five years, give or take; Emilio's muteness, four times that.

### 18. PORTRAIT OF A HUNTER

Right from the start it had been evident that Vincenzo had aspirations to be celebrated as the most eccentric of all the children the Notary had by both wives, and perhaps also those he had left dotted around outside the traditional confines of marriage. Elegant and sophisticated like his father, Vincenzo possessed an additional dash of exuberance and flamboyance, a particular yen for the unusual and an instinctive enthusiasm for the non-codifiable, all of which set him apart, albeit at the cost of occasionally bordering on bad taste out of an excess of aestheticism. His acid-bright shirts were legendary, his checkered pants renowned, his floppy neckties memorable. But it was in his hunting attire that Vincenzo's inventiveness reached heights unparalleled.

Like his father, he loved English fabrics. Both anxiously awaited the annual arrival of the Gutteridge catalog, which was sent to them from Naples, and together they picked out the tweeds, flannels, and Scottish lisle cottons that the shop in Via Toledo assured its select clientele. The Notary's eldest two sons displayed no interest in this kind of thing, but Vincenzo happily consumed enough for three people, and for this reason alone his father forgave him failings that would have cost others rebukes, dressing-downs, and reprimands. However, while the Notary confined himself to selecting patterns that were refined but predictable in taste, Vincenzo unselfconsciously indulged in the never yet seen.

This passion for fine clothes was not the only symptom of eccentricity. In a family where the dominant religion was that of humanist culture, and books were considered an indispensable tool of learning—about the world and oneself—Vincenzo favored the open air and amusement in general. As far as he was concerned, Bacchus and Tobacco stood at the apex of the pantheon. As for Venus: no one ever did discover whom it was he spent his nights with.

Ernesto, who was only three years younger, shared Vincenzo's predilection for fun, but lacked his brother's self-possession and the cavalier and roguish nonchalance with which he asserted the body's primacy over the soul. Ernesto was certainly a pleasure-lover, but tended not to flaunt it in front of the family and especially not in front of his father, whereas Vincenzo asserted his own nature without the least bashfulness.

A clamorous example of this was offered by his expulsion, at eighteen years of age, from "all schools in the Kingdom," as the result of a class test in Italian. The essay question dictated by the schoolmaster required the pupils to sketch out a profile of the most significant and influential man of modern times, he who had restored Italy's ancient grandeur—the excellence and glory of the Roman Empire. It was taken as read that they would all be writing about Benito Mussolini. Vincenzo instead produced—with an elegant turn of phrase and uncommon skill—a portrait of Rudolph Valentino, who had been dead for a number of years but whose legendary exploits had, in his opinion, truly regilded the nation's reputation.

The following day, the boy was summoned to see the headmaster, who instructed him, first in a roundabout way and then explicitly, to rewrite his essay and devote it to the Duce, whose majestic figure had been so profitably described by every one of Vincenzo's fellow students, without exception. Vincenzo not only refused categorically but went so far as to declare, in front of numerous terrified witnesses, that Mussolini in comparison with Rudolph Valentino was an amateurish ham and, what is more, a great deal uglier, what with that bald head and overgrown jaw of his. At which point disciplinary action could not be avoided.

The young man was not, therefore, able to attend university. A fact that earned the headmaster his gratitude. And in fact, he sent the man a brief letter of thanks for having freed him from the yoke of that school that was, wrote he, "as useless as it is ghastly."

In lieu of his studies, Vincenzo dedicated himself body and soul to hunting. He considered that activity to be the most ancient and noble manifestation of the intelligence of the species *sapiens*, so ancient as to predate the species itself, and therefore a direct expression of the divine. Hunting was rivaled only by card games, since, while the former reveals man for what he is (among other things, a victim to the glamor of the chase), the latter is an enactment of the human compulsion for masquerade and mimicry: in a word, for deception. Because, self-evidently, any successful card player is first and foremost a cheat. As for armed conflict: far from being a protracted, grand-scale version of hunting—as more-innocent souls maintained—it was, in the eyes of Vincenzo and Vincenzo's close friends, a grotesque collapse of the principle of individuation.

For which reason, after Italy entered the Second World War on 10 June 1940, in order to avoid possible future call-ups, Vincenzo, who was almost twenty-six years old, made for the hills. But he did so in a breezier and more ironic fashion than his father. After all, he wasn't a wanted man; no one—for the time being—was demanding his presence in the army (when called up for national service, he had been sent straight back home on account of a minor heart complaint). Nonetheless, the young man felt it might be wise to disappear from circulation for a few weeks.

This decision, made on impulse and rather lightly that summer, would over time turn out to have been a much more momentous choice than was foreseeable at the point in question. Vincenzo went into hiding, but unlike his father, who reemerged from his own hiding in 1943 substantially unaltered as far as his cardinal principles were concerned, Vincenzo underwent a truly unexpected transformation. He vanished from the town almost as a game: for the first few months he simply roved the surrounding countryside in solitude, and then, little by little, moved ever farther away. But most important, he left as a dandy and returned a partisan commander.

## 19. TAMARA ALSO SETTLES ON A PLAN OF ACTION

The circumstances were unquestionably exceptional. Another war. The first had lasted an eternity, but she had only been a few years old: she retained a few memories of privation, but since Lea had always been somewhat miserly, those recollections of penury and hardship ended up blurring with other similarly cheerless memories of early childhood. This time round, though, things seemed different right from the outset. Tamara was a young woman, not a little child. Time was, for her, no longer an abstract and incomprehensible dimension belonging to the adult world. Now she herself was an adult and could therefore legitimately wonder: How long would this new conflict last? Not to mention the racial laws. And the horrifying news coming out of Germany: true or exaggerated? What in heaven's name was happening? Collective, across-the-board lunacy, it seemed.

One form of madness being equal to another, Tamara realized all of a sudden that she wanted to get married. She was about to turn twenty-seven. She could have been said, for the era, to be very late to the game. Her mother, at twenty-seven, had already had her first child. Whereas she, Tamara, had up to now doggedly refused all wooers. Only the Lawyer had persevered. And now there was the war. She couldn't dillydally ad infinitum. Her days went by with a visit or two to the dressmaker, a little gossip with Cousin Margherita (who wasn't the sharpest tool in the box), and a few hours behind the counter in the pharmacy, compensating for paternal laziness. But what kind of life was that?

Her elder sister had only just left home, marrying a man called Gaetano whom she didn't love. But she had decided to marry him all the same, because according to her, he was kind and affectionate, and also to escape Lea's miserliness and her cast-iron rules about what could or couldn't be done, about what was better said or better not said, about whom one should fraternize with and whom not, et cetera. (Tamara's sister had once admitted that she longed to get married simply in order to be free, when the mood took her, to eat two hard-boiled eggs and not just one.)

After Maria's wedding, Tamara had found herself alone. Giorgio was living in Naples because of being at university, and had just been drafted back into the army as—in view of his training—a medical sergeant. Nina didn't count because children don't count: she was only twelve, what could she know about men, engagements, and marriage?

Tamara's thoughts turned to the Lawyer. For a long time now he had been courting her discreetly but tenaciously. Secretly, he had already made one proposal. Why didn't she say yes? Why didn't she say no? Who was she kidding: Tamara didn't know. To begin with, she had thought he wasn't the right one. To tell the whole truth, to begin with she had, if anything, thought that the right one might just be Ernesto, because he seemed to be a sensitive young man and because he had a disconcertingly beautiful pair of eyes. But over time Ernesto had become like a brother to her; he practically lived in their house. Added to which he was younger than she was and had a certain fame—or so said Giorgio, laughing—as a lady-killer.

She tried reasoning the way her sister would: calmly and without too much sentimental silliness (Maria often used that expression derisively—sentimental silliness). The Lawyer was a serious person, a hard worker (and even Lea said that). Unlike his father the Notary, famed for his short temper and his lovers, the Lawyer had a reputation for tolerance and level-headedness: and in effect, that was her impression of him too. He would remain faithful to her—she couldn't have told you why, but she was certain of it. The Lawyer didn't seem to be the type who played the field. Far from it. He respected women. One had only to look at how he had treated Elvira, his stepmother, being there for her at every stage of her illness, accompanying her to the doctors, taking her up to Naples for surgery, and throughout all this never a word of complaint, never a word out of place. A correct man. A generous man. No question. Over time, little by little, she would come to love him, yes, she would love him unreservedly. Now she was sure of it. And she was also sure she wanted to marry him. But when?

Right now it was out of the question: the Lawyer's family was in full mourning for the death of Elvira. The two of them would have to wait. At least until the end of the summer. But in the meantime, how would the war play out? Would it soon be over, as the radio and newspapers said? And what would happen if Hitler and Mussolini really did become masters of the world, or even just of Europe?

Tamara felt confused. She even felt like crying. Now that she had decided to take a husband she couldn't get married because life—what a stupid thing to discover!—wasn't going the way she wanted it to, and reality was frighteningly more complex than she had imagined. She looked at herself in the little mirror above the dressing table, which up until very recently had always loyally returned her gaze with an image of plenitude and control. Now she looked wan, she looked plain. Horrible.

In any case, better not to cry.

## 20. LATEST NEWS

The bleak summer of 1940 came to an end. France was broken up, and in London the bombs were raining down.

"Perfidious Albion" was now Italy's enemy, and so Tamara's family attempted for the first and, it has to be said, only time to shake off—unsuccessfully—the label "English," which in earlier times had denoted not a threat but foreignness (and perhaps also affluence). In September Italy signed the Tripartite Pact with Germany and Japan, and one month later declared war on Greece. Those who immediately paid the price included Ernesto, sent off to fight without any real training, ill-equipped and iller-fed, together with a considerable (but insufficient) number of soldiers from the Royal Italian Army, who ended up being pushed back, bombed, forced to retreat, and massacred, until, in the April of '41, the Germans came to their aid.

Before leaving for the Greek front, Ernesto found time to impregnate Italia, the daughter of his Neapolitan landlady. He continued to care nothing for the young woman, who was almost ten years his senior and too large in the hips, but he had carried on making love to her, partly out of laziness and partly out of kindness. Added to which, since the death of Elvira, Ernesto had begun looking at women in a less predatory way, and while knowing that Italia would never become his wife—for the simple reason that there was no chance he would ever fall in love with her—he did feel a sort of gratitude that made it easier to yield to her entreaties. So he had agreed to spend a whole night with her on the eve of his departure. And although, over the course of those hours, he had been tempted to confess that he didn't love her and that perhaps it was better they say their goodbyes, in the end Ernesto had kept his own council, and had taken away with him fond memories of those final kisses.

Approximately three months after the young man first found himself on the front line, in January '41, when reports from the Balkans already spoke of defeat, Giorgio had also been sent to the front, to serve in a field hospital. And, at an encampment alongside the river Kalamas, he had come across Ernesto, lying abandoned on a cot, racked with a high fever and a cough, delirious, and forty pounds lighter than he had been.

George took his friend to the infirmary, which for all that it was poorly equipped and chaotic, was in any case a safe place in which to recover. For almost three weeks, he looked after Ernesto without ever neglecting the other patients, but nonetheless, very cautiously, always secretly prioritizing him. As soon as he was up to stringing together words that made any sense, the invalid had sketched out a gloomy, sorrowful tale in which the recurring themes were the rain, the cold, the mud, and his antediluvian Carcano M91 rifle.

Giorgio avoided telling him immediately that Italia was pregnant and that he would soon be a father: Ernesto's health was still very precarious, and his friend hoped that, suspecting tuberculosis, the command might send him home—where the interested party could preannounce the happy event herself. Unluckily, that's not how things went. The follow-up physical examination found Ernesto fit enough to return to the front line. At the end of February, he left the infirmary and was assigned to the Eleventh

Army, which was due to launch an attack in the Desnizza valley, between the Trebeshina massif and the Mali i Qarrishtës ridge, their objective being to retake the Albanian town of Klisura. Only at the very last minute, as they were embracing and swearing to meet again soon, somewhere in this or that version of hell, did Giorgio tell his friend that Italia was expecting his baby.

Ernesto's eyes had widened, his face surprised, astonished. He had flapped his arms and had started making bizarre, rather disjointed gestures with no obvious point to them. And in this way Giorgio had sufficient time to notice that, in response to the news of that imminent paternity, the dominant expression on the face of his almost-brother was one not of shock but of wonder—in both senses of the word. On closer inspection, however, Ernesto's much-loved face told him one thing and one thing alone: "I am happy." But more than once . . . "I'm happy, I'm happy, I am happy."

The two young men would never meet again. Not in the land of the living.

## 21. GOOD NEWS, BAD NEWS

Many years later, when that cruel and ashen period was but a distant memory about which one could even crack jokes, the Lawyer would find it amusing to tell his own version of his nondeparture for the front. While his father and Vincenzo were fighting in the ranks of the antifascists, while his two brothers Giuseppe and Ernesto were respectively busy in North Africa and in the Balkans with the Royal

Italian Army, he had, he maintained, received the call to arms sometime in 1941. He was to present himself at such-and-such a barracks in Bari. From there—went the anecdote, which was accompanied by a whole series of nods and winks—he had been sent on to Brindisi for a short period of training, at the end of which the battalion he belonged to would leave for Russia. However, having learned what their destination was to be, and suffering greatly at finding himself so far away from Tamara, his Mara, the Lawyer—and herein lay the narrative stroke of genius—had preferred to return home, explaining to a friendly and very pleasant lieutenant colonel that Russia was too cold: he wasn't used to a climate so inclement. So it would be better if they recalled him at a later date, just as soon as the army had identified targets better suited to a southerner like him, who happened to feel the cold rather badly. And so, with a cordial shake of the aforementioned lieutenant colonel's hand, the Lawyer's experience of the Second World War came to an end.

Patently, things had in reality gone differently. Yet with the excuse of having a laugh, this would remain the only officially sanctioned version of events. In May 1941, the Lawyer really had been sent to Puglia for military training, and it is equally true that he had come home again a few weeks later, but the reason for his sudden reentry remained unclear.

At the time, the Lawyer had been not quite twenty-nine years old. He was practicing his profession in his father's office and supporting a family composed of his brother Arnaldo (nineteen or twenty years old, and a student), his half siblings Vita (eleven) and Tecla (seven) and the last-born,

Emilio (three). As if that in itself weren't enough, he also had a father on the run who was accused of seditious assembly and of having slandered the Duce, and a brother (Vincenzo) who was also on the run and accused of the very grave crime of desertion. Were these perhaps the motives that determined his failure to leave for the front? The fact, in other words, that this young man was shouldering the burden of a family in disarray? Or had there instead been medical justifications—real or putative?

Whatever the truth of the matter, the Lawyer returned to the town, and he and Tamara began discussing the date of their wedding. The whole of 1941 went by, and then the better part of 1942. In the meantime, the Lawyer would have occasion first to worry unnecessarily about his own safety, and then to face fresh and unexpected sorrow.

Evening after evening, while making his way home, he had noticed a shadow trailing him, always a few yards behind. Nearsightedness meant he was unable to tell whether the individual was known or unknown to him. On the first few occasions he had brushed it aside, and then he started to worry. How likely was it that the local Fascist command had arranged to have him followed on a daily basis in order to confirm that he had—as he claimed—no contact with that father or that brother of his, who were both wanted by the militia and the army? Effectively, it was very likely. But how come the tailing was exclusively being done by a lone individual? It had to be just the one person, because even someone as myopic as he was could see that the complexion and movements were always the same.

After ten days or so of being followed, the Lawyer turned for help to Peppo from the posthouse, who was to follow him very cautiously at a distance and try to uncover the identity of the mysterious figure. The first attempt came to nothing: the shadow at the end of the street noticed that someone else was present and disappeared in a flash. The second time, however, something happened that was, then and there, inexplicable: the Lawyer caught sight of the now-familiar silhouette, and an instant later Peppo from the posthouse leapt on it, but rather than a scuffle or the two men yelling, what followed was a warm embrace. After which both of them fled. So, was Peppo from the posthouse—the Lawyer wondered, aghast—also an assassin in the pay of the regime?

The mystery was cleared up the very next day. With great embarrassment and a degree of fear at the idea of being accused of conniving with a figure the authorities held to be a criminal, poor Peppo from the posthouse confessed that the mysterious shadow was Vincenzo—who feared for the safety of his brother: the only member of the family left in the town on whom the Fascists could still vent their ire.

Newly buoyed up by the good news that Peppo from the posthouse had brought him (Vincenzo was well and would shortly be leaving for Naples, where he was to meet their father), the Lawyer settled down to thinking exclusively about the wedding and Tamara, his Mara. In any case, other news—this time terrible—was about to rain down on him.

## 22. BACK IN THE ATTIC

Giorgio came back to the town on leave, for Christmas 1941. He was tired and thin, and his eyes were focused on things far away. He greeted the family vaguely and hurriedly, and told them that he had been in Vlorë, a town in the south of Albania, that he had been traveling for ten days and that he wanted to sleep. No, not eat—or perhaps yes, but later on. Sleep. Right now he just wanted to sleep.

He vanished into the attic, up into the realm he had once shared with Ernesto. The twin beds. The little table with a chair on either side, so that they could study facing each other. The green lampshade. The warped coatrack. The chest of drawers too small for the two of them (and in fact Ernesto left his clothes lying around all over the place). The books—almost all of them Giorgio's—lined up on the low shelves and in the recess of the dormer window. It was dusty. Cold. The sheets smelled of damp. On the bedside table, the reproduction of the *Sleeping Hermaphrodite* from the Louvre, which Ernesto had been given by old Uncle Giorgio. Giorgio ran a finger over it and smiled. He had . . . he really had to sleep. He lay down still fully dressed and closed his eyes.

He opened them again many hours later. He had been dreaming of a long, thin strip of land, very far away but also nearby, and a frightening amount of water that was perhaps rain because it splashed down from somewhere above him; and then darkness, an inky, brutal darkness. He had dreamed he had something lodged in the middle of his chest, something that hurt him very badly, and so he had to find pads of sterile gauze and blot the wound dry before it could become infected. He had dreamed of Ernesto, who slid out of their last embrace and stared at him with eyes filled with irrepressible joy.

He shut his eyes again. He didn't want to see his friend's face, but in that room, as soon as he lifted his gaze, he saw it everywhere.

Giorgio leapt out of bed. Was it day or night? From the little dormer window with its frame of books, he couldn't see anything, no terrace, no house, no sky. The world seemed to have come to an end. Pitch-black. To orient himself in that bare, silent void, he switched on the green table lamp, and an instant later saw him, right there, sitting in front of him, while they both tried to study in the suffocating heat of the attic. Ernesto, as usual, was not concentrating; he was rolling his eyes and gesticulating theatrically to stress how much he hated Latin. The dictionary with its curling pages. Their books open at a passage from Cicero. Instinctively, Giorgio switched the light off.

He got back into bed again, among other things because he was cold, but this time round he had pulled off his clothes, which stank of mud and of railway carriages, and he had chosen, from one of the drawers in the chest, a pair of stripy, blue, lightweight flannel pajamas that Ernesto had used only rarely, in order to avoid wearing them out—he who had never cared what he wore and who let his dirty clothes pile up on the floor. Those pajamas, however, enjoyed a special status, being the one and only gift he ever received from his father in all twenty-four years of his life. They were the present Ernesto had been given to mark his graduation from high school, the same graduation that, thanks to the munificence of old Uncle Giorgio, had heaped upon Giorgio himself a cornucopia of shoes, shirts, cufflinks, tie pins, shaving sets, travel-size hairbrushes, silk scarves, a gold wristwatch, and a small fortune in cash. Giorgio had in any case shared everything with Ernesto: some of the cash had been used to pay off a gambling debt his friend had accrued, the silk scarves were often seen knotted around Ernesto's neck, and it seemed obvious that the shaving set should belong to Ernesto, because at that point Giorgio still had no beard.

In bed, with those pajamas on, he felt a sense of deep warmth and well-being, as though a clot of icy coldness inside him had suddenly melted, a coldness that had been tensing his muscles for God knows how long.

Once again he fell asleep, and once again he reopened his eyes several hours later. Someone was knocking at the door and muttering something: in came Lea. She was carrying a small tray with a bowl of hot soup, some bread, and a piece of cheese. There was also a glass of red wine, which Giorgio downed in a single gulp.

He was undeniably hungry, but more than that he longed to be caressed, held in her arms, welcomed home. Lea sat down at the foot of the bed and waited for her son to eat. They didn't exchange a word. The young man was conscious of an awkwardness and a coldness in his mother that were sadly far from unfamiliar to him: Lea had always taken care of her family with determination and efficiency, ensuring that each of them lived a healthy and adequately comfortable life, but without ever yielding to the seductive charms of superfluity, which in Lea's eyes meant luxury. And feelings. Wafting around his mother, for as long as Giorgio could remember, there had always been an air of organization and cleanliness, of methodicalness and scrupulosity. But anyone living in hope of a gratuitous display of affection, of a little tenderness, would be disappointed. If anything, it was their father, the Pharmacist, to whom one could turn—he was the one capable of showing warmth. Albeit in a disorderly, rather haphazard fashion.

All the same, that evening Giorgio tried turning to Lea, and as the woman placed the dirty plate and cutlery back on the tray, the young man stretched out toward his mother's body, seeking her embrace. She said something like "What's this about? What's this babyishness?" and she moved to one side and then hurriedly disappeared back out toward the stairs.

Having shut the door behind her, Lea paused for a moment. She sensed the young man's terrible anguish, although she didn't know the reasons for it; she sensed his fear, the terror of something experienced at the front that must have broken him, but there was nothing she could do beyond bring him warm food and check that his room wasn't cold. Lea would have liked, somewhere in the further reaches of her mind, to have been one of those mothers who also took their children in their arms and dispensed physical warmth, but she was incapable of it: she couldn't do it, and the reason she couldn't was so ancient and elementary as to be entirely obscure to her.

Lea heard a few sobs from the other side of the door. Poor Giorgio. He had always been such a gentlemanly little boy. Who knows what he had gone through in that dirty Fascist war. Silently, taking care not to make any noise, she made her way downstairs.

## 23. MARIA DEL NILO OR THE CAT?

Relations between Tamara and her mother had been tense for a while now. To be precise: ever since Lea had voiced concerns regarding her daughter's engagement to the Lawyer. Tamara had spent a long time making up her mind, but once it had been established that yes, she did want to marry, and the husband-designate was indeed him, the Lawyer, Tamara didn't appreciate being reminded of the hesitation and misgivings that had preceded her decision. Moreover, she found her mother's objection frankly inopportune: the young woman herself was not especially concerned that not one but two members of the Lawyer's family were on the run from the law. The Notary was, in the eyes of his daughter-in-law-to-be, a professional man of good standing and immense culture, not a delinquent; his run-ins with the authorities were down to motives of principle, of politics: the man hadn't sullied himself with some gross act of criminal violence. The crimes he was accused of were crimes of opinion. And the same was true of Vincenzo, who was likewise opposed to the war and to Mussolini's regime. And then, in any case, why bring the Notary and Vincenzo into it? She wasn't going to and had no desire to marry either one of them. So, if Lea had something to say on the matter, let her refer to the interested party, without beating around the bush and bringing up the question of his relatives.

The house had been humming with the quarrel for months. Fortunately, the Pharmacist mediated between mother and daughter, attempting to explain the positions of one to the other, but his was an almost hopeless diplomatic cause. Because the truth was, Tamara and her mother were very alike, both in their obduracy and in that mental coldness that as we have seen secretly caused Lea great sorrow. Obduracy and coldness that the Pharmacist was wont to summarize, with a shrug of his shoulders, in the following words: "Both of them are fond of their own opinions." Having said which, he would—whatever the time of day, or of night—find an excuse and disappear off into the pharmacy.

The eldest of the three sisters took Tamara's side. Actually, if anything, she was even more radical, maintaining (but never right there on the spot) that their mother really had no right to be interfering or expressing any opinion regarding the bridegroom-elect, because they were no longer living in the Middle Ages, were they? And then—Maria reflected—in Tamara's case it wasn't a question of "sentimental silliness" (she was particularly fond of those two words and trotted them out whenever the chance presented itself), if anything it was a question of common sense: because no son should ever be held responsible for his father's iniquity. From the town twenty-fiveish miles away that she had moved to after having married Gaetano,

Maria wrote long letters to Tamara in which she stood up for her sister, urging her to hold her ground in the face of maternal fundamentalism. Only to melt like snow in the sun the minute the discussion took place in Lea's presence. At that point, Maria became even more conciliatory than the Pharmacist: she equitably agreed with both her mother and sister and then privately explained to Tamara that this was a tactical move.

One afternoon between Christmas and New Year's Eve in 1941, Maria came back into town to see their brother, who, having just returned from the front, was apparently not on good form: since arriving home he had never once come out of his room in the attic, not even for the Christmas Eve meal. The woman had held Giorgio in her arms and had hugged him tight, stroking his hair and speaking words full of tenderness, but within minutes the two of them were plunged into all the silence, awkwardness, and foreignness that adult life wraps around family relations, and so she had left him there, alone in his room.

Down in the kitchen, Lea and Tamara had found an excuse to snipe at one another. This was happening increasingly frequently: they would attack each other over some trifle and were capable of then spending days at a time making sly digs at each other. Maria del Nilo was sitting in front of the fireplace, peeling a mountain of lemons in preparation for making Giorgio's favorite marmalade. As soon as Maria appeared at the door leading onto the staircase, her sister seized the chance to begin berating her mother. The phrase that would subsequently be defined as incriminatory went more or less along the lines of "You are heartless, everyone knows that when you cook mushrooms you always make her" (pointing at Maria del Nilo, who was luckily deaf as a doorpost) "taste them first."

Lea rose to the bait. How dare the brass-faced Tamara accuse her of being a murderess, an assassin, a Nazi, a madwoman? She would never dream of using Maria del Nilo as a guinea pig. If anything, she might have done it a few times with Emanuele, the family's pet cat.

At which it was little Nina's turn to begin yelping: Emanuele was her cat, a present her father had made her for her tenth birthday—how could Lea have thought of using *him* as a guinea pig? What a monster she was! What callousness!

Utter chaos. Lea, Tamara, and Nina accused one another, using various epithets, of all kinds of domestic wickedness; the Pharmacist rushed into the house on hearing the hullabaloo, and he too raised his voice in a useless attempt to make himself heard over the female shrieks; Maria gave her backing first to one and then to the other and gesticulated hysterically, while Maria del Nilo seraphically carried on peeling her lemons and thinking how happy Giorgio would be to eat his favorite marmalade. Eventually, three or four knocks were heard through the ceiling: the young man was protesting against that shameful hubbub by banging his military boots on the floor. Within minutes they had all fallen silent. And Maria del Nilo smiled to herself, as mysterious as a cat.

## 24. SAVE ME FROM THIS EMPTINESS, I BEG YOU

The days went by, and Giorgio still hadn't poked his nose out of the attic. Up and down the stairs of the house there was a great to-ing and fro-ing of pans of hot coals to warm his room, trays laden with food, and Lea and Maria del Nilo, who took turns carrying up clean linen, collecting the clothes he had dirtied, and in the meantime trying to persuade the young man to come down to the kitchen. Tamara and Nina also took turns going and seeing their brother, although both of them had the feeling they were paying visits to a stranger. Giorgio didn't speak. He stared at the ceiling or at one of the two chairs flanking the little table, and he gulped down his anguish.

On the night the year ended, the Pharmacist also put in an appearance. He climbed the stairs very slowly, pausing between one tread and the next. It had been years since he last ventured up into the attic, and he was surprised to discover that he now lacked the puff to make it up that steep, yes, but not very long flight of stairs. Almost as if, now that Uncle Giorgio was dead, it was his turn to play the part of the old man in the family. And the Pharmacist discovered in the course of that short journey that the role fitted him much more snuggly than he had anticipated. He had aged.

He knocked softly on his son's door. Silence. Perhaps the boy was sleeping, even if it was only seven o'clock in the evening. He waited for a moment and then, just as he was turning around to leave, from inside the room he heard a muffled voice asking who it was. For a second it occurred to the Pharmacist that the voice seemed to be that of a child, not a twenty-four-year-old man. But he banished that thought immediately. He said, "It's me, your father."

From inside, Giorgio said, "Come in, Father, please."

The room was almost in darkness. Only the lamp on the bedside table lit up a very small strip of space that enclosed an open book, Giorgio's hands, the edge of a bedsheet, and two or three cigarettes scattered across the dark blankets. There was an acrid smell of smoke and youth. Moving toward the bed Giorgio was lying in, the Pharmacist tripped on the rug and very nearly tumbled to the floor.

"Be careful, Papà," sighed Giorgio.

"I'm sorry if I'm disturbing you," responded the Pharmacist.

Then both of them fell quiet, as though they had already exhausted all available topics of conversation. At a loss for what to do next, stuck on his feet in the middle of the room, the Pharmacist said, "I'll open the window a bit." And he made a fanning gesture. Once again, he tripped on the rug and yet again risked tumbling to the floor. Finally, he sat down next to the little table. He sighed. Then he sighed again.

"Giorgio," he said, but added nothing else.

"Tell me, Father."

With one hand, the Pharmacist smoothed out his double chin. He would have smoothed his hair back too, but no longer had enough of it to justify the gesture. His son stared at him as if it were he, the father, who ought to be speaking, to be explaining his behavior of recent days and the fact that he had remained barricaded in his room, indeed mostly in bed; in short, it seemed to be Giorgio who was waiting for a word of explanation from the Pharmacist and not the other way around.

The man emitted a disorderly series of fresh sighs, and had the room not been engulfed in semidarkness, the young man would have glimpsed a thick and sudden flush spreading across those paternal features.

By way of encouragement, Giorgio repeated, "Tell me, Papà."

At that point, the Pharmacist rose out of his chair, shuddering like a large cetacean straining to reach the surface of the sea and spout its jet of water; timorously and unsteadily he took the few steps that separated him from his son and then, a split second later, embraced him, clutching him tightly as he said, "What is it, my boy? What's going on here? Tell me, I beg you. Please."

It was then that, in the kitchen on the floor below, they heard the young man's howl. A piercing, primitive howl like the cry of a wounded animal trying to escape its captors. A timid, testy animal. A porcupine, for example. The quills he was unleashing at the world took the form of a handful of words—repeated, obsessive words, like a mantra or a litany: "Save me. Please save me from this emptiness, I beg you, Papà. Save me from this emptiness..."

The Pharmacist let the young man weep it all out and continued to hold him tight, cradling him almost the way one does with an infant. And so, in fits and starts and hiccupping, liberatory sobs, Giorgio told his father the tale of how, just a few days before his leave began, he had gone to the aid of a group of soldiers who had been caught beneath the enemy's bombs somewhere on the outskirts of Klisura. Their bodies had formed a single lump of blood and mangled limbs. Ernesto, alas, had been among them, his face so muddied that it had looked like a terra-cotta votive mask. The young man had lost a great deal of blood and was delirious. The field hospital's medical captain made it clear right away that for Ernesto and the others there wasn't much that could be done, apart from pumping them full of morphine so that they didn't feel the pain. Cleaned up, medicated as well as he could be, watched over night and day in the hope that he might show some sign of improvement, Ernesto had gradually slipped away, his eyes closed, occasionally mumbling incomprehensible words. In those final hours, with Giorgio sitting beside him, the young man had more than once sought his friend's hand. When the two of them were finally pried apart, because Ernesto had to be buried, Giorgio had become aware of a monstrous, piercing emptiness at the center of his being. At times it took his breath away.

## 25. FINALLY MARRIED

Inevitably, following the news of Ernesto's tragic passing, Tamara and the Lawyer's nuptials were once again postponed. This time round, their grief was doubled, because there were two families directly impacted by the loss: the Notary's, but equally and perhaps even more so, the Pharmacist's.

As if that in itself weren't enough, their grief could not be expressed or elaborated. Ernesto had no funeral, and for years no one even knew where he was buried, because Giorgio couldn't remember precisely where it had been. Only a great deal later, when the war was long over, did Ernesto's friend try, via the Italian Army, to locate the grave of his almost-brother, and once it had been found he invested much time and money (a great deal of money) in attempting to bring home Ernesto's remains, but without success. The dead man thus became a sort of specter or, to be more precise, an undead man for both families. With the exception of Giorgio, who had been with him right to the very end, for everyone else the young man's passing acquired the abstract quality of certain very vivid dreams during which we are, in spite of that vividness, immediately conscious of their unreality. Ernesto was dead, but at the same time he wasn't. Or not entirely: there was nowhere they could take him a flower, no tombstone certifying his death, and every one of them, in both families, remembered him young and full of life. Ernesto had simply gone away. He had left, and they knew he would never be back. None of them, apart from Giorgio, could superimpose on those remembered images of a young man in the full splendor of his youth the picture of a bomb-mangled corpse.

Without exchanging a word, Tamara and the Lawyer tacitly agreed that setting a date for the wedding was out of the question. Their grief over Ernesto's terrible death fused with the generalized grief of wartime, reducing the present to a mucky sludge of coldness, fear, and insufficient food. Hard even to imagine a party.

The Lawyer reacted to the death of his brother by sinking himself up to his neck in work, also because the weight of the family—or rather, the weight of what was left of it—rested entirely on his shoulders. And since the three children born of the Notary's second marriage were still very young, he also had to set about finding a housemaid who possessed at least a modicum of maternal instinct.

In this, at least, luck came to his aid: Cicia was by now looking after Emilio full-time and would continue to do so until the little boy was big enough—toward the end of 1945—to be returned to his father's household; as for their sisters Vita and Tecla, and his own needs, and those of their brother Arnaldo, who at that point was twenty and about to begin his university studies, he instead found a very young woman, Rosa, who moved in with them and did everything for them and who, in a future still remote, would one day become the chief organizer of the Lawyer's political career. Needless to say, the expenses the poor young man had to cover were considerable, but at home at least there was now a semblance of normality, meals not lavish, perhaps, but regular, an orderly life. His longing to marry Tamara was still urgent and deep-seated, but if nothing else he no longer had to cope with the domestic emergencies that had arisen first as a result of the premature death of his mother, and then the Notary's flight, and then, after that, the demise of the man's second wife. Not to mention the additional flight of Vincenzo, and then finally the death of Ernesto. In the space of not much more than fifteen years, the Lawyer had had to cope with so many setbacks, and such serious ones, that at this point waiting a few months longer before finally being able to wed Tamara, his Mara, was hardly likely to daunt him.

As for Tamara, she understood the situation all too well, and without batting an eyelid accepted what, for the time being, appeared to be an indefinite postponement. Ernesto's death had been a much harder blow than she ever let on, rekindling memories of the short-lived passion the young woman had, many years earlier, briefly nursed—in the privacy of her own dreams—for the thought of that young man's intensely bright eyes.

The whole of '41 was spent in the relentless and remorseless void of war; a good part of the following year was swallowed whole by the same ferocious beast. However, on 17 October of 1942, a Saturday, within a few hours of what would go down in history as the last cavalry charge ever made by the regular Italian Army during the Second World War—the charge on Poloj, on the Yugoslav front—Tamara and the Lawyer finally tied the knot. She was twenty-nine years old, an enormity in those days; he was thirty. The wedding took place at home and was celebrated in the Pharmacist and Lea's bedroom by a priest of Greek extraction who spoke rather sketchy Italian. The guests were few, and the food and drink even scanter. Responsibility for the first toast fell to the Pharmacist, who also stood in for the father of the groom. He pronounced a handful of words brimming with emotion, and wrapped things up with an imprudent cry—in Hebrew—of *Lehayim!*

# CHAPTER TWO

## 26. WHAT THE LAWYER WAS THINKING

In some ways the Lawyer was happy that the only members of his family present at the wedding were his brother Arnaldo and their half sisters Vita and Tecla—two little girls. Aside from the fugitives, not even his elder brother Giuseppe had been able to participate, because he was off at the Egyptian front, and at what was almost the very last minute, on account of the British offensive that was, at precisely that point, being led by General Montgomery, his leave to reenter Italy had been revoked. As for little Emilio, he was only four years old, and throughout the simple reception that followed the ceremony he remained glued to the skirts of Cicia, his nursemaid.

For almost the entire duration of the little party, the Lawyer had been thinking about his mother, Vita. She had been dead for nigh on twenty years now. He remembered very little about her. Those hands. As small as a child's. Whenever she had risen to her feet to upbraid him, with a forefinger pointing in his direction, he had found it impossible to take her seriously and had had difficulty suppressing a laugh. Those soft, rosy cheeks. The way she moved around the kitchen while preparing her famous pasta with lentils, which her children adored and the Notary loathed. Certain words of encouragement, often repeated during his early years at school: "Do as your father does, study and read the way he does. He's a great man."

As it happened, the Lawyer was happy not that his brothers were absent but that his father wasn't there. Because, he now realized, he couldn't stand the man. The Notary had treated his wife like a slave. Or if not quite that, like a member of the household staff; to say nothing of the countless times he had been unfaithful to her. And when Vita died, in 1924, he had replaced her, a few years later, with Elvira. But not even Elvira had been loved, not even she was of any account to that self-centered, unfeeling individual: when poor Elvira was suffering from cancer, it had been he, the Lawyer who had taken care of his stepmother, while the Notary remained focused, body and soul, on political plotting and intrigue. Elvira had died without her husband even being aware of it. And now the Lawyer missed her too, in the same way that he had been missing his mother for almost twenty years. He wondered if Tamara, his Mara, was any good at making pasta and lentils.

In any case, on that Saturday, 17 October 1942, the day of his longed-for wedding with Tamara, his Mara, the

Lawyer swore to himself that, lentils or no lentils, he would, come what may, never behave like his father; he would never follow his father's example.

Then again, father and son could not have been more dissimilar. The former was as tall and elegant as the latter was stocky and unprepossessing. They had the same resonant voice, the same very black hair and certain way of arching their eyebrows, but in everything else one seemed to be the polar opposite of the other. Even in his practice of the legal profession, the Lawyer promised himself, he would not follow in his father's footsteps: for one thing, he would not become a notary; for another, he would be devoting himself primarily to criminal law, while his father's expertise lay in the civil domain. As for politics: he couldn't very well renounce the socialist leanings he had inherited from the Notary, but his would be purged of any abstract intellectualism; he, and the family he and Tamara were founding today, would not take sides with the masses in an aristocratic and condescending way. They would belong to them. Their home—bought for them by the Pharmacist with the money old Uncle Giorgio had left for Tamara's dowry—would be unostentatious and sober, with none of the silver and luxurious furnishings that had filled the Notary's house until Elvira was forced to sell off many of the better pieces to keep things afloat. And as well as being modest, it would also be a home whose doors were open to anyone truly in need: for a start, he and his wife would offer free use of the first-floor rooms—next to the rooms where the Lawyer intended to open up a legal practice of his own—to their cleaner, who also happened to be their cook, and additionally happened to be a childhood friend of Tamara's. Maria-la-pioggia. Who had very recently married Santo, who was unemployed and the son of an unspecified father. The couple had nowhere else to live.

### 27. THE MAGNITUDE OF MARIA-LA-PIOGGIA

Over the following decades, Maria-la-pioggia would come to play a major role in the lives of the Lawyer and Tamara, on whose behalf she would keep the house clean, cook every lunch and evening meal, and see to an infinite number of everyday chores. Apart from a painful final parenthesis, she and her husband and their numerous offspring would always live in the two bedrooms plus bathroom and kitchen provided by her employers, rent free. And while living in those two bedrooms plus bathroom and kitchen, she would raise Valentino, one of the four children the Lawyer and Tamara would bring into the world.

Unlike Maria del Nilo, who was effectively a monument to discretion (the Pharmacist maintained she went deaf out of a surfeit of minding her own business), Maria-la-pioggia loved being at the center of domestic affairs. She adored chitchat, she handed out advice, and she fussed over all of them, plying each of them with such attention and care that she eventually made herself indispensable in all contexts. Maria-la-pioggia was an indefatigable worker: early every morning she went out to buy food for the day; she cooked with passionate enthusiasm; she ate with an equally passionate enthusiasm; she washed and she cleaned and she tidied. And while the Lawyer and Tamara applied themselves to their ritual postprandial siesta—a habit they would forgo not once in the course of their very long married life—she devoted herself to darning, patching, folding, ironing, and putting away socks, underpants, bras, handkerchiefs, and undershirts, until it was time to start sorting out supper.

Maria-la-pioggia was tall and robust, a sizable woman. She was four years younger than Tamara, but acted as though she were twice Tamara's age. As little girls they had been the closest of friends, and back then Tamara used to say, conspiratorially, "The two of us are the cleverest girls in town." But now that they were adults, Maria-la-pioggia often insisted, with no respect for chronology, that Tamara was like a daughter to her. Her eldest daughter. When she married Santo, a month to the day before her friend's wedding, Maria had demanded Tamara be her bridesmaid. After all, it had been Tamara who asked her mother to buy double the fabric needed for her own wedding dress, so that she could pass the excess on to Maria-la-pioggia. To begin with Lea had refused, because she didn't want to spend more than had been budgeted for, but in the end the cousins Levino and Margherita had charged a very reasonable price, so Lea had caved in. And then the making of the dress had cost hardly anything, since Farà, the dressmaker who was going to be sewing Tamara's bridal gown, was arm-twisted into running up a second dress (in a less la-di-da design) for the young woman's friend.

Which was why Maria-la-pioggia would forever be loyal to Tamara, even when the latter was capricious and disagreeable; even when, with the excuse of a headache, she shut herself into her bedroom for days on end, turning her back on the Lawyer's silent moodiness and her children's noisier version of it; or when she failed to hold her tongue and called Santo a drunkard (which was not entirely inaccurate) and called her, Maria-la-pioggia, a hapless nuisance who brought bad luck (which was plainly ridiculous). Even then, Maria-la-pioggia forbearingly forgave Tamara, because each time it happened Maria-la-pioggia would think back to their respective weddings, or even further back to their childhood, and would, each and every time, remind herself that no other person on God's earth had ever been as selflessly generous to her as Tamara. Certainly not her father, whom Maria-la-pioggia had never known—for the simple reason that nobody knew who he was. And not her mother—whom everyone knew as "Rain or Shine" because she conscientiously plied her trade on the streets however bad the weather, and who, had the Pharmacist's daughter not intervened, would have forced Maria-la-pioggia to sell herself too. And Tamara had also been more selflessly generous than all the relatives who were ashamed of Maria-la-pioggia, and all the neighbors who did their best to avoid her. Tamara was the only person who had ever given her anything, and little though it was, to Maria-la-pioggia it seemed huge.

Besides, everything about Maria-la-pioggia was sizable: her body, as was plain for all to see, and also her intellect, as one day far into the future she herself would come to realize.

## 28. THE SECRET LIFE OF THE PHARMACIST

These words: "The darkness, here comes the darkness." And then some disconnected images: washing hanging in the sun to dry, very white, dazzling (he can hear the wind slapping at it violently); a little print of Millet's *The Angelus*, a gift from old Uncle Giorgio, which suddenly comes alive and warns him that his wife might be betraying him; his own mind like an arid stretch of land vanishing off into a distance made up of scrubby bushes and stones, and which looks like the first few yards of the desert in southern Morocco that he'd visited with his grandfather as a small child. Then words again: "Wait, wait for me, wait"—said like a prayer, to Lea, and repeated again and again until they turn into a rasp, a smothered yelp, or something resembling a growl.

Ever since December 1921, when his eldest son died at the age of nine, the Pharmacist has been having these moments of crisis. Moments of crisis that, following the arrival of Uncle Giorgio at the end of July '34, have been growing more frequent and more painful. No one understands, except Lea, who nonetheless pretends to see and hear nothing. All of a sudden the Pharmacist starts mumbling those words to himself (*The darkness, here comes the darkness*, and then: *Wait, wait for me, wait*), and repeating them in a keening singsong, his upper body rocking backward and forward as if he were shuckling at the Western Wall; and right after the words, filling his head, crowding out the possibility of doing anything else, here come the images of the drying clothes, of the *Angelus* talking about betrayal, and of his mind being like a desert. At this point the Pharmacist abandons whatever it is he is doing: he rushes out into the street and makes his way off, out past the edge of the town, along hillside tracks that lead down toward the sea. It doesn't matter whether it's winter or summer, whether it's raining or a day of bright sun: the Pharmacist abandons the house and his work. He needs to be alone, he needs not to make public his affliction (which was once just called grief but now also goes by the name of jealousy). And then, once he is far away from everything, once he feels he is surrounded by nothing if not those repetitive and disconnected images of drying clothes, of angels and of deserts, and—inside his head—those dark, obsessive words that haunt him, then something in him seizes up and he feels that he too is dying, that he, just as his little boy did, is suffocating, and that no one can help him. Not even Lea, who has perhaps betrayed his love.

Over time, Maria and Tamara will get used to their father's abrupt and inexplicable fugues. Tamara will also get used to taking his place in the pharmacy, as though she were his efficient, miniature deputy, and she will learn how to prepare a few of the simpler medications. And he himself will begin growing a beard—a thick, black beard that lends his pale eyes a new hint of madness and mystery—and he will continue wearing it long and well groomed until the August of 1939, when old Uncle Giorgio dies. At which point the Pharmacist will decide that this mourning for the death of his eldest son and this agonizing jealousy over Lea can—in fact must—come to an end.

And so, from that moment on, every time the Pharmacist senses those ill-boding words approaching (*The darkness, here comes the darkness*, and then: *Wait, wait for me, wait*), and every time the images—of that washing flapping in the wind, and of the *Angelus* preannouncing betrayal, and of the desert in his mind—begin to materialize before his mesmerized eyes, instead of escaping out into the street and roving the hills like a madman, with the townsfolk whispering "The Englishman's not right in the head," the Pharmacist rummages around in the wardrobe and pulls out his violin and plays all the tunes he has stored away in his brain—Mendelssohn, Édouard Lalo, Paganini, and others besides—and in this way the anguish of his jealousy and the burning memory of his little boy dying with eyes staring wide into that nothingness are transformed into something lovely, into something tender that, instead of repelling the world, welcomes it in, and which anyone who happens to be listening will find rather moving. The townsfolk no longer tell one another in whispers that the Englishman's not quite right in the head, but loiter outside the door of the pharmacy and listen very willingly to those unexpected and improvised concerts. And—since none of them has ever set foot in a concert hall or a theater—they earnestly agree that the Englishman must be a great violinist who, for some secret reason, has abandoned the world of music and his country of origin, and has come to that godforsaken corner of Italy to heal its people with those medicines he often dispenses free of charge, asking for nothing in return, because he pities those who have nothing to give.

Therefore, it is perhaps more in memory of the little boy who died twenty years earlier, and more as a way of finding relief from the agony of his jealousy than it is in honor of Tamara and the Lawyer's nuptials that the Pharmacist gives a little performance on his violin, while the guests eat the wedding cake and Lea keeps an eye on the children—her own daughter Nina, but also Vita, Tecla, Emilio, and Maria and Gaetano's little ones. The notes spread out through the rooms, throb into the furniture, envelop the guests. And although they do deposit a seed of melancholy, which sooner or later will sprout and bloom in all those minds, here and now they put everyone in the mood to party. The dancing is about to begin. A gramophone is brought out and takes over from the violin.

## 29. SILENCE

At a certain point the guests had all congregated on one side of the room that opened out onto the terrace—the room in which old Uncle Giorgio spent his final years and had died. Today it was unrecognizable: apart from the uncle's chair and a pair of tapestries on the wall, everything else had disappeared. There were no rugs or precious knickknacks, the bed was gone, and so were the two little Gauguins that no one gave any thought to and which were now hanging somewhere in one of the corridors. Up against the wall where the wardrobe stood, a long, low chest of drawers was acting as a buffet table, and on the stool sitting next to it, the gramophone had suddenly appeared. Around the edge of the room a row of dining chairs and armchairs had been set out, and older folk were sitting down. Everyone else was crowding around the French doors, and a few people had moved outside into the open air (this was, after all, one of those mild Octobers which are so common in—and unique to—the south).

The bridegroom's friends had slipped off their jackets and were now in shirtsleeves, still sweating, almost every necktie loosened. The girls smoothed down their skirts, waiting for vigilant parental eyes to signal permission to dance. A large number of hats in felt and thick corduroy. Caps and boaters and berets: hot though it was, the men hadn't relinquished their headgear. A gramophone record was trilling, "*Ki ki kiss me little lady / With your pree pree preety little lips / Give me lo lo lots of little kisses / Ta-tara tara tara ta-ta,*" but no one yet dared make a move. The record continued: "*Chee chee cheeky little baby / You're such a bree bree breezy little lady / Your charms are irr-re-sis-ta-ble to me / Tee-teree teree teree te-tee.*" In the pauses between one verse and the next a few rumbles of complaint could be heard: in some folks' opinion, that song was a little too audacious.

But just as Alberto Rabagliati's voice began intoning: "*Bee and bo and beh and bee / Darling, sing the syllables with me / Bee and bo, bee or boo / Sweet syllables of love from me to you,*" something that no one would ever have expected to happen took place. Maria del Nilo threw aside the white apron she had been wearing just a minute earlier, launched herself into the center of the room, pulling her son Franceschino along by his arm, and amid the perfect silence of her deafness, started dancing with all the undulant grace of an expert. For a thirty-two-year-old manual worker who was as shy as a boy of sixteen, her son made a damn fine job of it too, but she was sensational.

Smiling at the thought of a melody she couldn't hear but which accompanied the movements of her body astonishingly well, for a few minutes Maria del Nilo abandoned the role of domestic help to which she had for a lifetime remained tenaciously faithful, and she etched herself into the memories of all present, in the form of a pint-sized Terpsichore, a down-at-the-heels goddess of dance. And this would be the most vivid and enthusiastically treasured of all the memories that, once the partying was over, the guests took home with them and jealously conserved through the horrible years to come.

Then everyone started dancing, beginning with the bride and groom.

### 30. FOREVER SISTERS

At every point in that immensely long day, Tamara had literally and metaphorically looked out for her sister. She was keeping an eye out for her because she was worried that Maria might tire, what with two little children to chase after, and a third—on the way any moment now—in that low-slung belly, which was as taut as a hot-air balloon; and also because, now that she, Tamara, was finally, actually married, she was feeling a trepidation and even dismay that perhaps only her sister could placate. During the ceremony and then during the meal served by Lea and Maria del Nilo, the two young women hadn't managed to exchange so much as a glance. Maria hadn't stopped running around after little Lea and Pepe, and seemed distracted and remote; while Tamara had the impression that everywhere she turned she was met only by the dark, apprehensive eyes of the man who would, from that day forth, be her husband.

Finally, having offered everyone a small piece of the somewhat-pitiful wedding cake (eggs and milk were in short supply, and in the kitchen one had to work inventively, finding new uses for everything possible, including potato skins), having danced with the bridegroom, having exchanged a word at least once with every one of the guests, Tamara slipped off toward the stairway leading up to the attic, certain that that was where she would find Maria. Making her way up wasn't easy in that long dress: those stairs were as steeply pitched as her heart. When she got to the top, she found the door gaping open and her sister stretched out on Giorgio's bed. Maria was pale, her eyelids lowered. She looked dead.

Hearing the swish of Tamara's gown, Maria opened her eyes and made a move to get up, but then seemed to change her mind immediately and slumped back down on the mattress. She was tired, she said, and had really needed a little time to herself. When you have small children, she added, time to yourself becomes the most precious of all commodities—time to yourself and sleep.

Tamara felt almost guilty for having disturbed her, and made a gesture to suggest she would leave. But her sister whispered, "Come here," and made room for her on the bed, squashing herself up against the wall. Tamara curled up around Maria's enormous belly, almost as if trying to listen to the life of the little being contained within it: Would it be a boy or a girl? Everyone swore it was bound to be a girl, because of the shape of Maria's belly. Maria had even chosen a name already, seeing as Gaetano never meddled in these things—truth be told, he never meddled in anything and limited himself to working like a dog and slicking his hair back with pomade. The little one was going to be called Assia, after Assia Noris: because Assia Noris was a movie star and because when she met Hitler she had announced that he "had a face like a snowman," which showed she had a lot of guts.

The two sisters remained silent for a while. Both of them breathing heavily, Maria squeezed Tamara's hands. The hubbub of the reception in progress on the floor below reached them but was muffled, as if filtering up from an underwater world. As little girls, the two sisters had often sought the refuge of the attic, to escape the inquisitorial side of Lea. Back then it wasn't yet Giorgio and Ernesto's room; in fact at that point they didn't even know Ernesto, because he would not begin frequenting the house until the two girls were in their teens. Therefore, with its steeply sloping ceiling and its central dormer window and its profusion of moth-eaten objects that, expelled from the everyday world, seemed to have escaped there in order to carry on living, that enormous room was still—and despite more recent memories (Giorgio, for instance, barricading himself into that space to elaborate his grief in the wake of Ernesto's death)—the two sisters' secret hideout. A powerfully symbolic space, that on that October day Maria and Tamara would take their leave of forever, because henceforward neither of them would properly belong there. Not just in the attic, but in every room of that home.

They gave each other's hands an even tighter squeeze. The younger of the two women had wanted to ask the other what to expect of her wedding night and all the other nights to come, but in the end didn't have to, because Maria got there before her, saying simply that she didn't need to be frightened, that she shouldn't be frightened of her husband, but if anything should teach him, with kindness, what to do. She would feel some pain to begin with, but then, if she trained him well, and above all trained him not to be hurried or selfish, as men have a tendency to be, he would over time become a good lover and perhaps even a friend. And babies would follow naturally, just as summer follows on from winter.

Tamara's eyes moistened at the thought of her babies being like the seasons. She was on the point of saying something about her uneasiness at the idea of getting undressed in front of a man, but then all the nerves accumulated over the previous days and the sound of Maria's deep, slow breathing suddenly made silence seem preferable. And so the two sisters lay there quietly, wrapped in each other's arms, surrendering themselves, for a moment, to the shared dream of remaining forever sisters—not wives and not mothers.

## 31. ANOTHER SILENCE

For the entire duration of the ceremony and then of the party, Emilio has remained firmly attached to the skirts of Cicia, his spherical, hard-as-a-chickpea nursemaid. He is four years old now and getting bigger by the day, to the point of making one wonder if he won't sooner or later end up being classed a giant. He has a big, wide, full-moon face. He hardly ever cries, and he hardly ever laughs. Most of the time he is busily focused on playing a private game of his own invention, which involves lots of imaginary objects but none that are physically tangible: he moves around and gesticulates and spins on the spot and looks over his shoulder in reference to a reality that no one, apart from Emilio himself, can see.

Emilio is always hungry (over the course of his half brother's wedding lunch he has eaten a first course of pasta and potatoes and a second course of suckling goat served with greens, as well as two helpings of the dessert that, if we are to be entirely honest, was far from sweet); when sitting at any table, perched on Cicia's knee, he is more than capable of trying to take a bite out of even his plate. He is a methodical, determined eater, even though this is wartime and food is rarely tasty. Emilio capitulates before nothing and no one:

if something is edible, he eats it. He even loves lemons, black olives, chicory—all the sour, bitter foodstuffs children normally abhor. He shovels it all in without batting an eyelid. When focused on his chewing, he has every appearance of being engaged in a complex, demanding exercise from which no one and nothing must distract him. He widens his eyes a little and stares out into the void, at a point remote and abstract, almost as if attempting to pinpoint not flavors but a meaning. Something hard to comprehend.

Even so, the most striking thing about him is the fact that he doesn't speak. He doesn't mumble. He makes no sounds. Cicia is a simple woman and consequently shrugs it off. His older sisters, Vita and Tecla, are themselves just girls of twelve and eight, so they don't notice it. But among the adults—starting with Tamara—a worry begins to insinuate itself that Emilio might be mute. Not deaf, though, because if somebody calls his name, he turns around, and in the main, when spoken to he evidently understands. The problem is he doesn't talk. Even though, as a newborn babe—Cicia remembers it very well, all those times when she lifted him out of his mother's arms—the little thing used to screech like a fire alarm. In reality—judging from what the Lawyer says he remembers—Emilio vocalized for as long as Elvira, his mother, remained alive. Only afterward did he stop emitting any sounds. Or at least that was the Lawyer's impression. And the other one of Emilio's half brothers still living at home, Arnaldo, had the same impression too. According to Giorgio, who is now almost a qualified doctor (he still has to take a few exams, but will need to wait until the war is over before he can finish his degree), Emilio simply has some mild learning difficulties, nothing very serious. He'll catch up.

At any rate, throughout the wedding celebrations, Emilio remains wrapped in Cicia's long, tiered skirt and his own intangible silence.

### 32. NINA'S GHOSTS

On the day of Tamara's wedding, while the priest of Greek extraction pronounced incomprehensible ritual phrases and everyone present allowed their thoughts to drift off elsewhere, Nina's gaze was scanning the male faces crowded into the room: that of the bridegroom, naturally, but also those of her father and her brother Giorgio, and Peppo from the posthouse and Cousin Levino, and many others besides. And so it was that the young girl suddenly came to realize that the only face she was really looking for in that little crowd was the face of Gioacchino. A face she was looking for even while knowing she would never find it.

At the precise moment when she turned ten years old, Nina had discovered that ghosts really do exist. Old Uncle Giorgio was still alive, and she was forbidden from entering his room without first knocking repeatedly at the door and then loudly asking for permission, because the old man didn't hear very well. Here it should be pointed out that Nina was a very sensitive child, possessed of an imagination easily excited, but she was in no way shy: aware that her father had a soft spot for her, she enjoyed showing off and enjoyed being praised, and as a result she tended to behave the way adults wanted her to.

On 11 August 1938, the day of her tenth birthday, Nina knocked again and again at her uncle's door, but no one answered. Yet she could clearly hear the old man's voice. The young girl was carrying a tray with a glass of cold lemonade, a slice of cake, and a late-flowering yellow rose cut from a plant on the terrace. She set the tray down on the floor and knocked harder. Nothing. Through the door, the sound of heated debate filtered out, but no one came to answer. Not wanting to wait any longer, Nina walked in, and at the precise moment in which she burst into the room, saw a shadow slip out through the French doors. Her uncle was on his feet, his shirt collar unbuttoned; he looked as red as a beet and was staring at her with a look of consternation on his face.

The young girl said, "Uncle, the lemonade will get warm if you don't drink it right away."

The man pointed at the little table next to the yellow armchair he always sat in. As Nina began to mention that there was also a slice of her birthday cake, her uncle hurriedly put something away in a drawer. The little girl had been expecting the old man to turn around and walk over to thank her, and who knows, perhaps even present her with a gift, but seeing that he was still fumbling around with his back to her, she asked him, "Who were you talking to?"

"Gioacchino," her uncle replied without a second's thought, as if that name should be familiar to the girl.

"And who is Gioacchino?" Nina instead asked, never having heard of him.

"I can't believe you don't know who Gioacchino is, that can't be true."

"No, Uncle. I don't know who he is."

"But he's lived in this house since before you were born."

Nina's face arranged itself into an expression of utter bewilderment. "He lives with us? But where?"

At which point the little girl was called back outside by her mother, her uncle said he didn't have time now to tell her the story of Gioacchino—who, what is more, detested nosy little girls—and an instant later little Nina found herself accompanied to the door.

Whereupon Nina knew no peace. Until later that evening, when she learned from Maria and Tamara that Gioacchino was the ghost of an extremely irascible—but not wicked—man who carried off children he found to be excessively curious and shut them up in a prison that could only be reached via the attic. Should they then, once incarcerated, continue to poke their noses into other people's business, Gioacchino made a meal of them (albeit reluctantly), cooking them in a kitchen no one knew the whereabouts of, using all manner of inventive recipes. The fact that Giorgio and Ernesto slept in the very room that acted as Gioacchino's general headquarters should come as no surprise to her, since—according to Maria and Tamara—all males are in cahoots, and while the two boys weren't cannibals like Gioacchino, they did egg him on. Besides, while it was true that Gioacchino was built like a big-boned ogre and was over six-and-a-half-feet tall, he was for all that still a ghost, who could therefore make himself invisible and thus take up very little room.

Over time, Nina grew fond of the figure of Gioacchino, who had been invented by her uncle to cover up a secret that Nina would one day figure out for herself, and who had then been dramatized by her sisters with an eye to defending their teenage intrigues from the threat of future snitching. As the years went by, Gioacchino became a permanent fixture in Nina's imaginary world, and from potential enemy morphed little by little into a solicitous and amiable ally, very severe and dangerous to others, but friendly and well disposed toward her. As if that in itself weren't enough, the figure of the six-and-a-half-foot tall ogre, the reluctant eater of human flesh, was then embellished, in Nina's head, with the addition of a tragic past (his wife had abandoned him, taking with her their numerous offspring—a whole band of naughty, scheming children), a passion for literature (especially Dickens's *A Christmas Carol*), and a handful of rather singular habits (for example, reading while standing on his head).

Nonetheless, despite growing fond of Gioacchino's benevolent persona, in some ways Nina would, in her heart of hearts, continue to find him frightening. It was as if she knew that this was an invented character, one that her own fantasy had helped to shape, but one who, at the same time, was better not provoked with an excess of cynicism—who could tell whether or not Gioacchino might take umbrage and, from the world of her dreams, come rushing out into the real world to exact his revenge?

Which was why, at her sister's wedding, Nina—who in August had turned fourteen and was therefore a fully fledged participant in the world of adults, or at least according to the daily homilies inflicted on her by her mother—was scouring the crowd with her eyes for Gioacchino's face, while in her head she knew perfectly well that she wouldn't find it. And then, a few hours later, as the party was ebbing to a close—after the wedding cake had been cut and eaten, the bride and groom and some of the guests had danced, but people were beginning to leave now and Lea and Maria del Nilo were already putting things away—when she found herself at the foot of the stairs leading up to the attic and clearly heard the sound of muttering from behind the shut door on the floor above, Nina said to herself that it must be Gioacchino, chatting away with the ghost of Ernesto, who, from the foreign land he'd been killed in, had come back home for his brother's wedding to Tamara. Of whom, Nina knew, he, too, was particularly fond.

### 33. HAVE A REST, LEA

The kitchen is as good as tidy, but the rest of the house is still a war zone. Put old Uncle Giorgio's bed back in its usual position! Push the chest of drawers back over to the other wall! Away with those glasses and plates left lying around in random places! The gramophone and its records need to be taken into what used to be the girls' room and from now on will just be Nina's. Almost everywhere stinks of smoke: throw open the doors and windows!

While Maria del Nilo is cleaning up the bathroom and the hallway, Lea finishes straightening out the rest of the house. Giorgio gives her a hand, carrying a few old dining chairs back up to the attic, a little armchair, two tables. Their uncle's room is back to being what it used to be, more or less, including the two Gauguins that, for a time, after the old man died, had been exiled to one of the corridors. Lea has now rightly decided they should be moved back to where they hung when Uncle Giorgio was still alive—in other words, the wall at the foot of the bed. A bed that she has, for a while now, been using for her siestas, so that she and the Pharmacist can each spend an hour or so on their own, without disturbing one another. And, whenever she lies there brooding, with her eyes half-closed, Lea enjoys peering at those two very colorful little paintings that the old uncle spoke so highly of. Now too, leaving Maria del Nilo the task of finishing off the final chores, Lea lies down for a moment to rest.

By evening, the house has reacquired its usual calm. Tamara has left with her husband. They will be living just a few dozen yards away: coming out of the pharmacy, you go straight up the road, up the hill, and then turn right. It's the first building on the left—the house where Tamara and the Lawyer will live for the next twenty years and more, and in which all four of their children will be born. Who knows how Tamara will fare tonight—her wedding night? Lea secretly wonders.

Now that her eldest two daughters are married, Lea tells herself things will be easier. It's true, there is still a war on, but their chief financial worry has been resolved: Maria and Tamara are now the responsibility of their respective consorts. As for Giorgio: apart from his university degree being temporarily delayed by the chaos of war, he certainly won't have any worries; the old uncle has left him a fortune—so much money that a tiny fraction of it was enough to buy the house that Tamara has received as part of her dowry. (Giorgio is generous, and when Lea told him his sister would be getting married, he also insisted on paying for the reception.)

There remains Nina, who is fourteen years old but still seems far from ready for life as an adult, although Lea has lately been having lots of little talks with her, during which she pretends to be addressing Nina woman to woman. Nina worries her, but not—for once—because of money: Lea's worry is that Nina is rather plain, and that sooner or later, compounding the problem, she is going to need glasses (Lea and the Pharmacist have both noticed that their daughter continually screws up her eyes, and when reading holds books very close to her nose). Lea fears the girl will have trouble finding a good match—a concern that, this evening, on Saturday, 17 October 1942, might perhaps seem premature, given Nina's age, but which over the years will grow and eventually ripen into a certainty. Because Nina will never get married. And she won't marry, not because of the thick-lensed glasses she has to wear once the war is finally over, but chiefly because that imaginary life of hers will continue expanding at the expense of her real one, and figures like Gioacchino will become increasingly important, if not indispensable.

But for now, let us not get distracted from Lea and her thoughts, which are shuttling back and forth between Uncle Giorgio, her daughter, Gauguin, the past and the present. The woman is about to fall asleep: the day now drawing to a close has in effect been as tiring as a week or more would normally be. Among other things, because preparations for the wedding began long before this Saturday, and the accumulated fatigue is overwhelming Lea now. She can feel it between her shoulders, in the middle of her back. She feels the tension and anxieties of the last few weeks, and perhaps also weeks less recent. All the usual things: money, of which there is never enough; the terror that something might happen to her son who is off fighting at the front; the fear that Fascism will sooner or later track them down, Lea and her family, here in this godforsaken corner of the south; her husband's moods, which at times take a nosedive, especially when he picks up that darned violin of his; Italy, the whole of Italy, which seems to have slid well beyond the brink of the abyss; not to mention the guilt she feels over poor Uncle Giorgio, toward whom she had, not infrequently, been vile.

Now that she is tired and has given in to torpor, at the end of this memorable day, Lea can finally admit it: her husband and Maria del Nilo, and Ernesto—for as long as he was alive—and perhaps even her elder daughters, and Cousins Levino and Margherita, all knew that Uncle Giorgio kept a secret. But—and this is the thing that really counts—all of them had thought the secret related to her. The family (Lea is convinced of the fact, and in this interval of calm can confess as much to herself) believed she had been having an affair with Uncle Giorgio. What is more, and what is worse, looking back on it now, she had let them believe it. Even though it wasn't true. For this reason, at a certain point she had started addressing the old man gruffly. For this reason, she had begun treating him unkindly and even, at times, humiliating him. To cover up their uncle's secrets, to protect him from the catastrophic consequences those secrets could have unleashed, Lea had opted to plant and nurse in everyone's minds the idea that she herself was the key to those secrets. And this is something she cannot forgive the old man, even now, three years after his death: because it is hard to forgive those who oblige us to be generous.

She rolls onto her side, her face pressed up against the wall. And by degrees—as if this is a war of position—triumphing over the need for control that makes of her a twenty-four-hour-a-day worrier, Lea falls asleep. All at once, like a theater curtain, reality slides limply off to one side, leaving the stage free for dreams to walk it. Which is a blessing, because this way 17 October 1942—a Saturday—can draw to its conclusion; which means the business of remembering can now begin.

# CHAPTER THREE

**34. 1943**

And then the war came to an end, without really finishing. Armistice—that was the word being used. And it didn't mean peace, it meant chaos. The Notary came home, and to begin with no one recognized him; then again, the little tribe he had left behind him had long since fallen apart and dispersed. At home he found Rosa, the housemaid, who was keeping the household going and—while Arnaldo came and went from Laura his sweetheart's house—looking after the younger children, Vita, Tecla, and Emilio. When Emilio first saw the face of that tall, haggard man, the man with the aquiline profile who said he was his father, the little boy started mewling like a cat, his lips contracting in panic.

Characteristically, the Notary furnished no explanations. He told no one where it was he arrived from or what he had been up to in recent years. Strapped to his belt he had a revolver, which he casually plunked down on the desk in his office, and then he sent them to fetch the Lawyer and was briefly filled in on the fate of his other children, starting with Giuseppe and finishing with Ernesto. He already knew that Vincenzo had thrown his lot in with partisan groups with links to the Communist Party, which irked him considerably because he himself was now a member of the center-left antifascist Action Party: the young man's choice seemed to be a deliberate snub. At any rate, he told the Lawyer—who was initially very happy to see his father, but then promptly exasperated by the man's self-absorption—Vincenzo was currently in Naples and would soon try to make his way home, or at least this was what he had heard via his friend Pasquale, the young medic from up in the Sila mountains, with whom he was still in touch, notwithstanding the fact that Pasquale, too, was a communist.

The Lawyer informed his father that two weeks earlier, his own firstborn child had been delivered: the baby had been christened with his grandfather's name. But instead of voicing thanks or expressing any satisfaction, the Notary started questioning the decision—very questionable, in his opinion—to have the babe baptized. The Church, in his view, had shown its true colors with the election of Pope Pius XII, an ignoble man who had turned a blind eye to the persecution of the Jews. And true though it was that there were many priests who, in many circumstances, were lending a very real hand in the fight against Nazi Fascism, any assessment of the Vatican as a whole couldn't but favor a repudiation of Catholicism in toto.

The Lawyer—who was not a believer but felt a residue of friendly sympathy toward the Christian faith (connected with his few remaining memories of his mother)—tried to change the subject, and redirected his father's attention toward the family's financial travails. The man could surely see for himself that the household was short of everything (the little ones survived almost entirely thanks to the generosity of Rosa and Cicia), that many of the better bits of silver were missing, that Elvira's jewelry and all her clothes had been sold, and that they had even had to pawn some of the more valuable pieces of furniture and paintings. The real estate they owned, moreover, no longer brought in any money and had fallen into terrible disrepair. The house itself was in urgent need of repairs and renovation. The Notary had, after all, been away for five years. Before her illness struck, Elvira had had to make do and mend amid a thousand difficulties, and she had left behind her a parlous financial situation that the Lawyer had attempted to administer as shrewdly as possible, permitting Arnaldo, for example, to avoid abandoning his studies, but at the cost of enormous sacrifices.

The Lawyer continued his chronicle of those grim years, describing the death of poor Ernesto, who had perished on the Greek-Albanian front. He was giving a drawn-out account of the enormous efforts his brother-in-law Giorgio had gone to, helping and comforting his friend in the field hospital where he had been working, when he realized that the Notary wasn't listening to him: the man had started rearranging his books, and as he did so, reciting a sort of muttered litany that was, in reality, a list of all the important matters he needed to attend to over the next few days.

There was a moment of silence, during which the Lawyer, appalled at his father's insensitivity, was about to take his leave—in part to avoid a quarrel—when, all disheveled, in burst Rosa, shouting, "The patrolmen are here! The patrolmen!" The Notary instinctively grabbed his revolver, pointing it at the door. The Lawyer started to say that there were no patrolmen, as Rosa called them, in town these days; ever since 8 September, the Fascist militia had melted away, and from the local carabinieri there was nothing to fear: he knew all of them personally, and every last one of them hated the Duce. But before he could finish making his point, a tall man walked into the room. A man as tall and gaunt as the Notary, but with a less aquiline, and indeed rather more phlegmatic, even ironical, look to him. It was the Canadian Lieutenant Colonel Xavier Reid, come, on behalf of the Allied forces, to ask the Notary, as a figure of note among the local antifascists, to produce a list of names of people in the area who had been complicit in and had colluded with the newly former regime.

The Notary invited their guest to take a seat and sent Rosa off to find refreshments of some sort—coffee, a cup of tea, or maybe a drop of liqueur? A look of astonished dismay formed on the woman's face: they had nothing in the house. Eventually it was the Lawyer who took himself off downstairs to the kitchen, in search of dregs at the bottom of some bottle or other. He emerged soon afterward holding a tray on which there sat three glasses and a carafe containing a dark liquid claiming to be port.

The Canadian spoke a fairly incomprehensible version of Italian. The Notary enquired as to exactly where it was he came from. The man said he lived in the province of Manitoba but hailed from Quebec, Montréal, thus speaking both French and English; and so the Notary proposed—with a certain hauteur—that they continue the conversation in French. Back in his university days, he and Magda had often chatted in French.

Reid explained that the Allied forces intended to begin a purge of the Fascist ruling classes. It was important, he said, that in the new Italy that would emerge at the end of the war there should be no risk of the Nazis' old allies finding themselves in positions of power. The lieutenant colonel clarified that he was not referring solely to the leadership of Mussolini's party, but also to district prefects, police superintendents, and the high-ranking bureaucrats who ran the machinery of state: it was essential that a clean break be made with the past; instances of *trasformismo* had to be avoided. Both the Notary and the Lawyer signaled their assent: Absolutely. Of course. We agree entirely. But while the latter limited himself to a few firm nods of his head (the French language was one he understood, but he would sooner have thrown himself out of the window than try speaking it), the former launched into a long and very self-satisfied disquisition, in which he explained that *trasformismo* had always been *the* great shortcoming of the nation's ruling class.

In the end Reid cut him off short, and addressing the Notary directly, said that he would be back in a few days' time, on the 18th, to pick up the list of the names of people who were to be gotten out of the way. He said, "Think about it carefully, *cher Monsieur.* You Italians won't be getting *une seconde chance.*" Then he snapped to his feet, made a military salute with an elliptical flourish, added a grin, and left.

The Lawyer followed him out as fast as he could.

## 35. LUIGI, ALSO KNOWN AS SCIAMMERGA

Luigi, also known as Sciammerga—which means, more or less, cape, cloak, mantle, hood: essentially any heavy, slightly moth-eaten garment you wrap around yourself—makes his first appearance in this story during approximately the same hours in which the Lieutenant Colonel Xavier Reid, a native of Montréal but resident in Winnipeg, in Manitoba, Canada, goes to find the Notary who has returned home after five years on the run, asking him for a list of people to kill. Apart from their temporal contiguity, the two events do not as yet have much to do with one another. Luigi, known as Sciammerga, is a good-looking young field hand: he has much success with the ladies and not a penny to his name, and with the Notary he has nothing in common. If we were to define the family he comes from as poor, we would be promoting it to a higher social class. Since this is a status shared by all the other peasant families in the district, Luigi-known-as-Sciammerga is organizing a protest, on 20 September 1943, that will involve the occupation of fields owned by a local baron who has, in reality, commandeered what should actually be public land. And therefore, in his role as local firebrand, Luigi-known-as-Sciammerga now has a meeting with Lieutenant Colonel Xavier Reid, who has just come away from the Notary's house.

Reid is certainly not a communist or a radical, but by now he has seen enough of the living conditions enjoyed by agricultural laborers in the south of Italy to be of the idea that the aforementioned baron and his ilk may not perhaps have misappropriated public land, but are, even so, slave drivers, because the day rate they pay for work in the fields, for toil from dawn to dusk, is, not to put too fine a point on it, shameful. Apart from anything else, in this part of the world, in recent years, what with everyone being called off to the front, the male workforce has been trapped in the maelstrom of war and the only ones left to eek a living out of the land are women, children, and old folk, who are exploited to a degree as cruel as it is unimaginable for a man like him. Which is why, upon meeting Luigi-known-as-Sciammerga, who communicates the date and time of the protest he is organizing, Lieutenant Colonel Xavier Reid, while not understanding very many of the words being used to justify the protest, hints that the Allied forces under his command in the area will not get in the way of the picket. The important thing is that everything is done in an orderly manner, Lieutenant Colonel Reid attempts to urge. The important thing is that the demonstrators are not violent. (And here it cannot be ruled out that the Canadian, overestimating southern Italian farmhands, may have in mind some or other cautionary tale from his homeland, such as the Red River rebellion of 1869, with all its dramatic repercussions.)

Luigi-known-as-Sciammerga will reappear in this story several years later, by which time Lieutenant Colonel Reid will have made his way happily home, and a new wave of land occupations will be shaking not only the town but the entire province. He will turn up again because, on 29 October 1949, when the peasants march on Baron Berlingieri's Fragalà estate, and the police sent in by Minister for the Interior Scelba fire off a fusillade, leaving three victims in the dust (twenty-nine-year-old Francesco Nigro, fifteen-year-old Giovanni Zito, and Angelina Mauro, who is twenty-three) and a further fifteen people wounded, Luigi-known-as-Sciammerga will be one of the leaders of the revolt, and at that point, pursued by the forces of law and order, he will turn to the Lawyer for help. Thereafter, the pair will establish bonds of friendship so deep as to nonplus even themselves, so intense and enduring that Tamara will tell people—usually amid gales of laughter from her listeners—that Luigi-known-as-Sciammerga has been married three times in his life, and not at different times but simultaneously and for keeps: to Gemma, his legitimate spouse, from whom he will never separate; to Virginia, the first of his lovers, whom he will never leave; and to the Lawyer, whom he will never let down.

For the time being, however, Luigi-known-as-Sciammerga is a young man of thirty-four, recently back from the Russian front, where he took part in the siege of Stalingrad, ruining his lungs in the process. With all the fierceness of a returning soldier, he has been devoting himself to the cause of agrarian reform and to jumping from Gemma's bed into that of Virginia, and many other beds besides. The Notary he knows only by name; he has occasionally caught sight of the Lawyer in town (Luigi doesn't live in the town, which clings to the side of the hill; he lives down on the coast, where the houses haven't yet been electrified). Both of them, father and son, are men he admires for their steadfast opposition to the Fascist regime. And now that the Duce has hightailed it and the Allies are here, both the Notary and the Lawyer—and Luigi-known-as-Sciammerga would stake money on it—will have a role to play in the Italy that is about to rise up from all these ashes, an important role. And so will he. It seems almost that this Lieutenant Colonel Xavier Reid (his name is printed on the public notices that have appeared on the walls of the town, but who knows how it's supposed to be pronounced? Luigi wonders) means to acknowledge as much even now, because, instead of dissuading him from organizing the farmhands' protest, the man's expression and gestures suggest he considers Luigi a serious and trustworthy interlocutor, in other words an equal. In other words, a big cheese.

## 36. NAPLES WON'T BURN

At the beginning of September 1943, Vincenzo arrived in Naples. To be more precise, Vincenzo turned up at 148 Via

Roma, as Via Toledo was called back then, at a little store that sold products for philatelists and was a safe rendezvous for antifascists. He found the city radiant but also spectral: a few days earlier there had been a dreadful bombardment. The umpteenth. Since the Anglo-American air raids first started, Naples had chalked up tens of thousands of deaths and other casualties, and ten times that number of homes had been razed to the ground. Drinking water was rationed, food now at a minimum, rubble everywhere. People were, for the most part, living underground in the bomb shelters. The Allies had now reached Salerno, while the Germans still seemed uncertain what to do: they weren't sure whether to give ground and retreat, or attempt to push back the troops just landed.

So, Vincenzo found the city in its state of ruin spectral, but at the same time radiant with a light he had never seen in any other part of Italy. It seemed to him that the people here, and not just his antifascist friends, but all the inhabitants of the city, had in their bodies an energy that might unleash itself from one moment to the next, flattening everything, like an explosion with incalculable consequences. Maybe it was an effect created by the sunlight reflecting off the surface of the sea; or maybe it was the hunger paring down all those profiles, sharpening them, making them vulpine; or maybe (again) it was the news that the Allies were close enough to give them all hope that things would very soon be changing: the one thing we can be sure of is that, arriving at the little safe house at 148 Via Roma, Vincenzo felt for the very first time that he was party to an energy that would alter both the course of history and Vincenzo himself. To put it another way, he felt afraid.

The room at the back of the little store was crammed with young men. Apart from the proprietor, who Vincenzo knew was a friend of Amadeo Bordiga, the Communist official who had been expelled from the party because he disapproved of Stalin, the others, as far as he was concerned, were all unfamiliar faces. All of them seemed to be in their very early twenties, and although they were all very scruffy, with several days' worth of stubble, and although all of them gave off a pungent odor, he found them inexplicably very elegant. Particularly Dante, who came, like the little store's owner, from Forio, on the island of Ischia. All of them would lose their lives in the next few days, but Vincenzo would forever remember them smiling and immortal, as they were at the instant in which they welcomed him into the group they had formed, named after Spartacus.

From them, he learned that various attacks were being planned on the Germans. In effect, numerous clashes and scuffles had already taken place between the local population and the troops led by Colonel Schöll, who would shortly be assuming overall command of the city. Many Neapolitans had been fighting back against the roundups and the pillaging, and there had already been civilian deaths and casualties. At the end of the meeting, Vincenzo made sure to be paired up with Dante, because he thought, without entirely thinking it through, that if he were to perish in the course of one of the operations being planned by the group, he should like the last thing he ever saw to be creation's infinite beauty mirrored in his comrade's face.

The group's plans would in any event be torpedoed by what happened the following day—Sunday, 12 September—when the German army began systematically destroying Naples, blowing up factories, public buildings, and all the cornerstones of city life. Dante and Vincenzo ended up watching the university library burn, and realized that, if action wasn't taken immediately, the Nazis would reduce Naples to an ash heap. The very same day, Commander Schöll's first proclamation was issued, declaring a state of siege and a curfew from ten o'clock at night to six o'clock in the morning—in addition to which, for every Teutonic soldier wounded or murdered, one hundred Italians would be killed; and finally, anyone possessing a firearm was to hand it in to the military command.

Within a few days, the city was awash with terror. Vincenzo and his group participated in a steady stream of guerrilla operations. The Nazis were progressively inflaming the population's nerves with their pillaging and gratuitous violence, and decrees imposing "obligatory military service" on all young Neapolitan males; but when, on the 23rd of the month, they also ordered the evacuation of the entire seafront, forcing approximately two hundred thousand people to leave their homes, it became clear that Naples had taken as much as it could, and the rebellion became unstoppable. Vincenzo's group and all the other groups operating in the city were taken by surprise and found themselves caught up in an insurrection that no longer had any time for leaders or any form of organized politics. It was like an immense and terrifying howl of protest rising from the city's bedrock.

Violent clashes took place everywhere, in the old city center and outside it, in Vomero, Ponticelli, Poggioreale . . . People attacked in any way they could: shooting, if they had firearms; throwing furniture out of their windows if they heard Schöll's soldiers making their way through the alleyways; and jamming the streets with automobiles and trams to stop the Nazis crossing town.

Vincenzo and Dante remained constantly together until the evening of the 29th. They slept on cellar floors, they shared what little food they could find, and they smoked an incalculable number of cigarettes. They took part in operations carefully planned by the proprietor of the little store on Via Roma (whose name sometimes seemed to be Mario and at other times Mimì), and in a series of ambuscades and shootouts that appeared not to be fruit of any organized political or military strategy, but initiatives launched by a few individuals that lots of other people then immediately joined on impulse.

Their last night together, the night between 28 and 29 September, was spent in a cellar somewhere near Porta Capuana. It was rat infested and damp. Vincenzo and Dante chatted and smoked cigarettes they had found in the pockets of dead German soldiers, until they fell asleep. They slept for what might have been just a few minutes, but could equally have been an eternity. From out in the street the crackling sound of something burning could be heard; then there was an explosion, and they both woke up with a start. Remaining immobile for fear of being discovered by the enemy, they exchanged a few whispered words. Vincenzo said he feared that the Nazis, given the way things were going, might set the entire city alight before pulling out and retreating up toward Rome. Dante made a clicking sound with his tongue and replied, "Don't you worry, Vincè, Naples won't burn." His hand reached out in the dark to find that of his comrade. Then they fell asleep again.

The following day was one Vincenzo would remember as a series of disconnected and dreamlike images: the sun already high when they emerged from the cellar, and the city gate at Porta Capuana seething with life but strangely silent, as if no one wanted to make any noise; Dante's tired face turning watchfully to look at something as they set off together down Via dei Tribunali; the morning's first cigarette being smoked wordlessly, as though it had suddenly dawned on both of them that after having slept hand in hand it would be hard to let the day go by without acknowledging it; a small loaf of undercooked bread donated to them by a girl who had two more of the things in a shopping bag full of bundles of rosemary (they ate the loaf, panting with hunger, but left a few bites' worth for an old man who was staring at them from the other side of the street). Then finally, the rendezvous at the back of the little stamp-collectors' store belonging to Mario (or Mimì): less enthusiasm and more nervousness than a few days earlier, but above all exhaustion—an exhaustion that was something of an elephant in the room.

Armando and Antonio hadn't turned up: Armando had apparently been wounded in Via Indipendenza; no one knew what had happened to Antonio. People began talking over one another. There was a lot of news, much of it contradictory. Everyone had their own take on the events of those days, which seemed to be passing at a speed that was different than normal, both faster and slower. Mario (or Mimì) had shaved off his moustache, and behind the tortoiseshell frames of his glasses his expression was alarmed and slightly childlike. Dante, in contrast, seemed more self-assured, and his hands, which Vincenzo had held tightly in his own just a few hours earlier, looked big and decisive, potentially even intimidating. Everyone listened to what the others had to say, but each of them was thinking something that couldn't be said.

Then, in the room at the back of the store, news arrived that three panzer Tigers were making their way down from Capodimonte toward Santa Teresa, where a barricade had been erected. The tanks were firing their cannons and machine guns, against which rifles and hand grenades were of very little help. There were already many casualties. The Germans were heading for the Archaeological Museum, and beyond that, on toward Piazza Dante.

The meeting disbanded. Splitting into pairs, they reached the Basilica of the Holy Spirit and positioned themselves, ready for the tanks. One arrived, and they started throwing hand grenades at it. Vincenzo was shooting, shooting, and shooting at that behemoth, which seemed to have gotten stuck, twisting round on itself, suddenly unable to advance forward or retreat, at the center of a crossfire of bullets pouring in from every side. And so he didn't immediately notice Dante. A few yards away, to his right, the young man had been hit in the chest and lay dying. A little further on, Mario (or Mimì) had also been wounded: carried off to the hospital with the other two when the first tank began to retreat, he would die a couple of days later.

Vincenzo flew across those few yards that separated him from his comrade, and knelt down next to him. He lifted Dante's still-warm hand and held it to his lips. He was so convulsed with tears that he couldn't tell whether Dante was dead yet. "Help! Help!" he screamed—or it may be that he didn't scream anything, and those screams all stayed caught in his throat. The group's surviving members were at his side seconds later. Three of them grabbed hold of Dante's body, to drag it away from there as fast as they could. Vincenzo refused to let go and ran alongside them, keeping a tight hold of Dante's hand. It would only be many days later, during his tortuous journey home, that Vincenzo realized he didn't even know if Dante was his real name.

## 37. INSOMNIA

Many years later—when this story will already, as was entirely foreseeable, have ended in the most unpredictable of ways—Valentino, one of the Notary's grandsons, will be invited to a book festival to talk about the relationship between creativity and insomnia. And in front of a paying audience of at least a thousand people, late one evening in one of northern Italy's most beautiful piazzas, he will rather awkwardly have to admit that he of all people is the least qualified to expound on the topic, if for no other reason than that he comes from a family of incorrigible and enthusiastic lie-abeds. At home, no one had ever so much as laid eyes on a bottle of sleeping pills—and yes, his maternal grandfather was indeed a pharmacist. Never had he heard any mention—on his father the Lawyer's side of the family, or on his mother Tamara's side—of anyone having a sleepless night, let alone abstaining from the ritual of an afternoon siesta. No difference existed, no distinction was made, between adults and babes: at certain hours, the homes of the Notary, the Pharmacist, and, later on, the Lawyer, although packed to the rafters with children, grandchildren, daughters-in-law, brothers- and sisters-in-law, et cetera, fell abruptly and so obdurately silent that even the notoriously deaf Maria del Nilo could have heard a pin drop.

A single and noteworthy exception is recorded and deserves to be remembered: that of the night between Friday and Saturday, 17 and 18 September 1943. Its protagonist was the Notary. Witnesses: his bedroom, the office on the same floor of the house, and his nine-year-old daughter Tecla. As Tecla would subsequently recall: "Papà was walking in and out of his rooms, which is why he woke me up; the doors were squeaking on their hinges, the sprung bed he slept on squeaked too, that whole night was one long squeak; Vita woke up as well—she had the bed next to mine; Emilio and the nursemaid, no: they didn't wake up because they slept in two little rooms with communicating doors down at the end of the corridor, and there was one door before that, and then a second one; and Arnaldo? He was at his sweetheart Laura's house."

Question: Could the Notary not sleep because of the news that had arrived from Naples, which was where Vincenzo was? The fire at the university had been on 12 September, but rumors of it had only reached them that evening. Or was the chief cause of anxiety—and its close relative, insomnia—the catastrophic family finances he had returned to after five years' absence? Answer: neither of these things. If any sentiment could be said to have traversed the entirety of the Notary's existence and have rendered it exemplary in terms of—if nothing else—fidelity, that sentiment had to do with, in equal parts, politics and his own person. Everything else counted for little or nothing, with a heavy bias toward the latter. And since he was a man as partial to sleep as others are to alcohol, on the night between 17 and 18 September 1943, the Notary must evidently have found the two halves of his sole passion simultaneously at issue. How could he sleep, knowing that in the morning Lieutenant Colonel Reid would be coming back to see him, expecting a list of the names and surnames complicit in the now-former Fascist regime? How could he, to put it another way, condemn one or more of his political adversaries to death? If he were, as the Canadian officer had suggested, to do it for the nation's sake, would his conscience (in other words, his ego) ever forgive him? Hence the insomnia.

### 38. AN UNGODLY HOUR

She didn't like getting up early, but sometimes fear overtakes and outstrips our loves and hates. Which is why Tamara dragged herself out of bed a few minutes before six o'clock on the morning of Saturday, 18 September 1943: because she was worried that politics might now have reached such levels of barbarism, thanks to fascism and the war, that it risked tumbling definitively over the edge, overtaking and outstripping the last remaining vestiges of human kindness. To put it more concisely, she was worried about the so-called law of retaliation. And to put it even more concisely, she was worried about the Notary.

It was daybreak. Outside the big kitchen window, the mismatched roofs of the houses and a strip of sky were visible and brightening minute by minute. The baby—who was not yet a month old—was asleep in the room next to the master bedroom. The Lawyer was asleep too, marinating in his dreams of justice. Tamara made a pot of chicory coffee, and as she did so, summoned Maria-la-pioggia using a special signal they had devised: two sharp knocks on the floor with the broom handle, in a spot that corresponded, a floor below, with the bed where the housemaid slept together with her husband Santo and little Sisina. The knocks were to be repeated at fairly regular intervals, four or five times, until a little knock of reply was heard from downstairs.

Tamara had been repeating her little speech to herself like a litany: ever since the Lawyer had told her about the meeting between the Canadian officer and the Notary, she had thought of nothing else. Her father-in-law was in many respects an odious man, but culturally speaking he was rather refined. Not that she knew him especially well—all things considered, the image she had of him was the one he wanted to give, of a humanist and philanthropist with, Tamara would add, a choleric disposition—but the little she did know was enough to give her some idea which arguments might best help her to make her case: for example, that justice can never be justice if it's done in haste, the way the military wanted it, or reduced to pure and simple vendetta, and that even a pair of monsters like Mussolini and Hitler have the right to be tried in court, once the war is over and Europe has time to start mourning its dead. Otherwise, what difference is there between antifascists and fascists? Between us and them?

Tamara knew that once she was face-to-face with the Notary the words would come out garbled, and that she would probably lose her thread. That man was intimidating at a distance, let alone in person. But if not even his son the Lawyer was brave enough to tell him what he thought (to say nothing of the Pharmacist, with all his fragility and insecurities), someone had to do it. At the end of the day, Tamara resembled her mother, and Lea was a woman of mettle—perhaps excessively so. And so Tamara had repeated the little speech to herself several times, and that morning she was ready. Or at least she thought she was.

As soon as Maria-la-pioggia appeared from downstairs, Tamara went back into her bedroom to dress. She carefully chose the clothes she would wear, and took them into the bathroom so as to avoid waking her husband. In the mirror, she was satisfied to note, she looked elegant but not overdressed: elegant and dignified, comme il faut. Old Uncle Giorgio would have approved.

The Notary's house was in the higher part of the town. To get there, Tamara had to walk up the main street, cutting across the piazza with, on the left, its church and the memorial to the dead of the Great War, and the courthouse on the right. The town center was already relatively animated, but it was a stilted kind of animation that seemed rather aimless: there was none of the usual, orderly to-ing and fro-ing of people and animals going about their work, but noisy and untidy little knots of people and, in the middle, dusty jeeps and foreign soldiers. She realized she was the only woman out and about. So she put on her haughtiest expression (Tamara would be hostage to it throughout her life, often being mistakenly thought standoffish) and walked on in the direction of her father-in-law's house. Mentally, meanwhile, she polished her little speech.

When she got to the Notary's, she found Tecla preparing a breakfast of chicory coffee, evil-smelling goat's milk, and chunks of dry bread that had been warmed on the brazier: the young girl was so small that in order to reach the higher cupboard doors she dragged around a stool that she climbed up onto and down off continually. Sitting at the round table in the kitchen, there were Vita, Emilio and Arnaldo, who had only just gotten back in from his sweetheart's house. There was no sign of Rosa the maid, or of Cicia, Emilio's nursemaid.

Tamara was offered a cup containing a warm liquid that she carefully avoided ingesting, because it stank. She had really just wanted a glass of water: walking across the square on her own, surrounded by all those ragtag groups of men, had made her sweat immoderately, and now she felt terribly thirsty. The Notary—Tecla and Vita told her—had gone out very early that morning, carrying with him some sheets of paper on which he had scribbled a series of illegible words. He had urgent concerns, they added, and had spent the whole night—Tecla continued—walking up and down the corridor between his room and his office, smoking, and banging doors shut, until he woke Tecla, and then also her sister. Rosa had gone out too: she had needed to run over to her parents' house, for motives that had nothing to do with the Notary's insomnia. But Cicia would be here any minute now.

Arnaldo got up from the table and disappeared upstairs without saying a word, but with that poetic and vaguely revolting je ne sais quoi that all young males have the first time they fall in love. Emilio looked around benevolently, like a little Asian divinity: five years old now, he was getting quite fat, notwithstanding the lack of plentiful food; added to which, he continued not to speak, although his eyes radiated good humor and intelligence. Only in front of his father did that little Buddha ever scowl, emitting sounds that put one in mind of abandoned kittens.

Tamara settled down resignedly to wait for her father-in-law to get back. She worried she might have turned up too late for the thing she had in mind. On the other hand, the man's children weren't able to tell her where it was the Notary had been headed when he left the house at dawn, so she had no choice: all she could do was wait.

Her son would need a feed in half-an-hour's time. But on that account she had nothing to worry about, because Maria-la-pioggia would see to it: she had a generous bosom and milk galore, plenty for both Sisina and Picchio. Rather than sit there inert, in front of a still-full cup of the liquid she had no intention of drinking, the woman got up to give Tecla a hand, and together they tidied up the kitchen. Meanwhile, she noted that Vita, who was older than her sister by almost a full four years, acted like an honored guest and made no effort at all to put things away—an attitude that the other girl accepted without protest, as if it were natural. Eventually, Vita stood up and announced that she was going to withdraw to her father's office to read a novel, Tamara remarked, "Isn't life nice... for some people," and Tecla carried the now-cool brazier out into the courtyard.

## 39. AWAY FROM PRYING EYES

Early on the morning of Saturday, 18 September 1943, the Notary decided it was preferable for him to go see Lieutenant Colonel Xavier Reid, rather than the other way around. He worried that at home there might be too many ears, and that those ears accompanied a necessarily smaller but no less efficient number of mouths, and that—to cut a long story short—his meeting with the Canadian army officer would become public knowledge in next to no time—which was the time it would take to translate it into Italian, or rather (and preferably) into the local dialect, at which point it would bounce off into all four corners of the town and then spread like wildfire throughout the district. Better to be prudent. Better to meet Reid at the Allied Command and ask him for an appointment immediately afterward, away from prying eyes, somewhere on a country road far from the center of town.

Reid found the Notary's prudence a little excessive, perhaps, but couldn't help admiring him for it all the same. Up to now he had been inclined to think of southern Italians as sunny natured but unreliable: only ever tight-lipped with those they considered outsiders, they instead—he was sure—chattered a great deal among themselves. Proof of which lay in the fact that everybody always knew everything about everyone else's business, and one could never count on even an iota of discretion. Thus, after the initial surprise of seeing the Notary appear in his office at first light, Xavier Reid agreed without batting an eyelid to the proposed appointment out of town.

It was a beautiful day—mild, and with none of the summer's muggy heat—and the sky was so blue that it looked like something freshly daubed by an eighteenth-century landscape painter. With the sun still low, the air was soft; the light seemed to have gotten itself tangled up in the lower branches of the olive trees. Despite the war, this countryside didn't appear to be suffering from neglect: the vines were ready for the harvest, and the scent of the citrus groves was strong enough to knock a man out, even though the blossoms had long given way to oranges, lemons, and bergamots, which in a month or so would be ripe enough for picking.

Walking along in silence, Reid thought to himself, first in English and then in French, that he would never forget this ravishing landscape, where from one moment to the next, at every bend in the road, one could conceivably bump into a pagan god, or a nymph. Or even Pythagoras, who once lived in this neck of the woods. Here and there, poking out from the vegetation, the remains of columns hung suspended like exclamation marks halfway through a sentence, and there were blocks of white marble with chipped edges, perfectly rectangular, like bricks for building castles in the air. The lieutenant colonel stopped for a moment and gazed down into the valley spread out below him: off in the far distance one could see the Ionian Sea, its blue as deep and ancient as the color the sky had been daubed with—so ancient as to make one want to go back to school and study the Greek of Sophocles and Euripides properly, and learn how to speak it effortlessly. At that hour of the morning, with that light and the perfectness of that panorama, it would make much more sense to express oneself in iambic trimeter than almost any other way. Following the mildly schizophrenic thread of his own bilingual thoughts, Reid felt he was beginning to see why geography—which must surely have been invented somewhere in this area—was so well regarded: because here there was no gap between nature and history, and the latter of those two seemed to have spawned the former, in exactly the same way that classical architecture seems to beget the land beneath it, and not the other way around.

Reid—as has already been mentioned—was a tall, gaunt man, like the Notary, and it may well have been this resemblance between the two that, from the moment they first met, had inspired a measure of fellow feeling. Although, unlike the Notary, who had dark, worried eyes and an aquiline nose that seemed to tip him forward and closer to his interlocutor, the Canadian officer gave the impression of being detached, held back by his own gray-green gaze, at a distance both ironical and forlorn. Therefore, and even though they had similar complexions and similar, slightly affected physical foibles, the two men were effectively one another's opposites—which was probably the real reason for the aforementioned fellow feeling.

They met up beneath a very lovely olive tree, all twisted in on itself—its contorted outlines well matching the emotions of both men, although Reid made more effort to hide his than the Notary did. It was hotter now. The sun was fully up, and the walk had put heat into muscles and emotions. The Notary pulled out of his jacket pocket two sheets of white paper stiff with the blue ink he habitually used. He held them out toward the lieutenant colonel, who took them from him, glanced rapidly at them, and said, "I don't understand. What's this supposed to mean?" He said it in French and then repeated it in English. He tried saying it in Italian too.

There was an awkward pause. The lieutenant colonel stared at the other man with an expression that was, all of a sudden, severe, as if someone were attempting to play games with him and he wasn't having any of it. The Notary didn't know where to start. They studied each other for a moment or two, each unsure whether they should trust the other simply on the basis of a vague physical resemblance, or whether they should set little store by the fact that they happened to find themselves on the same side of history.

Reid repeated, somewhat impatiently, "So what is it supposed to mean?" And he held the ink-stained sheets of paper out toward the Notary: there were a fair number of words written on them, columns of words, but all redacted very carefully, hidden behind darker blots of the same ink.

The Notary smiled an artificial, nervous smile; all his body's thinness seemed to be condensed somewhere between his nostrils and his mouth. It occurred to the soldier that the man's tight smile reminded him of Victor, his Jack Russell. He said, icily, "Answer me, please."

The Notary began speaking, making a rather roundabout job of it, but Reid interrupted him brusquely: "I didn't come all the way out here to listen to another one of your stately little speeches. You were asked for a list of names and surnames, and you bring me pieces of paper covered in illegible doodles. Where are the names I asked you for? Give me a clear, straightforward answer. I do not have time to waste listening to your prattle."

The Notary's face took on an expression of bewilderment—a look his features were not accustomed to wearing. Reid sighed noisily. "Forgive me," he said, "I didn't mean to be rude, but I don't understand what it is you're trying to do."

Again, the Notary smiled nervously, and again Reid was put in mind of his dog. Then the Notary explained that he had spent the previous night drawing up a list of people in the area who had held positions of importance during the Fascist regime and had proven to be particularly vile or cruel toward its opponents and the Jews. The odd judge, two or three lawyers, a district prefect, a police superintendent, even a bishop; various podestàs (but all things considered, not very many of them, compared with other lines of work) and soldiers. He had worked on the list for hours: he had wanted it to be precise, detailed, fair—void of any great oversights or heavy-handed inclusions. He had wanted it to be as accurate as possible: an exemplar worth imitating in other parts of Italy liberated by the Allied forces.

And yet, as the night gradually slid into morning, as the hands of the clock seemed to speed faster and more eagerly round than was normal, and ever less time remained for polishing, correcting, and reconsidering decisions already made, the Notary had found himself feeling increasingly confused, increasingly unsure of himself, like a student who has learned by rote many of the formulas useful in an exam he has to take, but hasn't understood the first thing about the subject he is being tested in. And so, as soon as he wrote down each name, position, profession, he immediately backtracked and crossed it all out, like an irascible—and also male—Penelope. Not one of those notes had survived, and across every line of each sheet of paper there now lay a thick, messy skein of ink.

"I can't do it," concluded the Notary, "I can't condemn these people to death."

He took back his sheets of paper and tore them into a thousand pieces.

Reid didn't move a muscle; he made no comment. In his heart of hearts he told himself he probably would have done the same thing, had he found himself in the Notary's shoes. Ultimately, what he had asked of the man was to transform himself into an informer, and therefore into an individual worthy of contempt, even if the people he would have been denouncing deserved to be taught a lesson, considering all the evil they had done. In any case—Reid also told himself—that man who was as tall and gaunt as he was, and who was now staring at him without any hint of a canine, Jack Russell smile, would in future regret that decision of his on many occasions, execrating himself for having been too indulgent or excessively generous, or just too human. He would curse himself every time he saw a former Fascist Party official elected to parliament, or a murderer of partisans enjoy a brilliant public career. And to this we should add that Lieutenant Colonel Xavier Reid's prophecy would eventually come true, right down to the very last detail: had he pronounced it aloud, on that morning of 18 September 1943, the dirty, sordid pact we all call history might well have unraveled rather differently.

### 40. NO NAMES

If only Tamara, his Mara, had told him why it was she had slipped out of bed at first light, silent as a thief, to go over to the Notary's house; if only she had confessed, when she returned from her mysterious mission, the motive for that visit; if only she had made some reference to that morning expedition, without necessarily going into any of the details, the Lawyer would not have been left thrashing around in the agony of a man who doesn't know how to give vent to his jealousy, but instead remains in thrall to it. He pretended nothing was wrong. He didn't ask; he didn't pry. And yet he could think of nothing else: Why had Tamara, his Mara, left at dawn to go over to see the Notary? In other words, why had she gone to see a man to whom she was in no way close and had in fact hinted she couldn't stand? How and why had she overcome lack of familiarity, mistrust, shyness, her dislike?

When she came back home on the morning of 18 September, Tamara didn't say a thing, as if she had never left the house. She got on with her normal chores, baby included, and started racking her brains for ways to produce a lunch: she sent Maria-la-pioggia off to look for some of the wild greens that grew in the meadows on the edge of town, she popped round to her mother's house to ask for a few tomatoes (but Lea gave her nothing and instead complained about her husband, who hadn't left his bed all week, forcing her to do the work of two people, looking after the house and the pharmacy), she handed over a ridiculous number of Allied Military Currency banknotes in exchange for a skinny shank of lamb that wouldn't stretch to one full portion, and she called in on Cousins Levino and Margherita in the hope of cadging a couple of potatoes. When she got back in, Maria-la-pioggia was boiling up a dark-green slop. Tamara set to work at the stove, attempting to give the meat some sort of flavor with the addition of garlic and wild rosemary, and she waited for her husband to come home for lunch.

The Lawyer arrived at around two o'clock, sat down at the table, and began discreetly cross-questioning his wife, employing a whole range of insinuations and roundabout phrases, to which Tamara responded very vaguely. They were both of them being so evasive that at one point—in an attempt to come to Tamara's aid and break the vicious circle of a conversation that was going nowhere—Maria-la-pioggia intervened to say the greens were ready: Would Tamara and the Lawyer like some? No, no, they didn't want any, or perhaps yes, maybe just a spoonful for now, or maybe later, can it wait a few minutes? Getting those two to state anything plainly was impossible.

Then, blessedly, silence descended. The Lawyer asked himself why it was that he couldn't express himself frankly, while his wife, for her part, wondered why on earth her husband was so ill at ease and querulous, when with other people, outside the family, he seemed so easygoing, so chatty and witty. At heart, the answer to both these lines of questioning was a relatively simple one, but neither husband nor wife appeared to be capable of seeing it. For which reason, the mute awkwardness continued for several days, interrupted only by nocturnal yowls from the baby and Maria-la-pioggia's clumsy efforts to initiate a conversation of some sort, any sort, whenever the young couple sat down at the marble-topped kitchen table. Even Lea noticed that something wasn't right between the two, and one evening when they were round at her house for supper, she made a futile attempt to force an improvement, urging Nina—who as a small child had loved being the center of attention but now that she was fifteen had discovered she had a bashful streak—to show them a card trick, in hopes that it might melt the ice between Tamara and her husband.

At times, at night, the Lawyer's eyes raked the dark, looking for the sleeping profile of Tamara, his Mara, and if and when he located a piece of it, and if and when he managed to identify correctly a small section of it, he felt like roaring for happiness, but he also felt like howling in misery. He wanted to hold her, Tamara, his Mara. He wanted to touch her, but out of pride he held back. He was sure she was keeping something from him. Something unimaginably horrible.

And so the weeks went by, and Maria-la-pioggia was now in despair. Every evening she went back home (downstairs) and held Santo tight, offering him many memorable moments of joy and also, nine months later, little Enzo, who—although blithely unaware of it—would live to see the end of the war in the closing days of April and the first few days of May 1945, but thanks to a bout of pneumonia was unfortunately not around for the proclamation of the republic on 2 June the following year.

Christmas was approaching by the time Tamara broke the silence. By this point, she had become convinced that the Notary had not denounced anyone to the Allied forces, because no one—in town, at least—had suddenly disappeared from circulation. She couldn't have sworn to it that the man hadn't pointed a finger at some or other high-ranking Fascist Party official from Cosenza or Naples (her father-in-law had just gotten back from Naples, where, from 18 to 20 December, he had attended the Action Party's southern delegates' conference), but certainly no one she, Tamara, knew personally. So, on the morning of the 24th, no longer having anything to fear—in other words, thinking that if she were to confide in her husband it would not now lead to a row or a family crisis—she serenely told the Lawyer all about that visit back in September: about leaving at dawn in the hope of intercepting the Notary before he could reduce himself to an abject snitch; about waiting in vain at the man's house and giving Tecla a hand tidying up the kitchen, while Vita took herself off to read with that air of spoiled entitlement that Tamara found so irritating; and about returning home frustrated and frightened, and wondering if the Lawyer, too, might not be complicit in the paternal wrongdoing—which would perhaps have explained why her husband had lately grown so silent and hostile.

The Lawyer felt at least a decade falling magically off him. And since that didn't count for much (all things considered he was only in his thirties, and at that age rejuvenations don't have much of an impact), he also felt himself growing several inches taller (his height was a sore point) and an equal number of inches disappearing from his midriff (a second sore point). He didn't dare confess his jealousy—a sentiment he would always despise—but he did confirm that his father had been careful not to involve him in the decision made with regard to Lieutenant Colonel Reid's request, and that he himself had often since wondered what the man had elected to do. After all, the Notary's silence could have been every bit as indicative of ratting as of its opposite. In any case, a sufficient number of months had now gone by that he and Tamara, his adored and beloved Mara, could safely infer that the Notary had named no names.

At which point, in a manner of speaking, the couple's second-born son was brought into the world: perhaps not according to the registrar of births and deaths, but as far as the two of them were concerned at any rate. And that being so, hostilities came to an end.

# CHAPTER FOUR

## 41. THINGS CHANGE

On the morning of Thursday, 6 June 1946, at around half past nine—the air was pleasantly warm, this summer was promising to be kind but firm—the Notary met with himself.

A man who must have been fifty years old, give or take, but wore it well (tall, slim, dressed with slightly excessive care), had just then knocked on the Notary's door. It had been opened by Vita, who, suddenly feeling rather awkward in front of this stranger—there was something familiar about him, like a street or a town square one knows one has been in but can't remember the name of—had led him into her father's office and asked him to wait there for a minute. When, shortly afterwards, the Notary appeared, there had been two sharp intakes of breath, each man seeing his own mirror image.

That morning, the front pages of all the papers were yelling out news of the proclamation of the Italian Republic and the imminent departure of the ex–royal family following the handover of power to De Gasperi, the provisional head of state. In the Notary's eyes this represented a personal success, repaying his recent defeat in the local elections (the Action Party had won only 1,428 votes, while the Christian Democrats had raked in a thousand more than that), because from boyhood onward, even before he had first espoused the socialist ideal, he had always been firmly pro-republic. He felt he could be accorded some merit for the fact that here in town, in the referendum held a few days earlier, the voters in favor of a republic had heavily outnumbered those who expressed themselves in favor of the monarchy (2,618 votes to 2,251), while in the rest of Calabria the losers turned out to be greatly in the majority. Which is why, after that first glance, during which the Notary had the disturbing sensation that he was standing in front of himself—a younger and possibly even thinner self—he had smiled a hesitant but inevitable smile and a look of expectancy had formed on his face: What did the stranger want?

The latter looked the Notary up and down, gave a smile of his own, and seemed to be rather embarrassed. Eventually, his gaze running across the shelves of the bookcase as if he were thinking of dusting it, he said very simply, "My name is Giulio, and my mother was Dinda, your parents' maid."

The expression on the Notary's face promptly altered: now it was watchful and defensive.

Giulio, however, had not come here looking to assert any claims. Giulio had studied engineering in Bari, where he had completed his university degree and had begun his working life on the huge construction sites that, under Fascism, had reshaped the city's waterfront and had brought into being the vast exhibition center known as the Fair of the Levant. After Bari's liberation by the Allies, he had found work for himself chaperoning Americans round the city. Then, following the terrible bombardment on 2 December 1943, he had, as an expert engineer, collaborated with the Allied forces, keeping an eye on the situation in the harbor district, a situation made all the more delicate by the fact that the American ship SS *John Harvey* had been chock-full of mustard gas bombs—information that was highly classified. Giulio had handled the emergency tactfully and assertively, and his social standing had soared.

And now he had come back to the town to pay a brief visit, because Dinda, his mother, was dead and he wanted to meet the man he had always known was his father. The Notary was cool as a cucumber. The individual facing him inspired confidence, although he didn't particularly like him. And in any case, he had to admit the man was a carbon copy of him. He called Rosa and asked her to bring coffee and pastries for their guest, and an hour or two later had learned that Giulio was married but childless, and had promised he would acknowledge Giulio as his son, giving him the legal right to use the family name, if Giulio would, in exchange, take his half sister Vita back with him to Bari, and ensure she was educated and looked after in a manner appropriate for a girl born into the upper classes and possessed of considerable intellect but unfortunately not possessed of a private income.

Giulio agreed, because every time any document of his bore the words "father unknown" the humiliation of it and the sense of defeat slammed a fist into his professional achievements. But he also said yes because he had always dreamed of having a daughter, and Vita looked so like him that he could at least now wallow in the fantasy.

And so it was that, after two days of frantic preparations in which trunks were filled and tears were shed, as if Vita were going off to live on the moon and not, rather more prosaically, to Bari, the family gathered in front of the Notary's house to wave off the girl who was, together with her half brother, about to drive off in an American-made automobile packed full of luggage and covered in dust. Contrary to Tamara's expectations, Vita wept uninterrupted tears, while Tecla remained controlled and practical right to the last. Only as the car drew off, screeching, did Tecla glance at her sister-in-law and remark, "Isn't life nice... for some people." And that was that.

## 42. THE WORDS AND THE ORDER OF THINGS

On the third or the fourth day the Pharmacist spent in bed, refusing to get up despite there being nothing physically wrong with him, Nina started quarreling with Gioacchino. Gioacchino contended that Nina, who was now a young woman (time had gone by, and this summer she would be turning eighteen), should not be working in the pharmacy as her father's stand-in: it wasn't right for a young lady to be spending every God-given hour of the day dealing with the hoi polloi. Nina, however, found it fun, whether standing behind the tall counter and folding powder papers, or simply deciphering the abstruse and labyrinthine tangle of handwriting on the prescriptions: it was like a game that had the magical property of freeing her from the maternal realm. Because at home the atmosphere was one of strict control, as dictated by Lea and her steely sergeant, Maria del Nilo, but in the pharmacy Nina could do as she saw fit and give free rein to the cheerful disposition she had inherited from who knows where.

Nina loved company, and found something of interest in everyone. She asked questions, she made inquiries, and she knew pretty much all there was to know about whoever came in to ask for this or that medicine: where they lived, what problems they had, whether or not they led a respectable life. She knew whether a particular husband was well behaved even when drunk, or if he beat up his wife and children; whether harmony reigned in his household or quarrels were the order of the day; whether the children were well fed or hungry. Had she been able to study at university, Nina would undoubtedly have studied pharmacy, or would have looked for a job in some other field that involved contact with the public, because it was in dealing with other people that she gave the best of herself. But she hadn't gone to university, and as for a job, it was out of the question. In those days, war or no war, girls from good southern families didn't work. And then her galloping nearsightedness had seen to the rest.

Nina was so good at dealing with the clientele that whenever her father absented himself and she stood in for him, the pharmacy filled with people. First, the women of the town felt more comfortable talking to a young woman, and so they went into the pharmacy less reluctantly. And since the women were more inclined than their respective parents, brothers, and husbands to try out new products and devote a minimum of care to their own bodies even when healthy, the pharmacy made much more money when Nina, rather than her father, was in charge.

Of an evening, when Nina shut herself into her bedroom, Lea heard her daughter chattering, laughing, and—lately—vehemently arguing some point or other. Because it was of an evening that Gioacchino materialized in Nina's head, and at that point the quarreling began. He criticized the Pharmacist and levelled accusations at him, going so far as to ridicule the man's weakness of character—and this she refused to put up with. Hence the rows and the squabbling.

Then again, Nina always hit a brick wall during those tiffs, and she got to that point by continually asking herself the same questions: Why, instead of working like everyone else, instead of providing for his family with that modicum of grimness or of resignation characteristic of all the other men she knew, why did her father wallow in his own melancholy, clamming up and locking himself into a secret, inaccessible, and in many ways sinister world? And what did it mean, precisely, scientifically (if there were a science that contemplated its existence), that word—depression? A word he used now and then as a sort of universally valid safe-conduct, an authorization to travel into a dimension where there were no family ties or responsibilities or anything. Nothing except the endless, cruel freedom to be oneself.

Ever since the war had ended, in other words after the armistice and the arrival of the Anglo-American troops, after the veterans had returned (even Vincenzo, the Lawyer's brother, had finally made an appearance, at the end of a long disappearance), after the desperate hunger and the grief over those who had remained trapped in that war forever (the town's war dead numbered thirty-nine, as a memorial tablet would confirm three years later); after the horror of Piazzale Loreto, with Mussolini being hung from his feet; after the black market; after the shame of discovering that they were all craven and squalid; after all the evacuees; after the happiness and relief of getting back to an ostensibly normal life; after the referendum that had ratified the republic, the Pharmacist had begun using that queer, mortifying, indecent word—the word "depression," which Nina imagined being like a cudgel or a blunt instrument—increasingly often and with increasing enthusiasm, in the same way that others say "I'm feeling a little out of sorts" or "I don't feel great." That word formed on the Pharmacist's lips at the least predictable of moments, with its lingering air of mystery and incompleteness; it sounded allusive and unripe, and—throwing Lea and the entire household into a panic—it blew through the house like a dry, abrasive wind, threatening to leave only desert in its wake. And yet that deathly, obscene word did have something positive to it, something deceptive and at the same time protective (it was like a mirror—if one can mirror oneself in a word), because for the time being it usefully hid behind it another more potent, dizzying word, one which hadn't yet been held up to the light of conscious awareness. The word "Holocaust."

### 43. GIVE OR TAKE THE ODD SECOND

From the second in which Dante had exhaled his last breath, his hand held tight in that of his friend, two years, eight months, ten days, nineteen hours, and fifteen minutes had gone by, give or take the odd second: at precisely 10:45 on the morning of Sunday, 9 June 1946, Vincenzo came home. In all that time they had had no news of him, and at a certain point, going by the latest information to have reached the Notary—in other words that his son was in Naples on the eve of the famous four days of insurrection at the end of September '43—it had been assumed that the young man had been killed in the clashes with the German troops under the command of Colonel Schöll. But no. Vincenzo wasn't dead, even if, in a sense, his heart had stopped beating precisely two years, eight months, ten days, nineteen hours, and fifteen minutes—give or take the odd second—before he knocked at the door of the house he was born in.

What he had been up to and why he had never bothered to send word of any kind to his family he would confess only to Tamara. But not right away—a week after his return. Getting home, Vincenzo—who had grown very thin and had lost the foppish air he used to have, as if he'd misplaced it somewhere, like losing a pair of gloves—wanted only to sink into a tub of hot water, use a great deal of soap, pull on clean underwear, and climb into bed between freshly laundered sheets. He slept for twelve unbroken hours. When he woke up it was almost four o'clock in the morning. Hungry, he went downstairs to the kitchen and raided it of everything edible. Then he went back upstairs and shut himself up in his room. Tecla, who slept in the room next door to his and who, as we have seen, was in the habit of keeping an eye on the household's sleep, had the distinct impression her brother was weeping. She held her breath in an attempt to confirm it, but couldn't hear a thing. At half past six on the dot, she got up to make breakfast with Rosa.

Vincenzo had lost weight and had also lost interest in clothes and fashions, but in recompense he had gained in allure. His physique had become better defined, his profile seemed better designed: everything about him appeared to be more detailed and in better focus. He spoke less than he used to, and his gestures were measured. He didn't smile, and his face was frequently grave. But in all of this there was something virile and mature that unquestionably rendered him more attractive.

Ever since the evening of the day of his reappearance, the Notary's house had been bristling with friends, relatives, and neighbors. Vincenzo was sleeping, so none of them could see him or ask him any questions. Before he went off to bed, the Notary had tried pressing his son with a volley of questions about his disappearance, but the young man had replied in monosyllables: the only thing he let slip (but perhaps it wasn't a slip of the tongue, perhaps he wanted his father to know it) concerned Magda, the Polish noblewoman with whom the Notary had had a tempestuous affair back in the days of his Neapolitan youth. Vincenzo, it seemed, had met her, Magda Świr (he used her maiden name, as proof of their encounter), but how, where, and when exactly that had been he didn't clarify—which the Notary found maddening.

The only one of them not to join in the procession of people trying vainly to pay Vincenzo a visit, now that he was back from the hereafter that his relatives and acquaintances had consigned him to for nearly three years, was Tamara. The Lawyer's wife didn't turn up at her father-in-law's house until a week after the young man came back to life. She chose a time in the morning when, she was fairly certain, the head of the household would not be there.

Vincenzo was in his room, lying on the bed. It was a hot day, and the young man had left the window flung open; the shouts of women and children floated up from the lane below, together with a strong smell of fried onions. Tamara knocked at the door, and Vincenzo welcomed her in without effusive displays of emotion, but affectionately. He suggested his sister-in-law take a seat in a wobbly little armchair, and he lay back down on the bed. Both of them were lightly dressed, she in a pale shirtdress that had seen better days but set off the blue of her eyes; he in a sky-blue short-sleeved shirt and striped trousers. To begin with they sat in silence, then Tamara got the conversation off to a start with a few generic remarks about the weather.

That morning, Vincenzo told Tamara about Dante and about himself, about those days in Naples and everything that had followed, talking with an ease and sincerity he had never thought would be possible. He began with the moment of Dante's death and the small steps he had then had to take, day by day, working his way toward comprehending the fact that his friend was no longer alive. He talked about that 29th of September, almost three years ago now, but then he pushed on further back to describe the moment he saw Dante for the very first time, in the back room of that little philately store at 148 Via Roma, when he had thought (but that wasn't the right word for it, because if anything he had *sensed*) that all the beauty in the world was amassing right there in that little back room, turning his life upside down in the blink of an eye. And then, the instant in which Dante had died, just a few days after they met, he, Vincenzo, with the warmth of his friend's hand still there in his own, had understood that he would never forget that very brief interval of time in which it had all taken place, because deep inside him it would never come to an end.

On the evening of 29 September he had found himself on the outskirts of the city. Going south, going home. But the roads were as good as destroyed: bombarded first by the Allies and then by the Germans, the countryside seemed featureless, it had no landmarks. So he had started to zigzag.

Days later—how many? he didn't know—he had arrived in Sorrento.

Mercifully the weather was still mild, pleasant, even though they were now deep into autumn. Sometimes the people he encountered were hostile, sometimes they were kind. In Sorrento he had been taken, for heaven only knows what reason, to the house of an old Polish countess who was lending the antifascists a hand. Magda Świr. The same Magda his father had lived with back when he was not much more than a boy. Vincenzo made no mention of it initially; that fate should have brought the two of them together was so absurd that explaining any of it to her didn't feel right. But then, in '45, when she made up her mind to return to Poland, on the eve of her departure he had confessed whose son he was. Magda was by this point desperately poor; in those months spent living with her and acting as her domestic help and factotum, he had understood that, beyond a shadow of a doubt. Yet when they said their goodbyes, she gave him a little diamond broach. "Use it as a tiepin," she suggested. "Or if you don't like it, give it to that reprobate of a father of yours." She had pronounced that phrase with the addition of many extra *r*'s, *p*'s and *b*'s.

Magda had never asked him anything in all those months they had spent under the same roof. She knew that Vincenzo had taken an active part in the liberation of Naples, but the motive behind his evident sadness and the tears he shed in private had never been a subject of curiosity. In Magda, Vincenzo found a maternal figure—because she pampered him—and also a moral compass, because she forced him to look everything in the face. She was, to boot, a fairly intransigent employer.

Following the noblewoman's departure, Vincenzo stayed on in Sorrento for a couple of months, until the lease on the house ran out, and then he set out for home and took what seemed to be forever to get there. Sleeping in his childhood bedroom again seemed to have reignited memories of Dante, and sometimes they burned so fiercely that, regardless of the time of day, he was forced to leave the house and go for walks that lasted for hours, out in the countryside (Magda had apparently often told him that a good walk sorts everything out). In bed at night, though, those memories were paralyzing and left him sobbing the desperate tears that Tecla strained to decipher from the other side of the wall.

When Tamara got home that day, she found the Lawyer already sitting at the kitchen table, waiting for her. Thankfully, Maria-la-pioggia had thought to get lunch. Tamara sat down too, but wasn't hungry. She was thinking about Vincenzo and the immense gesture of friendship he had made by telling her his story.

The Lawyer noticed that his wife was troubled by something, that she was distracted. He asked, "Did you go to see Vincenzo?"

Tamara nodded and lifted up her right hand, palm facing outwards, like Buddha giving a blessing. Except in her case it meant: Don't ask me anything more about it, please.

So the Lawyer sang the praises of Maria-la-pioggia's spaghetti *al pomodoro*.

## 44. WELL-TIMED VISITS

Every morning, around nine o'clock, Peppo from the post-house dropped by the pharmacy, and since he invariably found Nina busy behind the counter, wordlessly took a seat on the bench just outside, in the street, and waited. As soon as Nina had a moment free she went out to join him, giving him a chance to ask after the Pharmacist's health.

In truth, Nina had no idea what state her father's health was in. Despite the ophthalmologist having expressly forbidden any attempts to read by the light of "weak and unreliable electric lamps," Nina spent her evenings immersed in books precisely in order to find that out. She told Lea they were formularies and pharmacopeias useful for work; in reality she was compulsively poring over psychology textbooks, in search of an explanation for her father's behavior. She was desperate to understand exactly what it involved, that confounded depression she had heard him refer to. But by slow degrees, as she waded through whatever volumes she managed to get hold of, Nina developed the increasingly distinct impression that psychology was a haphazard and erratic brand of tarot-card reading—which she happened to adore. In effect, she was getting no closer to understanding what was happening to her father's mind. Above all, she still didn't understand why it was that his anxiety attacks had recently grown so much more intense, and so frequent that they were now chronic.

For his part—and while almost always to be found lying in bed nowadays, or, at best, barricaded in his room, and appareled at all times in pajamas and dressing gown—the Pharmacist did nothing to hide his malaise. And if anyone asked how he was, he shrugged his shoulders, hands outspread, and said, "My health's all right, it's my head that's all wrong."

Unlike Nina, he knew what was going on in his head: the words and obsessive images that had tormented him in the past (the darkness, the laundered clothes hanging in the sun to dry, Millet's *Angelus* coming to life and transforming the landscape around it into a desert scrubland like the Morocco of his childhood, and then finally that sort of litany or chorus—wait, wait for me, wait) had hollowed themselves out, they had lost all significance: at this point they were gauzy, neutral words and images that provoked nothing any more, apart from indifference. Because his anxiety, or more precisely his horror, sprang from reality now. Or better yet, from any account he could give himself of it. And there we have it: it was the accounts that terrified him, the accounts of what had gone on in Berlin and Vienna and France and even in Italy, although thankfully not here in town and not in the rest of the region either, as far as he knew. But if he thought about Berlin or Vienna, or about France, where his relatives had vanished into thin air, or the north of Italy, where so many friends had been loaded like animals onto trains and taken off to those icy places they were beginning to read about in the papers, if he thought about all this horror, which included and predated his own private horror, well, at that point the Pharmacist no longer wanted to live. He simply couldn't face it. And perhaps he would have preferred to have been put—him too—on a train, like an animal being carted off to the slaughterhouse, and not have had to feel this pain, this heartbreak relentlessly tearing him apart, the guilt of being alive, of having survived a massacre he had barely been aware of.

He would never play his violin again. Besides, who was there to play it for? For an audience of the dead? All of them, all of them were dead: even Lea and Nina and his married daughters and Giorgio, who was a surgeon and pretended to battle against it, that death. They would all be dead forever, forever and forever. Humanity was dead. The world, the planets—dead. A dead world. Dead planets.

Before the war he had never thought about Judaism. His life had been lived in a world where Jews hardly existed. To please Lea's father, who was a gentile, he had agreed to convert to Catholicism, promising to educate his children as Catholics. But neither of them (Lea was Jewish too, thanks to her mother) had really given a fig, and the children had actually been given a secular upbringing. Naturally, after the racial laws came in, he had thought about his own roots, but by now they were remote: he had converted thirty years before that loathsome legislation came into being, and any ties with the family had been extinguished when old Uncle Giorgio died in '39.

Those remote, hazy roots had come crashing down on him like a mountain of stones only now, now that Fascism had been defeated. All of a sudden, he found himself remembering the summers in Morocco, and his grandfather who took him out to see the desert, and young Aunt Fanny, with whom he had been in love—possibly because she was always sweetly perfumed and everything around her smelled of it—and the cousins from Paris, who were so unpleasant, and his older brother, who had his nose in a book all day long . . . He suddenly remembered every detail of those long-lost roots, and it seemed to him that all the happiness in the world was contained in those summers, and that it was inevitable that the noisy, hot days of that period should have been followed by a chill, dark season: one had only to screw up one's eyes and peer a bit harder to see as much. And yet, even the age of darkness and ice had now run its course, and history—that concatenation of illusions—had been set back in motion. It had taken a war and an unspeakable number of murders, but time had, in the end, begun flowing again. It was just that the stench it left behind was so fetid that one couldn't help but be disgusted by everything that had survived.

In May the Pharmacist had turned sixty-seven, an age at which the past is more astonishing than the future—to say nothing of the future's codicil. There was little left to lean forward into, little in the way of tomorrow and the day after that. If he was really going to have to keep on living, he wanted no surprises, because before you know it surprises turn into nightmares. If anything, he hoped for a life of gray routine, neutral, noiseless, its repetitiousness as tranquilizing as a Veronal tablet.

This routine took the form of Peppo from the posthouse.

## 45. EVERY DAY A GOOD DAY

In the late summer of '46, and while not returning to work (Nina had by now seized firm control of the pharmacy counter, with the complicity of Lea, who had noted a tripling in the volume of business), the Pharmacist got into the habit of sitting down every day, together with Peppo from the posthouse, next to the door of his own premises, and smoking his pipe. And the passersby began to think of that big, tired, laconic man who benevolently returned their greetings with a nod of his head—as if to say "Yes, I see who you are"—as a sort of comforting and propitious deity; and while in the past they had limited themselves to asking him for hurried advice about some or other medicine, nowadays they happily lingered to give him detailed descriptions of their more intimate ailments, their worries, and their troubles, for which they expected no medical cure, but sought assistance of a much vaguer kind. Over the course of that exceptionally hot summer, the Pharmacist interlarded every word and every sideways glance at Peppo from posthouse with a mopping of his brow, as if expressing his views on this or that case were an additional exertion, supplementary to the business of coping with the heat. His answers were always thoughtful and sympathetic. He would turn to look at Peppo from the posthouse as if seeking confirmation of his own opinion, and rarely did he voice a criticism. Generally speaking, he had something of the air of a cheerful and disinterested parish priest. Those who consulted him—to wit, the whole town, parish priest included—seemed to consider him a threefold authority in the field of life: as a foreigner, as a violinist, and as an individual who had not been ashamed to let others know of his own suffering. Because everyone in town had known for months that the Pharmacist had been feeling so out of sorts that he couldn't get out of bed, and the irony of it was that for that ailment of his no effective medicines had yet been invented.

It had been Peppo from the posthouse who dragged him—unwittingly, of course—out of bed. Because Peppo had sat down every day on the bench outside the pharmacy and had waited for him. And every lunchtime, Nina had gone home for a bite to eat, had knocked at her father's bedroom door and had spent ten minutes or so sitting at the end of his bed: she was endeavoring to keep him in touch with the outside world, with tales of how so-and-so was in bed with the flu and such-and-such had had an attack of kidney stones overnight. And before going back into the kitchen and sitting down to have her lunch, she never failed to remark, "I almost forgot... Peppo says to have a good day and that he's waiting for you."

Day after day, that vision—of a man sitting there alone and quietly waiting, for as long as the pharmacy remained open—made deeper inroads into the Pharmacist's aching psyche, becoming a sort of lifebuoy, or a bright signal sent out from a lighthouse to a boat that, with bad weather on the way, runs the risk of not making it into the harbor for the night. And so, the Pharmacist's depression begat both an enduring friendship and a legend—regarding the number of handkerchiefs he owned (all of them white, all of them abnormally large, and all of them used exclusively for the purpose of mopping the sweat from his brow).

### 46. DARNED STOVE!

No two ways about it: she was hopeless in the kitchen. She had no imagination. Ideas died between her fingers as soon as she picked them up. She would start out planning to cook something new, something moderately but not exaggeratedly sophisticated, and the result would unfailingly be a fiasco. Her sauces were too watery or too thick. Her pasta was pitifully overcooked or jaw-punishingly "al dente." And her meat dishes? Raw, or stringy. Or oddly reminiscent of shoe leather. Fish we will avoid mentioning. There were times when, having labored over a new recipe, and faced with now-certain failure, Tamara wanted to weep: quiet tears, discreet tears, so that Maria-la-pioggia wouldn't notice and laugh. Under her breath, so that no one would hear her, she imprecated: she cursed the "darned stove!" At moments like this, that famed sense of humor, of which the Lawyer was simultaneously the favored target and the greatest admirer, went up—appropriately enough—in smoke.

Maria-la-pioggia, on the other hand, cooked superlatively well. When she did it she didn't even seem to be doing it, because in the meantime she would be dusting, or washing a shirt, or tidying up a cupboard and explaining that her husband Santo had gotten himself woefully drunk last night and that little Sisina wouldn't stop arguing with her baby brother, and then suddenly she would pull a mouth-watering pasta *alla Genovese* out of her proverbial sleeve. Or two plain old poached eggs (Tamara called this *shakshouka*), magically transformed into a veritable delicacy. Or two pounds of whitebait, cooked in a pan with a couple of hot green peppers and a tomato (the Lawyer called the combination *catamascia*) and become ambrosia fit for the gods. Tamara hated her for having this skill, although that hate morphed very quickly into gratitude, and even ecstasy, just as soon as she sat down at the table and tasted all those culinary masterpieces.

In the early years of their marriage, Tamara did at any rate try. She did her best to learn. She tried above all with artichokes, which happened to be her great passion (with a meat stuffing, given a quick fry in batter and then popped into a heavy pot, with a tomato sauce as delicate as delicate could be). She practiced the dish hundreds of times, to be sure it would turn out right. She asked for tips from her mother, who although not an especially expert cook, did have a feel for it; she took notes, to avoid making basic errors; she went to the butcher herself, to ensure the meat was of the very best quality, and to the market, to ensure that the parsley and celery were the freshest possible. Then, faced with the inevitable debacle, she felt like screaming. And in the end, she admitted defeat—she threw in the towel.

The Lawyer did all he could to encourage Tamara, his Mara: he insisted, despite all evidence to the contrary, that chicory was delicious when it was bitter as gall; that spaghetti was cooked to perfection when, with a fork, it could be lifted off the plate in one compact, dripping lump; that a poached egg was perfect when visibly hard-boiled. He lied shamelessly, if he thought it would spare her blushes. But Tamara, his Mara, was not ingenuous, nor did she lap up false praise: her capacity for self-deprecation was as bottomless as the scorn she reserved for others. Thus, not trusting the Lawyer's judgment, or for that matter anyone else's, she decided cooking didn't suit her, and quit for good.

To the eternal gratitude of her husband and their existing and future children, she delegated responsibility for the stove to Maria-la-pioggia. She stopped going out to buy groceries. She became so estranged from the kitchen that she almost never set foot in it, except at lunch and suppertime (breakfast she preferred in bed). Her interest in food was archived definitively, and replaced—very successfully and to the evident satisfaction of all parties—by an interest in reading, with a particular focus on crime news and celebrity gossip.

## 47. HARD TIMES

The referendum in June '46 and the interlude of the Constituent Assembly (which, in December '47, approved the republic's founding charter, with 453 votes in favor and only 67 noes) were followed by a period of political turbulence. In the lead-up to the general election of 18 April 1948, with the Christian Democrats and the left-wing Popular Front at loggerheads, Italy lived through its first republican-era psychodrama. When the results came in, in town they were the inverse of those recorded nationally, albeit by a whisker: the alliance of socialists and communists had won 46 percent of the vote, putting them ahead of the Christian Democrats. The breakaway social democrats, led by Giuseppe Saragat, who were considered to be chiefly to blame for the leftists' peninsula-wide defeat, did not win even one local vote.

The following year, the farm revolts ushered in a period of fresh tumult, culminating in the Fragalà massacre and Luigi-known-as-Sciammerga emerging as undisputed local leader of the peasant movement (and also definitively ratifying his bigamous relationships with Gemma his wife and Virginia his lover). Nineteen forty-nine would also see the birth of his friendship with the Lawyer—who would go on to defend Luigi-known-as-Sciammerga pro bono in the many criminal cases that would be brought against him precisely as a result of his commitment to the farmworkers' cause (the Lawyer would even end up offering the man sanctuary in a barn he owned, during the time Luigi spent a few weeks on the run right after those first clashes with the police).

In '51, after the inaugural edition of the Italian Song Festival in Sanremo, which was supposed to herald a return to a more wholesome ideological vernacular best summed up in the phrase with which Italians have always told each other to get a grip: *canta che ti passa* (singing might take your mind off it), lo and behold another moment of political and human drama... Taking advantage of the recently passed Local Self-Government Act, the area around the marina split away from the rest of the town and declared itself an autonomous municipality. A sort of collective shudder ran through the town's remaining neighborhoods: Cannone—where Tamara and the Lawyer lived, as did the Pharmacist, Lea and Nina, and the cousins Levino and Margherita, not to mention Maria-la-pioggia, Santo, and Maria del Nilo—was all abuzz with female mutterings; Bandiera—where the Notary and his household lived, as did Rosa and Cicia—shook with indignation; Valle—the working-class neighborhood where Peppo from the posthouse had his home—was on the point of manning the barricades; and similar discontent wreathed its way through the fringe districts of Acuto and Acutetto. It was a very real laceration in the social fabric: what had, just a day ago, been one of the town's districts—the neighborhood where the fishermen lived and the wealthier families had their seafront second homes—by othering itself from its hillside roots, seemed to have withdrawn from the town even geographically, almost as if it had pushed off out into the waters of the Ionian Sea. From that day onward, living in Marina became a synonym for traitor.

Just a year later, another round of elections: municipal this time. As if to confirm a certain bias toward inconstancy in the Italic temperament, the outcome was '48 turned on its head: the Christian Democrats won, with 1,533 votes against 1,247 for the Popular Front (an alliance of communists and socialists, but not the Notary's Action Party, which had disbanded). And since nothing here on the shores of the Ionian Sea has more of a future than the past, the mayor-elect happened to be a former Fascist official who would certainly have featured on the famous list that Lieutenant Colonel Reid had asked the Notary to write a few years earlier. As prophesied by the Canadian officer, when confronted with the reality of that nomination the Notary cursed himself—for the first of what would be many times—for not having heeded the words of the military man from the Allied forces. But in a mocking sort of recompense for that old antifascist, the Lawyer was also elected to the new town council.

Henceforth—or more specifically, from December 1952 until June 1966—the Lawyer would be a key and constant feature of local political life. A fact which resulted, on a municipal level, in a sewerage system worthy of its name and in the beginnings of a local welfare system, and on a personal level in at least two consequences of incalculable significance: the employment of Ciccio Bombarda as a chauffeur and, in due course, the first of two major breakdowns in relations with Tamara, his Mara.

## 48. BEING CICCIO BOMBARDA

Let us take a look at a snapshot from the early 1960s. Ciccio Bombarda has now been the Lawyer's chauffeur for nearly a decade, despite never having had a driver's license. This is a black-and-white photo. In the foreground, a little three- or four-year-old boy is standing next to a man who is crouching down to make himself more or less the same height as the child, so that he can hold the child's left hand in a two-handed grip. The little one's hand looks like it has been placed gently between the man's fingers, which are big and strong. Both of them are staring into the camera: the child looks skeptical and perhaps a little lost. There is something faintly Asian in the set of his eyes. The man is serious, his brow furrowed: he has something resolute and protective about him. Both of them are dressed smartly but comfortably, neither of them is in their Sunday best. One would guess they are about to set off on a journey. And behind them, in fact, we catch a glimpse of the front of a bus. In the background, on the right, there's another man, a little older than the first (he could easily be in his fifties, while the first man is closer to forty).

Observe: between the man in the background and the one in the foreground there are many similarities. The black hair. Its cut—swept backwards and very slightly puffed up. The short, neat moustache. The plump, round face with its wrinkled forehead, the left eyebrow lowered and the right eyebrow arched. The suit in a thin pinstripe, the solid-colored vest and very discreet grid-check shirt, worn here with a rep-stripe tie. Dress boots with laces and a stacked heel. A wristwatch by no means small. Could the two men be brothers? Possibly. Similar complexions, almost the same height... Yet the impression one has is of a resemblance less biological than cultural. Or rather: they have the air of a long- (and one hopes happily) married couple who have ended up looking identical. But the two men in the photo are obviously not a married couple. They are the Lawyer (the one in the background) and Ciccio Bombarda, his chauffeur from the spring of 1953 to fall 1966.

Ciccio Bombarda happened to have absorbed much of the character of his own surname. Wherever he turned up (and turning up is effectively the whole point of chauffeurs), he created a sort of noisy excitement, as if he were there to announce an event that would be joyful and jolly—a party of some kind, with plenty of fireworks. He was a cordial, expansive individual with a razor-sharp practical intelligence, thanks to which, from simple chauffeur, he had grown to be the Lawyer's right-hand and left-hand man, his best friend and his alter ego.

The circumstances that led to Ciccio Bombarda's employment had been entirely fortuitous, as is often the case with legendary encounters. The Lawyer had never gotten around to acquiring a driver's license, but his professional and political commitments meant he was increasingly having to travel not just around town but pretty much all over the province: apart from the Police Court, which was in the town square, some of the local district offices were down in Marina, while the District Court was in Corone, not to mention the Appeals Court over in the provincial capital. Traveling by bus was a nightmare and very inconvenient: besides being uncomfortable, the buses were few and far between, and he was often forced to spend nights away from home. Trains along the Ionian coast were almost nonexistent. And so, not long after his election to the town council, the Lawyer decided to look for a driver. There was no lack of available manpower during those postwar years. So much so that, now that it was no longer blocked by war, many young men without employment were taking the old route out and emigrating. It was just that in the past they had mostly looked for work in the United States or Argentina, but now they went to Germany instead.

Being a newly elected councilor belonging to an opposition formed of socialists and communists, the Lawyer enjoyed a special rapport with the less-privileged classes, including the town's many unemployed. He therefore saw at a glance that Ciccio Bombarda was the man for the job. For one thing, Ciccio Bombarda wasn't illiterate, which in that period and in that part of the world was a rarity. In addition to which, he was well turned out and quick-witted. And lastly, he had a reputation for being sensible and reliable. Only problem: he didn't have a driver's license. The Lawyer signed him up for a course of lessons at the driving school, but Ciccio Bombarda failed the test on his first and second attempts. And yet, he was very good behind the wheel. Except when he was being examined. In view of which, employee and employer jointly concluded that the important thing was the knowing how to drive, not the possession of a document certifying the fact. The Lawyer made a gift to Ciccio Bombarda of a pair of his own suits, to ensure he looked the part, and they stopped worrying about the license. Despite being "Ciccio" (which is short for Francesco, but above all means roly-poly), Bombarda was a little thinner than the Lawyer, so Rina, his wife, had to make a few small alterations to get the suits fitting nicely. After which a Fiat Topolino was bought, and Ciccio Bombarda was straightaway so proud of it that it might as well have been his own.

Ciccio Bombarda's working day was generally of two halves: in the morning, he took the Lawyer wherever he needed to be for work or for political motives (at the Socialist and Communist Parties' provincial headquarters, meetings were far from unusual); in the afternoon, he helped his boss out at the office, mainly by welcoming their clients, or he drove Tamara and other members of the family around when they had errands to run. All of which very quickly made him indispensable, and not just to the Lawyer.

Ciccio Bombarda was polite and thoughtful: with the Lawyer's children he shrewdly played the part of the avuncular friend; with Tamara he was impeccably kind and discreet. Little by little, he began repeating a few of the Lawyer's characteristic gestures, using certain turns of phrase of his, the same facial expressions (such as, for example, raising his right eyebrow to indicate perplexity). His spoken Italian began to feature sprinklings of legal terminology (employed, furthermore, very aptly); his use of language became more refined. He dressed like the Lawyer, with whom he not infrequently ate the same meals at the same table (when they were out of town on business, they would go to restaurants together, and the chauffeur, who was not used to dining out and didn't want to make a mistake, ordered whatever the other man was having); he shared the Lawyer's beliefs and ambitions; he cultivated similar foibles; he read the same newspapers (the Lawyer read them in the car, en route; Ciccio Bombarda read them on arrival, while waiting for his employer to get back to the car; and the newspapers were then handed over to Tamara, who, stretched out on one of the sofas as soon as lunch was over, flicked compulsively through them before conceding to herself that it was time for a siesta).

The chauffeur's gradual but inexorable metamorphosis did not trouble the Lawyer. On the contrary, the Lawyer was secretly amused by it, and in some ways gratified. It was odd and in its own way instructive, seeing one's good points and flaws repeated in someone else. At any rate, Ciccio Bombarda was a very competent driver, and with each passing day was also revealing himself to be a conscientious and efficient secretary who never brought him anything but credit.

The Topolino was soon replaced with the newly launched Fiat 600. In other words, the Lawyer was earning three times what he used to and now had clients across the whole region. Thanks to the resulting increase in his own salary, Ciccio Bombarda was able to move his wife and son into a more comfortable house closer to the Lawyer's, where he set about arranging for a correlated increase in the number of his offspring. The apogee of Ciccio Bombarda's social advancement was reached in the spring of 1957, when his fourth son—Cecè—was born, and the Lawyer was elected mayor.

## 49. SOUTHERN QUESTIONS

Throughout her labor-intensive life, Tecla was motivated by contrasting feelings toward her sister Vita. The contrast, however, was not between love and loathing, as the history of Western literature teaches us it should be, but between two forms of love destined to conflict: the devoted and fundamentally servile love of a mother for her cub, and the exasperated and possibly vindictive sentiment of a lover betrayed or offended, or—more accurately—disappointed. Odd though it may sound, given that she was the younger of the two by four years, Tecla felt a powerfully and sometimes obscurely protective instinct toward her sister: in her eyes Vita was a doll-like figure, incapable of looking after herself, because she was too clever, or too sensitive, or whatever it was (it wasn't entirely clear). She therefore had to be taken care of, as far as was possible, so that she would never want for the solicitude and warmth that all of them—Tecla included—had felt the lack of ever since Elvira had died in 1940.

At the same time, however, the younger of the two sisters was irritated by the ingratitude of the other, who seemed impervious to any kind gesture, any thought paid to her, any demonstration of affection—precisely like one of those animals that, with the excuse of being delicate and endangered, rip whoever crosses their path to shreds. Sometimes Tecla had the sensation—it was an incoherent, nebulous thought, to be immediately bundled off and locked away in the dark chamber of her subconscious—that she herself was like one of those unrequited lovers who nurse a frustration that then increases their desire, which in turn fosters fresh disappointment, and so on, ad infinitum.

Therefore, ever since her sister had been towed off to Bari by Giulio, Tecla had periodically felt relieved that she no longer had to take care of her. As if looking after the Notary, Vincenzo, Arnaldo, and Emilio—who continued not to speak a word—wasn't enough. But at one and the same time she was hostage to a terrible nostalgia, because at the end of the day Vita had been the only female presence in the house (given that Rosa was effectively a Prussian soldier and Cicia had eyes for no one except little Emilio).

The two sisters began corresponding. Tecla's letters were perhaps a little ungrammatical and not infrequently confusing, but they always shone with a natural fondness that made them cheerful and full of enthusiasm. Whereas Vita's seemed to have come straight out of a primer instructing young ladies of good breeding in the arts of etiquette and affectation. While one of them relayed jolly and even slightly outré anecdotes about the neighbors or their brothers, the other replied with tedious lists of her own daily activities, principally made up of piano lessons and the paying of teatime visits. Tecla wrote letters from a southern Italy that was wretchedly poor but high-spirited, while Vita replied from another southern Italy that was dull and, in all honesty, phony.

In any case, one of them missed the other, and both of them hoped they would see each other again very soon—and maybe even be able to quarrel again. But the years went by, and opportunities failed to present themselves. As a result, things between them were never exactly idyllic. Until the beginning of '57, when Vita came home: there was a local election coming up that spring, and the Lawyer was running as mayor. So not one vote could be wasted.

## 50. OUR MUTUAL FRIEND FRANK

At the end of April 1956, a year before the Lawyer was elected mayor, the town woke up to find itself overflowing with banners, posters, and leaflets enthusiastically lauding our mutual friend Frank, wishing him long life and prosperity, and also vowing him eternal gratitude. In the bar in the town's main square, what seemed to be a program of civic events appeared, announcing—over the course of the following week—a series of activities and public celebrations to welcome the aforementioned mutual friend.

Among the many interpretations given to that unexpected frenzy of initiatives, the Notary was inclined to favor a political reading of events, thus offering proof both of his own acumen and of the southern Italian tendency to see conspiracies and intrigue just about everywhere. As it happens, our mutual friend Frank was none other than Signor Franco Rizzuto, who had emigrated to the United States in 1909 at the age of eighteen. Rizzuto had settled in Brooklyn, where he made his fortune in the food industry (he had owned a chain of butcher shops), remaining a bachelor and very attached to the family of his birth. Contradictory rumors abounded: some folk insisted he was very religious and particularly devoted to the Blessed Virgin, some would have him a ruthless member of the New York Mafia, and others saw no contradiction between the two things. Now an old man, Franco—who had evolved into Frank forty-seven years and a few million lire after his departure from the town—had decided to come back for a few weeks, to convince his nieces and nephews—for the most part unemployed and hard up—to join him in New York, where he would offer them a financially untroubled future in exchange for a little affection and company in his fast-approaching old age. And since he was coming back after almost half a century away and wanted to offer a tangible demonstration of the riches he had accrued, Frank Rizzuto had also made arrangements for a conspicuous donation to the town church, which was in need of a new roof and a general refurbishment. Hence the little posters and the banners welcoming and thanking him.

Nonetheless, Frank Rizzuto's visit happened to be taking place twelve months before fresh municipal elections were due to be held—which explains why the Notary chose to give a political interpretation to the civic celebrations in honor of a fellow townsman who, returning to the place of his birth after so long away, had not concerned himself with the living conditions (mostly wretched) enjoyed by relatives, friends, and neighbors, but had first and foremost helped out the local parish—thereby furnishing an extraordinary argument in favor of, and offering a considerable number of dollars to, the political bloc headed up by Father Marcello and the Christian Democrats. As a result, the celebrations marking Frank Rizzuto's arrival ended up splitting the townsfolk into two camps. Those who took part—and perhaps even managed to wrangle something small in the way of a cash handout, in addition to tinned food, decent cigarettes, and packets of chewing gun—were immediately labeled bigots, lickspittles and mafiosi, while those who resisted the siren song of consumerism and sanctimony in the person of Frank Rizzuto were immediately written off as priest-eating communists.

During the few weeks in which Frank Rizzuto stopped over, the town seemed to live through a preview of the following year's electoral campaign. To coincide with all the programed celebrations, Cicia and Rosa organized open-air events in the evening in the traditionally left-wing, working-class Valle neighborhood, with plenty of wine and card games, and a gramophone or two wafting the notes of "The Internationale" and "Bandiera Rossa" through the velvety May air. Within the walls of his own home, the Notary gathered together the more cultured local souls, to whom he explained, with elegant flights of rhetoric, the historical–juridical significance of the newborn Constitutional Court, inaugurated on 23 April with Enrico De Nicola as its president. Meanwhile, in the town's main square and in its better-off households, folk feasted on pork chops and veal steaks—which in those days very few people could afford.

This all goes some way to explaining why the wave of novelty and change that the arrival of our mutual friend Frank brought with it did not correspond to any effective improvement in their collective life, and would in fact subsequently be remembered with a mixture of embarrassment and coolness: because it reawakened memories of other bygone revelries accompanied by a sense of hostility and angry resentment; and also because, apart from converting the town's main church into a ghastly meringue, its only material consequence was the removal of the

Rizzuto family from the local population register. All of them, in fact, emigrated to the United States not long after Uncle Frank's visit. Uncle Frank, however, never had time to savor an old age surrounded by nieces and nephews and great-nieces and great-nephews, because on 20 September 1958, he was struck down, on the doorstep of his comfortable Brooklyn home, by a round of bullets from a submachine gun.

### 51. ELECTORAL CAMPAIGNING

You can't begin to imagine what things were like in the town during the electoral campaigns of '57, '61, '65, and '66—a sequence of numbers that would have had even Fibonacci trembling. You can't begin to imagine the passion, the rows, the plots, the betrayals, the vendettas, the exaltation, and the grief produced by that numerical sequence. Excitement overflowed, ardor was the norm; so was fear, and day and night were indistinguishable and inverted, amid myriad noisome cigarettes, leaflets scattered every which way, and promises and disappointments.

On each occasion the same two teams contested the race: the left-wing alliance, now known as "the Trumpet," and the Christian Democrats. Belonging to one or the other meant automatically having to sacrifice almost 50 percent of oneself. Because, while the first of the two claimed victory in two consecutive rounds, tied for first place at the end of the third, and lost the fourth, it was always by only a handful of votes. As a consequence, rifts opened up within individual families—and even within individual individuals—not infrequently giving rise to dramatic partings of ways.

The Lawyer himself risked an estrangement from his wife. Not that Tamara, his Mara, was indifferent to his political proposals: unlike many young gentlewomen of her generation, Tamara had always kept track of political goings-on at a national level, and read the daily papers with a close attention and an acuity that would have made her a top-notch political pundit. What the woman couldn't stand, at a local level or anywhere else in Italy, was the rancor, the hostility, the sectarianism that were animating (and in her opinion perverting) the public discussion of ideas. As she saw it, there was no need for all that strength of feeling. An adversary did not necessarily have to be an enemy. As well as threatening more or less openly to return to her father's household, it would be in this period that Tamara developed her Anglophile leanings and the resulting determination to encourage her children to join the Italian diaspora. When, in '66, the Lawyer finally lost an election, she was inflexible: either active political life was to be abandoned or they would separate.

In short, these weren't years of grand Italian comedy, even if, at the Reda Cinema just behind the town square, *Cops and Robbers* and *Big Deal on Madonna Street* were going down a storm. If anything, the comparisons we should be drawing are with melodrama and Sicilian puppet shows. Or possibly the young composer Mascagni and his opera *Cavalleria Rusticana*.

As luck would have it, the wine produced locally—vigorous, generous, and stately, just as the ancient poets dictated it should be—sometimes helped soften the atmosphere and dispensed, in equal doses, hilarity and drowsiness. But by and large the mood was one of blistering tension, and the first victim it claimed was any sense of humor.

Heading up the Trumpet's list of candidates in all four rounds of elections was the Lawyer. And he benefited from the decisive support of what, half a century later, would come to be known as spin doctors. In his case they happened to be two women who up until a day earlier had busied themselves exclusively with kitchen stoves, diapers, and furniture in need of a polish: Rosa and Cicia. In other words, the Notary's housemaid and Emilio's nursemaid. The pair set to work with an energy and a dedication the likes of which had never before been seen. The two of them organized campaign rallies in different corners of the town, door-to-door canvassing, and fundraising dinners. They investigated and, with inventive élan, put into practice all possible forms of propaganda. It was they who united the women of the town in what was effectively a clandestine lobby intended to put pressure on husbands and adult sons, who would thus vote for—or at least not vote against—the Lawyer's list of candidates, who were promising kindergarten schools and help for the neediest, with a fundamental twist: instead of cash handouts—conventionally distributed to the head of each household, who would then invest them in demijohns of wine—it was to take the form of groceries and other essentials.

Rosa, who in '57 was a mere girl of thirty-three, had taken as husband an older man to whom, every time an election appeared on the horizon, she handed over responsibility for the care of the children and the house. She was tall, always very stern, and had a mass of curly black hair that put one in mind of a gorgon. Cicia, on the other hand, and as has already been mentioned, was short and stout, with hair that was now fully gray (she was hovering at a point somewhere over fifty) and worn up in a bun as if to underline her rotundity. Where Rosa employed the vehement language of invective and calls to arms, Cicia favored moral suasion, with a sprinkling of irony. Both, in any case, were permanent fixtures on the front row of every town-square rally, and theirs was the loudest applause during the speeches. The extraordinary thing was that, when the Lawyer once suggested to both that they should run for office as councilors—and they would certainly have been elected—both of them blushed like schoolgirls and declined. On the implausible grounds, which they themselves spent an entire decade giving the lie to, that politics wasn't a suitable activity for women.

Anyway, in 1957 the pair also attempted a mediation with Father Marcello, who was openly sympathetic toward the Christian Democrats' slogans. They requested, if nothing else, some form of neutrality—if he really couldn't bring himself to support the famously priest-eating left-wing candidates. The man of the cloth pretended to give it some consideration and to be carefully mulling it over, but then, during his next Sunday sermon, he cold-bloodedly launched an uncompromising and uncontestable attack on the Lawyer, the man's irreligious family, and the Trumpet's entire slate of candidates. At that point, galvanized by the element of surprise, Rosa and Cicia unbarred all holds: they embarked on an implacable demolition job targeting the personal and religious credibility of Father Marcello, going so far as to spread increasingly insistent and increasingly poisonous rumors regarding his private life. Rumors that, many years later, long after all the protagonists of this particular episode had left the scene, would lead to that poor man being expelled from the ranks of the priesthood.

After the defeat of '66, they followed the Lawyer's metaphorical lead and retired from public combat: Rosa and Cicia became two little grandmothers, all dressed in black, their energies focused chiefly on crochet and the saying of prayers for the dead. Seeing them in their twilight years (which in Rosa's case were admittedly rather brief), no one would ever have guessed that in those ordinary and toilworn old ladies there lurked the spirit of a passionate, generous age: the very spirit that had once inflamed Italian politics, back in the era now remembered as "the postwar boom."

# CHAPTER FIVE

## 52. NUMBERS

In addition to political passions and clashes between ideologies, Italy's so-called economic miracle, as experienced in town, ushered in indoor plumbing and a certain linguistic effervescence.

From the 1951 census it had emerged that only 7.1 percent of Italians had in their homes that combination of electricity, potable water, and a flushing toilet that we nowadays define as civilization. In the south the percentage was even more modest than that. So, as soon as he was elected mayor in spring of 1957, the Lawyer set about endowing the town with a decent sewerage system—meaning that the bulk of the town's population was finally introduced to the joys of personal hygiene. What is more, since the fiasco of the agrarian reform of 1950 had forced much of the local workforce to take the emigration route, initially to the Americas (the United States, Argentina, and Venezuela) and then to northern Europe (West Germany, Switzerland, and Belgium), the town also experienced an extraordinary increase in lexical wealth. It was not uncommon to hear neologisms such as, for the sake of example, "the Teutonicals" (to describe emigrants to Stuttgart or Munich who came back for the holidays with bouffant-wearing blonde fiancées in tow) or devil-may-care syncretisms like *i kids stanno giampando nella street* ("the children are jumping around in the road")—trotted out by someone who was back home after a few years living in Brooklyn.

In any event, the combined effect of soap and multilingualism led to the marvelous discovery of a hitherto unexplored continent—a continent not only solidly physical, but also, and in numerous respects, symbolic. In a nutshell, the postwar boom had brought to light the existence of the world of household appliances.

In this case too, one has only to look at the numbers. For instance, numbers regarding the manufacture of refrigerators: on a national scale, in 1951 a total of 18,500 were put on the market; in '57 the number increased to 370,000; ten years later it reached 3,200,000 units. Television sets: in 1958 only 12 percent of Italian families own one, then seven years go by and we're suddenly looking at 49 percent. Now let's widen the focus: the growth in GDP, in these years, oscillates between 5 and 6 percent. In a single decade, the industrial production index grows by 120 percent, average income by 78 percent, and the net output of the manufacturing sector alone by 103. And despite the numbers in the south of Italy being considerably less exciting, and the unemployment rate remaining high in comparison with the rest of the peninsula, and for all that the boom is dramatically intensifying the disparity between north and south, the deutsche marks, Swiss francs, and dollars being sent home by the emigrants do nonetheless contribute to an overall improvement in material living conditions, even in the most godforsaken rural hamlets. Sure, the sacrifices being asked of southern Italian males at the point when the economic miracle is in full swing are paradoxically greater than those of the past, when they were peasant farmers: having left a life of muddy open-air toil behind them, they have gained monetarily and now have regular wages, but they live crammed into tiny rented apartments in the grayest suburbs of Italy's northern cities or in the New World. They work gruelingly long shifts on the production line, they live lives devoid of sex and affection, they are the targets of racism and other forms of discrimination. Et cetera, et cetera. However, these dreadful sacrifices give rise to the greatest social and cultural transformation in Italy's history—and here a single number will suffice: in this period 30 percent of the Italian population—one in three people—relocate. It's just a shame that the word "transformation" doesn't always refer to steps taken upward on the evolutionary ladder.

## 53. GIOACCHINO'S INCARNATIONS

As her lenses grew thicker and her eyesight grew weaker, as the pharmacy's profits swelled but hopes of marriage shrank, Nina grew progressively more attached to Gioacchino, whose personality and physical appearance were coming into sharper focus. Besides, she had given the real world a try, but without much success: the various Giuseppes, Giovannis, and Robertos (although the sequence of names was actually much longer than that) had absorbed her mental energies to no avail. The minute she dropped any tentative hints about some form of future together (houses, babies, holidays), they all vanished, as if by magic. They melted away. They dematerialized. *Pfft!* For this reason, over time Nina had turned to the world of fantasy: at the end of the day, it seemed much less volatile, and, if nothing else, she could predict its next moves. So, she had devoted herself to Gioacchino.

To begin with she had created him as a sort of bet with herself—a mental game in which the sexual inhibitions of the era had played a certain part—and also as a way of keeping Maria and Tamara's children disciplined. Since time immemorial, nothing has ever done a better job of ensuring children behave themselves than the Bogeyman has (the trick sometimes works with adults too), and Gioacchino could in many ways be considered one of that fellow's more eccentric incarnations. It was no coincidence that when old Uncle Giorgio pronounced Gioacchino's name for the very first time, it had been precisely to deflect the, at that point, very young Nina's curiosity by instilling in her a certain fear. But Nina wasn't the type to be satisfied with a banal cliché, and over time Gioacchino, who began life as an evil ogre, had taken on the more complex and contradictory outlines of a mysterious lover. He still needed to inspire fear, but in a form more primeval than anything we expose children to—the fear that presides over life itself, a fear that is veined with desire, attraction, and repulsion. In Nina's mind, in her nearsighted eyes—which without glasses on saw a reality different from the customary version—Gioacchino became the personification of masculinity.

Little by little she started talking about him as if he were a flesh-and-blood person. And not just with her nieces and nephews, but also with Lea and the Pharmacist, with her sisters, with Giorgio, with the cousins Levino and Margherita. Within the space of a few years no one any longer paid it any mind: having emerged from the wordless and wildly irrational realm of the imagination, Gioacchino had become part and parcel of their everyday conversations—in other words, reality. And he had, as a result, become one of the family. Giorgio even joked about it with random girlfriends (he had a string of them, all of them vacuous and identical) and then with his equally random, vacuous, and identical wife (Teresa, known as Bebè—probably a mispronounced version of "baby"—whom he married in Naples in the fall of '49). Ever since he had settled down with Bebè in Corone and had begun working as a surgeon at the city hospital, whenever he came home to see his parents, Giorgio referred to the figure hatched from his sister's imagination as his roommate, because many years ago they had once shared the attic bedroom. And ultimately he preferred remembering that imaginary cohabitation and not the other real, material one, with Ernesto, in the same attic—a cohabitation that remained an open wound in his memory as a result of the early death of that friend whom he had loved like, and more than, a brother.

Gioacchino, to put it briefly, ended up becoming the symbol, for Nina, of everything her life had denied her. Which is to say good eyesight, a family and children of her own, married bliss, financial serenity. Gioacchino offered her as much as a generous but powerless subconscious could provide: a private life, a parallel but not secret or prohibited space; a shared—if entirely hypothetical—space in which she could live a life that was fun, a life overflowing with all the gifts that fantasies can bestow. In this sense, Nina was perhaps the luckiest of the Pharmacist and Lea's children, and not just because she lived a long life and enjoyed good health (apart from the bad eyesight that troubled her from a very young age), but because she was granted the privilege of a perpetual childhood. Whereas the others, having grown up in a hurry, set off to meet adult life almost defenseless: Maria would forever struggle with her health and with a husband she never did love, Tamara would harbor a phobia of Germans and disease, and Giorgio ended up being prostrated by the overwhelming vacuity of his wife and children.

## 54. A BRIEF HISTORY OF TELEVISION

In Italy, the state television service makes its inaugural broadcast, from Milan, on 3 January 1954. On 19 November the following year the first episode of the legendary quiz show *Lascia o Raddoppia?* (Quits or Double?) is presented by Mike Bongiorno. It will then be on 4 June 1956 that a gargantuan television set makes its triumphal entrance into the Lawyer's family home. (Against all the odds that would have it the undisputed protagonist of the nation's living rooms and breakfast rooms, this particular set is—by order of an unequivocal and irremovable Tamara—installed in the kitchen.)

On that 4 June—a Tuesday—the *New York Times* goes to press with the story of the famous secret report on Stalin's crimes being read out by Nikita Khrushchev at the previous February's Twentieth Congress of the Communist Party of the Soviet Union. The scoop, however, has no effect of any kind on the viewing public in the Lawyer's house, since the news bulletin makes no mention of it. In front of the small screen that evening, only the family has gathered—with the small addition of the Pharmacist and Lea, Nina, the cousins Levino and Margherita, and Maria-la-pioggia, with Santo and the children. On the evenings that follow, especially on Saturdays, the Lawyer and Tamara's kitchen instead hosts an increasingly sizable throng of neighbors, who arrive bringing their own chairs and stools once things get to the point where there is nowhere else left to sit. Watching television on Saturday evenings at the Lawyer's house becomes an unmissable fixture in the Cannone neighborhood's social calendar—an excellent pool of votes to draw on for the following year's local elections.

Furthermore, it is in front of the television that the first dramatic symptom materializes of one of the two phobias that will blight Tamara's existence: her phobia of Germans (the other, as has been mentioned, has to do with diseases).

Since the end of the war, Tamara has displayed a growing and slightly morbid interest in literature and cinema inspired by the conflict. She has put much ardor into reading *The Skin*, and its author, Curzio Malaparte, could even be said to have become something of an idol of hers. She has subsequently devoured Primo Levi's *If This Is a Man*—the first edition, published by De Silva in 1947—and also *The Sergeant in the Snow*, by Mario Rigoni Stern, and Anne Frank's *Diary*, with a foreword by Natalia Ginsburg. On vacation in Florence (throughout their married life the Lawyer and his wife will always spend their summer holidays in Tuscany, and will do so alone, with no children in tow), Tamara has insisted on going to the movies and seeing all three films in Roberto Rossellini's antifascist trilogy—*Rome, Open City* and *Paisan* and *Germany Year Zero*. Up to now, all these stories about Nazism, partisans, and Jews being persecuted have moved and enthralled her, and her enthusiasm for them has steadily increased, but none of them appear to have struck a particularly distressing chord. That distressing chord's configuration is possibly determined during the months when her father, the Pharmacist, puts every one of his personal activities on hold, from his job to the pleasures of playing the violin, and stays in bed, crushed by the horror of having discovered the monstrous scale of what will come to be known as the Holocaust.

In any event, one Saturday evening toward the end of '57, in the kitchen belonging to the Lawyer and his wife, the customary little throng of friends, relatives, and neighbors has convened. Exchanges of pleasantries. The sound of chairs being moved. Contentedness. On television they are about to show a film on the war and Nazism, directed by someone none of them have heard of. About halfway through, in the middle of a rather dramatic scene in which viewers hear a few phrases pronounced in German, Tamara starts to tremble. Within seconds the woman is shaking from head to toe. She gets to her feet, she screams, she is weeping, she knocks over a glass and it smashes to the floor. The Lawyer tries to come to her aid, to the aid of his Mara, who is running into the bedroom, locking the door behind her and shouting, "Help! Help! Help me!"

What triggers this disconcerting reaction? Why, instead of containing Tamara's emotions, does the small screen seem to unleash them, amplifying them to a degree that leaves the rest of the little audience, Lawyer included, frozen in shock? What happens, what is it, in that instant, that snaps in Tamara's mind? And what role, if any, does the television set itself—that symbol of domesticity and comfort—play in this? (A few years later, the same television set will be the focal point of another minor family tragedy.)

Tamara will never come up with an answer. What is certain is that, from this day on, every time the woman hears German being spoken she will be visibly gripped with a profound sense of dread. And over time her phobia will become so pervasive as to involve anything in any way connected with Germany. To the point that, when Valentino, her youngest child (on the evening when the movie about the war and Nazism is being screened, he hasn't yet been born) will one day announce that he wants to study philosophy at Heidelberg, Tamara will succumb to such gloomy despair that her son will instead choose to study in Rome.

## 55. COUSINS FOR THE AGES

Business, in the emporium run by the cousins Levino and Margherita, was not very good. Midway through the 1950s the town's population was shrinking, thanks to all that emigration. Besides which, the type of merchandise sold in their store seemed to belong to an era irrecoverably bygone. Levino had lost nearly all his hair. And although lack of custom had not necessarily played a direct hand in bringing on his baldness, the fact that he now had a shiny pate seemed, if nothing else, to underline his extraneousness to the modern world (which in the space of a few years would soon be enthusing over long-haired young men). The older and less with-it he felt, the more he had the sensation that the same was true of his store.

Unlike her husband, Margherita had a thick head of hair, which she continued to color with dye that was blacker than the blackest corners of her heart. It was a dense, curly mane, which she spent hours lovingly brushing every evening before getting into bed, where Levino awaited her with a blend of enthusiasm and skepticism. The couple had no children. When they first arrived in town, following old Uncle Giorgio, they had been young enough still to think they didn't want any. But once the war ended, and with it the possibility of the Nazis swooping in and sending them off to a death camp somewhere, Levino and Margherita had begun planning an expansion of the family. Sadly, however, she never did get pregnant, despite the two of them having tried and tried again. Eventually, they came to terms with it. And she came to terms with it quicker than he did, partly because, behind all that sentimentalism of hers, Margherita was a practical woman, and partly because, over the years, she herself had come to realize that she had much in common with the monstrously insensitive man who had been her father.

The couple's day-to-day life seemed somewhat predictable. In the morning it was Levino who served their customers in the shop, and in the afternoon it was her turn, but an hour or so before closing time her husband would come back in, leaving his wife free to go home early and worry about supper. One evening a week, on Fridays, they ate at Lea and the Pharmacist's house. And again on Sundays, at lunchtime. When Maria and Tamara, and then Giorgio too, produced babies, Margherita turned out to be an attentive and sharp-eyed babysitter, much loved by the little ones—whose adoration of her can probably be ascribed to the fact that she was always cheerful and ready to turn the house upside down, as long as it made them happy; added to which, she baked lip-smackingly good cakes and she never used the word "No." As it happens, like most folk who make too ready a show of bountifulness, Margherita secretly inclined to selfishness: she baked those cakes because she loved eating them, and she left the children free to do what they wanted simply because she was lazy.

Neither Maria nor Giorgio lived in the town. They lived in two larger towns not quite twenty miles away: for which reason, their children were only entrusted to Margherita's care very occasionally, and mainly during the holidays, whereas Tamara's children spent an hour or two with Margherita almost every day. Which explains why it was in fact Tamara who first heard the news that the cousins were moving to Marina. Down in Marina, according to Levino, the emporium would have more potential: he had already found premises with much bigger rooms than the current ones. Right in the center and at a reasonable rent. Meanwhile, he was in the process of negotiating for a lovely modern apartment with a magnificent sea view. Marina seemed to hold out the promise of a smidgen of the modernity that had eluded him here in town. Along with his hair.

To Lea, Margherita confided that Levino had briefly considered moving back to Piedmont, but had then been dissuaded by all the difficulties connected with such a radical change in their lives, and also by the couple's sentimental ties to the town. Margherita had been more than happy about his change of heart, because—she confessed—moving back to Turin, erasing the past twenty years of their lives, would have been traumatic for her. Added to which, during the war a considerable chunk of her family had vanished, and her relationship with her father had always—to put it mildly—been problematic.

Marina was only a couple of miles away: on Sundays she and Levino could come over for lunch at Lea's, and in the summertime the assorted children—Maria's, Tamara's, and Giorgio's—would be able to spend their holidays at the seaside in that new apartment of hers, which had every modern convenience. Yet even as she said these things, Margherita was almost on the point of tears (not because she truly cared, but because she thought it was appropriate, given the circumstances), and she made to embrace Lea—who, always allergic to demonstrations of affection, parried the woman's advance with the excuse of needing to impart an urgent order of some kind to Maria del Nilo, and hurtled off down the corridor leading out to the pharmacy.

### 56. A MINUTE TO THINK

On gray days like today it was easy to believe that, by dint of having spent so long looking at each other, the sky and the earth had become a single substance. The Lawyer loved his own office, which was directly beneath his house, but he did everything he could to avoid the mayor's office at the town hall, because from the window of his own office the view swept uphill and downhill and then out toward the coast, giving a foretaste of the vastness of the sea, but the mayor's office instead looked out over the rooftops and the narrow streets of the town center, and that view was oppressive and cluttered. On gray days like this one, with the sky and the earth looking as interchangeable as two men who love the same woman, the Lawyer yearned for those moments of hiatus and quiet in his own office, when he had no need to justify himself to anyone, when he could tell Ciccio Bombarda that he was on no account to be disturbed before a certain hour, and he could retreat—not for long, perhaps just half an hour, just long enough not to feel that his clients were eating him alive—and he could stare out through the window into all that open space, and sometimes jot down a few lines dedicated to Tamara, his Mara, who would never, ever, be allowed to read them. And as he wrote them, calm and detached, he memorized them, those lines of his—because an instant later, just as soon as he had finished polishing them, he would condemn the sheet of paper to death, ripping it (in nearly all cases) into a thousand pieces, or he would hand it a life sentence and immure it in some weighty legal tome.

Whereas in the little mayoral office he felt exposed. The door was forever open, and the constant to-ing and fro-ing of people (council staff, committee chairs, members of the public) prevented him from mulling things over. Looming over him he felt the neither affable nor encouraging presidential gaze of Giovanni Gronchi, whose official portrait hung on the wall behind him. Ciccio Bombarda kept bursting in, demanding that attention be paid to this or that issue. Noise and confusion reigned. On gray days like this, when the sky was so close to the earth that everything between them was squashed, the Lawyer told himself that perhaps he had gone into politics chiefly to please the Notary, so that he could achieve the things that Fascism had prevented his father from achieving. Perhaps. Or perhaps not. Because his own enthusiasm was genuine, and his socialist beliefs sincerely held. Nothing, however, compared with what he felt for Tamara, his Mara: when he thought about her, no politics withstood the comparison, and socialism dimmed to an indistinct haze. She, Tamara, his Mara, was the center of his everything, the only true reality.

He snuck out of the little mayoral office. Without even noticing Ciccio Bombarda—who boasted of being his shadow—on foot, walking as close as he could to the walls of the town-center buildings so as not to be spotted, he reached the tranquility of his own office. He locked the door behind him. He threw open the window. He needed to think. He needed a little time to try to understand.

What had happened to Tamara, his Mara, while they were watching that film on the war and the Nazis the evening before? Those screams of terror had shaken him. And their children—both Picchio and Erri, who were now adolescents, and Vita, who was only seven—had been unsettled by that moment of maternal panic. Since then, the Lawyer hadn't managed to grab even a minute alone, to stop and mull it over. Because after that hysterical outburst, when everyone had gone home and he and his wife had found themselves face-to-face in the bedroom, she had given him no time to think, and had repeated insistently, "I don't know what came over me, I really don't know, you have to believe me." And given that he had tried—delicately, but he had tried—to ask a few questions, Tamara, his Mara, had said, all in a rush, "The truth is, the Germans scare me, if I hear someone speaking German I tremble like a leaf, I feel like a leaf." To which he—for the time being giving up on trying to understand, and partly to diffuse the drama of all this—had replied with a snatch of "Les Feuilles Mortes," imitating Yves Montand's voice, and then Tamara had said, "Oh for goodness' sake, that French accent of yours is horrible, and you're so out of tune it's pitiful." So they had laughed together, she had let him persuade her to sing a little, in that lovely French of hers, and they had made love. And it was probably right then that, in both their minds, they conceived the idea of a final child—the timing adds up—but in any case, those screams heard while watching the film still echoed in the Lawyer's ears. Even now that she was no longer singing and was instead moaning with pleasure.

Had they given him just a few minutes, the Lawyer would perhaps have gotten a foothold on the horror his wife had experienced the evening before. As he wrote something down on a scrap of paper, he felt he was on the threshold of understanding and therefore of sharing that monstrous emotion; he felt he was very close to being able to defuse and neutralize it. But at that very moment he heard a confused fuss of voices, and someone approaching, and a key turning in the lock.

In came Ciccio Bombarda.

### 57. PUT BRIEFLY

Tamara wouldn't go into it. She was a good-looking and spirited woman (in '57 she is forty-four years old and wears those years very well, for a woman of that era), and as everyone knows, the combination of pulchritude and a sense of humor tends to result in a certain briskness. So she wouldn't go into it then and there, and she didn't even go into it later on. She said, "When I hear German being spoken, I get anxious, I can't help it. End of the matter. Case closed. Let's talk about something else." If pushed, she might add, "It seems to me that the Germans did what they did because of the way they talk. Because of the tone of their language."

Naturally her children objected, especially Valentino, the youngest: And what about Goethe? And Schiller? And Thomas Mann, Rilke, Kafka, Musil? Can you not bear to hear them?

The Lawyer never objected. He narrowed his small, myopic eyes and waved his hand in a way that all of them took to mean "Let it drop."

Tamara didn't react to the objections. No, she never once reacted. She wasn't the type.

## 58. SPECIAL

From six to eighteen years of age, Emilio had irregular schooling. Every fall, from mid-October onward, he began studying at home with the help of various tutors; in June and July he took the end-of-year exam as a privately enrolled candidate, and—assuming he passed—after a couple of months of undiluted inactivity during which he ate and he slept, the following fall he was ready for another round. In actual fact, his schooling was irregular only in the sense that it didn't take place in a regular classroom, for in every other way it was much more disciplined and continuous than that of pupils at public schools. Thus, and despite a few hiccups and a great many difficulties of a practical nature, Emilio got through elementary school and middle school. Things became progressively more complicated as he approached his final school exams, and the handicap of his mutism acquired more relevance. For Emilio, therefore, 1957 was a pivotal year.

According to his teachers, Emilio was special—a remarkably sensitive boy. At the end of the war, Tamara and her husband had taken him to Naples to see a couple of renowned physicians, who had both very categorically ruled out the possibility of the boy's mutism being physiological. His vocal chords were intact, and no damage was apparent in his Broca's area, the part of the brain involved in verbal articulation. Not only that: his hearing worked perfectly well, which suggested that Emilio's mutism might, if anything, be of the selective kind. The trouble was, that particular disorder usually manifests itself in social situations (at school, for example) but not in the home: Emilio, however, didn't speak in either case. The Neapolitan doctors concluded that the issue was psychological, probably linked to the death of his mother, and they advised waiting for him to reach puberty.

Nevertheless, puberty came and went without anything changing. The boy's tutors continued to remark that he was gifted with unusual intelligence and astuteness. Although he didn't utter a word, although he had never emitted a sound, Emilio was a brilliant pupil. He loved literature, especially in Latin, but he also got by very well in mathematics and physics. He answered every question, in every subject, in writing, displaying a gift for brevity as well as a certain feeling for language (in those essays of his there was never a repetition, never a discordant note, never un unintentional rhyme). Year after year, the number of subjects to be studied increased, and he continued to demonstrate an aptitude for learning.

The problems began to emerge when, having gotten through adolescence, Emilio found himself having to interact, one way or another, with his peers. If they were boys, he became truculent and aggressive; if it was girls he was dealing with, he panicked. For instance, when he discovered that one of his tutors, Professore Giletti, had a daughter his own age, he no longer wanted lessons with the man. Rather than go over to the teacher's house, Emilio pretended to be ill, or he vanished from circulation and spent the day out of sight.

The situation got worse the closer he got to the tough exams at the end of his final school year. Emilio was studying less than usual. He seemed listless and almost always bad-tempered. It was chiefly Tamara and the Lawyer who kept an eye on the boy (the Notary never had concerned himself with his children, and he remained blithely uninterested). Despite already having fish of their own to fry (at the town hall, the Lawyer had to handle endless emergencies, while his wife was seriously concerned about their second-born son, Erri, who at almost thirteen was a fledgling hoodlum), the couple still found time to take care of

Emilio, hoping at least to manage to get him through his leaving certificate. So they checked that things were going as they should, they spoke to his tutors, they tried to find timely solutions to any problems that arose. Thus, when, in May '57, now just steps away from reaching his goal, the boy began skipping lessons, even disappearing for two or three days at a time, even not coming home at night, all the alarm bells started ringing simultaneously and Tamara and her husband knew the nettle had to be grasped.

They invited him over for supper one evening. But before sitting down at the table (Maria-la-pioggia had prepared a pasta bake that would go down in family history), they ushered the boy into the living room, safely away from Picchio, Erri, and their own little Vita—who like a trio of nosy monkeys promptly took up their positions and eavesdropped at the door. Nothing seemed to be coming of it: Tamara was being very loving and careful not to hurt the feelings of that exceptionally young brother-in-law who made her heart bleed. And the Lawyer was every bit as loving and careful, because his heart bled for his brother too. They gave their little speeches. They begged Emilio not to throw in the towel now that he was within spitting distance of his goal. They told him how proud they both were of everything he had achieved as a student, notwithstanding the disadvantage he had of not speaking. They encouraged him, they egged him on, they voiced their support in a way they possibly never had before, even with their own children. But nothing. No reaction. Emilio looked at them vacantly. He appeared to have gone deaf as well as mute. A mask of indifference.

Discouraged, and also a little embittered, Tamara and the Lawyer were already thinking of calling it a day and moving into the kitchen—the siren smell of Maria-la-pioggia's pasta bake was hard to ignore—when, rising up from the armchair to the fullness of the six feet and not quite one inch that made him the only one of the Notary's children who came close to competing with their father in terms of height, and clearing a throat that had, over the course of an entire lifetime, never once been cleared but which nonetheless produced a clear, firm voice, Emilio said, "I'm sorry."

Tamara very nearly fainted. On the other side of the door, Picchio and Erri whistled. Only Vita didn't understand what had just happened.

From that moment on, Emilio never stopped talking. Actually, it felt like everything he had been keeping bottled up for years and years was coming out and slamming into the world like a bullet. Or, more precisely, like a hail of bullets. Welling up out of that enormous mass of silence, his words rang out with a surgical, remorseless precision. These were not careless words: Emilio had brooded over them for a very long time. He had formulated them in the darkness of his mind, day after day, and now it was time for them to glitter in full daylight. In all their vehemence.

The principal target of that slew of projectiles was the Notary, his father. Emilio had realized he hated the man with every ounce of his being. Had he been asked, he couldn't have fully explained the motives for it. One way or another he held the Notary responsible for Elvira's death, but that wasn't the point here. What Emilio hated about his father was a whole constellation of ideas and attitudes: that self-confidence, the arrogance of always believing himself in the right, the utter conviction that reason was on his side. They were ideas and attitudes that horrified Emilio and at the same time fascinated him in some obscure way, as if, at the end of the day, their forcefulness attracted him more than it repulsed him. Had he considered his father a cretin, Emilio would perhaps have been able to forgive him: at any rate, it would have been much easier to belittle him and consequently shake him off. But the Notary was an intelligent man, a cultured man, and it was this that spurred Emilio to want a confrontation, or rather a showdown. And it was this that led Emilio to believe, in the summer of '57, that the only effective means of hurting his father was to aim that salvo of bullets at himself.

Which was how, being unable to punish the Notary in any other way, and even though he was sorry to disappoint Tamara and the Lawyer, Emilio failed his final exams, handing in an essay, for Italian, that was full of glaring errors, deliberately mistranslating the Latin and Greek texts, and turning up half-drunk for the oral exam. Days of angry scenes with the family followed, at the end of which Emilio disappeared for what would be many weeks.

## 59. THE SUMMER OF '57

Almost as if swapping places, just as Emilio vanished Vita made it known that she couldn't bear staying in Bari, with Giulio and Letizia, a moment longer. Her half brother and sister-in-law spoiled her, that was undeniable, but even so, Vita was homesick for the town, for Tecla (she missed quarreling with her sister), and in general for a life that didn't feature piano lessons as exhausting as they were pointless, and paying polite afternoon calls, and endless plates of raw fish—which she loathed. She didn't dislike the strolls taken along Via Sparano, in the city center, to look at all the latest fashions in the store windows, but if her sister-in-law came with her the pleasure was diminished, because Letizia seemed incapable of enjoying life and therefore always found something to complain about—too many people, too few people, too much breeze, too hot, too cold. Walking along arm in arm with her half brother didn't much improve things: Giulio was a handsome man, despite being almost in his sixties, but everything he did was done in a hurry; heaven forbid it involved being forced to dally in front of a ladies' boutique, of all things. His impatience was beginning to verge on boorishness.

For reasons known to no one, least of all the interested parties, Vita enjoyed a privilege largely unheard of as far as the other women in the Notary's life were concerned: the privilege of being able to decide what to do and when to do it. It is true that she had been sent to Bari, almost ten years ago now, without anyone asking her what her views on the matter were, however in that case she had been very happy to leave the town: she had been a teenager back then, and felt like she'd won the lottery, going off to live in a big city. But now that she was a woman and no new circumstances of any note had presented themselves (a fiancé, for example, or just some proper girlfriends), Vita felt her roots calling compellingly—apart from anything else, because roots meant Tecla, and therefore squabbles, bickering, and tiffs, but also peacemakings, shared confidences, and complicity. That recent spring visit to vote in the local elections had simply fanned the flames of her nostalgia.

Tecla was both happy and worried about her sister's imminent return. She, too, missed their evening chats, the giggles, that gleeful and slightly naughty atmosphere one would expect to find at a girls' boarding school every time she and Vita shut themselves into their bedroom with its twin beds, and, before falling asleep, conceded themselves the silliest joint fantasies. However, she also dreaded her sister's supercilious and spiky character, having gotten used to living without it: Vita pontificated about everything, but never lifted a finger, and there were times when Tecla would have happily wrung her neck. For a while now, in her own head, Tecla had called her the Viscountess.

And since the Viscountess clearly couldn't travel by train (although it has to be admitted that southern Italy's railways have always been grim), Ciccio Bombarda was sent to pick her up. And since it was not fitting for a Viscountess to travel alone in a car with a man, Rosa also set off. Which created a few problems on the way back, because Vita was accompanied by a spectacular number of suitcases.

From the day she got home, the Viscountess exempted herself from all activities associated with housework. She unfailingly behaved like an honored guest, and except during the moments of quiet complicity shared with her sister at close of day, she stressed her indifference to domestic affairs by adopting a detached and mildly resentful air. Her only daily chore consisted of the hours of reading done for the Notary, whose eyesight was worsening with age. Accordingly, Vita's cultural baggage—which up to that point had accommodated the sentimental novels of Guido da Verona and Luciana Peverelli—was gradually enriched with Salvemini's essays on Italy's "southern question," with Pietro Nenni's political meditations, and with Paul Sweezy's writings on capitalist development. Thus, when the Notary eventually died and the family intellectual's scepter passed to her, it would become perfectly normal for Vita, who now mostly consumed women's glossies like *Grazia* and *Annabella*, to trot out what were sometimes rather startling references to Marcuse's *One-Dimensional Man* or to Isaac Deutscher's books on Trotsky.

The Viscountess had been back at base for quite a while by the time news of Emilio finally arrived. The young man was in Naples, at the Hotel Vesuvio. He hadn't been seen at reception for a couple of days, the room was locked shut from the inside. Finally, the staff had forced open the door to find Emilio drunk as a skunk, in a lake of vomit. Asked to leave the hotel, he had confessed to being unable to pay the hotel bill because he didn't have a lira to his name.

Yet again, Ciccio Bombarda was charged with getting into the car and fetching the castaway home. Since Emilio was male, and there were therefore no social codes to respect as there had been in Vita's case, the chauffeur could set off alone, without a chaperone appointed by the family. In

Naples, Ciccio Bombarda paid the Hotel Vesuvio's bill and was given Emilio in return. He was in a hurry to get back to the town because his youngest son, Cecè, was due to be baptized the following day, in grand style.

## 60. OTHER SONS

Peppo from the posthouse's two sons were called Luigi (nicknamed Gigino) and Oreste. Number one was two years older than number two. They had grown up in their maternal grandparents' house, because their mother, Lucia, had died when they were both very tiny, and as we already know, Peppo from the posthouse had never remarried.

Their father was as mild-mannered, courteous, and reserved as his two sons were full of themselves, noisy, and immoderate: especially Gigino, who never passed up a chance to make a show of himself with his empty boasts. Oreste seemed to favor the role of *éminence grise*, because he was arrogant too, but in a shrewder, subtler way. It was evident that, of the two, he was the thinker; Gigino was too busy being loutish and rowdy to have any time to cogitate.

Peppo from the posthouse seemed astonished, even appalled, to have ended up with two sons like this. Toward them he harbored ancient feelings of guilt, for not having wanted to start another family back when he had been widowed, and for having handed the little ones over to his mother-in-law, almost as though they were two parcels to be gotten rid of in a hurry. It probably had been the wisest thing to do, or if nothing else the most prudent, but in his heart of hearts Peppo from the posthouse had quickly begun to nurse feelings of shame and inadequacy with regard to the two little boys. As those babes grew—faster than he could ever have imagined—he had ensured they lacked for nothing, but all the same realized he had condemned both of them to the depressing and pathetic status of orphans. And perhaps it was precisely as a reaction to that pitiful condition that the two brothers grew up so unruly and impudent. Whenever Peppo met them in the street he would say hello almost timorously, as if expecting that sooner or later they might make him the object of their mockery—or worse, an act of physical violence.

After Lucia's death, Peppo from the posthouse had devoted himself almost exclusively to old Giorgio Attali, the most refined, elegant, and self-effacing man he had ever known. He had looked after the properties the old man owned: a pair of rather good vineyards and a nice piece of land with a thousand or so olive trees, and then the houses in the center of town and down in Marina. In actual fact, Giorgio Attali had invested relatively little in land and bricks and mortar, preferring to keep most of his assets in a pair of Swiss bank accounts. Although he did keep a sizable quantity of money in the house, and many objects of value. Peppo from the posthouse knew this because, when the old man died, in '39, he had inherited a discreet sum in cash, the man's gold wristwatch, a wonderful early eighteenth-century Gobelins tapestry, and a pair of cufflinks with two large rubies that he had never had the courage to wear.

Whenever he thought about the old man, Peppo from the posthouse's eyes moistened. Giorgio Attali had changed his life, and that was the truth. He had made, of a coarse and penniless young man, a respectable, self-possessed, and self-confident person. When they first met, Peppo from the posthouse had known nothing of what really counts in life, but by the time the old man died, only five years later, he had developed enough of an eye to be able to tell a Savonnerie rug from a Burkhara and a Burkhara from an Aubusson. If only they had met a little earlier, or at any rate before Fascism fully degenerated, the old man would surely have taken him to Paris, and then perhaps around the world. They would have lived a life that was free and full. They would have become like real family to one another. The old man had certainly been a father figure—the father Peppo had never had—and maybe even something more than that.

Now that he thought about it, Peppo from the posthouse couldn't help comparing the relationship he had with his two sons to the bond he had shared with the old man. Why, he wondered bewilderedly, why had he not been able to create the same magic with Gigino and Oreste? Why had he never talked to his sons about the things that really count in life? Of course, he—Peppo from the posthouse—was no equal to Giorgio Attali. Of course with Giorgio Attali there had been something—something impossible to put into words—that united them more strongly than any blood ties could have. Of course his sons' characters were emphatically different from his own. And yet Peppo knew he had failed without even trying; in fact, with those two boys he had written off from the outset any chance he might have had of success, and now that they were adults they intimidated him, because he sensed something primitive and uncontrollable in them. Something so alien that it was threatening.

Conversely, he had grown fond of the Pharmacist, offering his wordless but stubborn support during those long months when the man had been suffering from depression (Peppo from the posthouse liked to say that the Pharmacist was very "sentimental," by which he meant sensitive). On the Pharmacist he had focused maybe not quite his own paternal instincts, given that the other man was approximately twenty years his senior, but to a certain extent at least, the protective side of his personality. Which, of course, reached its fullest expression in the context of young Giorgio—young Giorgio, who had inherited almost all of his uncle's worldly goods. Which Peppo continued to take care of.

Toward the end of the summer of '57, Gigino, the elder of his two sons, was murdered: a revolver was emptied into him in the main town square. A week earlier, the doorstep of the house where the young man lived with his grandparents had been smeared with excrement. The homicide had three consequences that would, over time, prove catastrophic, or at least in the sense mathematicians ascribe to the term: the breakdown of a previously stable morphological and structural equilibrium. The first consequence was the conversion of Peppo from the posthouse into a religious zealot: the instant in which Gigino was buried, he began frequenting Father Marcello's church, convincing himself, as time went by, that his own sins had been visited upon his son. The second consequence was the start of a blood feud that would mark the birth, at a local level, of that constellation of rage, erotic frustration, and business-minded ferocity that goes by the name of *'ndrangheta*. Lastly, it resulted in the extraordinary metamorphosis of Oreste, who, having been a dissolute, preening youth, although less rowdy than his brother, now morphed into a boss as taciturn and reserved as he was ruthless.

### 61. TIME FLIES

It was probably due to the gravitational dilation of time, but 1957 went by in a flash. After all, the town was well above sea level, and ever since Einstein everyone knows that up in the mountains the course of events runs faster than it does down on the plains. As if that in itself weren't enough, that year, on the night between 4 and 5 October, Radio Moscow announced that the first man-made satellite, Sputnik 1, had been placed into orbit, adding momentum to human history in aggregate. The space age had begun, and this story's protagonists and supporting actors hurriedly jumped to the appropriate conclusions.

On 3 November Giuseppe Di Vittorio—the head of the Italian General Confederation of Labor, Italy's largest trade union—died; the Notary had met him in France, during those years on the run. Their paths had never crossed again, but in the fall of '56, following the Hungarian uprising, he had written the man a letter of unstinting appreciation and esteem, because, despite being a Communist, Di Vittorio had been brave enough to criticize the Soviets' military occupation of Budapest, dramatically distancing himself from the official line being taken by his party—at that point led by Togliatti, whom the Notary detested.

Unlike his father, the Lawyer felt no particular hostility toward the Communists, and indeed ran the town with their help for almost a decade. All the more justifiably, therefore, the loss of Di Vittorio so saddened him that he went along to the funeral, which took place three days after the union leader's death. During the service, when Pietro Nenni got up to speak, the Lawyer was quite overcome with emotion and couldn't hold back his tears. Afterward he would forever be a fan of Pier Paolo Pasolini—both the man and his work—because, ten days or so after that funeral, the Lawyer read a magazine article by the poet, who, with genuine emotion—the same emotion he himself had felt, thought the Lawyer—described the funeral cortege in which the Lawyer had taken part, moving through the streets of Rome.

Upon his return from the capital, where political business had kept him for a few days longer than planned, the Lawyer discovered that the calendar was now rolling rapidly toward Christmas. He scolded himself for not having realized sooner, when he was still in the city and could have bought a few gifts for the children, and above all for Tamara, his Mara, from whom he had never been separated this long since the day of their wedding, exactly fifteen years earlier.

At the beginning of December, the suppers and parties began—suppers and parties that, as mayor, the Lawyer could not opt out of. Contemporaneously a procession formed, made up of clients, vague acquaintances, assorted mendicants, and distant relatives, who knocked hourly at his door, each of them carrying a crate of oranges or bottles of liqueur, or a brace of pullets, or a hamper filled with salamis and cheeses. Before the holidays finally drew to a close—which we can take to mean sometime after Epiphany, on 6 January—a good 70 percent of the victuals necessary to feed a hungry African state would make its way down the street leading to the Pharmacist's house, and from there to Maria-la-pioggia's, Maria del Nilo's, and Cousins Levino and Margherita's. The Notary's home was excluded from the recycling operation, because on one occasion the viands—chickens, eggs, and sweetmeats, sent over by Tamara via Peppo from the post-house—had been returned to their sender without a word of explanation. Always the snob, had thought Tamara, and the experiment had never since been repeated.

The most eagerly anticipated revels—preparations for which occupied weeks of their time—included those to be held at Ciccio Bombarda's house. And Ciccio Bombarda had more than one reason to celebrate: in the space of a year he had gone from being a member of the ancient southern brotherhood of the unemployed to being the right-hand man of a much-loved local mayor, and his own popularity had soared accordingly; added to which, his wife Rina had presented him with a fourth son, Cecè, who goes on to play an important part in this story.

On the evening of the party, decked out to resemble a very convincing and—in more than one way—disconcerting doppelganger for the Lawyer, Ciccio Bombarda positioned himself at the door of the house, ready to welcome in his guests: he said to his wife that for nothing in the world would he have passed up the chance to exchange salaams with all the people he had invited, enemies and detractors included.

In dribs and drabs to start with, by seven o'clock the march-past had already begun, even as the finishing touches were still being put to the decorations.

Accompanied by Tecla and Vita (the latter got up, as befits a viscountess, in a ruffled gown entirely inappropriate for an occasion that was more in the spirit of a village fete than a ball at court), the Notary made a brief appearance at Ciccio Bombarda's house: as soon as he caught sight of Emilio, who was already passably inebriated, he gestured to his daughters that a quick getaway had to be made. As a matter of fact, Emilio had not yet imbibed a great deal, but seeing his father arrive, had pretended to be drunk, in the sure knowledge that this would have the Notary hightailing it at almost the same velocity with which that man's conscience chased away regrets. His objective achieved—the Notary having made his escape together with Tecla and the Viscountess—the young man was then able to dedicate himself peacefully to the business of getting himself truly blotto.

There were umpteen people, that December evening, crowding the not many square feet of floorage in Ciccio Bombarda's house. Rosa, Maria-la-pioggia, and Cicia brought along their respective families and made themselves very useful, helping the lady of the house bring the food out to the long table that stretched through the living room and off into the entrance hall. Lea and the Pharmacist dropped by, but just to raise a quick glass, accompanied by and then leaving behind them the cousins Levino and Margherita, and Maria del Nilo, together with her son Franceschino and his wife Mena, who all stayed on till late, while Peppo from the posthouse sent word that he wouldn't be coming because he was still in mourning for the death of his son. The Pharmacist and Lea went home early, with the excuse that Giorgio and Bebè were due to arrive the following morning for a short and longed-for vacation (now that he was at the hospital in Corone, Giorgio worked backbreaking shifts), but the truth was both of them felt old and tired, and thought their lives no longer offered any cause for celebration. Along with the cousins and Maria del Nilo, Nina also stayed on, and after supper, spent most of the evening dancing with Gioacchino—in other words, dancing alone.

Both Ciccio Bombarda and Rina, as well as the Lawyer himself, had made tearful pleas to Tamara, begging her to come along to the party. In the end she had relented, and for the first and last time ever the Lawyer's wife was seen at a supper party somewhere in town that wasn't her own house or her parents': as far as reservedness was concerned, over the years Tamara would become something of a legend, like a local version of Greta Garbo. In any event, that evening, holding Ciccio Bombarda's minuscule heir in her arms and looking into his opaline eyes, and despite already having turned forty-four, Tamara found herself thinking nostalgic thoughts about maternity. A few days later, the aftereffects of the crisis brought on by the film about Nazis being shown on television would see to the rest. Nostalgia morphed into imperativeness.

Vincenzo was also part of the crew that evening at Ciccio Bombarda's, and at one point forced his sister-in-law—with whom he shared a time-honored bond of complicity in the mocking of the Lawyer for his soppiness—to join him in a waltz, which was greeted with unanimous but rather formal applause. Vincenzo had gone back to being the elegant and slightly foppish figure of earlier times, before his days in the Resistance, but he no longer hung around with his old pals, and he had acquired the tics typical of those who prefer their own company to that of others and who constantly flaunt the fact, as though it were a badge of nobility. And so he often laughed quietly to himself, or hid behind that face people pull, with one eyebrow arched, which is supposed to suggest self-reliance but which actually betrays a form of fear. In reality, and although he wasn't aware of it, everyone thought that, since the war, Vincenzo had become a sad man.

# CHAPTER SIX

## 62. GRAPE PICKING

One September morning—as Tamara was giving birth to her fourth and final child, who for reasons unimaginable just a few days beforehand, would end up being named Valentino—it dawned on Vincenzo that he had become an individual with a past so cumbersome that it had already enveloped what little he could identify in the way of a future for himself. He was walking alone in the countryside just to the north of the town, in the direction of the vineyards that had once belonged to poor Elvira and which he now took care of. The sky was a solid blue, showing very little inclination for nuance, and the warm air made no pretense of acknowledging the fact that fall was fast approaching. This was a landscape seething with life, and yet the whole scene was oddly silent. There was a strong scent of rosemary. Vincenzo paused for a moment to light a cigarette and enjoy it in peace. In a flash, he found himself reliving that morning at Porta Capuana, in Naples, when he and Dante had smoked together and the air had been soundless and saturated with the smell of their own bodies, and then they had set off in the direction of Via dei Tribunali and a fate as brief as it was interminable. More than a decade had gone by since then. That seething morning, its strange silence, the scent of the rosemary and of a slowly smoked cigarette—it was all repeating itself, it all seemed exactly the same as that day. 29 September 1943. Vincenzo's past seemed to be contained in and confined to that date.

He remembered having looked at Dante, trying to imprint the image into his memory, almost as if knowing he wouldn't have another opportunity to do this. Over time, however, his friend's likeness had lost its precision: it had become a little blurred. Vincenzo was losing him, he was losing Dante. He wondered if and how he could fight it, that inexorable process of decay that our past always ends up facing. He focused on his friend's voice. Could he still hear it? It was a deep voice, with a youthful ring to it. What had it sounded like? What had it sounded like when he had said "Don't you worry, Vincenzo, Naples won't burn"? He had clicked his tongue, Vincenzo remembered. It had felt as if he were being spoken to by another human being for the very first time. The very first time he had ever been looked at that way, the very first time that... How many first times had he shared with Dante in that handful of hours their closeness had lasted? In a sense, there had been so many of them that he seemed to have used them all up, his first times—consumed in the space of a night and a day.

He recommenced walking. It was still very early in the morning, but he wanted to get there before the bins full of bunches of grapes were taken into the cellar and emptied into the tubs where the men were ready to begin crushing the fruit with their bare feet. It was a ritual he had always found beautiful and perturbing, the crushing: it wasn't uncommon for the men to do it not just barefoot, with their pants rolled up past their knees, but stark naked; and that nudity, which had no ulterior motives, which was dispassionate, which was exhibited in such a primitive, straightforward way, represented—in Vincenzo's eyes—one of the most erotic sights the world had to offer. During one grape harvest, when he was a child, someone—seeing him staring, entranced by the scene in front of him—had muscled him into one of the tubs, in the middle of all those unclothed bodies. Vincenzo remembered it confusedly: all those male body parts glistening in the candlelight, the shadows on the whitewashed walls, the smell of the must, the lightheadedness brought on by the gases released during fermentation—if he had known of the existence of the frescoes in Pompeii back then, he would have said he was in one of them. There had been the same grace to it. The same suspended quality, halfway between light and mystery.

Not far off, he heard two voices—one male, the other female—chasing after each other and rolling through the fields of high grass. Two kids, making out on the sly. They were speaking mumbled phrases to one another and then laughing, and then laughing again. Vincenzo would happily have watched them at it, but resisted the temptation. He couldn't, however, help envying them. And it wasn't their youth he envied: at little more than forty, he still felt young, he exercised every morning, and his body showed no signs of sagging. Rather than that, what he envied was the fact that the two of them could, without even knowing it, count on the world's approval. As Vincenzo saw it, those two kids had the blessing of at least two thousand years' worth of received wisdom and ethical and aesthetic conventions—which he himself could effectively see no way of circumventing. If, instead, someone were to have witnessed the same scene, but played out by two actors of the same sex—Vincenzo himself, for example, and Dante—laughing and whispering those same words and rolling around in that same high grass on a September day in any given year of the Christian era, that someone would be very unlikely to have approved. It all boiled down to a point of view—just a banal question of standpoints, nothing to snivel about. And yet he would have given almost anything for a shift in perspective.

As he walked briskly on toward the vineyard—and he could already hear the wail of the female farmworkers' tuneless songs tainting the air—Vincenzo told himself that it had perhaps been no accident that when he had truly loved someone, that someone had been Dante. Because in his friend he had encountered something profoundly akin to himself: an identical reticence. Like him, Dante didn't enjoy discussing his own life and his own relationships; he wasn't interested in declaring what he was or wasn't (as if any of us can know what we are or what we aren't); he didn't give a fig about all the psychology that lovers' conversations are freighted with. Dante was capable of saying nothing; Dante was like him, and the two of them were like no one else on earth...

Stop right there. Stop it. He was ashamed at how trite those thoughts were.

By the time he arrived, Rosa was already preparing the morning's first meal: tomatoes sliced into segments, with stale bread that had been dipped in water and then olive oil, red onions, salt, generous quantities of oregano. Any slices of bread still hard enough were to be used as spoons. A pair of enormous pitchers of wine were being passed round, but Rosa was also serving coffee. Vincenzo opted for the coffee. He was hot, after the long walk here. He sat down on a stool beneath a gigantic oak tree. For a second, he worried he might have a headache coming on. He half closed his eyes and listened to the malevolent, insistent buzzing of the flies. His breathing slowed.

Yes, he was losing hold of Dante's image, of his face. Beneath his eyelids, Vincenzo could no longer picture it.

## 63. VALENTINO

Somewhere between nine o'clock and half past nine: as attested by Picchio, the eldest of Tamara and the Lawyer's children—who, on that September morning in 1958, has very recently turned fifteen and is therefore an old enough young man to be a reliable source. The baby weighs an unexceptional eight pounds six ounces. It's a little boy. A little boy with very thick black hair, long hands, a round face (although there's not much one can say as far as newborn babies' faces are concerned, given that they do all seem to emerge from the same mold—two molds, at a pinch).

The birth has taken place at home, without any noteworthy complications. Present at the birth: the town's elderly doctor (Italo Gigli, toward whom the as-yet-nameless little one will forever nurse a blend of trust and terror); a four-months-pregnant Maria-la-pioggia; Lea; and Giorgio, who has just now arrived from Corone in order to be present for the event (not wanting to hurt his elderly colleague's feelings, he insists he is only here in his official capacity as the baby's uncle). Crowded into the room next door are the Pharmacist and Peppo from the posthouse, Maria del Nilo with her daughter-in-law Mena, and Rina, Ciccio Bombarda's wife, with little Cecè in her arms. They talk in low voices, they whisper, they mutter. Whereas in the kitchen a great din is being made by the assorted children (Tamara and the Lawyer's: Picchio, Erri, and Vita; Maria-la-pioggia and Santo's: Sisina, Enzo, Antonietta, and Silvana; Franceschino and Mena's: Gigino, Maria, and Rosetta), whom Nina is vainly attempting to keep in check. Ciccio Bombarda's other children aren't there, but nobody actually notices.

When news of the birth reaches the kitchen, Picchio lifts his eyes to the clock hanging on the wall above the television set, and announces in a firm but still-teenage voice, "It is twenty minutes and seventeen seconds past nine." And, all together, everyone else says, "Dongggg!" partly in imitation of the radio and partly because it makes them all laugh.

The news of the birth is followed by resounding compliments and congratulations and hugs and kisses. But who's going to tell the Lawyer? Picchio and Erri are sent off on that mission, and run all the way from the house to the town hall, where the baby's father is in a meeting. As soon as he sees them, Ciccio Bombarda understands what has happened and asks, "Boy or girl?" Erri, who at fourteen is constantly thirsty for jokes, immediately answers, "Twins, a boy and a girl." But then he bursts out laughing and Ciccio Bombarda cottons on. "Boy or girl?" he repeats slightly frantically.

The deputation of two boys and a chauffeur knocks at the door behind which the mayor's meeting is in session. Ciccio Bombarda waves a bottle of the worst sparkling wine to be had: "Congratulations, congratulations! It's a boy!" No one knows who or why, but a split second later, just as everyone is raising their glasses and exchanging bear hugs, from the windows opposite, at full volume, the stirring proletarian notes of "Bandiera Rossa" suddenly blare out.

The latest arrival does very little in the way of bawling and quickly falls asleep. By the time his father finally peers into his crib, he has already been cleaned and clothed and is deep in dreams bustling with shadows and unfamiliar shapes, which sporadically convulse his little arms and then drop them back down onto the sheet.

As of yet, the baby is not availed of a name. Tamara has Sergio in mind, but not for any special reason—she just likes it, simply that. The Lawyer is instead thinking of

Giustino, for the sibling who died in 1925 and also as a tribute to a famous relative. Instead, the following day, the little one's name will be registered at the town hall as Valentino, a name no one had predicted and that—as was typical of her—represented an extreme attempt on Tamara's part to bring a note of levity to even the darkest of moments, summoning up a happy memory from their youth, one that had to do with her brother-in-law Vincenzo.

Nina, on the other hand, had no doubts, and from day one called the baby Chiquito, because Nina adored Dora María, "La Chaparrita de Oro," especially when she sang "Amor chiquito acabado de nacer / Tu eres mi encanto / Tu eres todo mi querer."

## 64. IN COUNTRY SLEEP

It was the silence that woke him. The others had finished eating and were sitting quietly for a moment, before getting back to work. Vincenzo hadn't been asleep for more than a few minutes: waking up, he had the distinct impression that someone had been sitting there, next to him, and had just slipped away. Between that very short sleep and reality a sort of doorstep remained, and Vincenzo had tripped up on it.

Up on his feet again, he smoothed down his bottle-green cotton pants and corduroy jacket. He felt crumpled, as if that quick sleep had left a series of wrinkles in his thoughts as well as his clothes. He drank another drop of coffee, washed down with cold water.

The harvest was not an excellent one in terms of quantity, but in recompense the wine would be better than usual. Not that he liked the local wine—too strong and rough. He preferred the wines they made in the north—in his opinion more refined. In any case, this year's vintage would be of a superior quality, so the price these grapes would fetch had gone up slightly. He set off toward the building with whitewashed walls—the building they called the cellar—where the baskets were gradually being brought in and put on the weighing scales, and then emptied into the tubs. The grape treading would begin later.

Vincenzo talked to a pair of farmworkers about how the day was to be organized. Then he decided that he too would pick a few bunches of grapes, the table grapes they grew on the other piece of land, further on down the road. He slipped off his jacket and shirt, leaving only a neckerchief knotted at his throat, and set off, bare-chested, toward the other vineyard.

The temperature was rising, and the atmosphere continued to grow more animated: he could hear things snapping, things juddering, birdsong, whistles, rustling, and again the ghastly singing of the female farmworkers (to whom Vincenzo dedicated a heartfelt curse).

When he got to the vineyard, he realized that this was where most of the singing was coming from, and bitterly regretted having chosen to tackle the table grapes. But now he'd arrived there was no point standing there worrying about it. He steeled himself, stopped listening, bent over, and got methodically to work, giving the plants a good tidy and pulling off the ripe bunches, taking care not to cut his hands. He had brought with him, in the back pocket of his pants, a light-colored hemp cap: he pulled it out and put it on, to avoid getting sunstroke. He worked on until the others stopped for lunch. Then the group assembled beneath a mulberry tree; a large, stripy oilcloth was spread out on the ground, and plates and food were laid out.

A few minutes past twelve. Rising to his feet, Vincenzo felt his bones creaking: clearly, spending hours bent double in that unforgiving heat was rather exhausting, even for an athletic man like him. He was hungry and would be glad to eat the cold pasta salad the women had prepared. He sat down and stretched his legs out, a few feet away from the cloth on the ground. Shortly afterwards, Cicia made her way over with a plateful of pasta, a spoon, and a glass of red wine. Vincenzo smiled at her gratefully. He said, "Come and sit next to me, let's chat."

Cicia gestured to say he would have to give her a minute: first she had to serve her husband and her eldest son (who was not a child, but a tall, strong young man—the exact opposite of his short, round mother). Then the woman prepared a plate and a glass for herself and came over to sit down with Vincenzo.

They ate in silence and then finally she said, "Do we know if the Lawyer's baby has been born?"

Vincenzo gave a shrug and continued devouring the pasta: it had just the right amount of chili in it, and there wasn't too much onion mixed in with the fresh tomatoes.

Cicia continued, "And you? Shouldn't you be thinking about having a child? You're no spring chicken…"

"Age is an issue for you ladies," he replied, "but to us gentlemen it doesn't make a jot of difference. And anyway, my sister-in-law's a year older than I am and she's giving birth as we speak."

"I am aware of that, but if you don't get married, how are you going to have a family? Your father's had lots of families. And good for him."

"My father has simply gone around being an asshole. Each time that man sets up home with someone, what he's setting himself up with is a dedicated staff. Look how he behaved with the countess, Magda, and then with my mother, and then poor Elvira. And now with Tecla. My father doesn't give two hoots for family roles and responsibilities. Wives, daughters, lovers—they count for nothing. The only thing he notices is who will or won't be of use to him."

"You're exaggerating," said Cicia. "And that's not the way one should talk about one's parents. Besides which, the fact remains, if you don't get a move on and get yourself married, you'll soon be too long in the tooth."

"Excuse me, but if I'm old at forty-four and you're fifty, what does that make you? Methuselah?"

"I've done everything I was meant to," concluded Cicia. She gave Vincenzo a sideways look. Then she added, "You haven't."

Vincenzo put down his plate and spoon and lay down, stretching himself out under the tree. Christ, he thought, he hadn't done any of the things he should have, Cicia was right. He hadn't even made the effort to discover what Dante's surname was, to find out where he was buried, or to take a flower to his grave. What a superficial idiot, what a selfish cretin. Maybe he wasn't so different from the Notary. He closed his eyes, hoping sleep would come swiftly. That sleep that is the gift of the god of fools.

### 65. A BADGE OF HONOR

Afterward, Tamara will take refuge in the dark embrace of a migraine, sinking into a depression all the more painful because it is unvoiced. She has probably sensed that this final birth is catapulting her into that period of claggy obscurity which is the menopause. Or perhaps, now that the baby has arrived, she is reacting like many other women do, withdrawing into herself and feeling empty and useless. What we do know is that, following the baby's first few days of life, she retreats into her bedroom, refusing to have any contact with the world. She has a headache, she needs silence and semidarkness, she cannot breastfeed. The little one is handed over to a wet nurse.

Nonetheless, before things take this turn, it is Tamara herself who, with panache and intelligence, solves the puzzle of which name should be inflicted on the baby. Sergio, Giustino, and the other hypotheses rapidly wither and fade following Vincenzo's sudden death, the day after the baby's birth. The news reopens the sore of the excessive number of premature deaths in the family, and so, for an instant, the Lawyer tells himself that the very best way of honoring that brother of his (that only-just-younger brother who had, during the years of the dictatorship, unexpectedly revealed himself to be not the frivolous swell appearances suggested, but a sort of partisan hero, possessed of a strength and generosity never previously exhibited), the very best way of preserving his memory and simultaneously negating his passing—which is such an absurd idea that it skims the edges of the paradoxical—would be to give the baby his name.

Why not? Vincenzo is a fine name, derived from the Latin, evoking victory. And the Lawyer's brother had been victorious, during the war. Yet it seems to Tamara that using the name immediately, before the funeral has even taken place, would be a little sinister, perhaps even inauspicious for the little one. And since not only the Lawyer but also all the other components of the family—first and foremost Tecla, who only a few hours ago found her brother's lifeless body in his bed—agree, Tamara pulls the name Valentino out of her proverbial hat. It was Vincenzo himself, back when he was in the third year of what should have been five years of high school, who had embarked on his own antifascist adventure by writing an essay whose subject—a role model for all Italians—he decided should be Rudolph Valentino and not the Duce. That class test had won him endless reprimands and expulsion from "all schools in the Kingdom" (as was spelled out in the letter informing him of the disciplinary measures to be taken). Now the moment has come to turn the negative consequences of that deed on their head and make of it a badge of honor. Something to be justifiably proud of.

By calling the baby Valentino, they will be keeping Vincenzo's memory alive not via a dull and, given the circumstances, rather lugubrious nominal reiteration, but in the form of one of his most anticonformist and daring deeds: and deep down, concludes Tamara, weren't those the two adjectives that best defined him? Yes, agree the Lawyer and even the Notary, Vincenzo certainly was an uncommon man, and despite being reserved to the point of neurosis, courageous in a way that very few people are.

So Ciccio Bombarda is sent off in great haste to the records office at the town hall, and the name Valentino exits the realm of hypotheses and makes its official entrance into our tale.

## 66. WITHIN A BUDDING GROVE

The heat had gotten unbearable. Vincenzo pulled off the handkerchief he had knotted round his neck, wrung the sweat out of it, and poured a glass of water over it. He wrung it out again. Almost everyone was back at work. Only Cicia's eldest son was still lying beneath a tree, groggy with fatigue and wine, the clean-cut features of his face melting into an expression at one and the same time infantile and sensuous. The crickets were chirping furiously.

There was no more water left in the jug. Vincenzo regretted having wasted so much of it on freshening up his neckerchief. He could have walked the dozen or so yards over to the well and pulled up a bucket of water and done the same thing there. But he hadn't thought to do that because he was maladroit and whenever he was faced with doing something practical he got snarled up in a tangle of pointless and self-defeating gestures. Over the course of the many months he spent fighting as a partisan, he had acquired a sense of practicality and a certain self-assurance, but when the war ended it had mysteriously vanished, leaving the old ham-fisted Vincenzo to reemerge. Dante would certainly have teased him, had he seen the cockeyed way he cut the bunches of grapes and how clumsily he shoved them into the basket, or the way he rinsed out his handkerchief, twisting it at an angle that had ended up soaking his pants.

Vincenzo attempted to imitate the quick, neat movements made by Cicia, who was squinting at him surreptitiously, keeping watch on him from a distance. Just a moment earlier, had that been a flicker of desire she had seen in his eyes? Innocence is always a paradox, and on that particular day—the final day of a life that had been a difficult one, but ultimately happy because it had, even if only on one occasion, been touched with grace—in the eyes of Cicia and the other workers, Vincenzo represented the most extreme of paradoxes.

The hours went by, and the countryside smoldered with an incandescent heat. His joints were burning, his eyes were burning, and so were his hands and so were his thoughts; his whole body was aflame. And his thirst was feeding the blaze. With an enormous effort of will, Vincenzo hoisted himself to his feet and hurried over to the well. Without moving from where she was, Cicia, who was still keeping an eye on him, yelled out, "Don't drink from the well! That's not a good idea!" But a day or two earlier he had seen a pair of farmhands greedily drinking that water to no ill effect. So he dipped a glass into the bucket and gulped it down. And then another one.

Nothing happened, or at least not immediately. His thirst momentarily quenched, Vincenzo announced that he would be going home that evening. He was feeling too tired to help with the grape treading, or to stay on for the night, together with Cicia and the others, in the nearby hunting lodge they used as a bunkhouse at harvesttime.

He set off for home. As he walked, he could feel his knees and legs reacquiring their efficiency. All the way home he hummed cheerfully, thinking of the sleeping profile of Cicia's eldest son.

Destination reached, he washed thoroughly, ate a light supper in his bedroom, and switched off the light: tomorrow morning he wanted to be back in the vineyard early; in a sense, he couldn't wait. He found time to concoct a few fantasies involving the pillowy lips of the sleeping youth, before falling asleep himself. He dreamed that his belly was distended, that it was racked with a sharp and surprisingly insistent pain. He dreamed that, in his pain, he had collapsed to the ground at the foot of the same mulberry tree he had been dozing beneath a few hours earlier, and that Cicia, her son, and the other workers were crowding around him, all of them standing and staring at him, with the sunlight at their backs. The shadow of the young man fell directly across him, and for a second, he felt deliciously cool.

# CHAPTER SEVEN

## 67. THE DECADES FLY BY

Let us recap. Or, to put it another way, let's take a quick look at the future that, by the time this story of ours picks up again, had already become the past.

June 1963: the Lawyer is still mayor (they had reelected him two years earlier); Tamara seems only recently to have emerged from the recurring migraine that has been used as a pseudonym for her lengthy postnatal depression; Valentino is still not five years old but has already made up his mind that he must, at all costs, go to school; and Ciccio Bombarda's youngest son, Cecè, has wonderful golden curls. (Should direct causal links be inferred between these latter two developments?)

On a broader scale (and working backwards): Pope John XXIII, who ascended to the self-styled throne of St. Peter in 1958, has just died in Rome, after having set the Catholic Church all atwitter with the Second Vatican Council and the world of politics all atwitter with his encyclical recommending "Peace on Earth." Since May '62, the president of the republic has been Antonio Segni, who won't last long, on account of being an amateur putschist. That October ('62), someone—but no one knows who—murdered Enrico Mattei, the founder and chairman of the government-owned oil group Eni: he wasn't much liked by the Mob because, by dealing directly with oil-producing states, he bypassed the big American oil companies; and he wasn't much liked by the CIA for exactly the same reason. In '61 it had emerged that Italy's rural population amounted to 6.2 million (it had been 8.6 million back in '51). Also in 1961, in January, the United States swore in a Democratic Irish-American Catholic president, and—ignoring his military attaché Vernon Walters, who proposed a military intervention in Italy should the Socialist Party ever end up in a coalition government—John F. Kennedy summoned Amintore Fanfani, the leader of Italy's Christian Democrats, to Washington and gave him the go-ahead to form a coalition government of the aforementioned kind. Before these overtures, however, there had been a government led by Tambroni (spring and summer 1960) which was, thank heavens, short-lived: long enough, though, to revive the ancient custom of having police shoot at people protesting in the street. Again in 1960, the XVII Olympic Games were held in Rome, and Italy came fourth in the final medal table. It was an auspicious year, was 1960, because in January the *Financial Times* awarded the Oscar for most stable currency to the lira; to say nothing of the theatrical release of one of the most beautiful films ever made—Fellini's *La Dolce Vita*.

All in all, and as has been remarked in other contexts, the decades fly by, even while some afternoons never seem to end. And our narrative has thus, in a matter of minutes, taken its leave of the twentieth century's sixth decade and, not without alarm, has welcomed in the sixties. The cause for alarm lies in the fact that, observed with all the well-known benefits of hindsight, the new decade makes its entrance brandishing the banner of ideology. And where ideology starts, literature stops.

### 68. POLITICAL DRAMAS, MARITAL DRAMAS

With the exception of Vincenzo, who, while not a signed-up party member, never concealed his communist sympathies (his eccentric, anti-conventional, and anti-Togliattian communist sympathies), the Notary's influence on his children was indelible: perhaps not on a human level, because they would always be openly critical of his behavior, but on a political level at least. Over in Puglia, Giulio, the son he had only recognized as his own at the end of the war, was very supportive of the local Socialists, and as an entrepreneur didn't turn his nose up at opportunities to do business with them in the construction sector; Giuseppe, a professional soldier, would never say so aloud, but in the privacy of the polling booth cast his vote for the party his father had helped to found; Ernesto had died too young to have had time to give voice to his own ideological sympathies, but when chatting with Giorgio he had never pretended not to lean the same way as his father; Arnaldo—now settled in Naples with his wife—was a party functionary; ultimately even Emilio, with whom the Notary had always had an openly conflicted relationship, counted himself a member of the socialist electorate. In the case of the two girls, as far as anyone knew no opinions had ever been declared, but Vita the Viscountess considered everything her father said and thought to be the gold-plated truth (especially when it regarded etiquette, and above all the correct positioning of knives and forks) and Tecla was too astute ever to admit to any potential difference of opinion. The long and the short of it was—should it not yet be obvious—that in the Notary's household and in its immediate and indirect spinoffs, the air breathed was that of socialism.

Caveats, however, were in no short supply. For instance, Arnaldo was firmly pro-government (in December '63, the party leader Pietro Nenno had become deputy prime minister), while the Lawyer's sympathies lay with the radical wing led by Lombardi. The Viscountess acted as a sort of family *Pravda*, but with a soupçon of snobbery more in the style of *The Tatler*. Tamara, who was in any case merely affiliated with the clan, zigzagged her way through the Left, from time to time expressing an interest in this or that political group, but always with a slight bias toward the heretical and the antiestablishment, and a growing enthusiasm for what were nominally referred to as civil rights.

The ISPPU (the Italian Socialist Party of Proletarian Unity—the same name the original Italian Socialist Party had had in the 1940s) came into being in January '64 with the secession of thirty-eight ISP deputies and senators, who disagreed with the decision to enter the coalition government. In the Lawyer's eyes this was an outright tragedy: many of his dearest friends went off to join the new organization, which reeled in something in the region of 20 percent of the old party members, including a figure for whom he felt profound esteem and fondness: Vittorio Foa, the then secretary general of the Italian General Confederation of Labor. At which point, wordlessly and imperceptibly, the first crisis in his marriage to Tamara, his Mara, began.

Not that he was unaware of the failings of the first, second, and third of Italy's center-left governments, all of them led by Aldo Moro between late '63 and '68. On the contrary, the Lawyer saw all too well that the program of major reforms that his own political party had drawn up (from town planning and higher education to agriculture, regional government, and the economy) had stalled, rendered unworkable by the Christian Democrats' immobilism. Yet he believed Italy was so close to the brink of a precipice, at the bottom of which he could see there being a new fascist regime, that he became convinced the only defense lay in remaining in government. Even a disappointing, sapless government. He was wrong, but only up to a point. And when it came to light many years later, General De Lorenzo's infamous "Solo" plan—an attempted military coup not dissimilar to the one that took place in Greece in '67—would in many respects prove him right.

At the time, however, neither he nor anyone else, apart from those directly involved, had any way of knowing anything about it, and so disagreements and quarrels with Tamara, his Mara, became staple fare. It should also be added that, owing to his mounting political responsibilities, the Lawyer's professional life was being rather badly neglected, and the disastrous financial consequences of this did not take long to make themselves felt. Those were years in which—at least for a huge section of the political class on the left (and on the right)—being politically active required a significant sacrifice of private resources. It certainly wasn't the financially rewarding occupation it would later become.

Tamara complained about those economic sacrifices, and the Lawyer accused her, more or less openly, of being untrue to her own radical principles. You act the communist but then you expect to live like a lady, he thought—not aloud, but intensely enough to be heard. And although at a local level he remained the leader of a coalition with the ICP, a coalition that had never once resorted to making deals with the Christian Democrats and the social conservative bloc, Tamara, his Mara, didn't refrain from criticizing him all the same, attacking the contradictions and delays in his political program.

## 69. HUMILIATION

Valentino hated the scene that was reenacted in their house every morning. It was a ridiculous scene, a humiliating scene. His father would scuttle quickly downstairs to avoid being intercepted by his mother, who then unfailingly caught up with him at the very last second, right on the doorstep, and asked for money for the groceries or for the children, or some other urgent necessity. The little boy wondered why it was that his father—the Lawyer, the Mayor—always tried to duck out of that strange appointment, sneaking away like a thief. And why did his mother—an intelligent woman, a well-read woman, and a rather imperious one at that—stoop to that squalid domestic pantomime just to plead for a few lire?

There was a single plausible explanation for it: the family was poor. External appearances suggested otherwise—indeed, the family gave every appearance of being comfortably off, with a television set in the kitchen, leather armchairs and sofas in the living room, and a driver ready to chauffeur them wherever they fancied (or wherever *he* fancied). But that was obviously just for show: a way of reassuring his grandparents, leaving them to imagine a state of affairs behind which a very different reality lurked.

His grandfather the Notary certainly wasn't a poor man. He was closefisted (in fact he never pulled so much as a coin from his pocket to give to Valentino) but not poor. Every time Valentino was taken round to his house to pay a visit—these were, to tell the truth, rare events that occurred at Christmastime, and then that was it for the year—he was struck by the elegance of that old man, who always sat in a big, dark-green velvet armchair and who spoke a very correct, vaguely nineteenth-century Italian, and who had his coffee served in delicate porcelain cups, with silver coffee spoons and a silver sugar bowl and white linen napkins. The

Notary was intimidating. Sitting in front of him, Valentino kept still and quiet, frightened that at any moment he might do or say something wrong.

His grandfather the Pharmacist was, meanwhile, a different sort of man. For a start, he dispensed coins without it even having to be Christmas, and then he gave Valentino hugs; he sang him funny little songs in an incomprehensible language; he invented games and riddles. In short, he was the very model of a model grandfather. Nonetheless, Valentino did not enjoy being wrapped in his arms, because his grandfather the Pharmacist smelled of old man. There was, in fact, an odor that emanated from his jackets, or maybe it was his shirts, or who knows what it was, that Valentino associated with death—a concept that had first presented itself in his mind at a very young age, because one day a little boy who lived opposite had fallen from the balcony of his home right before Valentino's eyes (he remembered the muffled thud of the body, a second of silence followed by the screams of a woman, that smell of something musty in the air).

In reality, Valentino didn't enjoy being touched by anyone except Cecè, his playmate. He had other friends—Massimo, for example, Maria del Nilo's grandson—but Cecè was his favorite by far. Cecè was a year older than he was, with blond, curly hair and the extraordinary gift of knowing how to do anything with his hands. He could repair a tin soldier, sculpt with clay, or retune the television set. He could do anything with those hands of his. He picked grapes from the vine like an adult, he could safely peel a prickly pear, and, by pressing at a watermelon's mottled skin, he could tell if it was or wasn't ripe enough to eat. Those hands were magical. And beautiful. And big. What's more, Cecè knew all the dirtiest swear words.

Valentino's young friend explained to him that his family was not, thank goodness, poor. On the contrary, they were rich enough to be able to employ a chauffeur—his father, Ciccio Bombarda. Perhaps—insinuated the little boy, with a wink—the Lawyer and the Signora (that was what he called Tamara) chased after one another every morning as part of an enjoyable little game they played as a couple. Valentino stared at him in surprise. As far as he could see, the point wasn't games, it was money—but in any case, what did that mean? What kind of little games was he talking about? At which point, Cecè put on a knowing air that Valentino found irresistible, and gave him a potted lesson in sexual education that, while in no way dispelling the fog that surrounded the aforementioned little games, had the effect of persuading Valentino that he would, the following October, have to go to school together with Cecè, regardless of the fact that he himself was still far too young. For nothing in the world—he saw it clearly now—would he spend every morning away from his friend's side, while said friend was in class doing magical things with his hands and saying dick and butt and pussy.

## 70. MADE IN ITALY

In June '63, following a depression that had left a few wrinkles, she might have been a stone's throw away from her fifties, which in those days were synonymous with old age, but Tamara had no intention of relinquishing her looks (she would, in fact, never relinquish them). She colored her hair once a month with a deep, honey-colored dye, slightly darker than her natural color; regardless of whether or not she was leaving the house, she spread a light moisturizing cream over her face and neck every morning, and then applied an almost-invisible veil of face powder; she didn't make up her eyes (except very rarely and in later years), but she wasn't averse to a touch of lipstick; no polish on her nails, but they were, nonetheless, always neatly manicured.

With the passing of the years, her beauty had lost the perhaps slightly insipid character it had acquired in the thirties, and had become sterner and more austere. She dressed with an elegant sobriety, favoring muted colors (beige, gray, powder blue), she loved graduated pearl necklaces, she always wore the same diamond earrings (a late nineteenth-century pair inherited from old Uncle Giorgio), and always and scrupulously matched her purse to her shoes (the inside of her purses gave off an unmistakable scent of face powder and reticence, along with a hint of bergamot).

For almost the entire duration of the sixties, while Italy and the rest of the Western world (not to mention the globe's northeastern quadrant and its hardcore elements, including Communist Germany, the Soviet Union, and China) postulated an unappealable divorce between intellect and body, and unashamedly favored the former, Tamara pursued a cautious but stubborn policy of peaceful coexistence between the two competing extremes. In some respects, her position appeared to be a classically Platonic one: καλὸς κἀγαθός (*kalos kagathos*), the necessary and harmonious correspondence between beauty and virtue. But in reality, at the heart of this underlying and perhaps even unconscious philosophy of hers there lay a hidden kernel that, had it been revealed, or become mindful, or simply been voiced, would in those days have been considered an outright heresy. Because, in Tamara's eyes, beauty took precedence over virtue. In other words, aesthetics came before ethics and actually gave rise to its rival.

Accordingly: at that stage in history, Tamara's primary occupation—or rather, her preferred occupation, the one that inspired her to express all that was noblest in her—was the making of late-afternoon visits to the house of her dressmaker, Signora Farà, to whom she took along fabrics acquired whenever the chance presented itself (on her own or other people's vacations, or during her husband's pre-electoral tours of northern Europe, or the Viscountess's sojourns in Bari, or even via correspondence, picked out of the Marzotto and Gutteridge catalogs): wools, silks, linens, hemps, piqués, bouclés, and macramès that were, with the help of clever paper patterns, transformed into exquisite but simple dresses, unfussy but sophisticated in cut.

From June 1963 onward, Valentino was allowed to participate in these afternoon expeditions to Signora Farà's house. To begin with his sister Vita had also joined in, but then, having grown up (in '63, Vita was thirteen years old), the young woman got into the habit of going to the dressmaker's on her own or with her best friends, Rosalba and

Maria—although in private they called themselves Stellina (little star) and Rosellina (little rose) and Carla Boni (like the singer who sang "Casetta in Canadà").

The expeditions were primarily mounted from early summer onward. The afternoons began lengthening, and after their siesta, mother and son, dressed up to the nines as if on their way to an opening night at the theater, would set off through the narrow streets of the town and head off toward Valle. The journey was made calmly, hand in hand, every so often contentedly noting a lovely Tiepolo pink outlining a lone cloud on the horizon, down there, down near the sea, or addressing brief hellos in reply to those of people walking past, or even stopping to watch one of the groups of women they occasionally spotted gathered on their porches to recite a novena: Valentino had no idea that these were religious rituals; he thought—and was encouraged to think so by Tamara—that those women were chanting their litanies for the pure pleasure of it, like singing in a choir. Walking along, side by side, she was as tall and solemn as a statue, and he worshipped her from below.

Arriving at their destination, the couple was ushered into the biggest room in the house, a room that doubled as living room and as Signora Farà's atelier. For Valentino, this was the least interesting part of the trip, because Tamara seemed all of a sudden to start speaking a language that only the dressmaker could understand. The two women talked in quick-fire volleys of words, and they rearranged chairs, scissors, pieces of cloth, tissue paper, and thin sheets of cardboard. Tamara went in and out of a changing cubicle of a sort, set up behind a flowery curtain, and every time she reappeared with a new dress on, Valentino's heart thudded with excitement. More often than not, Signora Farà offered Tamara a coffee and Valentino a homemade and very hard cookie. The cookies were almost impossible to eat, but he would forever remember them with huge nostalgia.

Heading home, their calm made way for a certain hurriedness: the sun plunged below the edge of the horizon very suddenly, and where, seconds beforehand, shades of red, purple, and crimson had triumphed, seconds later there would be nothing but shadows and barking dogs. Waiting for them at home, though, there were delicious treats that were the fruit of the bottomless fondness (and appetite) of Maria-la-pioggia. All the more reason to quicken their pace.

### 71. LEA, ALWAYS

Unlike the great majority of human beings, who are by definition—and perhaps of necessity—fickle, in the eyes of those who knew her Lea embodied an almost unparalleled fidelity to self. Instead of growing old—which would have meant acknowledging time's official status as an intransigent and unequivocal deity—Lea grew into focus. The only change she underwent as the decades went by was, in fact, to shrink. In every other way, she was always identical.

In the photos of her that survive, her devotion to constancy is clear as day: her face, her body, and the style of her clothes seem immutable. As a thirty-year-old she dresses and poses in the same way she does at eighty. Her features have an identical softness. Her hair grows paler but remains thick and is combed in the same manner. Her hands seem to be big and rather imposing, quite significantly so given the economy of her overall anatomy. Young or old—categories that are in her case essentially irrelevant, judging by the photos—Lea resembles a Minoan idol, one of those commanding figures who emanate directly from the land of which they are goddesses or priestesses.

After Giorgio finally got married in '49, and after having understood that Nina, in contrast, would never make it to the altar (or tie the knot at the town hall or even under a chuppah), Lea decided she would take care of her grandchildren. Had she not settled on this plan of action, she would have had to do simultaneous battle on two fronts: with her husband's continually spiking depression and with her youngest daughter's not infrequently deranged imagination. Which was why she turned her attention to her grandchildren's education: out of a healthy, practical realism. With her grandchildren, she thought, she stood some chance of being useful, while with the Pharmacist and Nina she would never have managed that. And with Maria's children, at least, it proved to be no trouble: for one thing, there were lots of them, so she could, in a manner of speaking, shoot randomly into the crowd; and what is more, the girls could be put to use in the house as unpaid manpower. As a result, one after another, little Lea (named after her grandmother), then Assia (like Assia Noris), and finally Rosalba (a name chosen entirely at random) spent their childhood years and early teens up in the town, at Lea and the Pharmacist's house.

Of Tamara and the Lawyer's offspring, only Picchio spent very long living with his grandparents, chiefly for preventative pedagogical motives—in other words, to protect him from the influence of Erri, who was a year younger but perfectly capable of leading his brother into mischief (Lea called Erri "the rascal" and, more occasionally, "the dybbuk").

Nevertheless, even with the other grandchildren Lea refused to relinquish her role as educator, an educator whose lodestar, whose cardinal principle, and, we might as well add, whose rock-solid foundations lay in the idea, and above all in the practice, of penuriousness. Basically, virtue consisted in knowing how to abstain from everything. To which there is no point adding that terms such as "beauty" or "pleasure" were by nature so alien to her as not to be contemplated in her vocabulary.

And yet when, in '49, Giorgio set up home in Corone together with Bebè, and insisted, quite rightly, on taking possession not just of the cash and the property but also, ten years after the old man's death, of the objects that were rightfully his as part of their uncle's legacy, Lea made various attempts to hold on to the two little Gauguins, which should instead have belonged to her son. And her efforts were not motivated by the monetary value of the two canvases, of which Lea was entirely unaware. Long hidden away in a dark little corridor, those paintings appealed to the woman in a way she herself couldn't have explained or perhaps even admitted to. Because it was, when all was said and done, a weakness.

But, without batting an eyelid, she let Giorgio carry away rugs, tapestries, and silver that, in Lea's eyes, were worth a great deal more.

## 72. THE LIFE OF THE GAUGUINS

From Paris, where they had both come into the world just as 1883 hovered into view—in other words, just after the catastrophic collapse of the Union Générale, which transformed one of the bank's respectable employees into a penniless great artist—the two little paintings by Paul Gauguin that belonged to old Uncle Giorgio would, ten years later, move to Turin.

In the Piedmontese city they first took up residence in a room in Via della Rocca, where Giorgio Attali, contrary to all expectations, would live for a considerable length of time; then they moved to the backroom office, behind the first of his stores selling fabrics (wholesale). In this locale, looking out onto Piazza Bodoni, the two little paintings resided for a long time before moving, again, to the nearby Via Mazzini, where old Uncle Giorgio would live, until the point when he decided to sell up and move down to his nephew's, in the south. In that vast apartment in Via Mazzini they chose to live separately for a little while: one of them, representing an ethereal autumnal landscape, stayed on in the entrance hall, to welcome visitors; the other, a self-portrait that looked to be a preparatory study for the famous *Les Misérables*, painted in 1888, hid itself away in Giorgio Attali's study, a square, minutely proportioned room where, in addition to the painting, there was an English Regency desk with a little armchair and a bookcase occupied exclusively by French-language editions of the beloved Maupassant (numerous other books were scattered throughout the apartment).

On arriving in the town, at the Pharmacist and Lea's house, the paintings found a lodgment in the high-ceilinged (but not particularly spacious) room with French doors leading onto the terrace, which was to be the uncle's headquarters. The two works of art billeted themselves at the foot of the bed, so that their owner could contemplate them in comfort every morning, as soon as he woke up.

Following the old man's death, for a time the paintings roved around, feeling rather lost, without finding a satisfactory berth. Until one day Lea decided to shut them into a windowless inner corridor, where they were barely visible. Yet she liked the two paintings. She liked them very much, as became apparent at the point when she reluctantly had to part company with them (when his wife Bebè pointed out that his mother had made an attempt of a sort to hang on to them, Giorgio, their legitimate inheritor, a genuinely generous man, felt ashamed at not having left the works of art where they were, but never did have the courage to bring the subject up with Lea).

In any case, in the very lovely apartment that Giorgio had bought in the old historic center of Corone, the two paintings would live a long and happy life. Curiously enough, here too—almost as if they sensed that the shared name of their old and new owners was a coded message—they split up again, the self-portrait taking up residence in the library, and the autumnal landscape in the living room, where, as the years since their painter's death steadily multiplied, the many guests whom the owner of the house enjoyed entertaining on Saturday evenings would admire their quality, and in the meantime their market value soared.

A couple of decades later, not long after the end of this story, the two works of art would vanish off the face of the earth, stolen and in all likelihood sold off for a pittance by ill-informed dealers in stolen goods, who were almost certainly experts in the field of opiates and their derivatives but incapable of recognizing two little jewels of figurative art. But then, Giorgio had also very recently vanished off the face of the earth, thanks to a pulmonary carcinoma.

## 73. EVENTS

In addition to the death of Pope John XXIII, the events of the summer of 1963 unarguably included two that were rather important for—respectively—Tamara and Valentino. The one that concerned Tamara had a Russian name, with all that implied at the time in terms of secretiveness: Valentina Tereshkova, the first-ever female cosmonaut, launched into space for a full three days and forty-eight terrestrial orbits. Question: Was Tamara struck by the fact that the young woman had been a dressmaker before beginning the career that would catapult her up through the earth's atmosphere and into the upper echelons of the Communist Party of the Soviet Union? Whatever the answer, what is certain is that the astronaut's feat, with its aureole of exceptionality, seems to have revived our heroine's dreams of a socialist world and sexual equality—which on this side of the Iron Curtain was still very far from being achieved (in parenthesis, it mustn't be forgotten that the Lawyer's wife had not been given regular schooling, because, when she was young, it had not been customary in the south for young girls of good family to attend public schools, much less university). In any case, her admiration for Tereshkova rekindled the polemics in her marriage (among other things, the Lawyer was categorically anti-Soviet).

The second significant event of that summer concerned Valentino. On 14 July (also a momentous date for many millions of Frenchmen) the little black chick Calimero made his broadcasting debut on the Italian state broadcaster's one and only television channel. Valentino was instantly smitten: for reasons impossible to put into words, he immediately felt that he too was small and fuliginous, just like the cartoon animal. By way of Calimero, he came to see that he himself was misunderstood and rejected. And yet he had no concrete motive to believe that. Which would suggest that in certain cases conscious thought is so quick that it jumps to the right conclusions well in advance of itself. The peoples of the East would call that the third eye, but this story is set in the West—and what a West! We are in full-blown Magna Graecia, which means the lands of Pythagoras, which means—by derivation—Plato, Galileo, and Kepler. So, we can forget about the third eye. Instead, we can hypothesize that Valentino (and those like him) perhaps already keep the other two orbs wide-open from a very tender age. There was, in fact, only one other little chick who did not make our extremely youthful protagonist feel small and fuliginous, and his name was Cecè.

Be that as it may, this business of Calimero also uncorked other feelings. Feelings that, it would seem, had already taken up residence in a not particularly well-lit area of Valentino's brain. Which was why, one very hot day, still in the summer of '63, when the only people in front of the television in the kitchen were Valentino himself and Maria-la-pioggia—who had one eye on the programs being broadcast and the other on the tomato sauce she was cooking—Valentino clearly saw the television set, which in those days was a heavy, solid sarcophagus of a thing, advancing menacingly toward him. For a few minutes the little boy endured it all in silence and in a cold sweat, but when it seemed that the monster was on the point of reaching him, he started screaming in a way that was really quite frightening, and trembling so hard that he couldn't control his limbs.

Unfortunately the episode was repeated more than once that summer, and since it was always the television that provoked these moments of crisis (as the showing of the film on Nazism had done for his mother), at a certain point the object was interned in a heavy cloth and locked up in a broom closet. It was just a pity that no one knew how to put a halt to the cavalcade of nightmares that marched through the little boy's dreams every night, leaving an inevitable stream of pee in their wake.

In any case, from those first vaguely epileptic episodes onward (although, luckily, no specialist would ever grade them as such), Valentino had good reason to think of himself as small and fuliginous. And he had good reason to become increasingly attached to Cecè, who not only expressed apprehension regarding his friend's fits, but one day went so far as to pierce him with an arrow that would knock him right out. He said, "You're not ill, you're sensitive. You're more sensitive than all the rest of them put together." Words which, addressed by a child just six years old to another child of five, could easily be something straight out of one of those books of aphorisms and famous sayings. Or, likewise, could well be proof that the world's great seducers are what they are from a very young age.

All in all, it seemed that that year—from summer onward, at any rate—had ushered in a muggy ill wind. Because, on 9 October, there was also the Vajont Dam disaster, up in the Alps near Belluno, with its two thousand victims wiped out by the wall of mud; and not much more than a month later, on 22 November in Dallas in the United States, President Kennedy was shot dead—President Kennedy, the symbol (rightly or wrongly) of peace and of hope, and an idol in the eyes of half the world—including the Lawyer. (Tamara, his Mara, worshipped the man's wife, Jacqueline Bouvier, who would later become Jackie O, and who in her eyes embodied the only true ideal of femininity to survive all fashions and seasonal fads.)

## 74. THE SECOND PRINCIPAL ABODE

In September 1958, to celebrate the birth, very late in the day, of their youngest child, the Lawyer had bought a piece of land down at Marina where he planned to build a vacation home. To begin with, it was supposed to be a small, modest building, a low building. But as work progressed the plans had gotten bigger and bigger, spawning an unpretentious but two-story house with a large kitchen, three bathrooms, and a backyard. The work took years, but by the summer of '63 it seemed to be nearing completion.

Almost every morning that summer, Ciccio Bombarda loaded up the car—which was now no longer a Fiat 600 but a commodious, dark-blue Fiat 1100 D (very presidential)—with the Lawyer's four children and Nina, who was to act as chaperone, and took them all down to the sea. Whence they returned many hours later, starving hungry and brown as berries. From time to time, especially if Picchio and Erri abstained from the trip, Cecè would join them, and maybe even Maria or Rosalba, Vita's best friends. Less frequently, Tamara also took part, and when she did, she flaunted elegant sundresses and rigorously one-piece bathing suits, usually light blue (whereas the Lawyer was never once observed setting foot on a piece of sand).

On their way back from the coast, after also paying a flying visit to the cousins Levino and Margherita, who were very busy with their new fabric store, the group often stopped to take a quick look at the work being done on their future second home. Which it never would become, because to begin with it was rented out, in the deluded hope of clawing back some of the exorbitant cost of the building work, and then it became the family's principal abode. The Lawyer was particularly proud of the three bathrooms, and especially of the master bathroom—very spacious, and with a ridiculously big corner tub that gave the house a Hollywoodian touch.

When Cecè joined the day-trippers, Valentino's heart jumped for joy. At the seaside Cecè was free to perform his finest repertoire of stunts, such as swimming very fast, putting his head underwater while keeping his eyes wide-open, breaking a few records for sprinting on the beach, collecting a steadily increasing number of sea urchins (which he then prized open with a knife, offering the fragrant orange pulp to Valentino), filling his mouth with salt water and then spraying it, in a sneak attack, all over someone who was peacefully sunbathing, and then challenging anyone and everyone to beat him in any sort of competition, and letting off volleys of swear words. In effect he never stopped, even for a second—befuddling and dazing Valentino, who trailed along behind him admiringly and absolutely exhausted. An exhaustion which only served to fuel yet further admiration.

When Nina was with them, the two little boys had no inhibitions. Because—with those ubiquitous and enormous sunglasses sitting on her nose and further reducing her visual acuity—Nina had a lovely time stopping to chat with all and sundry, giving free rein to her own most authentic self in the form of a cordial and sunny-natured person, and as a consequence she left the boys at total liberty (but the greatest relief was that felt by Vita and her friends, who were hovering somewhere between thirteen and fourteen years of age and considered themselves very adult). If, instead, Tamara was the chaperone, the rules of behavior ended up being so strict that she seemed to be every bit as startled as everyone else: Was it possible that deep down she was starting to resemble Lea? Which is why, in order to take her mind off her children, and seeing as she didn't want to chat with anybody on the beach, Tamara took along a novel—to keep her well removed from reality. That summer she read the two bestsellers of the season, Primo Levi's *The Truce* and Natalia Ginsburg's *Family Lexicon*, as well as Sartre's *The Age of Reason* (which left her cold) and *Boredom* by Moravia (from which point onward, she acquired the tic of asking, in entirely random situations, What are you up to? Are you bored?).

Back in those days summer finished in late September, because the school year began on 1 October. Apart from Picchio, who was at university in Rome, Erri (who, for the umpteenth time, was repeating a year) and Vita would be moving to Corone to attend high school there (he was going to live in a rooming house, she as a boarder at the school). Valentino desperately longed to be enrolled in first grade and make his debut in the world of education alongside his best friend. But as it was—unhappily for him—things went differently.

## 75. MAGICAL THINKING

No one has more direct experience than a child does of what Ernesto de Martino called "the crisis of presence": because a child is, by definition, defenseless in the face of the world. If that child should then, during the daytime, see the family's television set walking threateningly toward him, and at nighttime miserably contemplate an endless to-ing and fro-ing of nightmares with diuretic side effects, it is easy to see that—more than even a shaman would—he might feel obliged to ritualize his own experiences, to render them stereotypical and repetitive, precisely in order to avoid the risk of losing the precarious, faltering life that Mother Nature has only recently bequeathed him.

To simplify: in an attempt to exorcise his own demons, Valentino lumped them together with the fits that shuddered through him, and he invented a numerical system of a sort, via which he perused, interpreted, and ultimately predicted reality. Of course, had he been an adult he could have resorted to sex or religion, or maybe even astrology, all three of which are ultimately branches of magical thinking, and the thing would have gone no further (no one is ever surprised when an adult overrates their partner, their god, or their horoscopes). But this being a little child, and what is more, a little child born at a latitude and in an historical era congruent with Ernesto de Martino's ethno-anthropological research (the reader is invited to consult *Magic: A Theory from the South*), he ended up excogitating a series of mathematical calculations whose function was to distract him from his anxieties. For example: if, on television, a particular word was repeated a specific number of times, the television set would behave itself and remain where it was, without threatening to crush him. Or if, as he went to bed in the evening, a preestablished series of circumstances were to occur, Valentino's dreams would then not uncork his urinary tract. By means of these calculations of probability and this micromanaging, the poor little boy did his level best to take the edge off the feelings of terror and humiliation that promptly followed every fit and every pee-soaked bedsheet.

In '63 the works of de Martino were already in circulation, but unfortunately neither the Lawyer nor Tamara, both of whom were enthusiastic readers, had come across them. This is not an unimportant detail. Because, had Valentino's parents interpreted their child's "problems" (we'll put it that way, between a nice pair of quotation marks) through the eyes of the great anthropologist and historian of religions and philosophy, who died prematurely in Rome two years after the events we are narrating, this episode would very probably have taken a different turn. For a start, from 1 October 1963 onward, Valentino would have sat at the same school desk as his beloved Cecè, thus logging an abrupt percentage jump in his own happiness index, which would have outperformed even Italy's GDP (which itself, as we have seen, was surging): a psychological boom (psychology, as everyone knows, pertains to economics, and as a pair they form part of the wellness package). And we should not discount the possibility that the effects of a psychological boom of that kind might have swept away all fits and nightmares and fear and humiliation, resulting, if nothing else, in a much-improved urinary function.

But that is not how things went. Valentino was not enrolled in first grade; for a long time he was unable to see his best friend, and his demons multiplied. Instead of being left in peace to contemplate his beloved during school hours, he was taken on a tour of all the leading pediatricians, endocrinologists, and psychiatrists in Italy. This is, after all, the early half of the 1960s, and never before had science (including that pseudoscience commonly known as medicine) enjoyed such renown: faith in its efficacy inspired the belief that for every malady there existed a label that would surely unmask it and a pill that would certainly cure it. The tour, which commenced in late September, concluded in triumph approximately two months later, at the end of an electrifying final round of clinical examinations, X-ray investigations, and aptitude tests, with the following feedback from pediatricians, endocrinologists, and psychiatrists in unison: there's diddly-squat wrong with the little boy. Although, no: if we're to be precise—one ear, nose, and throat specialist consulted in passing did spot a mild ear infection.

In the absence of organic root causes behind Valentino's daytime fits and nocturnal micturition, and perhaps also to de-dramatize things a little and to archive—with a little laugh—any fear of heaven knows what psychic or somatic dysfunctions, the Lawyer, Picchio, and Erri decided that they might as well pull Valentino's leg about it. The quips and jokes—about the television set moving around like Frankenstein, and about peeing one's pants—multiplied exponentially. And as a result, what medicine hadn't managed to do, the family achieved. The damage was done. Henceforth, the little boy would remain convinced he was a freak and deserved to be jeered at. And without there being any need for them to cart him around Italy, spending money on expensive specialist appointments, but here at home—for free.

As is traditionally the case for all freaks, Valentino was left with no choice but to beat a retreat, to turn in on himself, to hide his face. He refused to eat in the company of others, he avoided leaving his room; the holidays and parties terrified him because that meant people being around. All of a sudden all he had left was himself, with his shame and his own bad smell. Solitude became more essential than even Cecè. Because, out there in the world, every which way he turned there were eyes teasing him, mocking him, laughing at him.

Then something happened that would put a halt to the torture, the wisecracks, and the ragging. The pain, however, didn't let up.

## 76. DEATH OF A PHARMACIST

In the spring of 1964, the Pharmacist felt the urge to put his life in order.

He had been born in 1879 in a land whose tongue he no longer remembered and into a family with whom, apart from old Uncle Giorgio, he had had no dealings since getting married. If asked to, how would he have defined his own existence, now that he was nearly eighty-five? He hadn't the faintest idea. He had fallen in love two times: with his violin and with Lea. Lea he had married, back in the year dot; the violin lay neglected at the bottom of a wardrobe. Of course, he had also loved his children, but that was a different kind of love, closer to what one feels for God. In addition to the pharmacy and a body that was big, fat, and weary, he owned a few vineyards, the house he lived in, and not much else. The savings in the bank were held in Lea's name, they were hers. He didn't possess riches, but what with everything that had happened in Italy and the rest of Europe during his lifetime, he counted himself lucky. No one had touched a hair on his head or on the heads of his immediate family. At the end of the war he had heard about relatives killed in the Nazi concentration camps, but for him they were just names linked to his childhood: he hadn't seen them since. In any case, he had paid for his good luck with an endless and exhausting to-and-fro between optimism and depression. All his life long he had shuttled back and forth between those two halves of himself, but since the war, once he had learned what there was to learn of the camps and the murdered dead, the second of the two halves had reared its ugly head, with an eye to liquidating the former. And so the violin had ended up in the wardrobe.

In recent years, he had begun talking aloud to himself. Lea told him, "You talk to yourself so much that it's made you gaga." But he wasn't gaga. He was worried. And in particular he was worried about Nina. Because, while their other children now had families of their own and the wherewithal to keep body and soul together, Nina had neither family nor means. She worked in the pharmacy with passionate enthusiasm: ever since she had taken the reins, business had always been good. However, when the

Pharmacist died she would have to shut down and sell out: Nina had no qualifications and, by law, could not continue working unless supervised by a college graduate, who also had to be the business's owner. At one point, a few years earlier, the Pharmacist had thought he could count on another Lea, his eldest daughter's eldest child, who had enrolled at university to study pharmacy, but then she had become very attached to a young man and would soon be marrying him, and going off to live with him who knows where.

Which is why, in the spring of '64, the Pharmacist decided to put things in order, and summoned his children one by one, starting with Maria: the thorniest issue, because she was the one in the stickiest financial situation.

He laid out the facts in the simplest and plainest way possible. He said that, given his age, the moment had come to make plans for the future, after his death. Of course Lea would inherit everything that belonged to him: not a great deal, but still enough to cushion her old age: the house and the proceeds from the future sale of the pharmacy and the two vineyards. He made no mention of the little hoard in the bank, held in his wife's name, because he himself had no idea how much it amounted to. The problem—he continued—would arise once Lea died: the small estate would have to be split into four chunks, one for each child. Tamara and Giorgio—of this he was certain—would happily forgo their quotas in favor of their youngest sister, who was neither married nor had a trade, while the two of them were both well set up. Could Maria see her way to making the sacrifice he was asking of her? Whatever her answer—he quickly added by way of conclusion—he would accept it.

Maria had been expecting that little speech. Not because she was mercenary—she was anything but—but because she was aware of her father's worries, and had plenty more of her own. So she answered without hesitation. In effect, she said, she and Gaetano weren't having a particularly easy time of it, from a money point of view. But they had a proposal to make: Maria would forgo her share of the house and of the money in the bank accounts, if there were any, but not her share of the pharmacy and the two vineyards.

Once again, the Pharmacist said nothing with regard to the savings on deposit in the bank, and felt vaguely guilty about it. Maria's proposal was a reasonable one, and he accepted it right there on the spot without even consulting Lea (for the first and only time in his life), and that very evening, in his happiness, he pulled the violin out of the wardrobe and promised himself he would start playing it again. He could go back to practicing Beethoven's *Kreutzer* Sonata: the Andante con variazioni had forever been a passion of his and a bugbear, because he never had managed to play it as it should be played.

Over the next few days, both Tamara and Giorgio agreed without a second thought—just as the Pharmacist had expected they would—to their father's proposition. And at that point, the man thought fondly, he could finally claim to be at peace with the world. Whatever time he had left he would dedicate to music and to all the good things life had reserved for him. Life, however, is always hard at work. She is also generously unstinting with other lives to come, even when she herself looks rather jaded and seems to be well past her prime. And so the Pharmacist fell ill. It was his heart. And in August a series of mild myocardial infarctions completely overshadowed the death of the Communist Party leader Palmiro Togliatti.

The Pharmacist was forcibly persuaded he should be admitted to the hospital where his son Giorgio worked as a surgeon. He was given all and more than the appropriate medical care and attention, but two weeks later they sent him home: his advanced age made open-heart surgery inadvisable, in addition to which, the man was champing at the bit to leave. Giorgio wanted to keep him in Corone for a little while longer, at his place, but like all old people, the Pharmacist was no lover of novelties and was convinced that he would feel better just as soon as he got back to his normal routine. And so, at the beginning of October 1964, he returned to the town, where Nina welcomed him joyfully, and Lea, who was in seventh heaven with the relief of it, didn't let it show, but in recompense made sure he found his violin waiting for him on his side of the bed, almost as if to make amends for the past, wordlessly asking him to play for her.

The very next day the Pharmacist died. So, no Andante con variazioni. No *Kreutzer* Sonata, nor any of his favorite pieces by Édouard Lalo and Mendelssohn. To which, what is more, at around seven o'clock in the evening, upon feeling his breath beginning to fail and, all of a sudden, all the memories, people, and gestures of a lifetime retreating into the distance, and while withdrawing into himself, into a knot of incomprehension and unexpected joy, he devoted not even the shadow of a thought.

## 77. MORPHOLOGY OF THE FOLKTALE

Coinciding as it did with the beginning of his school career, the Pharmacist's funeral confirmed Valentino's suspicion that death—that discipline only ever mastered by other people—was the one and only subject deserving of further study. Religion was another fan of this line of research, but he had no way of knowing that, because he had no religion, nor was he yet familiar with what he would later discover is the mother of all religions, namely literature.

Seeing that the death of his grandfather had rattled the little boy, Tamara took to sitting down next to her son on his bed every evening and easing him into sleep with a story. She started with "Cinderella" and "Little Red Riding Hood," but then gradually began inventing new ones, which for the most part described their own family life. They featured brothers who seemed to be Picchio and Erri, a sister very like Vita, and a father and aunts and uncles in every way indistinguishable from the real ones, or at any rate very obviously resembling them, although devoid of flaws, as if the copies had turned out a great deal better than the originals. Now and then, but always in borrowed guise, Maria-la-pioggia and Ciccio Bombarda and even the cousins Levino and Margherita popped up in these stories; Cecè, however, was never to be seen, and this irked and distressed Valentino, who, although he now saw his friend much less frequently than before because they were in different classes at school, continued to love him as though he were the brother—of almost exactly the same age—that life—aka Tamara—had denied him. An older brother, although not as old as his real ones, who were decades older than he was. But nonetheless a considerate, protective older brother in whose eyes and voice there was never a trace of mockery—a brother with magical hands, who said dick and butt and pussy.

But no, Cecè never featured in his mother's stories; he didn't even join the ranks of minor characters, bit parts, extras. He didn't even crop up in a footnote. The plot included no lines for him, no fleeting appearances somewhere in the background. Nothing. Cecè simply wasn't there. In Valentino's mind, his friend therefore began to resemble the air: not there, because invisible, but present always and everywhere.

## 78. HOW EVENTS PLAYED OUT

From the fourth chapter of this story onwards, mention is made of two marital crises between Tamara and the Lawyer, crises—as has been said—with very costly repercussions: one crisis with origins in politics, the other in matters of the heart. In reality, now that we are getting closer to the nub of both of them, we slowly discover—no thanks to a narrator who is rather less omniscient than he would like you to think—that the causes are actually indistinguishable and circular, and that both of them—the first and the second of these crises—nicely combine, ex post facto, to form that famous slogan according to which "the personal is political."

Let's take another look at the calendar. In December '64 Antonio Segni steps down as president of the republic. The excuse used is the precarious state of his health, but as we have already seen, there are ulterior motives: the man had entertained the idea of a coup d'état together with General De Lorenzo. As you can see, in this case too, the personal is political. In lieu of Segni, Giuseppe Saragat, a Social Democrat, is appointed. It would seem to be a victory for the left wing, but will not turn out that way. Then again, the Italian Socialist Party (this much we already know) has just survived a schism and is mixed up in a government being led by Moro that, as far as the much-trumpeted program of reforms is concerned, is looking very shaky. Meanwhile, the Italian Communist Party, "forced into the somewhat sterile role of a semi-permanent opposition" (as Paul Ginsborg wrote in *A History of Contemporary Italy: Society and Politics, 1943–1988*), has lost its longtime leader (Togliatti) and much of its membership, despite gaining votes.

This long phase of deadlock, discord, and inconclusiveness on the part of the nation's left wing is reflected in the municipal election results in town, in the spring of 1965: Christian Democrats 1,302 votes, the Trumpet (ICP + ISP) 1,320, Italian Socialist Party of Proletarian Unity 75. Since the last of these three has failed to take enough votes to win them even one seat on the council, the result is ten seats for one side versus ten seats for the other. Dead heat. Interim, government-appointed acting mayor.

For the Lawyer it was a very hard blow. The idea that his friends in the ISPPU had scuttled a project that had now been ongoing and successful since 1957 had an element of the absurd to it, as well as being upsetting. The Left lost control of the town council not because the Right had won, but thanks to their internal divisions. In other words: the oldest story in the book.

Caught up in the atmosphere of rancor and recrimination that had befogged his own side, the Lawyer hadn't been capable of seeing, at an early enough stage, that this was no longer his moment and that it would therefore be wiser to step aside. Tamara, on the other hand, saw it clearly, and for her all the bitterness over that electoral defeat ripped the veil from the left wing's sempiternal suicidal urges and the fundamental vulgarity of politics. From that point on and for a great many years she would refuse to vote, simultaneously launching a full-scale campaign aimed at persuading her children to make a run for it, as far as they possibly could, from the town and from the south in general ("They're all barbarians" was its inaugural slogan).

On top of the overt political dissent, there was also a purely personal question. Toward the end of the summer of '65—just a few months after the electoral setback—Erri, who had finally, very belatedly graduated from high school in Corone, baldly announced that he had gotten one of his schoolfellows pregnant. He hadn't been expecting anyone to open a bottle of champagne, but neither did he foresee that it would unleash a conflict of biblical proportions.

The personal got stirred into the political, and the cocktail they formed was lethal. Essentially, the differences of opinion between husband and wife spilled over from the postelection analysis and engulfed their emotional lives, and to cap it all brought with them a curious inversion of roles. In politics, the Lawyer took a conservatist, moderate line, announcing that in the next round of council elections, which were being brought forward to the following year, he would be standing once again at the head of the same old Socialist-Communist alliance as always; but as far as the private question was concerned, he took on the role of the intransigent anti-traditionalist, resolutely opposing the suggestion that his son should marry his high school companion and above all opposing the idea that Erri should legally acknowledge his paternity of the child. Quite the opposite of Tamara, who was convinced that her husband should abandon his political life immediately and move, with his family, to the house in Marina, where there was plenty of room for the girl Erri ought to be marrying and for the baby they had on the way.

Which was how a marriage that had been about to reach its twenty-third happy year, and whose protagonists (once her initial hesitation had been overcome) had desired and loved one another like no other couple before them in either of their families, a marriage that had survived a world war intact, and racial persecutions on an industrial scale with their associated mountains of corpses, and the atom bombs and the Cold War still in progress, then morphed into a battlefield on which an unbroken sequence of open hostilities, ambuscades, duels, and skirmishes took place for more than six months, in an increasingly acrid series of victories and defeats.

The final outcome was decided by the fresh local elections in May 1966, just a few days after the murder, at the university in Rome, of the socialist student Paolo Rossi, a friend of Picchio's who was assassinated by the neofascists (and from that moment onward, Tamara began worrying obsessively about her eldest son's safety). In town, the electoral campaign took on an epic and dramatic hue. Whoever won would do so by a narrow margin, and everyone knew it. Rosa and Cicia, the Lawyer's eternal paladins, plugged away right to the very last. The sleepless nights were countless, the stump speeches proliferated, the battle was fought house to house.

The Christian Democrats won. Not long afterward the family moved to Marina. Erri tied the knot with his high school sweetheart, and the newly born baby girl was given the name Mara—an odd sort of compromise intended among other things to gratify the Lawyer, who was the only one of them who ever called Tamara by that diminutive. But in reality it was she who had triumphed. Tamara, written in full.

# CHAPTER EIGHT

## 79. A TOPSY-TURVY WORLD

Now let us put ourselves in the shoes of a young boy somewhere in the region of nine years old who, from one day to the next, finds his world turned upside down. The school he attends is no longer housed in a chilly fifteenth-century castle in which there are three hundred sixty-five rooms (albeit most of them in a state of disrepair that renders them unusable) and a legendary, mysterious treasure. Now, instead, it is a stifling garage, entered via a metal door that has rusted half through, on a half-paved road halfway out of town. His classmates are not the ones he has had for the past three years, but total strangers who throw emaciated, hostile looks at him. At home, Maria-la-pioggia and her four children have vanished, and above all, so have all the wonderful treats she bakes: instead there is Virginia, who doesn't know how to cook, and her lover Luigi, known as Sciammerga, a big, vaguely catatonic man who every morning picks up the grocery list, and then vegetates in the Lawyer's office in the afternoon. And where is Ciccio Bombarda, dressed just like his employer, whom he resembles so much that their respective families find it slightly disconcerting? Ciccio Bombarda, who is incapable of passing his road test but who drives like a pro? Where are the boy's grandparents, his aunts, and his uncles, including Uncle Emilio, who every so often disappears, and is then inevitably found to be in Naples, at the Hotel Vesuvio?

In Marina there are no grandparents or aunts and uncles, and Ciccio Bombarda has been replaced with a series of chauffeurs who have driving licenses but who are unequipped with names and faces.

And now, most importantly, let us put ourselves in the shoes of a young boy somewhere in the region of nine years old who has lost the better part of himself, the part kitted out with blond curls and magical hands and memorable swear words. How does that little boy react to a loss on that scale, to an amputation so major, to a privation as terrifying as it is gratuitous? Does he see a string of other television sets marching toward him, ready to crush him conclusively? Does he sink into a swollen river of nightly nightmares that, all of them, flow out into an ocean of pee? Or does he, as he would in a nineteenth-century novel, run away from home, back to the old town where Cecè is waiting for him, where together they assemble a gang of young boys who live happily out in the woods until one day, after an exhausting number of plot twists, the two protagonists discover they are brothers?

Regrettably, the era in which these events take place is not the nineteenth century but the second half of the twentieth. We may be in the south of Italy, which does slow down the pace of the story, but this is still a point in history when telephones are in use. Added to which, no Dickens is currently available. One has to muddle through with what one's got.

Valentino saw no new television sets making threats. He did not wet the bed, and nor did he make any nineteenth-century plans to escape. He didn't even cry, except on the very first night as he drifted off to sleep in his new bedroom in the new house—but just a little, because he promptly decided that crying was for babies, and also because he was keen to avoid other forms of mattress dampening. Instead, he knuckled down to his schoolwork methodically and doggedly, like an automaton; and thus discovering that devoting himself to his own improvement resulted in a certain degree of detachment from all that pain, he also started reading the books that lay around the house (including the ones by Dickens). And the more he read, the more he remembered and also forgot about Cecè, until he stopped looking longingly around for his friend and started simply looking for glimmers of him in the stories he was reading. Little by little, reality moved aside to make way for fantasy, and the latter turned out to be more interesting and richer than the former. In fact, he eventually began to get the feeling it might have been reality's prototype.

If beforehand he had been a member of that irrational and insecure category of beings known as lovers, Valentino now enrolled himself in a more select but equally irrational and insecure group: that of readers. He had discovered literature, and he would love it as he had loved Cecè. That said, he didn't swap one thing for another; he did not supplant his friend with books. Because love is always bigger than any one beloved, and Valentino therefore came to see that he could love both of them—books and Cecè. Ultimately, Valentino himself flipped the world into a new position.

## 80. FIREBRAND AND FORTUNE TELLER

There are times when, if he thinks back to the past, Luigi-known-as-Sciammerga finds it hard to believe. He thinks of the 1940s and the war, and the Russian front he miraculously came back from intact (apart from his lungs); he thinks of the women who slipped into his bed and then took their leave of it (apart from Gemma, his official wife, and also apart from Virginia, his lover-wife), and in addition to that he thinks of the land occupations back in far-off '43, and of the unionizing of the agricultural laborers, and the political scuffles and the ones with the police—and how could he ever forget the events in Melissa and those three poor souls who were killed, and all the people wounded, on 29 October 1949, a date stamped on his memory? And yes, if he thinks about all of that, despite the dead, despite the sacrifices and the hardships, despite all that, the past always glows in his mind. But with a light that gets feebler and feebler the nearer it comes to the present. And when it comes to the present, he does find it hard to believe.

There had once been a time when he was a feared and respected local firebrand: he still remembers the deference shown him by that Canadian officer, Xavier Reid (who knows how that name was pronounced?). Luigi has been harassed by Minister Scelba's police. He has been taken to court more than once and has been imprisoned for his beliefs, and it is only thanks to the Lawyer, who defended him without taking a penny for it, that he didn't rot there, in jail. His has been a life faced with countless difficulties, but it has been a life full of pride and satisfactions. And now?

Now, at not even sixty, Luigi-known-as-Sciammerga feels like a decrepit old man. Had it not been for the Lawyer moving to Marina, where he himself had already been living for quite some time, and offering him a job (in the morning he goes to the market and does the grocery shopping on Tamara's behalf, and in the afternoon he acts as secretary in the Lawyer's office), he wouldn't have known how to scrabble together lunch and an evening meal. He has two wives to maintain (although Virginia now thankfully works in the Lawyer's house too, and so weighs less heavily on the household finances) and an adopted daughter (a niece who'd been orphaned). Had the Lawyer not moved to Marina, Luigi would have been in serious trouble.

In recent years, he had, to be honest, invented a trade for himself. He was ashamed of it, he didn't much like to talk about it, but it did bring in a few lire. He was a fortune teller—or, as Tamara described it, laughing until she cried, he was a wizard. He read cards, coffee grounds, and palms—he wasn't choosy and didn't make subtle distinctions. He did spells (in the sense of putting a hex on someone or other) and undid spells (still in the aforementioned sense, but in reverse). He rustled up love potions and relative antidotes. Clients were received at home, in one corner of the single, large, first-floor room, where he had set up a little writing desk groaning with several hundredweights of old copies of *Avanti!* (the Socialist Party newspaper) and *Unità* (the Communist Party newspaper). It was there that, wearing a pair of reading glasses held together with sticking plaster, he welcomed his clientele. The gentleman, or more frequently the lady, client would sit down in front of him, he would ask them to explain what the problem was—the reason for consulting him, and then he would set to work. For the most part he made it all up on the spot, but did so with a faint air of condescension that by this point came quite naturally to him anyway.

But lately, since being employed by the Lawyer, Luigi-known-as-Sciammerga has been gradually cutting down on the work. He is worried he'll be ridiculed for it and he needs the money less than he used to. He is mortified whenever someone knocks at the door of the Lawyer's house asking for a wizardry-related appointment. If it is Tamara who happens to answer the door, she understands in a flash and sometimes laughs it off, and other times she gives the caller a dressing down, telling them that these practices are medieval and that they shouldn't be throwing money away on such nonsense. But she's more likely to laugh. When news of these incidents reaches Luigi's ears, he apologizes profusely to Donna Tamara—"Mistress Tamara" (he prefaces the names of all the members of the family with *Don* or

*Donna*, except for the Lawyer, who is always "the Lawyer"; even Valentino, only nine years old, is Don Valentino).

Luigi-known-as-Sciammerga arrives early every morning and goes to sit in the kitchen. Tamara offers him a coffee and hands him the grocery list, the weather is briefly discussed, and then the man jumps on his trusty bicycle and comes back a couple of hours later with the food he has purchased and that day's papers. Now that Ciccio Bombarda is no longer around to flick through them while waiting for the Lawyer, the newspapers are read in a different order: Luigi-known-as-Sciammerga browses them first, followed by Tamara, and then, finally, the Lawyer. In the evening Luigi takes them with him when he leaves and deposits them on the little writing desk he has at home—his own private news archive.

But what Sciammerga excels at is the drawing up of the weekly accounts summarizing foodstuffs purchased. Tamara occasionally picks up the pieces of paper with Luigi's big, lopsided, but very neat handwriting and loudly declaims: "Nice, red, fresh tomatoes, . . . lire; large, round, local articchokes, with two *c*'s, . . . lire; good, yellow, juicy peaches . . . lire." The adjectives, which are always in triplets—Proustian, if you will—follow a precise semantic order, in a crescendo of gustatory enthusiasm that sends Tamara into raptures.

For many years, she conserves those pieces of paper in a huge glass jar that she keeps in the kitchen, on top of the fridge. She says will publish them one day, at her own expense, as a tribute to all the joy they have given her.

## 81. MIGRANTS

Lea and Nina, having sold off the house and the pharmacy, also moved away from the town. For Nina it was, after a fashion, an electrifying experience, but for Lea the novelty represented a trauma. She had seventy-seven years under her belt and no desire to change. Her dead—in other words her husband and old Uncle Giorgio, not to mention the two little children she had lost—were all buried there in town, and sooner or later she would have liked to lie down next to them, in the bare earth. A year to the day after the death of the Pharmacist, Lea had returned to the cemetery, as she had also done—in keeping with tradition—a week and then thirteen days after the funeral. But now that she was moving to Corone, who would take her to the graves of her loved ones when she wanted to pay them a visit?

For Nina it was different. She wasn't yet forty and still lived in hopes of finding a husband, sooner or later. What is more, Corone wasn't a little town inhabited by relatively few souls, but a small city with a population of fifty thousand, and with numerous factories; it was a reasonably wealthy little city with nice stores downtown, and it clearly offered greater scope for making new friends. And one thing might lead to another . . . Of course, being separated from Gioacchino was, for Nina, a little bit like being divorced from her own dreams—and in effect, in Corone, despite the optimistic prognostics, she would always have the impression that she was looking at things through a veil of vague melancholy, as if her nearsightedness weren't bad enough.

It was almost a sense of nostalgic regret and a feeling that she wasn't at home any more, but a guest, foreign and fundamentally different, whereas in the town, especially back when she had loomed commandingly over the counter in the pharmacy, she had thought of herself as a queen, right at the heart of the chitchat, the gossip, the desires, and the secrets of the people who flocked to stand in her presence.

In Corone, mother and daughter set themselves up, for a short while, in an ugly apartment on the second floor of a building that was depressingly squalid, albeit right in the center of town. It was a temporary solution while they were waiting to buy a house, but for as long as they stayed in those rented rooms, Lea and Nina felt like exiles in an honest-to-goodness no-man's-land: Lea because she didn't dare leave the house and consequently felt she was trapped; Nina because, in those rooms where there was no sunlight to be had for love or money, and where they had to keep the lights on all day long, she had the impression she was seeing even less than usual. The upshot of which was to make her ham-fisted and bad humored.

Giorgio lived in the city, together with his wife Bebè and their three sons (the youngest was still very tiny). It had been one of the things that had encouraged the two women to move: Lea was elderly, and having her doctor son nearby was reassuring. Relations with Bebè, however, didn't seem to be easy.

Bebè was a rather comely woman—a cascade of black curls, tar-black eyes, olive skin: a typically Mediterranean beauty, her features strongly marked without being coarse.

She dressed with care; she wore a lot of jewelry, most of it inherited from her father, who had been a jeweler; she loved bold colors, like many women from Naples—the city she came from. She had integrated well into life in Corone, and, since she and her husband enjoyed throwing parties and giving dinners, she had a fairly intense social life. The trouble was, that extroverted, worldly character of hers clashed jarringly with Lea's stern aloofness. And since Bebè knew that her husband would never dare say a word against his mother, she took her frustrations out on poor Nina, who was the same age as her and whom she considered dreary and provincial, as well as blind as a bat. To put the finishing touches to this picture, it should be added that Bebè had a tendency to express herself with a slightly crude frankness of which she was not remotely ashamed—quite the contrary—and she therefore made no attempt to conceal or even to tone down what she thought of her sister-in-law.

As a result, Lea and Nina reduced all contact and any encounters to a minimum. Every day, when he finished work at the hospital where he was now a senior surgeon, Giorgio would drop by for half an hour to say hello to his mother and sister, and would sit with them and, perhaps while sipping at a cup of coffee, would chat about this and that, and then go home. Whereas Lea and Nina never set foot in his house, and made the reason for that abundantly clear by calling Bebè (but never in front of Giorgio) "the Chatelaine."

## 82. OTHER MIGRANTS

Together with one hundred twenty thousand other southern Italians, various inhabitants of this story of ours migrated to the north in 1967. They left because they had to; the town emptied out. Maria-la-pioggia left, and so did her four children. They were supposed to be joining Santo, who was already in Germany, in Stuttgart, but then the poor man fell under a bus on the very day of the family's arrival. Luckily his two eldest sons immediately found work, blunting the financial impact of the tragedy. Any hopes they may have invested in receiving compensation for the loss of Santo evaporated very rapidly: the payoff they were offered was miserly to the point of being offensive. They accepted it anyway, and little by little integrated into that new world, although the mother and her youngest daughter would move back to Italy many years later, to a place near Varese, where Silvana found herself a husband. Maria-la-pioggia lost a dramatic amount of weight and gave up baking all her wonderful treats, partly out of a lack of time, given that she was working in a shoe factory, and partly because she had ceased to care for food. She also considered the ingredients for sale in northern Europe—the vegetables and tomatoes, the spices, the meat and the eggs—to be so insipid and lacking in flavor that the mere sight of them brought on depression. Instead she began taking evening classes and, remembering what Tamara always used to say when they were little girls—"The two of us are the cleverest girls in town"—for once in her life she invested in herself. She took her elementary school exams, then graduated from middle school, and in the space of a few years became the most influential trade unionist in the province of Varese: so much so that many people began calling her Maria-la-rossa (Maria the Red). But in her own head she simply and only ever thought of herself as Maria-la-pioggia.

And Ciccio Bombarda too, who was once again unemployed, packed his bags, and together with his family, went to join his brother, who was living somewhere near Zurich. He couldn't get work as a chauffeur, of course, given that he never had passed his driving test and in Switzerland they were much more pedantic than in the south of Italy. He got a job as a night security guard at a dairy, and a few years later was promoted to the day shift. He had no financial woes and even managed to send all four of his sons to college, but he did—very quickly—sadden. All of a sudden, he was no longer the jolly, noisy man he used to be; he grew as gray as the Swiss climate and retreated into his shell. It was Cecè, being the youngest of his children, who kept him company, especially after Rina's death. The other three left home as soon as they could, but Cecè remained at his father's side right till the end. Which didn't stop him becoming a famous designer.

But the most radical migration was Maria del Nilo's. In June 1968, having been left at a loose end yet again, her son Franceschino, along with his wife Mena and the rest of the family (their youngest, Massimo, Valentino's playmate, had just finished his third year at elementary school) pulled up stakes and decamped to the outskirts of Milan. One of Mena's relatives had found Franceschino a job as a factory worker. However, at the very moment in which they were piling boxes and cartons onto the bus that would take them to Corone, where they were going to catch the night train up to Lombardy, Maria del Nilo had announced, quite categorically, that she had no intention of leaving her home. There were discussions, there were rows, there was yelling. Franceschino and his family postponed their journey for twenty-four hours, hoping to talk the old woman round. But Maria del Nilo was deaf, and remained every bit as indifferent to their yelling as she was to their prayers. In the end everyone else departed, leaving the woman alone in a half-empty house.

News of what had happened reached Lea. She said to Giorgio that, just as soon as it could be arranged, she wanted to be driven back to the town. It was obviously not a request, it was a command, although she did specify a fairly reasonable period of time—ten days—within which the command was to be obeyed. Arriving in town, Lea knocked at Maria del Nilo's door, a few yards from the pharmacy and the house that had once been her own home, with its terrace overlooking the valley and the pots full of basil. She felt dizzy almost to the point of fainting, seeing her old world again—her old world that had so quickly grown foreign.

She knocked and knocked, but Maria del Nilo didn't answer, because she didn't hear the knocks and wasn't expecting callers. Lea sat down on the bench where her husband and Peppo from the posthouse often used to sit, and she waited. Everyone who walked past stopped delightedly to say hello, but she had never been a champion conversationalist, and so after a few minutes they all drifted off, sending their warmest regards and "very best wishes, bless her" to the signorina (the young miss), which as far as the town was concerned was Nina's name.

In due course, Giorgio arrived to pick his mother up and take her back to Corone. He too tried knocking at Maria del Nilo's door, calling out and throwing a few pebbles at the windowpane: they could see that the woman was at home, because there was a light on, but... nothing. There was no sign of her having noticed a thing. Disappointed and feeling powerless, mother and son set off home.

In the car, on the way back, Lea fine-tuned the speech she intended to make to Maria del Nilo next time round. The gist of it: Come to Corone, come and live with Nina and me, you can't stay here on your own, you're too old to be on your own, and anyway, I need you. This last bit was one she hadn't spelled out to herself very overtly during the outbound journey. Now, though, now that the expedition had been a fiasco, the thought was crystal clear in Lea's mind: she needed Maria del Nilo.

Not even two months later, she told Giorgio she wanted to go back to the town again. Once again her son did as she asked. But this time too, they failed to find the woman. The neighbors said that Maria del Nilo left her house early every morning and went out into the fields to do daywork. From what they said, she did look tired—because the heat was torrid, especially for the kind of work she was doing—but all the same, she seemed to be in good spirits and fit. She came back after lunch, and then no one would see her again until the following morning.

Lea begged various women who lived nearby to tell Maria del Nilo about her visits: they were to talk to her urgently, she emphasized. The following week she would come back again: it would therefore be best if Maria were to leave the front door open, so that her not hearing the raps at the door wouldn't be a problem. But all of them replied that it wouldn't be easy to do as she asked, because Maria del Nilo was getting increasingly deaf, and now, when anyone spoke to her, she never understood a word of anything she was told.

Lea came back to the town several times, each of them useless. The summer came to an end, and so did the harvest, and fall arrived with all its warm, rusty colors, and lent Lea's nostalgia an unexpected hint of desperation. At the end of the year, on 13 December, the news arrived that, not having seen her leave the house for almost a week, the neighbors had wrenched open Maria del Nilo's front door, and had found the body, lifeless, in her bed. She had died in her sleep.

## 83. MARINA

Unlike the town, which had a very distinct urban structure—not dissimilar to what one finds in hundreds of other ancient hilltop towns scattered throughout central and southern Italy—Marina was a disjointed, chaotic sprawl that had expanded very rapidly in recent years. It had a long, straight road cutting right through it, like a river drawn with a T-square, at the end of which there was the piazza with a couple of pretty, luxuriantly leafy trees, a café, and the church. Behind the church (vaguely Latin American looking, white and low-slung), there it was: the seafront—which everyone called the *muraglione* ("the great wall") because of the endlessly long brickwork parapet that marked off the beach.

By now, Marina had more inhabitants than the town that had spawned it. The fishermen were just one section of the population, a population that, during the summer, every evening at more or less seven o'clock, assembled to buy—at very reasonable prices—the fresh fish being unloaded from the boats just come ashore. There were also farmers and many shopkeepers, three lawyers, a brace of doctors, two pharmacies, bars, restaurants, and even two hotels and a campsite for the foreign tourists who arrived in the hotter months of the year, mostly from northern Europe.

Tamara and the Lawyer's house stood right on the main street, more or less halfway down it, at a point equidistant from the railroad crossing that marked the entrance to the built-up part of town and the piazza at the other end. It was a typical 1960s building, rectangular and unpretentious. On the side facing the road, above the front door, a big window let light into the stairwell that led from the first floor to the floor above. Round the back, an equally rectangular yard.

Making one's way on foot from here to the piazza, or strolling off in the other direction, seemed a silly thing to do, because it was basically like walking along the edge of a highway: the traffic was unremitting and noisy. It was anything but pleasant. The side streets were more interesting and lively, although frequently unpaved and therefore tiring to walk down in winter, because every time it rained enormous puddles formed and had to be circumnavigated. As in China, everyone went everywhere by bike.

To cut a long story short, the only truly lovely thing in that place that Picchio had once—while talking on the phone to some friend of his from Rome—defined as "a pustule by the sea," was precisely that: the sea. Blue and deep, as primitive as a founding myth. And accordingly both threatening and irresistible: even before you stepped onto the beach, onto those white pebbles that centuries had polished to a shine, you were overwhelmed by an urge to shake off all your clothes and anxieties and plunge into the sharpness of that water. One could expend vast amounts of time on that sea, safe in the knowledge that no investment would ever reap better returns from the point of view of mental wealth. Without counting the fact that for many families in a precarious state of hygiene a spot of bathing close to shore brought excellent sanitary benefits.

The sea was so much at the heart of the famous pustule that, one winter, when for reasons of its own it flew into such a rage that it devoured the *muraglione*, the entire community was left feeling suddenly bereft and thrown off-balance, as if they had lost their raison d'être; and they took a very long time not just to repair the fairly considerable damage but also to recoup all that joyfulness that, particularly in summer months, encouraged them to peel their clothes off at all hours of the day and night and dive into the waves.

The other notable feature of the landscape—an unmistakably indigenous feature—was the already notorious criminal underworld, which goes by a number of monikers but is most commonly known as *'ndrangheta*—a phenomenon that in the old town was somewhat shadowy and rarefied, but down in Marina had acquired a modern, entrepreneurial complexion and strong exhibitionist tendencies. As luck would have it, Oreste, Peppo from the posthouse's surviving son, had recently been proclaimed leader of the organization; and, thanks to the serious-mindedness that Oreste's father had bequeathed him (consoled by his faith and the presence of at least one sacristan, the man had now died), this turn of events resulted in a period of relative social calm in the late 1960s, after a decade-long bout of effervescence.

## 84. BARRICADES

According to some historians, and as per *The Best of Youth* (a lovely film by Marco Tullio Giordana that takes its title from a book by Pasolini), the flooding of Florence on 4 November 1966 and the ensuing mobilization of hundreds of youngsters—the so-called "angels of the mud"—who rushed to the city, and not just from Italy, to save the artistic and literary masterpieces that the cataclysm had put at risk, was the first test bed for the values and conduct of what would, under the name "student movement," occupy universities and the front pages of newspapers across half of

Europe just over a year later. A hypothesis anything but far-fetched, if it is true that the student revolt of 1968 was not just an expression of protest against the school and university system (considered discriminatory, anachronistic, and, to cap it all, badly organized), but also and above all a radical ethical revolt against capitalist individualism and its direct descendant: consumerism.

Picchio was still a long way from graduating in economics when, together with three of his friends, he jumped on a train going to Florence. For days no one heard from him. Then again, the task awaiting him was a desperate and dispiriting one: hours and hours immersed in all that sludge, attempting not always successfully to retrieve a manuscript or a codex held at the Biblioteca Nazionale Centrale, the national library, whose depositories had been devastated by the waters. He and his friends had no time even to glance at their surroundings, and for the entire week they spent slogging away from dawn to dusk, eating very little and sleeping even less, it never once occurred to any of them to look for a phone and call their respective families.

By the time Picchio finally got in touch, Tamara was close to having a nervous breakdown. From the people at the lodging house where the young man lived in Rome, somewhere near Piazza Bologna, she had heard that her son had left for Florence, and from that moment on remained on tenterhooks until she heard his voice reassuring her that he was well.

That was the context in which Tamara came to discover that she was an anxious person. In the past this side of her personality had remained hidden, or at any rate in the shadows; so much so that she had almost resigned herself to the prospect of resembling Lea much more than she wanted to: her ironic, detached character seemed to be an inevitable offshoot of her mother's chilly restraint. Instead, in November '66, having recently turned fifty-three and having lost her father two years earlier, with a certain relief Tamara came to realize that the Pharmacist had bequeathed her at least something of his apprehensive temperament. Perhaps it was no accident, she told herself, that this side of her had emerged as a consequence of her role as mother, exactly like the Pharmacist, who had given the best of himself in his capacity as parent.

In any case, she was so happy to discover that she was anxious and vulnerable that she resolved never to rein in that part of her nature. As a result, little by little, she exited the lives of her children, who began glossing over any detail that might provoke agitation, be it a head cold, a minor misadventure, or an airplane journey. And it was only thanks to the Lawyer's outrageous and healthy optimism, which acted as counterweight to his wife's catastrophizing alarmism, that the aforementioned children were able to access their rightful share of the happiness of youth.

In any event, Picchio's brief career as an activist, which in February 1968 took him straight from the Florence flood to the occupation of the university in Rome and the correlated clashes with the police—automobiles and buses in flames, forty-seven police officers in hospital, and a never-specified number of wounded students—was kept unmentioned by the family at home, and Tamara was thus able to read all about the "Battle of Valle Giulia" in the papers, thanking the heavens that her eldest son was not enrolled at the School of Architecture where the riot had taken place, and that he was only a couple of months away from graduating. And, at least as far as this second bit went, she was right: Picchio took his final exams in May, while Paris was burning, and immediately found gainful employment and ditched all his barricadist resolutions.

### 85. VACATION TIME, VACATION TIME!

As always in life, irony did not take long to put in an appearance: the Lawyer, who had strenuously objected to Erri marrying his high school sweetheart, was now thick as thieves with son, daughter-in-law, and even the baby. Whereas, despite having originally been the mediator thanks to whom the family crisis had been resolved, Tamara couldn't abide any of the three. In her opinion they were shiftless, rude, and irresponsible. The adults, at least. Little Mara was just rude.

Living together was not easy, and it was perhaps Valentino who paid the highest price: all of sudden, at more or less ten years old, he was no longer the spoiled and pampered family darling. Added to which, the atmosphere in the house was often electric with tension. His parents, who up till then had been serenely accommodating, a bit like grandparents are, suddenly seemed to be resentful and tetchy, and almost on the verge of separating.

Thank goodness Tamara and the Lawyer had kept up the habit of disappearing for three weeks every summer, treating themselves to a child-free vacation. That time dedicated simply and exclusively to themselves, at that particular point in their lives, worked miracles. They came back from it laden with gifts for everyone and with newly minted smiles. The domestic frictions were forgotten and for a little while even Marina acquired the status of a pleasant-enough place to be.

In reality Tamara increasingly despised their new domicile. The poverty and backwardness that had once inspired her compassion apparently now disgusted her. She loathed the way her new neighbors did things, their customs, and even the way they spoke, and couldn't help but see them as traitors who had divorced themselves from their roots. It was as if, somewhere en route from the town to Marina, she had lost her own coordinates: the old world, for all its limitations and flaws, had the merit of being homogeneous and therefore decipherable, whereas Marina seemed to her to be a hideous and cryptic mishmash, a smorgasbord of all the worst national shortcomings, with an added sprinkling of the vicious poverty typical of the south. It was no coincidence that the organized crime that, in Tamara's opinion, had barely made its presence felt back in town, here in Marina was already shooting from the hip, politically speaking, and as a consequence had shot straight to the heart of community life. In town the mafiosi were ashamed of being what they were; in Marina they flaunted it.

Which made those summer vacations (in Tuscany) all the more essential: they stitched the fabric of that marriage back together at points when it seemed it might be coming apart at the seams, and—if only very briefly—they took the couple off to a place far removed from an environment that she now made no bones about detesting and that he detested without saying so.

### 86. AN INTRODUCTION TO THE *'NDRANGHETE*

(A summary is offered, for the reader's benefit, of an episode that occurred on 7 July 1968, at approximately three o'clock in the afternoon, and that neatly encapsulates one analysis, put forward by Tamara, of the phenomenon of organized crime and its diverging anthropological-cultural performances in hilltop contexts and coastal settings.)

A muggy heat. A Sunday heat—so, compounded by a long lunch featuring spaghetti *alle vongole*, *surici* (the delicate local fish), lightly battered and fried, bell peppers and tomatoes sautéed with basil, a mixed green salad and boiled green beans, a homemade chocolate and almond *Caprese* cake (not entirely successful), fresh fruit, cheap white wine. High levels of relative humidity. A perfect, adamantine silence. All members of the family (in order: the Lawyer, Tamara, Erri with his wife and little Mara, Vita, and Valentino) have retired to take a postprandial nap in their respective bedrooms. Here it should be clarified that at the point in the year when the heat is at its most intense Tamara and the Lawyer do not sleep together: he continues to occupy the usual room;

she withdraws to a little sitting room on the inner side of the house. Much cooler. With a single bed in it.

Virginia too, who had just now finished washing the dishes and putting things away, is dozing in a wicker armchair in the kitchen.

The doorbell rings. First, a short, transitory chime. Then, after some hesitant pausing, a decisive ding. Finally, after a second, longer pause, a resounding dong.

Virginia shows no signs of life. She is tired and is a heavy sleeper. What is more, to avoid disturbing the others with the sound of pans and plates, she has shut the kitchen door. So Tamara gets up and goes to see who's there. She lurches toward the top of the stairs and the intercom buzzer, which can be used to open the door onto the street. She hadn't gotten undressed before lying down, and now her linen shirt is all creased, her skirt looks like an old rag, and her hair is a mess.

She presses the button. Metallic noises. The front door opens. From where she is standing, up at the top of the staircase, Tamara sees the heads of two men who start making their way up, one in front, the other behind him. She makes a hurried attempt to neaten herself up; in a matter of seconds, a little desperately, she smooths down her skirt and her blouse and her hair, just as, right at her feet, on the final run of stairs leading up from the landing, there appear first a young man who looks to be about twenty (he is actually seventeen), tall, an attractive physique, his hair and clothes disheveled (Thank heavens I'm not the only one looking a mess, Tamara has just enough time to say to herself), very nervous but also arrogant, cocky; and immediately behind him a forty-year-old wearing a dark suit, white shirt, and black necktie, almost a funeral getup, with—on his head—a wide-brimmed hat which he immediately sweeps off in a deferential salute, thus revealing that his face is that of Oreste, Peppo from the posthouse's second-born son and the recently elected incumbent of the highest criminal benefice in the area.

Recognizing Oreste's impassive and vaguely Asian features, which contrast powerfully with the younger man's antsy, extroverted persona, Tamara feels simultaneously relieved and alarmed. She has known Oreste since he was a truculent, motherless little boy (she remembers that Lucia, his mother, died giving birth to him), but all the same she is perfectly well aware of the position he currently holds. She hasn't, though, the faintest idea who the jittery pretty-boy is.

A brief exchange of pleasantries. The trio move into the living room. Tamara explains that her husband is resting. Must she call him? After a very theatrical pause, Oreste diffidently replies—employing a turn of phrase that if we simply define it as ceremonious will shorten this paragraph by several lines: "Yes, please do fetch the Lawyer, the matter is an extremely urgent one." Meanwhile, Valentino joins them, having been woken up by the doorbell and by the tiptoeing and whispers from the living room. In just under two months' time he will be ten, from which we can infer that his mind is at present—especially at siesta time—already occupied with thoughts intentionally lewd. In any case, as soon as he enters the room, Valentino's attention is irresistibly drawn to the younger man's restive hands and the way they dig into his pockets to pull out a packet of cigarettes and prepare to light one.

But now let us use a freeze frame. We'll pause this situation for a second. Tamara has just heard Oreste tell her that half an hour ago the young man (it's useless insisting: she cannot remember his name) killed someone, gunning them down in the street in front of no fewer than five or six passersby. Hence the extreme urgency. Tamara is stunned, terrified. On the one hand she wants to send them unceremoniously packing, and on the other hand she's frightened. But one way or another, her husband—she hurriedly reasons—must have been faced with more than one case of this kind, given the profession he practices and the region of the country he practices it in. And so, with Tamara immobilized by her own contradictory thoughts, with a stock-still Oreste staring at her fixedly, his eyes suggesting the route she will have to take if she is going to fetch the Lawyer, and with Valentino contemplating—in ecstasies—the hands of the twenty-year-old seventeen-year-old, we will unfreeze the frame and the scene can resume.

The young man lifts the cigarette to his mouth and makes a move to light it. At that precise instant, bringing a look of panic—the like of which Valentino will never again see her wear—to Tamara's eyes, Oreste lands an emphatic, sonorous slap right in the middle of the young man's face, flinging the cigarette to the floor along with the matches that were meant to light it. It all happens in a few seconds flat: Tamara tries to explain that smoke doesn't bother her, the twenty-year-old seventeen-year-old throws a furious but strangely submissive glance at his assailant, and he—the assailant, Oreste—scolds in a thundering voice, "Get rid of that cigarette, you jackass! A Lady is like a Madonna, and no one smokes in church!"

The pronouncement is so conclusive, so stentorian that its capital letters are audible, and so are the commas and exclamation marks.

(In conclusion: it is perhaps unnecessary to point the reader's attention to the fact that, in Tamara's eyes, Oreste embodies every aspect and every nuance of the old, hilltop, local *'ndrangheta* that is on the wane; and the young man with the restive, seductive hands is the new version, still immature but eager to plunge into the sea of major international crime.)

## 87. DEAR OLD COUSINS

It has to be acknowledged that, had it not been for the cousins Levino and Margherita, Tamara would very probably not have remained in Marina for more than a couple of months. With the intention of definitively wresting the Lawyer away from the yoke of local politics, it had been she who pushed for the move; so to begin with she hadn't risked stating it openly, but eventually she put her cards on the table: Marina was worse. Her contempt for the place was such that she had resolved never to step outside the front door if not in exceptional circumstances and for exceptional motives. But, as luck would have it, the cousins lived only a few blocks away from the house, not far from Levino's very central fabric store, and so Tamara could violate her own injunction by braving the short route that separated her from the two relatives. Who, as you will remember, were not relatives.

Since having had, a couple of years earlier, his first heart attack, Levino had adjusted to a new routine: as soon as he woke up, before going off to the store, he went for a very brisk stroll, skirting the *muraglione* for a mile or two. The walk never lasted more than thirty minutes. In months when the light and weather permitted it, he repeated the early morning walk in the evening, this time with Margherita on his arm. The pair were such creatures of habit and so reliable that, just as the inhabitants of Königsberg did with Kant, folk in Marina set their watches by the couple's movements: because everyone knew that at seven o'clock on the dot they would leave their house and that they would be back home an hour later. Levino and Margherita hardly spoke during their stroll, and even though business was now good, here in Marina they felt lonely, headed for a pitiful old age because it would be precisely that: lonely. One can quite see why the arrival of Tamara and her family was, as far as they were concerned, a bona fide godsend.

The second consequence of Levino's heart attack was the hiring of a clerk: Filippo, a young man of around thirty who looked at least ten years older. Slightly built and with perennially sweaty palms, Filippo had turned out to be a very good investment: courteous and conscientious, it was he who opened and closed the store every day; with the predominantly female clientele, he was eager to please without being inopportune; he was knowledgeable about the products he sold and had a certain flair. Margherita had been the very first of his fans, because Filippo's presence in the store meant greater freedom for her husband and less loneliness for her.

Then, since Tamara and her little tribe had moved to Marina, some old and much-loved habits, like Friday-night family suppers, had been resurrected, brightening up the couple's otherwise monotonous existence. Margherita started baking her famous cakes again, and every Friday she took one round to the Lawyer's house, to the joy of little Mara, who was a very greedy little girl, and to the horror of Vita, who, now eighteen, was in the process of launching her career in the diet sector (she was not a pound overweight, but was so certain of being fat that she had convinced everyone else of it too).

While the cousins' visits were regular fixtures, Tamara's followed a pattern not dissimilar to that of the appearances made by the Loch Ness Monster, which, in precisely 1968, that same year, the University of Birmingham was trying to flush out with one of the very first sonar machines: like the hypothetical prehistoric creature, she, too, could go a good long while without showing her face, but was then quite capable of materializing several times in one week. Not infrequently these visits were topped off with a quick trip to the store, where Tamara happily allowed the ever-attentive Filippo to inveigle her into buying cloth of all sorts for her husband and children, as well as herself. Of course, Signora

Farà's elegant cuts were by now a distant memory, but in Marina Tamara had, with Margherita's help, unearthed a little dressmaker who was far from second-rate, a little inexpert but very willing, and whose name has no bearing on our story, so might as well remain a secret.

## 88. WIFE OR WIDOW?

In this story of ours, 1968 will not be remembered for the terrible earthquake that in January hit the Belice Valley in Sicily, resulting in several hundred deaths, a thousand or so people wounded, and a new social category: the lifelong yet-to-be-rehoused earthquake survivor. Nor will it be reevoked on account of the student rebellions in May, in which Picchio would participate briefly without letting the family know much about it. The event that made this year memorable would unfold over the course of the summer and the fall. Its setting was Puglia. Its uncontested protagonist the Viscountess.

At the end of July, at Giulio and Letizia's insistence, Vita left for Bari. The plan was that she would stay at her half brother and sister-in-law's house for two or three weeks: it had been a long time since the woman had last been to see them; long gone were the days when she had lived with them, pampered and spoiled as much as and more than an only daughter would have been. The couple were now in their sixties, and Vita, the Viscountess, was approaching her forties, convinced she would remain a spinster. Like her sister Tecla, come to that.

In Bari, Giulio and Letizia had organized a series of divertissements for their long-awaited guest: hairdresser, beauty salon, dressmaker, jewelers, and a round of social engagements that included a chamber music concert (in memory of the bygone piano lessons inflicted in vain all those years ago), an evening at the theater, and a little party in her honor. Letizia had applied herself to the preparations well in advance, with all the zeal and lovingness of a would-be mother: both she and her husband wanted everything to be perfect for the return of their not quite daughter.

The reality surpassed their fondest expectations. First, the weather was exceptionally nice—not overly hot. And a few of the evenings were even pleasantly cool, as if this weren't the middle of the summer but the beginning of it, or earlier even—somewhere around the end of May, or early June. The Viscountess's old friends, informed of her arrival, offered to host what were in some cases tea parties and in others little soirees: they were all married and had children, and Vita's arrival reminded them of the golden days of their early youth, when life seemed to be one long carefree Sunday, especially after all the grimness of the war years. Vita appeared to be in excellent form: she had a lovely time shopping in Via Sparano, like back in the old days; she was grateful for the concert and the play (Thornton Wilder's *Our Town*—with Raoul Grassilli, Giulia Lazzarini, Gabriele Antonini, and Mario Carotenuto); and in every case she had fun and seemed appreciative and very sweet.

The most optimistic forecasts were exceeded, particularly on the evening when, in the luxurious apartment of a friend whom five pregnancies had aged very prematurely, Vita met Francesco, one of the hostess's cousins.

Francesco was exactly fourteen years Vita's senior, in other words, well into his fifties. Tall and florid, his face the color of claret, he had very white hair and the lively eyes of someone who rarely denies himself a pleasure. As a young man, he had enjoyed a certain fame as a lady-killer, but largely because he himself had done much to spread it. In reality he was a shrewd man, inclined to diffidence, which he hid behind the mask of a good-time Charlie. Whether out of a dislike of giving things up, or thanks to his reputation, or simply because he was diffident, Francesco had never married. Nor did he have a profession: all his life he had devoted himself to the management of the family inheritance, which among other things consisted of numerous real estate holdings on the Salento Peninsula, including three or four splendid country estates.

Between the two a spark of affection lit immediately. Neither one of them could have been described as conspicuously attractive, yet each—in the eyes of the other—possessed qualities essential in a partner: she was still reasonably young and fresh, she had a chic way about her, and she made him feel good about himself, even from a social point of view; he was possessed of a solid financial situation, and although older than she was, did not—at least visibly—seem to be a crumbling ruin like nearly everyone else his age.

Thus it was that Vita announced to the Notary that instead of the planned two weeks, she would be staying on longer with Giulio and Letizia. And thus it was that she announced to her hosts that she intended to accept an invitation to spend a weekend at the seaside, on the Salento Peninsula, in one of Francesco's houses.

Having packed and gotten ready luggage worthy of Queen Victoria, the Viscountess (accompanied by Letizia, for reasons of decency) was picked up by Francesco's chauffeur and delivered many hours later to said Francesco, who was waiting for her at his villa in Gallipoli. At the villa, effusively praised by Vita for its panoramic position, its art nouveau style, and the elegance of its furnishings (purchased direct from stock), there was also Francesco's sister, Lucia, with her husband Pepe and two babes, and their elderly mother, who was actually not a great deal more elderly than Letizia.

It was a weekend of gossip on the beach (Vita never swam), of long strolls at sunset, and of lavish meals. The Viscountess was very familiar with Apulian cuisine and the rhythms of Apulian life, and this nonchalantly alluded to expertise of hers gave her something of a cosmopolitan je ne sais quoi—or at least in the eyes of Francesco's mother, who was very rich and very rustic. To say nothing of the undeniable admiration (occasionally accompanied by a veiled disquiet) when Vita dropped a reference to Marcuse into the conversation, or an allusion to Baudelaire—names which meant next to nothing to those present or, on balance, to Vita herself.

More gatherings at the villa ensued, and on the fourth of these occasions Giulio joined in along with his wife and sister, among other things in order to begin sizing up Vita's potential and unexpected suitor. Francesco promptly took advantage of the presence of an older brother who was—considering the age gap—something like a father, and asked for Vita's hand.

The news bounced into town the very next day, straight into the Notary's house, where the only member of the household to demonstrate unalloyed delight for their sister was Emilio. Tecla was also happy for Vita but couldn't deny feeling a touch of envy, in addition to her sadness at suddenly being deprived of her only true coconspirator and confidante. As for their father, his first thought was for himself: while sure of being able to count on Giulio's support, he would, at least in part, have to provide a dowry for his daughter; furthermore, who would read his newspapers and books to him from now on? At ninety years of age, he could hardly delude himself into thinking his sight might improve. And then, Tecla had her work cut out for her, looking after the house; and with that shiftless idler Emilio he had forever been at loggerheads. In any case, the Notary condescendingly let it be known that he would not oppose the marriage.

The Viscountess came back to town a few days later, arm in arm with Francesco, to whom, knowing how much store the Notary set by elegance, she had in the meantime personally given a lick and a polish. The man stayed on for ten days or so, during which, like a touring statue of the Madonna, he was widely exhibited for public viewing. The Lawyer felt duty bound to roll out the red carpet and host a lunch, which ended up being a bit of a fiasco, since

Virginia—famously—cooked very badly, and Erri's little girl, swept up into her new great-uncle's arms, cleverly thought to pee all over him. In recompense, the gigantic meringue cake prepared by Margherita—a foretoken of the wedding cake in the offing—received excessive praise.

There were celebrations in town as well. And the bridegroom-to-be particularly appreciated the reception organized by Rosa and Cicia at the home of the latter of the two, because the homespun and unpretentious atmosphere led to merriment, wine, and, as the evening drew to a close, the dancing of *pizziche* and *tarantelle*. That evening, even the Viscountess lost a little of her customary aplomb and let her hair down to a degree unprecedented.

The wedding date was set for late March. The ceremony would take place in town, among other things because this would permit the elderly Notary to attend. At a later date Francesco planned to throw a party at the villa in Gallipoli, probably at the beginning of the summer.

On Saturday, 11 December, Francesco set off for home: in two days' time it would be his sister's name day and he didn't want to miss it. He also had a couple of pieces of business to see to. He would be back on the 22nd, to spend Christmas with his fiancée and her family. Regrettably, the man was never seen again. Because on Thursday the 19th, the very same day on which the Constitutional Court of the Italian Republic declared Article 559 of the Penal Code invalid—that monstrous law that had reserved punishment for female adulterers—Francesco had a massive heart attack and died.

Vita's grief was sincere, but for honesty's sake it should be added that she didn't make it out to be the end of the world.

What did come as a surprise, creating a few legal difficulties with the dead man's relatives, was that one of the pieces of business the man had needed to attend to back in Puglia concerned precisely her: his bride-to-be. Francesco had in fact managed to get to a meeting with his notary and had transferred into his future wife's name the full ownership of the villa in Gallipoli that she so loved from the moment she first set foot in it. It would have been his wedding gift. And so it was that, despite never becoming Francesco's wife, the Viscountess nonetheless inherited the beautiful house the couple would have lived in had they had time.

Yet again, Tecla might have commented on this latest turn of events with her usual line, first borrowed many years earlier from Tamara: "Isn't life nice . . . for some people." But in this particular instance it seemed somewhat controversial, so she said nothing.

## 89. EMILIO PACKS HIS BAGS

Just like black holes, calamities possess an extraordinary gravitational force: just as soon as one of them happens, in rolls another, attracted by the first at a speed outstripping the velocity of light. But then, and exactly like calamities, black holes are particularly partial to gloominess, and indeed gobble light up with a breakneck greed.

If 1968 became memorable for the Viscountess's marriage that wasn't to be and her subsequent ahead-of-its-time widowhood, '69 rounded the decade off in the worst of all possible ways. Although, for the Notary at least, it did mean for once in his life being forced to contend with a world to him unfamiliar. One that extended beyond his own ego. As would, inter alia, be the case for all the members of the human race, who, in July that year, watched the moon landing on TV. But all the same, the vista that both the Notary and humanity-as-a-whole saw stretching out before them was anything but comforting.

Emilio had lived through the past ten years in the most anarchic and subversive fashion imaginable. He was anarchic and subversive even from an ontogenetic point of view: while the students had been occupying the universities in May of the previous year, he had been turning thirty; and while they were right then first discovering Marx's early work and the anti-psychiatry of R. D. Laing and David Cooper, he had already ingested it all. As if that weren't enough, while the various student movements were talking in abstract terms about "total institutions," Emilio could offer an informed analysis, in full possession of the facts, given that he had twice been involuntarily committed to a lunatic asylum.

For a decade he had denied himself nothing. Alcohol and barbiturates. Disappearances from home and nights without sleep. Cigarettes smoked two at a time and paid-for sex. All mixed up with a burning need for human contact and a skin scraped so thin that it ended up repulsing others.

His idol, to give you some idea, was no derivative would-be like Bob Dylan (who perhaps not coincidentally would decades later win a Nobel Prize), but a true original: the poet Dylan Thomas (who perhaps not coincidentally would die an alcoholic while still in his thirties).

In his rare moments of calm, Emilio showed—to his sisters, his old nursemaid Cicia, and his few friends—a gentler side. He was affectionate, accommodating, capable of looking after himself to a degree achieved by very few members of his sex in that epoch and in those climes. He loved reading and he loved eating: of all pastimes, they were his favorites. With women he did not have an easy rapport: he adored them and he was wary of them, convinced that none of them could ever be interested in a loser like him. As a consequence, he neglected his appearance. He wore whatever old rags came to hand, he shaved if and when he remembered to, and on occasions he also forgot to wash (although it cannot be ruled out that, in addition and in parallel to the aforementioned insecurity, there may have been an element of rebellion at play here, against the extreme self-care practiced by his father).

He visited numerous prostitutes, particularly in Naples. Where he drank. Not to the point of being unable to tell his ass from his elbow, which often happened in town, but to reach that halfway stage where tipsiness casts aside all inhibitions and replaces them with a garrulous euphoria which permits even a shy man to transform himself into a devil-may-care Don Juan. At which point Emilio would walk through the door of one of his usual bordellos and entrust himself to the care of one or more of the women. He had favorites, of course, but he also liked a little variety, because by now he was very used to sex without intimacy and had come to the conclusion that, when all was said and done, the less there was of it—the intimacy—the more the sex seemed just perfect.

In some ways he regretted not having had a regular formal education. In all probability, had he not felt obliged to reject his father's odious, narcissistic authority—exactly as his father had done with the variety of paternalism that goes by the name of fascism—in short, had circumstances not compelled him to refuse to enroll at university, and renounce the premises for a life of bourgeois comfort and thus undermine the Notary's authority, Emilio would have studied geography. Because nothing is more ancient than geography, he thought, and nothing better resembles the human mind.

It was no coincidence that he loved reading. Poetry, especially, seemed to be an advanced version or, if you prefer, a recapitulation of geography's indefatigable description of the earth: the description of its physical characteristics as much as the organic ones—which are what change the face of it. As Emilio saw it, poetry began at the point where geography finished mapping out the surface of the planet; it was an attempt to give an account of historical and biological phenomena and of how they unfold.

Unfortunately, being the penniless son of a man of note in a town of very few souls (in an international context convulsed by a clash between generations) has its consequences;

and the most immediate of them was that an individual of this kind—if he was in his early thirties and quoted the century's most interesting poets while drinking like a fish, and if instead of accumulating wealth he acquired a tragic awareness of not having many routes of escape (apart from a couple of brothels and a hotel in Via Partenope, Naples)—could convince himself that he had to take his rebellion to its logical conclusion. And going from that to packing his bags was done in seconds flat.

And so it was that, on 11 December 1969, a Thursday, having scrabbled together a little cash thanks to thefts from his father's jacket and loans (mostly nonrepayable) from Tecla, Emilio made his way to Corone by bus, and there jumped on a train heading for Naples. He traveled by night in a third-class car in order to spend less money. He had enough to pay for two nights at the Hotel Vesuvio and something left over for cigarettes, alcohol, and sex (in that order of importance).

At the hotel he took his usual room. By now the staff knew him and treated him with a blend of fondness and concern, because they were aware that his moods could change course more rapidly than the most unpredictable of climates, and also because he was fabulously unstinting with both his tips and his drunken stupors.

Before leaving, Emilio had left no note at home explaining his absence, and so that very morning Tecla had telephoned the concierge asking if her brother was already there or if he had made a reservation. But he wasn't there, and none of the rooms turned out to be booked in his name. The concierge promised he would let her know, should Emilio turn up, and Tecla promised an umpteenth little bonus.

As soon as he got to his room, while the reception desk put in a call to the Notary's house, Emilio took a quick shower—he wanted to wash off the stench of the train—and went out onto the seafront. He walked with broad strides in the direction of Piazza Plebiscito; the air was cold and bracing. Still on foot, he made his way into Via Toledo and walked up as far as Piazza Dante, where he sat down in a trattoria and consumed a plate of pasta and a liter of red wine. The wine warmed him up and made him feel rather better. He instinctively lifted a hand to pat the inner pocket of his jacket where he kept his money and a half-empty bottle of sleeping pills. He ate up and drank up; he felt moderately happy; he went out into the street.

He spent the afternoon in an adult movie theater and moseying around the streets near Via Chiaia. Every so often he went into a bar and knocked back a shot of whisky. When it got completely dark, he knocked at the door of one of his favorite brothels and sank into its depths until daybreak.

By the time he got back to the hotel the day was timidly dawning, in fits and starts. The twelfth of December 1969 seemed unsure whether or not to launch itself up there in the heavens, or whether to go back the way it had come and retreat behind the clouds, declaring itself defeated from the get-go. Emilio was remembering all those years when he hadn't spoken. He started laughing at the thought. He thought of all the things he hadn't said, and admitted to himself that at the end of the day it had all been a colossal waste of time. Clearly, he had always had a screw loose: What other explanation was there for that nonsensical mutism of his, which had lasted so very long? Maybe the Notary was right. Maybe he was simply mad, and the alcohol, the pills, and the cigarettes had nothing to do with it. Not even his mother, who had abandoned him as a two-year-old child, had anything to do with it.

He felt a sudden anger toward Elvira (mentally, he had always called her by her name). To distract himself from that pointless anger he studied the sea in front of him for a moment: it was the color of chilly, rusty metal. And yet it was so beautiful.

Swaying, but with dignity—or at least, for the minute or so it took him to cross the hotel foyer and reach the elevator—he got as far as his floor and his room. He locked the door behind him, drew the curtains and lowered the shutters, because he never could get to sleep if it weren't pitch-black. He stripped naked. For a second he wondered if he should wear the pajamas he had in his suitcase: they were rather fine, in a blue-and-burgundy striped silk, a gift from the Viscountess. But then he decided that nudity has a nobility no outfit can replicate, and that morning he felt brushed with all the splendor and nobility the earth has to offer.

He rummaged around in his suitcase and found four packets of sleeping pills, saved up patiently over the previous months. The pills had different names, all of which seemed to him to be incredibly frivolous. He also pulled out the half-empty pill bottle he had in his jacket. From what he could see, it should be enough. He started gulping the pills down in little batches of three or four, mixing the shapes and colors and drinking an entire bottle of mineral water. Once he had swallowed the last little batch with the last remaining sip of water, he thought he felt tired and contentedly switched off the light on the bedside table. He closed his eyes. He heaved a sigh. Good night.

# CHAPTER NINE

## 90. THE SWORDFISH

Here it is. On a late-summer morning in 1969. In a couple of weeks' time Valentino will be heading out, moving to Corone, to Lea and Nina's house, to attend middle school there and then high school. But in the meantime, the arrival of this swordfish, stretched out to its full length on the marble-topped table in Tamara's kitchen, is reawakening the forces of the watery deep and of that inscrutable darkness in which men and lower animals live side by side, without distinctions.

It is approximately three yards long, but seems bigger in this domestic space. Its heft irrupts into everyday life with a vehemence directly descended from a world-before-time that only children and con men are capable of picturing. Laid out on its right-hand side, the beast seems to be staring at the ceiling with its enormous, wide-open eye, without a shadow of rebuke or resentment, but with an astonishment simple and ancient, older than history. At the point where its first dorsal fin begins, a red stain interrupts the body's metallic gray, which gradually fades to white as it reaches the belly. The same shade of red bloodies the upper jaw—the upper jaw that lengthens and flattens to form the sharp sword with which this beast mounted attacks and defended itself, cleaving through the water at a dizzying lick. It can't have been young, because it has no teeth; as for its sex, no one could tell you that, unless they happen to possess a good dictionary of classical mythology. But in this instance, we can justifiably toy with the idea of a hermaphrodite, capable of self-reproducing; because the origins of its species lie in an all-male group of warriors, the Myrmidons, who were sons of Zeus and Eurymedousa and under the direct command, during the siege of Troy, of none other than the hero Achilles—who not coincidentally has a soft spot for one of his counterparts (Patroclus). When Achilles receives a deadly blow to his famous tendon, the Myrmidons swear vengeance, but being unable to wreak it, because the surviving Trojans have fled, they opt to commit suicide, flinging themselves into the sea one by one. At that point, moved to pity, the nymph Thetis saves them by lengthening their jaws out of all proportion, thus equipping them with that rostrum with which they will be able to procure food, defend themselves, and plow swiftly though the briny deep—a rostrum which is also per se a phallic symbol, put there in anticipation of speculations to be made, several centuries later, by Dr. Freud.

Mythological and at one and the same time dramatically, physically real, the swordfish that has been brought as a gift for the Lawyer by one of his fisherman clients reignites in Valentino's mind those fears associated with the vast realm of human and animal metamorphoses that, back in town, before the move to Marina, once thronged his days. And above all his nights. Up in the town, in fact, when darkness descended, some men turned (far in advance of *The Twilight Saga*) into insatiable wolves, a danger to their own kith and kindred, and it was not uncommon for dirty old goats to confess, with a malign flash of their left-hand eyes, to a diabolical family pedigree; underground, the dead nourished an assortment of noxious and equivocal creatures, including vipers and toads; and the air itself teemed with souls in temporarily avian guise (the night owl, for example) or masquerading as bugs (the gadflies).

And now, to that long rosary of reincarnations and terror, even the sea adds new beads in the form of its own heraldic beasts, of which this large, blood-stained swordfish spread out across the marble-topped table in Tamara's kitchen is simply the epitome and apotheosis—a sort of savage, definitive *Deposition from the Cross*—one from a place somewhere beyond the reach of human history. But for this creature, so cruelly captured and crucified in the fantastical waters of the Ionian Sea, there will be no resurrection. Indeed, its body—hacked to pieces and cut into slices—will provide food for the family's members for many days to come, including the cousins Levino and Margherita, as well as Luigi-known-as-Sciammerga, his wife Gemma, his lover Virginia, and who knows how many others. They will devour it and metabolize it; they will, in a sense, absorb its mythical origins.

Around the animal stretched out across the marble-topped table, discussions spring up: How should it be cut up? Would it be better to grill it as steaks or moisten its meat with a light tomato sauce with some garlic and oregano? And what should be done with its mighty head, which reminds them of a heraldic shield? Should that be cooked too? And the rostrum? What is to be the fate of that sword that was once brandished a priori—and evidently with good reason—against lands dry and lands subaqueous? While the little community that peoples our story is busy debating and wondering, Valentino mechanically, and without even noticing that he is doing it, walks full circle around the animal, studying its storied, gray carapace and peering at the expression now fixed in perpetuity on its face. He bends down to take a closer look, and what he sees—in the unmoving, glassy eye of the fish—is himself.

## 91. POST POLITICS

The minute he set foot in Marina, the Lawyer abandoned any direct involvement in politics. He owed it to Tamara, his Mara, to whom he had promised a retirement from public life, and in a sense he also owed it to himself. Because during the ten years in which he had been the town's mayor, he had neglected a piece of himself that he would never have wanted the world to see, however important it was for him mentally. Literature.

It goes without saying—his ideological fervor remained intact. He continued to keep abreast of national issues, and to care about his own party and occasionally to dispense the odd piece of advice (mostly unheeded) to the youngbloods who were gradually coming to the fore. To the end of his days he would remain convinced that the only salvation for southern Italy and for the country as a whole lay in a politics of true, major reform enacted with surgical precision and not left hanging—as Italy's center-left governments had left it—in limbo. Reform that would, of necessity, impinge on established interests, positions of power, and oligarchies, and which could therefore only ever be carried out by an alliance of Socialists and Communists. But the Communists would have to relinquish explicitly their privileged and lethal ties with what was at that point known as the Soviet Union (in other words, Russia, in whose law-enforcement ranks Vladimir Putin would soon be getting his feet wet). It was unfortunate that, when Enrico Berlinguer's Italian Communist Party finally declared the long era of the privileged link with Moscow to be at an end, they simultaneously inaugurated the project known as the "historical compromise" with the Christian Democrats: in the Lawyer's eyes this basically amounted to a rehash, twenty years on, of the "center-left" envisioned by the Socialist Riccardo Lombardi. The grand reforms would get bogged down all over again, and the conservative bloc newly in power would remain intact. That was the trap his own party had fallen into, and that was what he saw in the offing for a Communist Party now engaged in the historical compromise.

All throughout the 1970s, there would only be two occasions when the Lawyer felt the old, deep thrill of an ideological allegiance: in May 1970, when parliament approved the Labor Charter, pushed for by the Socialist senator Giacomo Brodolini; and four years later, when the referendum to decide whether or not to repeal the recent law introducing the right to divorce—proposed by another Socialist, Loris Fortuna—was won resoundingly by the secularist front who were fighting to defend that law. In both cases, the Lawyer celebrated as though he had become the father of another two children: because, if nothing else, he could for once claim to be proud of his side of the political divide.

Even so, pride wasn't motive enough to break the pledge he had made to retire from active politics. Having much more time on his hands, with great joy he began reading again, and possibly also writing. But as far as the writing goes, nothing more can be added, since the Lawyer never mentioned it and kept private—and destroyed before he died—whatever papers were jealously locked away in one of the cabinets in his office.

Conversely, of the books he read and loved ample testimony does remain, in the form of marginalia, which he scribbled in pencil, at times filling every available inch of white space with observations and glosses that were often very imaginative. His most treasured literary companion, Franz Kafka's *The Trial*, was so crammed with comments that at one point the Lawyer stocked up on various editions. Apart from the first, which had appeared in Italian thanks to Alberto Spaini, the one he perhaps loved best was the Ervino Pocar translation, followed by Giorgio Zampa's and Primo Levi's versions, and then—as late as the 1990s—the translation by Anita Raja. In each of these copies the Lawyer composed, over time, a *Trial* of his own, a sort of parallel book—as Giorgio Manganelli would have called it—simultaneously a commentary and an entirely autonomous text. Above all else, what interested him in that spare, cruel tale was the idea of a paradoxical, murky justice—at bottom, the dark but unavoidable side of his own profession.

His other great love was Leonardo Sciascia. Here it is harder to point to one particular title, because almost all of them were annotated, although some more briefly than others. Alongside its analysis of the phenomenon of the Mafia, in the work of the Sicilian author the Lawyer perhaps found something akin to the overwhelming absurdity in the individual fate of Kafka's protagonist: or at least that is what some of the annotations suggest. In any case, Sciascia's works seem to have offered powerful food for thought in his professional life, because time and again, in the various courts of justice where he served as a counselor-at-law, he found excuses to quote the writer's words, and sometimes emulated their characteristic logic and deductive reasoning.

Whether or not, following the move to Marina, the Lawyer recommenced writing poems dedicated to his wife, no one knows. From time to time he would, as he used to, lock himself in his office, leaving Luigi-known-as-Sciammerga in the waiting room to watch over any clients; but whether or not he wrote poetry in there, or devoted himself to jotting down stories or kept a diary, no one ever discovered. By temperament and by zodiac affiliation (Capricorn), he loved secrets, did the Lawyer, and since he had no others (neither in politics or at work, nor in matters of the heart) he loved this one secret of his so much that he never shared it with anyone. Not even Tamara, his Mara—his muse.

## 92. BEYOND OLD AGE

That the Notary was a freak of nature, and not just physically, was already clear in the spring of 1951. One photo from that period—where he was pictured together with Magda, the Polish noblewoman who had been his lover during his university years in Naples—showed him looking not much more than a boy, despite being in his seventies. The photo was taken by Vincenzo, who—as we have seen—was also a friend of Magda's, and the occasion was the visit the woman paid the two men following various misadventures back in her homeland at the end of the Second World War (having returned to Poland in 1945, she had waited to see what the outcome of the elections would be two years later, and they had been won in dubious fashion by the Communists: at that point she put herself out of harm's way in France, justifiably fearing fresh political persecutions). When she arrived in town accompanied by the umpteenth of her lovers—he, too, an opponent of Poland's new philo-Soviet regime—Magda was in her eighties but sharper than ever. Standing at her side, the Notary looked so young that it verged on the miraculous, notwithstanding the lugubrious three-piece suit he was wearing for the photograph, which certainly did nothing to rejuvenate him. In his eyes, however, there was what one could describe as a hairline fracture, and Magda, who had last seen the Notary decades ago—this would be the final time; she would die just before Vincenzo did, in '58—had effectively noticed it right away.

Once the hairline fracture appeared, so did the cracks: the death of Magda herself, and very shortly afterward Vincenzo's; then the Lawyer's electoral defeat and his decampment from the town and from political life. But the real blow was Emilio's suicide. Life had unquestionably singled the Notary out, choosing to love herself in and via his person, but on 12 December 1969 that love seemed to abandon him for good. It is true that when Emilio removed himself from circulation the Notary was already ninety-two, a more than venerable age, but all of sudden he appeared to be twice as old.

Until a few months beforehand, he had been active and fit, incapable of sitting still either physically or mentally, well able to overtake his children while out on their habitual springtime and summer walks, but now he no longer so much as poked his nose out of the house. Actually, over the course of 1970 he stopped poking his nose out of his own bedroom. He moved backward and forward between his bed and an enormous armchair a few paces away from it. He barely ate. Even the books that the Viscountess continued to read to him every afternoon from four o'clock onward had started to bore him. In any case, after all the political essays and history books he had spent a lifetime greedily devouring, he now preferred nibbling at the Homeric poems, Ovid's *Metamorphoses*, and, ultimately, Dante's *Comedy*.

The Lawyer noticed that his father was talking much less than he used to, while Tecla noticed that he had begun talking to himself. In recompense, the Viscountess noticed nothing, because when she was declaiming the verses of Homer, Ovid, and Dante she only ever listened to the sound of her own voice. On one occasion, in the course of a pre-Christmas visit from his grandchildren Vita and Valentino, the Notary had apparently been so absent-minded and confused that he gave the young woman an exorbitant amount of money and to her younger brother handed a coin worth just a few lire, leaving both of them open-mouthed.

In the weeks following Emilio's funeral the Notary received a visit from Pasquale, the young medic who, during his period on the run, up in the Sila mountains, had been his chief refuge and comfort. Of course, Pasquale was no longer the young man he had been once upon a time: he was in his sixties now and a member of parliament with the ICP. He still had lively eyes and a ready quip, but his body, the way he dressed, and his posture had undeniably changed; he was, though, still the same open-minded and generous individual he always had been, with the same calm voice and those vaguely ceremonious and awkward gestures of his that betrayed his peasant roots. The Notary was finding it a huge strain to recognize his dear friend from the past, and at one point simply pretended—to avoid seeming rude. Only for an instant, when they were saying their goodbyes and the man embraced him, did the Notary register an echo of a camaraderie from long ago, an echo that reawakened somewhere within him images of big hearths with fires burning in them, of furtive shadows, tense nerves, and earthenware plates containing fresh cheese and black bread. But they were images from another realm. One he no longer belonged to.

In short, after the death of Emilio—that son whom he had denigrated and despised and with whom he had, for a lifetime, done nothing but quarrel—the Notary entered the minefield foreshadowing the end.

## 93. CONTINUAL ELECTIONS

Leaving aside the more obvious labels—the ones applied by the media now and at the time—the seventh decade of the twentieth century can be considered memorable for being an era of special but continual elections, however antithetical those two adjectives are evidently meant to be. (These were years in which the oxymoron unleashed its firepower and triumphed.)

The sequence went as follows: 1972, general election—Italy's first-ever snap election; 1974, referendum on divorce—Italy's first abrogative referendum, proposing the repeal of an existing law (the referendum in '46 that abolished the monarchy and ushered in the republic was an *institutional* referendum); 1976, general election—the first in which eighteen-year-olds had the vote (to his extreme disappointment, Valentino is, by a matter of months, too young to participate); 1979, general election (Valentino will vote for a very small far-left party); 1979, a few days later, European elections—the first vote for what at the time was known as the European Community and only had nine member states (in this case Valentino will atone for the frivolity of his previous vote, giving this one to the writer so admired by his father, Leonardo Sciascia, who headed up the Radical Party's list of candidates in the south).

Viewed from another perspective—a nominally more subjective one—the decade signaled a gradual political rapprochement between Tamara and the Lawyer (she moved slightly to the right, he to the left, and in this way they both ended up somewhere in the vicinity of the Radicals) and an ensuing period of domestic harmony, which received a vigorous booster shot when Erri, his wife, and their daughter vacated the family home; a harmony challenged, however, by concerns about the health of the Notary and Lea, both of them now very elderly, and by worries about Valentino, who like all teenagers worthy of the appellation, was going through that stage that is half saintliness and half slapstick, and that runs roughly from one's tenth to one's twentieth year of life (subsequent generations will find it lengthens considerably).

Recapitulating: the elections were special but continual; domestic life was serene but anxious. The oxymorons came pouring in thick and fast, all throughout the decade. Now, if here we add that the seventies began slightly earlier than expected, on 12 December 1969—the date chosen by Emilio for his definitive departure, and by the Italian secret services for the inauguration of the so-called strategy of tension, with all the innocent victims of those bombs placed in Piazza Fontana, Milan—one can see that, amid all that ferment of diverging significations and contradictory signifiers, sooner or later the decade in question was bound to decamp from the realm of linguistics, with all its neat rhetorical devices, and take up residence in the fiefdoms of delirium and of a nightmare harder to put a name to. The coup d'état in Chile, on 11 September 1973—which liquidated Salvador Allende's freely elected Socialist government and imposed a ferocious military dictatorship—would, in particular, be the emblem of that nightmare: because from that moment onward the left wing everywhere became a hostage to fear. As a result, it stopped thinking. Ergo, it ceased to exist.

## 94. CITY LIGHTS

Coming down into Corone, in this case by plane, the local airport presumably being open and fully operational (a hypothesis that appears to have more to do with riddles and brainteasers than with aeronautical science), one understands why the geography of which Emilio was so enamored continues to be taken so seriously. The beaches are perfectly white and outline a sea whose blue is nothing short of magnificent. As the land comes into view it is flat and perfectly geometrical, and seems to suggest elegantly but firmly that human beings must be of amphibian descent: basically, even before going through baggage claim, the natural urge is to jettison your luggage somewhere and run naked into the water. Once the plane has landed, however, one immediately understands that it is not geography but architecture or, if you prefer, town planning, that forms this place's nub.

Corone is a city cleaved in two. Although it stretches out metaphorically and physically toward its own mythical past in the form of the Capo Pilastro promontory, where the last, gorgeous remnant of a sixth-century-BC temple to Hera still sits, the city's nature has suffered catastrophically from the effects of modernity. The seafront seems to want to dissociate itself from what it once was, and has encircled itself with a bulwark of buildings, which isolate it, in a manner of speaking, from the old city that winds between the cathedral and the castle of Charles V, in a maze of very Levantine and mostly abandoned alleyways. The only point of contact between old and new lies in Piazza Pitagora, with its remarkably Nordic porticoes and a handful of old boutiques. Beneath those soaring porticoes, the city's students regularly storm the Moka café, where they feed on never-to-be-forgotten cream donuts and drink almond milk shipped in direct from seventh heaven.

As is almost always the case in Italy, the new bits are best ignored. Apart from anything else, because ultimately they all share the same characteristic: they rapidly crumble. Unlike the ruins from two thousand years ago that conserve, against the odds, a glimmer of their antique splendor, the only dazzling thing about the modern ones is their ugliness. That being said, we are now in the 1970s, so at least one element of novelty ought to be remarked upon.

Actually, two elements. Or maybe even three. To wit: Corone has a thriving manufacturing sector. As a result, rather than peasants, it is factory workers who make up the lion's share of the city's social fabric; which means that, unlike almost everywhere else in the south, Corone is an affluent city.

Which is why, when Valentino arrives here in September 1969, he is left quite literally awestruck. He sees buildings six or seven stories high, and to him they look like dozens of Empire State Buildings lifted bodily across from New York to the Ionian coast; he looks at the traffic lights and wonders if they mightn't be a local rendering of the fashion for all things psychedelic; he stares, enchanted, at the striped pedestrian crossings, with their open invitation to move in a zebralike herd, and he feels he is right at the heart of an asphalt jungle. But best of all, he discovers the concept of anonymity: because in Corone people don't all recognize one another instantly, nor does everyone know everything about everyone else like they did in the town, and then in Marina. The population adds up to over fifty thousand inhabitants—a giddying sum if your normal abacus only goes up as far as the number 2,000.

And what of the movie theaters, of which there are no fewer than four? In town there was only one. In Marina, zilch. And the stores? There is a whole long, straight street of them—the Corso, the main street—with all kinds of boutiques looking out onto it, jewelry stores, an imposing bank with pinkish, vaguely neoclassical stuccowork, a few cafés, an art gallery, even a bookshop (its name is Minerva, and Valentino will soon become such an assiduous client that he will know by heart almost every one of the titles on its shelves). Corone is an honest-to-goodness Shangri-la, it's paradise on earth, it's freedom.

Be that as it may, Valentino immediately has to reckon with a searing contradiction: in Corone he enjoys what could be defined as a supervised freedom, or a freedom under surveillance. Basically, a fettered freedom—we did already mention that this is a decade of oxymorons. Because, whereas in town he spent most of his time out in the street, in the roads surrounding the house, where automobiles even as a concept were still practically unheard of and Cecè and he could devise wild games to be played in and around the town's alleyways, the places where its streets widened, the roadside drinking fountains and doorways, all of this dilating in time and in space like a virtual reality avant la lettre; and whereas in Marina the aforementioned games were then domesticated and, on account of the frenzy of traffic on the main road, restricted to some backyard or other (the one behind the house he lived in, or the yard in front—his friend Sergio's—or the one a few blocks away that wrapped itself around Massimo's house), now, here in Corone, where he is living with his aunt Nina and his grandmother Lea, the only remaining province where his imagination can still run wild is the room he sleeps in. It is there that he spends most of his afternoons, especially during the three years when he is at middle school. He studies, he reads, and he daydreams in the space between his small bed and the massive desk, full of drawers, that once belonged to the Pharmacist. Sometimes he listens to the radio, and he falls in love on a daily basis—with rock 'n' roll, with the blues, with jazz. He even begins to flirt with classical music. He spends a great deal of time sitting in silence; it is almost his primary occupation. Simply put, by the standards of the time he is a model student. But the minute he expresses a desire to step beyond the front door, Nina's face darkens and he is asked to come back as soon as possible: an hour at most, and then he must come straight home.

And, accosted with all the liberty that Corone pours into her streets, whole rivers of liberty pouring out of those New York–style buildings, accosted with those electrifying promises of a life lived in neon that billow out on every corner of the Corso, the seafront, and Piazza Pitagora, Valentino feels even more of a recluse. But he says nothing and he never complains, because in some ways he enjoys being silent. And then also because he will start saying his piece in a few years' time—and won't ever stop—thanks to a friend, Luigi, who, here and now, he hasn't yet met, so Luigi doesn't yet exist. If not in the most secret of Valentino's dreams, in one of the drawers in the desk that once belonged to the Pharmacist.

### 95. TÊTE-À-TÊTE

Once Picchio had completed his degree in economics and had settled down in Rome, and once Erri had gotten a place in Bari and started to put roots down there with his wife and their daughter, and once Vita had enrolled at the School of Medicine at the University of Ferrara, and Valentino had been sent to live with Nina and Lea in Corone in order to attend the middle school there, Tamara and the Lawyer suddenly found they had an enormous amount of free time to spend together. To begin with, they were disoriented. They started frantically inviting Cousins Levino and Margherita over for lunch and for supper, but they very soon realized that that was a road to nowhere, if for no other reason than that, what with their advancing years, the two cousins seemed to be getting increasingly cantankerous and came round to the house begrudgingly, almost as if reproaching the others for having no children.

Meanwhile, going through the motions and putting on a show of being dissatisfied and even a little disappointed by life now that their brood was entering the gilded years of its youth, Tamara and the Lawyer started complaining about everything. They said they felt lonely, but you could see a mile off that that was a lie. Tamara complained that she missed Maria-la-pioggia's company, and that much was true, just as it was true that the Lawyer regretted not having managed to persuade Ciccio Bombarda to follow him down to Marina. Which was also true, apart from anything else, for a very concrete motive: although armed with a regular driving license, the latest chauffeur to perform the role had, in less than a year, wrecked two cars. In any case, the Lawyer really did miss the instinctive intelligence and the spirit of initiative displayed by his original driver, whom he would never cease to think of with nostalgic regret.

Over the years, husband and wife had ended up resembling each other. So, when one of them got tired of complaining, the other quickly followed suit. And since in reality they weren't remotely sad to no longer have their children underfoot and therefore to have time to do whatever they wanted, they launched one of the most successful examples of mutualistic symbiosis ever recorded in the history of animal biology. They traveled together, they planned improvements to the house, they discovered a passion for art auctions, and filled the walls of their home with oil paintings of no merit whatsoever, apart from the merit of being expensive. They looked after one another with scrupulous concern. She kept tabs on the state of his—for that matter, excellent—health, and he kept an eye on the very slight signs she showed of aging. So inseparable had they become that their children began to suspect they were using telepathy in order to exclude their offspring from their conversations. Which can't have been entirely true, if nothing else because they were often heard muttering together and then, soon afterwards, exploding into peals of badly stifled laughter.

True: they did still have worries. Their respective surviving parents were far from in the pink: although there was nothing specifically wrong with him, the Notary had now edged beyond ninety and was showing evident signs of structural failure; Lea suffered from an inoperable peptic ulcer for which, at the time, no effective pharmaceutical remedies existed. And then Valentino's hypersensitivity—after those famous pseudoepileptic seizures—worried them. They were happy that the boy had gone to study in Corone, at a highly regarded school and in an environment evolutionarily more advanced, but both of them feared that Nina's oddness, that morbidity of hers, might not be good for him. They weren't far off the mark, and within the space of a couple of school years, when, having sailed through middle school, Valentino made his debut at the high school that specialized in classical studies and was named after Pythagoras (an imposing building with an austere 1930s facade, geometric in style but with a little neoclassical flourish in its central *avant-corps*), Tamara and the Lawyer would be forced, for a moment, to step out of that perfect, fusional world of theirs and take peremptory action to avoid disaster.

### 96. NINA IN THE SKY WITH DIAMONDS

In Corone Nina found a substitute for her beloved Gioacchino in the form of a gaggle of girlfriends, all unmarried, just like she was, but for the most part older and spectacularly uglier. The age range oscillated between fifty and sixty; as for the ugliness, in some cases it was so elaborate as to provoke admiration: for example, Titina wasn't five feet tall, but she was five feet wide, and had two hypothyroidic eyes that unapologetically referenced Picasso's Cubist period; Tilda, on the other hand, had a torso, neck, and head all of the same circumference; Jole flaunted extensive hipster-style facial hair, while Alda, in contrast, suffered from alopecia and was almost bald.

The ingredient that cemented the group was their enthusiastic Catholicism. To varying degrees, Nina's new friends belonged body and soul to Holy Mother Church, in whose ranks they militated with a gusto that had discernable, albeit latent, erotic overtones. From this point of view, at least to begin with, Nina did have a few misgivings. Back in town she had never frequented the parish church, for at least two reasons: Lea and the Pharmacist never talked about it, but everyone in the family was vaguely conscious that their roots lay in another faith; in addition to which, Tamara had married the son of one of the region's most celebrated priest-eating socialists. All in all, it wasn't wholly appropriate to be seen at Mass on a Sunday or to turn up for the praying of the Rosary, the novenas, and all the other group activities so many women indulged in.

In Corone, however, Nina felt free to be herself, irrespective of her upbringing. And she therefore decided to adhere enthusiastically to the rituals and routines of her newfound friends. She filled the apartment with prayer cards featuring sword-pierced hearts of Jesus, the eyes of various St. Lucys offered up on plates, martyrs impaled and spit-roasted, and an entire, vast, splatter-oriented iconography from which Valentino took pains to avert his gaze. In the woman's bedroom a sort of domestic altar had materialized, caparisoned with multicolored garlands of artificial roses, fluorescent ex-votos, and little strings of frankly trippy Christmas lights. At home she imposed a complex dietary regime, according to which on certain days red meat was not to be eaten, in deference to this or that evangelical edict, and then the following day no milk or dairy products were to be touched, in observance of another catechistic precept. On Sundays too—a day that Valentino, like all boys, anxiously awaited, for the chance to grab an extra hour's sleep—she was gripped by a mystical/organizational fury, and so they had to be out of bed by seven o'clock in the morning, because her Mass was at nine, and before leaving the house she had to have everything and everybody perfectly shipshape.

In a word, Lea's ulcer worsened and Valentino began drawing up careful plans for escape.

### 97. FRIENDS, NOVELS, AND OTHER DISCOVERIES

Valentino's plans found excellent support in the form of Luigi, a boy his own age who also went to his high school, although in a different class.

Tall, very dark-haired, and olive-skinned, with strongly marked features and the athletic physique of someone who in any case puts no work into it, Luigi seemed to have walked straight out of one of those sixth- or seventh-century-BC bas-reliefs conserved in the local archaeological museum. In a previous incarnation he had surely practiced discus throwing and wrestling, and must have hung out with Milo of Croton. Now, instead, he preferred the megaphone he used when haranguing his school fellows into striking for their rights, and rather than some athlete or other, the company he kept was made up of individuals notable for their beards, long hair, and an aggregate shagginess that canceled out traditional markers of age, sex, and beauty. Luigi didn't really wear clothes, he wore wrappings. And his garments were always shapeless: sweaters several sizes too big for him, jeans so dirty they could walk unsupported by his legs, and to top it off the inevitable, preordained parka—the era's keynote and bona fide weapon of mass repulsion—the lining of which had to be a mandatory shade of gray that testified to that particular piece of clothing's many former lives. No shirt, and ideally not even a T-shirt: Luigi wore that scratchy wool sweater with nothing underneath.

In addition to possessing a great deal of sex appeal, in addition to being actively committed to the most disparate and unheard-of global causes, Luigi loved reading. And this inevitably attracted Valentino, who had, what is more, caught Luigi's eye because he was radically different from the people Luigi surrounded himself with: to cut a long story short, every aspect of Valentino's appearance suggested a classic case of still waters concealing a mammoth conflagration. And it was those flames that fascinated Luigi.

Drawn into one another's orbits, the pair began meeting up almost every afternoon. The fact that he was eluding Nina's control only added to the thrill of the moment, when Valentino finally stepped across the threshold into Luigi's little bedroom, where the walls were festooned with portraits of Jimi Hendrix and Che Guevara, the floor was piled high with LPs by King Crimson and Van der Graaf Generator and books by Hermann Hesse and Herbert Marcuse, the air was musty with the pungent odor of marijuana, and the disarray had such a grace to it that Valentino had the very credible impression he was standing in the kingdom of some generous, sunny-natured god who would protect him *in saecula saeculorum*—a god who, unlike the one worshipped by Nina, had—if nothing else—the merit of being equipped with a body a great deal more attractive than any consecrated host.

Together they read *Siddhartha* and *Narcissus and Goldmund* and reveled in the play of identities and the mirroring. They read *Tonio Kröger*, Rilke's poems, and novels by Kerouac and Pavese. They read *Les Fleurs du Mal*, Plato's *Symposium*, and Karl Marx on literature and art. They read the way other people pray, with the same conviction and the same euphoria; and all the while their bodies were conceiving and developing a joint splendor of their own, transforming them into inadvertent but immortal demigods. Only *Remembrance of Things Past* could not be shared, because Luigi was too impatient to plunge into that tourbillion of pages in which Valentino got waylaid, catching glimpses of his friend first in Gilberte, then in Albertine, and then also in Morel.

When they tired of reading, they listened to music at top volume on Luigi's stereo system (Crosby, Stills, Nash & Young's songs were so sweet! Grace Slick's voice was so powerful!), or they amused themselves by tuning in to Radio Tirana, where at around five o'clock every afternoon a program with the title *Marxist-Leninism: A Doctrine Forever Fresh and Scientific* was broadcast, a program that, if listened to with the aid of a spliff, generated a quantity of laughter directly proportional to the impassive tone of the Albanian presenter's voice.

Valentino's plans to escape from Lea and Nina's apartment envisioned him reaching a sole and inevitable destination: Luigi's little bedroom, and its lively, healthy chaos—a counterweight to the gloomy neatness of the desk that had once belonged to the Pharmacist. At which, into the bargain, the man had never once sat. No alternative end points were ever contemplated, and since Valentino wouldn't make up his mind, it was Luigi who eventually hatched the plot.

## 98. LEA'S THOUGHTS

She was no longer capable of slicing a loaf of bread, of holding it to her chest and tugging the knife through it, toward her, taking care not to cut herself. She was no longer capable of doing it, because that ancient, peasant gesture was at odds with the new reality of her ulcer. The pain was constant. In a spot near her breastbone. And it drilled through her chest, emerging halfway between her shoulder blades like the tip of an avenging angel's sword. She never mentioned it. She never said anything, because she didn't want to worry Nina. And given that the pain occupied the better part of Lea's thoughts, she pretty much stopped talking. She sat stiffly next to one of the windows in the living room, like an immobile cat who doesn't know how to purr. She glanced down at the street below, at the traffic, at the passersby, and that glance could last entire afternoons.

At around seven o'clock every evening Giorgio would call in to see her, coming straight from the hospital, a matter of yards away. He hung around for a while with his mother, chatting about the weather and asking her how she felt. Lea always replied that she felt fine, and half an hour or so later her son would go on his way reassured, picturing old age—which unhappily he would never experience—as a sort of call to order for the species, a settling of accounts purely animal in nature.

In Lea's head the few thoughts that managed to break loose from the tyranny of her ulcer were all devoted to Maria del Nilo. Not to the Pharmacist, whom Lea had loved and forgotten, nor to the children, who seemed to her to be so very distant even when they were present, but to the deaf household servant who at the end of the day had been the only true friend of a flinty lifetime. Why had she let Maria believe, all that time ago, that old Uncle Giorgio had been pestering her? The motive—she saw it now—had been so crass as to prove humiliating: Lea had noticed that her husband's uncle was sweet on Peppo from the posthouse, who by that point slipped in and out of the old man's room like a shadow at all hours of the day and night; and since Maria del Nilo had noticed something of it herself, Lea had decided to salvage the old man's reputation by sidetracking the housemaid with a muttered accusation—one much more disgusting than the man's putative sin. What an idiot she had been! And what vulgarity there had been in that lie! Lea wished she could make amends, or at least ask their forgiveness for that grossness of hers, but they were all of them dead now. Lea herself would soon be dead. Or at least she hoped so, because she really couldn't take much more of this pain in the middle of her chest.

## 99. CHANCE AND NECESSITY

Lea passed away in her sleep on the night between 5 and 6 February 1974. Earlier in the evening she had begun to feel the wolfish pains in her chest intensifying. Lying in bed, she had called out to Nina, asking her for some medicine to calm the spasms. Her daughter had realized that the situation was rapidly deteriorating and, terrified, had telephoned Giorgio. Her terror was made more acute by the fact that Valentino still hadn't come home. She called Tamara too, and told her without mincing words that Lea was dying and that the boy had been missing since the afternoon. It was past midnight. At that point Nina also summoned her little covey of sepulchral friends.

Giorgio saw immediately that nothing could be done for his mother. He injected her with a vial of morphine, he held her hand, and forcing himself to smile, he murmured to Lea that she should try to get a little sleep. Lea obeyed, glad to be free of that harrowing pain in her chest. She smiled an unforced, almost lighthearted, smile, then she closed her eyes and never reopened them.

Valentino was also sleeping deeply. So deeply that a trumpet fanfare three feet from his head wouldn't have woken him up. He had slid off to sleep buck naked, with Jim Morrison's voice still belting out:

*Come on, baby, light my fire*
*Come on, baby, light my fire*
*Try to set the night on fire.*

Luigi had encouraged him to drink and to smoke, and then, with the Doors playing those hypnotic, sensual, sometimes waspish, sometimes majestic songs of theirs, had very slowly pulled Valentino's clothes off. The two young men had gotten into bed, and having made love for the first and then the second time, Valentino had tumbled into a web of dreams as intricate and rapid as Luigi's breathing. Luigi, whose cock he continued to clasp in his hand, almost as if it were a bunch of flowers to be offered to the world in exchange for that simple rapture. Luigi stared at him with an odd sort of pride—the pride of having gifted his friend, and himself, the most ancient and justifiably celebrated of all human pleasures. He, Luigi, knew that out of that night of unalloyed joy, no love—in the sense that Valentino would give the word and would very probably have wanted—would emerge. But all the same he was convinced—and he wasn't mistaken—that it would give his friend's life a memorable thrust in the right direction. Toward personal happiness. In other words, toward his authentic self.

When Luigi's mother burst into the room the following morning, she noticed it smelled to high heaven of young male bodies. And since she was a simple woman with peasant roots, while she mustered her son and that friend of his whose face she couldn't see because he was barricaded beneath the bedcovers, it crossed her mind that, judging by that reek of maleness, she would need to change the sheets.

Out in the street, heading off toward school, the two friends chattered as if nothing had happened. Valentino was uneasy at the idea of returning home at lunchtime, but for now he was here with Luigi and nothing else mattered. They walked through the park in front of the Pythagoras Lyceum's school building. Although it was winter, the box hedges were luxuriantly thick, and in some corners the vegetation was so dense that it conjured up thoughts of a small and very neat jungle. The two young men melted separately into the crowd of other teenagers who were waiting for the bell to announce the first lesson of the day. When it rang, they nodded at each other from a distance, and each went off to join their own class.

The first hour's lesson would have been philosophy, Valentino's favorite subject. In the classroom, the teacher was standing next to his desk, waiting for his students to arrive. As soon as Valentino walked through the door with the others, the teacher called him over. In a few embarrassed words Valentino was told he must go straight home.

Alarmed and unsure what he could say to justify himself, he ran all the way to the building where he lived with his grandmother and aunt. He didn't really know what to expect, because he'd never before found himself in direct conflict with the adult world. His father and mother had never rebuked him, except very gently, and in any case no punishment had ever been inflicted. On the other hand, he had always done his best not to upset or offend them. But now that he had stayed out for an entire night without warning, how would they react, those parents of his who were so discreet and civil that at times they even seemed rather distant? Truth be told, it wasn't Tamara or the Lawyer he was worried about, and not even Lea, who had all but stopped talking; it was Nina, with her obsessive need for control and for tidiness.

Even in the building's stairwell, Valentino already noticed an unprecedented stir. His aunt's friends were coming in and out of the lobby as though in the throes of some mad collective twitch. He caught sight of his father at the door to the apartment, which had been flung wide open. Inside the door there was a fearsome crowd of people: neighbors; friends of Uncle Giorgio's; his uncle's three children with a woebegone air; Tamara's elder sister, Maria, with the eyes of someone who has recently been weeping. Aunt Nina was nowhere to be seen, but he could hear her voice shouting words with no sense to them. It was obvious that his grandmother had died. And equally obvious that Valentino would come to associate his first memory of sex with a burning, irredeemable sense of guilt.

For a week after Lea's funeral (she was buried in the cemetery up in the town, alongside her husband, old Uncle Giorgio, and the two babes she had lost as children), Valentino went back to stay with his parents, traveling in every day on a bus that left early and took him into Corone, to school, and then brought him back home at around three o'clock in the afternoon. He even toyed with the idea of asking his mother and father to let him continue commuting, but then convinced himself it would be a lousy life, and so he went back to his aunt's.

Over the course of that week, Nina descended into what was effectively a gloomy and self-destructive delirium. She wore head-to-foot black, she barely touched her food, she switched on neither radio nor television. That slightly crazy but, all things considered, sunny nature she had had in the old days appeared to have vanished. The woman did nothing but pray, finger rosary beads, and talk on the phone to her God-bothering friends. The only occasions on which she left the house were when she went to buy food (in ever-smaller quantities) or to go to Mass with one of the various Tildas, Aldas, or Joles.

Valentino was forced to keep curfew-style hours and was violently upbraided every time he transgressed or if his aunt came to hear of him being involved in any way in the student protests in support of the divorce law—the referendum for which was due to be held on 12 May that year. The tension between the two of them was so high that, one afternoon, taking advantage of the fact that the woman was momentarily absent, Valentino shut himself into the bathroom with two bottles of barbiturates in his pocket, guzzled them down without a second thought, and risked following in his Uncle Emilio's footsteps.

Nothing happened, thank goodness, apart from his stomach being pumped and Tamara and the Lawyer deciding to put an end to the domestic partnership between aunt and nephew. While waiting for the school year to end—following a landslide victory won by those in favor of divorce—the boy was temporarily parked at Giorgio and Bebè-the-Chatelaine's lovely home, where he was able to spy on the famous Saturday evening parties with all those spit-shined guests, the to-ing and fro-ing of uniformed, white-gloved waiters, and delicacies he had never seen or tasted before. And on the mornings after these events, while everyone else was still sleeping, Valentino would often slip silently into the big parlor where the reception had been held the night before, and would enchantedly inspect the tabletops, armchairs, and sofas for signs of the elegant little crowd that had assembled around them. And as he did so he would admiringly study the autumnal landscape by Gauguin (the other painting, the self-portrait, still hung in the library), each and every time noticing a new detail, an element that his previous investigations hadn't picked up on.

At the end of the summer, when he came back to Corone for the start of the new school year, Valentino went to live in the house of an elderly lady who had two other lodgers. Luckily the young man was given a room of his own, as recommended by an English novelist whose work he had recently discovered on the shelves of the Minerva bookshop on the Corso. The old lady's apartment was drab, dusty, and gloomy, but very close to his school (in the morning he could get out of bed at the very last minute and still not turn up late); what's more, the landlady was a good cook and had also given him a set of keys, so the boy could come back in whenever he wanted, without having to explain himself to anyone. In return for that undreamed-of freedom, Valentino studied twice as hard as before and never gave his parents any cause for concern.

Now that he was back in the city after the summer's hiatus, he picked up his friendship with Luigi and with their other friends from the student collective whose afternoon meetings he had started taking part in, along with all their other initiatives. Over the summer months he hadn't been in touch with any of them, which meant he was all the happier to be plunging back into that world of ideas.

It was a happy time, a period full of dreams and plans. He didn't see Luigi as often as he had the year before, but now and then he did sleep over at Luigi's, and on every occasion, found traces in the bed of the many girls who doted on Luigi and whose feelings were reciprocated. But in addition to Luigi there were also Francesco and Filippo and Domenico, Salvatore, Liliana, Claudia, Patrizia, Graziella, Mimmo, Fabio, Franco, Palmiro, Attilio—all his companions for that wonderful period, a period short-lived and immortal and soon to be left behind forever.

At the general elections in June 1976, although the majority of those youngsters didn't vote because they were a few months shy of the requisite eighteen years of age, the entire student collective mobilized spontaneously in support of a far-left party that would go on to win six seats in the lower house of parliament. As usual, each of them was assigned a task of their own, and Valentino's was to travel to the surrounding towns and villages and give campaign speeches in the piazzas. Wherever they went, the kids from the collective got straight to work, setting up an improvised podium and plugging a microphone and its accompanying loudspeaker into some unsuspecting storekeeper's electrical mains.

The defining characteristics of those election rallies were generally two in number: the paucity of the participating public—eight or nine idlers who wandered over to listen as a way of killing some time—and the guaranteed presence, albeit off to one side, of Oreste, Marina's *'ndrangheta* boss, Peppo from the posthouse's son. Valentino could not for the life of him work out how it was that that man who dressed like an undertaker with a wide-brimmed hat unfailingly glued to his head was invariably to be found standing—with the air of someone who just happened to be passing by—in the square of whatever town or village he was about to give a speech in. And as soon as the boy got started, the man would look at him from across the square and discreetly but decisively nod his approval. Valentino subsequently discovered that, as a token of esteem for the Lawyer, Oreste had decided of his own accord to keep an eye on Valentino's electioneering and ensure that nothing untoward befell him or his revolutionary friends. Which is how the far left came to be the unwitting beneficiaries of an extremely genteel example of *'ndrangheta* protection.

Then, finally, after the umpteenth protest march, after the umpteenth occupation, after the umpteenth rock concert organized to finance the collective's activities, along came his final school exams and with them the need to depart from Corone and continue his studies somewhere far away—as Tamara insisted—as far away as possible from that land of barbarians. In actual fact Valentino did not make his way as far north as his sister had, going up to Ferrara, nor did he hang around nearby, like Erri, who lived in Bari. He copied the eldest of his siblings, Picchio, who had after all played a comparatively important role in his discovery of the world of books: he decided he would enroll at the University of Rome. And so, one late-September evening in 1977, he caught a malodorous train that took twelve hours to get him to Termini station, and with the rumpled, euphoric and insecure air all immigrants have, he disembarked in the nation's capital and his own new life.

Just a few days later, Valentino learned via a phone call from Tamara that, at exactly one hundred years of age, the Notary had died. That day, as he always did, the man had eaten breakfast in his room, then he had climbed back into bed for an hour. In the afternoon he had settled into position in his usual armchair and had distractedly listened to his daughter reading aloud a canto from Dante, until it was time for the evening meal. His last words, according to the Viscountess, had been "I must get changed for supper."

# EPILOGUE

Many years later, at the tail end of a turn-of-the-century and turn-of-the-millennium April afternoon, in London it had stopped raining; the sky over Hyde Park had finally decided to concede itself an unapologetically gaudy, coloristic break after hours of being monopolized by very stern, gentlemanly grays. Heading for Marble Arch, Valentino skirted the snaking outline of the lake in the direction of the famous Speakers' Corner. The green around him was so bright, so true, that it felt artificial, and there was a bracing nip in the air. Perhaps even—fittingly for an island in the north—a touch of frost. And since the world seemed to be feeling refreshed and rejuvenated, Valentino, who was unconscious of the plummeting temperature, walked on through the alternating light and shade with a youthful enthusiasm of his own, almost as if, as a knock-on effect of the changeable North Atlantic climate, his age had mutated over the course of the day and was now at a point somewhere between twenty and twenty-five. Which would mean it had halved.

Then again, he was going to be the youngest person present at the event he was making his way to so eagerly—the youngest, not according to his birth certificate but for reasons of what could be called a technical kind. Because, of all the guests, he alone would be a novice, taking part for the very first time in a Passover supper—a seder. He had always had plenty of Jewish friends, not to mention his maternal roots, little though he knew about them, yet he had never before been invited to one of these ceremonies.

The idea had been Dina's, Dina, whom he had recently gotten to know here in London but who was, like him, Italian, and who had quickly become a steadfast presence in his day-to-day life. Dina's parents were going to be in town for Pesach, so she had decided to get a group of friends together for the traditional evening meal. The menu and everything at the table would be done according to ritual: the guests would read through the Haggadah, would sing songs in Hebrew, and would drink the prescribed number of glasses of wine; an overflowing cup would be left for the prophet Elijah, and the door would remain ajar in case he turned up. Valentino was so excited to be going to the party that he had set off much earlier than was necessary, opting to while the time away by walking the route that separated him from his friend's house in Marylebone.

That morning on the phone, already impatient for the evening to begin, he had told his father about the invitation, but the Lawyer, who was no expert when it came to Catholic festivities, let alone Jewish ones, and was also a little deaf on account of being almost ninety, had mistaken the seder for some eccentric new form of entertainment fashionable in London, and so said to his son, "Well, why not? Good for you! Go and have fun!"

As for his mother, it had sadly been a very long time since Valentino had last spoken to her. To be precise, it had been ever since she had ceased, in a way that brooked no argument, to recognize that anyone except her husband formed part of the vast, contradictory and mostly inane jumble of things that, for the exclusive purpose of consoling ourselves, we call reality. For quite some time now, Tamara had stopped consoling herself: reality no longer concerned her, if not at the point and the place in which it took the form of the Lawyer. In other words, fifteen years or so earlier Tamara had become Mara definitively, and since that name had always been the Lawyer's prerogative, she recognized only him. The Lawyer. Everyone else, children included, was lost to her, mislaid in the windings of her memory.

At seven thirty on the dot, Valentino knocked at Dina's door. Although actually this was a family home: it belonged to Dina's parents, Mirella and Giovanni. But for the time being it was home to their daughter—in London to study for her PhD at University College London. The interior of the tall, narrow building bore very few traces of Dina's presence (nothing really, apart from her obsessively collected CDs), but was chock-full of the pre-Roman antiquities that Giovanni collected and the Impressionist and

Postimpressionist works lovingly rounded up by Mirella. The pair were very rich and could permit themselves a liberal scattering of real estate and art collections dotted around various European capitals, and yet both of them retained a straightforwardness and a human warmth uncommon in their social latitudes. Mirella was fond of telling the story of how, during the Nazi occupation of Rome, she and her sisters had found refuge and salvation in the rooms of a famous brothel near the Trevi Fountain. The young prostitutes, who were working-class girls, had welcomed in those little escapees courageously and affectionately, and to some degree it was their legacy of candor that still gave a particular grace to Mirella's manners and features.

The supper was a drawn-out affair, once everyone finally sat down. There were nineteen of them, including a Nobel laureate in economics—an uncle of Giovanni's who was Roman but had been living in the United States for donkey's years now, and that was where he had flown in from a few days earlier, for a conference. Apart from a stereo system in one corner of the room, all the other furniture had migrated to the upper floors of the house and down to the basement, where the kitchen was. So the table occupied the entire first floor and was decked out with colorful plates, foods, candles, and decorations that were meant to allude to the celebration's theme, centered on the story of the quarrel with Pharaoh, the ten plagues that God visited on the Egyptians so that Moses could free his people, and then, finally, the flight across the Red Sea. For each of these stages, a reading of the relevant passages from the Haggadah was foreseen, but in recent years various communities, including the Roman one that Mirella and Giovanni belonged to, had made an addition to the text: a page that also commemorated the Holocaust; and it was these lines—in Italian—that were entrusted to Valentino, who was to read them aloud.

The man stood up and began reading in a calm, well-modulated voice, but hadn't even gotten as far as the second line when the tears started streaming down his cheeks. He was just as surprised as everyone else, perhaps even more so, almost as if it were someone else weeping, not him. Everyone present, every last one of them, felt duty bound to voice a gentle murmur of appreciation for that emotion displayed so spontaneously, so sincerely. And yet Valentino knew that his tears were welling up in reaction not to the terrible and painful remembrance of the Holocaust, but to a sudden, irrational recollection: the memory of the people who had thronged his infancy and early youth. People, names, stories, and emotions that, all of a sudden, he was frightened he had lost forever, irretrievably. At the time, he had wanted to put them behind him and to escape far away—as far away as possible from that land of barbarians, as Tamara had repeatedly put it. And he had; in the first place, to please Tamara. But now, now that he lived in London, in the civilized world, far enough away from the world of the barbarians, he sensed that he should instead have stayed close. Maybe not to the barbarians whom his mother had already erased from her memory, but—if nothing else—to what little remained of Tamara herself.

In short, what Valentino had suddenly become aware of was a personal and private holocaust. And in those seconds, while the other guests looked at him sympathetically, silently waiting for him to recommence his reading from the Haggadah, he came to understand that the past is not so much what bubbles to the surface of history, what wells up out of ruins and massacres and monuments, but a personal point of arrival. And accordingly, when those tears stopped falling, drying up as spontaneously as they had first begun to flow, he came to see that if we lose our connection with the past, we lose ourselves: because the past is vaster than the present. Never mind the future.

He recommenced reading in a tone of voice that was slightly gruffer, but controlled and dry; and when he finished Mirella gave him a motherly hug. Giovanni was having to suppress ruffled emotions of his own, and the other guests stood up from the table to stretch their legs and shake off the discomfort that the display of emotion had surely generated. Then a few songs by Roberto Murolo—chosen by Dina—did their job and mellowed the atmosphere.

By the time, that evening, Valentino made his way home, retracing his earlier steps across the park, it had started raining again—a fine rain, as thick and soft as a pang of remorse. As he gradually made his way forward between dripping-wet trees and the yellowish light of the streetlamps, the man felt drenched. Not with the water falling from above so much as with the thoughts and emotions that had risen to the surface while he read the passage from the Haggadah dedicated to the Holocaust. Sometimes, however, certain thoughts and emotions that affect us deeply need time and have to be left to rest in silence, at a distance, before they can be voiced. And so, the moment Valentino reached his house and, coming in, shut the door behind him, that evening's thoughts and emotions were left outside in the street and melted into the night.

After that, other years went by and other distances mounted up in Valentino's mind. His surroundings changed an incalculable number of times. Until, one morning, he learned, via his sister Vita, that Tecla, the aunt who still lived up in the town and whom he barely knew, had died the night before. She had been the last surviving member of their numerous and unhappy paternal family (the maternal side was already extinct). Valentino remarked to himself that at this point he no longer had a past. To put it very simply, he discovered there was no one between him and death. In that very same instant, as if something had short-circuited, he relived that London evening when he had burst into tears during the seder ceremony, and it dawned on him that from now onward Tecla, together with Tamara and the Lawyer who called her Mara, together with the Notary, the Pharmacist, and their identical but different wives, together with Maria-la-pioggia and Maria del Nilo, and Ciccio Bombarda and all the other heroes who move through this story as if dancing a drunken rumba, would constitute his future.

He was at the seaside, in a house directly overlooking the Bay of Naples. The sun was high in the sky and a scent of coffee filtered out onto the terrace, and then a procession of other aromas, with the smell of basil leading the way.

As he stared out at that exquisite, late-eighteenth-century vista that took in the slopes of Vesuvius, he heard an old Coldplay song bursting out from the sitting room, telling him that Dina had woken up. Swathed in a white caftan, his friend sashayed across the terrace toward him and, entirely unaware of what had just happened, took hold of his right hand and suggested, "Shall we dance?"

*Poggetto, Forio, and Crotone, 2018–19*